continued . . .

WISDOM
OF THE BONES

CHRISTOPHER HYDE

AN ONYX BOOK

ONYX
Published by New American Library, a division of
Penguin Putnam Inc., 375 Hudson Street,
New York, New York 10014, U.S.A.
Penguin Books Ltd, 80 Strand,
London WC2R 0RL, England
Penguin Books Australia Ltd, 250 Camberwell Road,
Camberwell, Victoria 3124, Australia
Penguin Books Canada Ltd, 10 Alcorn Avenue,
Toronto, Ontario, Canada M4V 3B2
Penguin Books (N.Z.) Ltd, Cnr. Rosedale and Airborne Roads,
Albany, Auckland 1310, New Zealand

Penguin Books Ltd, Registered Offices:
Harmondsworth, Middlesex, England

First published by Onyx, an imprint of New American Library,
a division of Penguin Putnam Inc.

First Printing, February 2003
10 9 8 7 6 5 4 3 2 1

For all the fallen heroes
For all the forgotten victims

"It's awful lonely here."
>—John F. Kennedy at the grave of his son,
>Patrick Bouvier Kennedy, August 1963

I have a rendezvous with Death
At some disputed barricade,
When Spring comes back with rustling shade
And apple-blossoms fill the air—
But I've a rendezvous with Death
At midnight in some flaming town,
And I to my pledged word am true,
I shall not fail that rendezvous.
>—WWI poet Alan Seeger;
>John F. Kennedy's favorite poem

Oh to be torn twixt love and duty
Sposin' I lose my fair-haired beauty
I'm not afraid of death, but oh,
What will I do if you leave me?
>—Dmitri Tiomkin, Ned Washington,
>"Do Not Forsake Me, Oh My Darling";
>Lee Harvey Oswald's favorite song

Prologue

The Monster sat at the scarred kitchen table in the shack and listened carefully to the night sounds of the dump: skittering animal noises, faint whispering from the screening woods that separated the mounds of garbage from the highway more than a mile away, the muffled crack and thud of ancient detritus giving way and sagging deeper down into the filthy strata of a hundred years or more of the county's waste.

He was reasonably sure that he'd hear the sound of a truck or automobile as it clattered down the long dirt road, or see its headlamps as their glowing beams of light swung across the filthy glass of the window in the shack, but he knew it wasn't likely, especially at night. The dump had been out of service for a decade now, its rotting geography long since picked over for anything of value, the caretaker who'd occupied the shack from dawn to dusk long since dead and gone. The stink kept young lovers from using the dump as a trysting place away from prying eyes and the rats stood guard against wandering hoboes and other jobless migrants fleeing from the cities and the nation's newly minted Depression. The fuming trash heap was his kingdom and his sanctuary, the shack his fortress and his castle.

The shack was small, not much larger than a prison cell, the corrugated tin roof sloping up from back to front, a narrow canvas-and-iron cot set up at the lowest point of the slope. There was a chair, the old kitchen table and a wooden McRay residential model icebox for furniture, a stained rag rug on the floor and bins and racks of salvaged objects of one kind or another against one side wall. A large wooden tool chest with his father's initials on it stood under the table. The only other object of interest was an old twenty-gallon whiskey barrel with a faded name stenciled in white: *N.B. Moll Wholesale and Retail dealer in Wines and Liquors, Green Lane, Montgomery County PA.* The Monster smiled to himself. A long way from home.

The Monster stood up and, stooping, shuffled across the floor in a pair of bedroom slippers he'd found one day on his rounds. They were red-and-black silk brocade with rubber soles and heels and looked as though they might have been a work in concert with a smoking jacket and a quilted robe. He reached the barrel and stood looking at it for a moment, letting the fingers of one hand trace around the top hoop and the smooth, dark-grained oak that made up the pickled wood cask. Finally he reached down and pulled up the top. Inside, curled into the bottom in a broken parody of a stillborn infant, lay the body of a small black girl, perhaps ten years old. Her head, bent back at an impossible angle, was facing upward, the eyes open, looking up at him imploringly, a trickle of blood dried on her baby-smooth cheek, draining down from the right socket where he'd stuck her with the needle-sharp engraving tool, a number six, which was just right for the job.

The eyes were drying out a little now, clouding over, and a few small flies were crawling across the swollen lips and thick, purpling tongue. He'd have to begin work soon or it would be too late to salvage what he needed. He thought about the time he'd spent with her before he'd killed her, feeling himself grow stiff and hard with the memory of how it had felt, but he stopped himself from thinking beyond that and dropped the top of the barrel back down, pushing the images crowding his head into some distant part of his mind for the moment, knowing that the memories could be brought forth any time he had need of them in the future.

He turned away from the barrel, crossed the room to the icebox and pulled up on the shiny steel latch. The inside was wood, heavily varnished, the shelf dividers made of slats of the same wood. He kept milk and cheese and a loaf of bread on the lower shelf, while the middle shelf held a rough pile of his leathery treasures, ready for use. On the top shelf, the coldest part of the icebox, there was a parcel wrapped in newspaper.

The Monster took down the parcel and took it to the kitchen table, setting it down carefully. He sat down in the chair and slowly peeled away the layers of newsprint to reveal what was underneath. It was the human head of an adult male; the wispy hair, once blond, was tipped with silver and the gray stubble on the cheeks had seemed to grow longer on the man's cheeks as the flesh on his face desiccated in the cold atmosphere of the refrigerator. The eyes were closed because the Monster had made sure of it by using tiny sutures through the flesh to keep them shut, but the mouth was opening up into a grin that grew wider with the passage of time as the muscles of the jaws began to thin out and shorten, pulling the lips away from the mouthful of small, pearly teeth.

The Monster stared at the head on the table a foot away from him, lost in the sensations it produced within him: the fear, the loathing and the strange power of it that seemed to flow into him like electrical current, an energy of death with the power to let him be whatever it was that he wanted to be. The power to kill and to live forever by killing.

As long as he had absolution.

The Monster crossed himself and closed his eyes, his strong, lithe fingers woven together in an attitude of prayer.

"Forgive me, Father, for I have sinned." And his father forgave him.

11/20/63
WEDNESDAY

Chapter 1

Ray Duval parked his Chevy in the underground garage and took the jail elevator up to the third-floor Homicide and Robbery Bureau. The old, slow elevator had shit-brown walls and smelled the way it looked. Normally it was used to transport felons from the cells on the fifth floor down to the basement, where they'd be taken to County Jail a few blocks away, but for Ray it was the easiest way to get to Homicide.

An operator sat at the elevator controls, protected from violent passengers by a steel mesh cage. Ray had never said more to him than good morning or good afternoon or thanks in all the years he'd been a Dallas cop. Riding up he stared at him and saw that he was thin, wore a brown smock, had a clubfoot and a twisted hand with the fingers all bunched up that he used to prod at the controls. A name tag on his chest said MICKEY.

"How's it going, Mickey?"

The man turned and looked at him and gave him a thin smile through the meshwork of the cage. His teeth were brown and he had a scar on his upper lip from a poorly done cleft lip and palate operation. He spoke with a nasal lisp and he knew perfectly well that neither Ray nor anyone else who rode his elevator gave a good goddamn how it was going. "Just fuckin' peachy," he said, then turned away again.

Riding up to the third floor Ray took off his hat and wiped the sweatband with his handkerchief, then put the hat back on. He was hot all the time now, being sick like he was, and any exertion made the sweat come up on him fiercely. It wasn't good sweat either, not the sweat you got on a hot day when you were working hard and an ice-cold beer would solve your problem. This sweat was like the kind you found on cheese left out too long, a sweat that was talking to you, telling you just what was coming, whispering that it wasn't too far off now.

The elevator stopped and thumped a little as Mickey tried to get the floors to meet. Ray stepped off into the small lobby in front of the toilets. He went out the pale green swing doors and turned right, pausing for a second at the water fountain for a long drink. Then he went along a few more feet until he reached the clear glass front door of Homicide-Robbery and pushed it open. Taking the regular elevator would have made the trip three times as long, and these days the fewer steps taken the better. He did exactly what his body told him now, which was ironic since he'd ignored it and taken it for granted through two wars and the better part of thirty years as a cop. Now mostly it was telling him he was dying. So was his doctor.

Ray took off his Knox fedora as he entered the bureau and gave a nod to Francis Ewell, who doubled as receptionist and secretary to Will Fritz, the Homicide captain. Like the entrance to Homicide-Robbery, Fritz's office had two glass panels, one just past reception, the other looking into the squad room. They were usually covered with venetian blinds, but you never knew when they were going to snap open and you were going to see the captain glaring at you for no good reason except to put the fear of God and Chief Curry into you in equal portions.

Ray went down the narrow hallway and turned right into the windowless squad room. There were twelve county-issue wooden desks crammed into the room, pairs pushed together in two rows, both rows facing the glass wall in Fritz's office. The more seniority you had, the farther away from the glass wall you sat. Ray's desk was as far back as you could get in the right-hand row and closest to the table with the big coffee urn on it, the old Kelvinator standing beside it.

Most of the other desks that far back were for the night shift but Ray had laid his claim years ago and nobody complained. The desk he butted up against belonged to his one-time partner, Ron Odum. Ron had quit the Dallas PD four months earlier after inheriting his daddy's oil stocks and his mansion in Vickery Place. Ron was talking about opening a car dealership, and given the state of Ray's ticker Fritz hadn't seen any point in pairing Ray up again.

There was a brown plastic radio sitting on top of one of the filing cabinets that ran along the wall behind him. It was a mid-forties Arvin that he'd coveted since rejoining the Dallas PD after the war, but there was no way he could walk off with it since everyone in the squad knew he collected and fixed old radios. It was tuned to KRLD and playing the Beach Boys singing "Little Deuce Coupe," a song he sort of liked but would never admit to. In fact he liked a lot of rock and roll, which he kept his mouth shut about in a room full of guys who thought Perry Como was the cat's ass.

Ray checked around the squad room. Most of the desks were empty, which meant the people who usually sat at them were out on the Job. Leavelle and Chuck Dhority were up

front closest to Fritz's glass panel and on the phone, while
Joe Perry was leaning back in his chair flipping through a
case file, but that was it. Ray picked up a paper clip from the
tray he kept at the front of his desk and flipped it toward
Perry. The younger detective looked up, scowling, then saw
it was Ray and smiled instead.

"Hey, Ray. How you doing?"

Ray did a fair imitation of the elevator operator's lisp.
"Just peachy," he said. "Who's catching? I can't read the
board from this angle."

The blackboard with the day's rotation on it was nailed to
the wall of the interview room on the right. The truth was,
Ray had left his glasses in the car and the blackboard was a
blur.

"You are," Perry answered. There was a little pause.
"Want me to take it if a call comes in?"

"Not unless some Olympic sprinter bumped off his
mother and I have to chase him around the Cotton Bowl,"
Ray answered. "I'm not dead yet."

Even without his glasses Ray could see the color rise in
Perry's cheeks. "No, no, I didn't mean nothing by it, Ray."
He paused and smiled. "Anyway, a sprinter like that'd be
some kind of nigger and you'd never catch him anyway unless it was at night and you caught his big old eyes in your
headlights."

Ray smiled back. He didn't feel too much one way or the
other about Negroes, but he didn't make fun of them. On the
other hand, he'd known from his earliest days on the Job
that the Dallas PD was full of Klansmen and John Birchers
and always had been. Dallas was a white man's city and all
the black folk around knew enough to keep their heads
down and their mouths shut. The same went for a Dallas cop

who even vaguely supported the principles of the so-called civil rights movement.

"So what do you think of this Kennedy thing?" Perry asked, trying to change the subject away from the state of Ray's health. The Kennedy thing was the presidential visit set for the twenty-second, with a parade and a big reception at the Trade Mart before lunch. Kennedy and the First Lady, as well as LBJ and the governor, would be in Fort Worth doing a day's glad-handing tomorrow and it was going to be even worse the day after that. Both the FBI and the Secret Service had been sniffing around for the past few days making a nuisance of themselves and looking down their noses at the locals.

"Well," said Ray, "I surely don't know. A couple of years back that Mink Coat Mob of so-called ladies spit all over Johnson and his wife in the lobby of the Adolphus and a year ago they did the same thing to Adlai Stevenson and almost flipped over his car."

"Maybe someone'll pee on the President."

"You have a piggy little mind, Perry."

"Don't I just." The detective grinned.

"Well, at least we don't have anything to do with it." Homicide was just about the only division not involved with the visit, and at least that was a blessing.

The telephone rang. Ray stared at it. Somebody was dead and if he picked up the telephone he'd be the one to take on the case, and that was the irony of it, and the fear. Somebody was dead and he was thinking about if he'd be a cop long enough to solve the murder, or even live that long. It was just about the only thing he cared about now—going out clean, they'd say that about him at least. But the telephone was ringing. "All yours," Perry offered. Ray picked up. At the same time he reached into the pocket of his suit jacket and brought out his red-and-black notebook for November. He turned to a new page and took a ballpoint out of the chipped and cracked Toby mug on his desk and wrote in the new date at the top of the page: 11/20/63. He listened to the voice on the other end of the line for a few moments, jotted down some brief notes with the pen, then hung up the phone.

"So?" asked Perry.

"Body in a refrigerator out at the dump."

"That's fresh," said Perry. "Like we haven't seen it a hundred times before."

"You ever seen one naked as a jaybird, cut up into pieces then put back together with twists of wire like some kind of puppet?"

"Christ on a crutch."

"More like Pinocchio."

Perry started humming an off-key version of "When You Wish Upon a Star." Ray gave him a raspberry in return, then made his way slowly out of the squad room. Fritz's big-jowled face looked up briefly from a desk full of paperwork as Ray passed the captain's open door but Ray avoided meeting the man's look. Most of his colleagues were overly solicitous about the state of his health, but Fritz's looks had nothing to do with sympathy; he was assessing Ray's competence, and the last thing Ray needed was to be sent down on sick leave, or worse, retired with a short pension. He was dead anyway, but without the Job he'd be dead a lot sooner, no matter what all the doctors said. Ray knew exactly what Fritz's look meant; Ray was due for his official DPD physical next week and he had no chance of passing it. He would be out in a few days, a month if he was real lucky. It was something he could barely let himself think about.

Ray used the jail elevator again, riding down with a silent Mickey, then walked behind the basement security desk and headed for his car. By the time he reached it he could hear the wheezing rattle in his throat. He sat in the car and waited until he caught his breath, then drove out of the underground lot, up the Commerce Street ramp and out onto the street. He turned south, eventually putting himself on State 75 and headed for the Dallas dump.

He felt the gurgling wheeze in his throat and upper chest recede and was careful to keep his leg and thigh from leaning against the door. Ten minutes of that and he'd have a gouge shaped like the door handle pitted into the puffy flesh of his leg that would take an hour to come back to normal. Ray twisted open the rectangular vent on his window and angled it so that the wind blew directly onto his face, drying the cold sweat.

He drove with his right hand, propping his left forearm on the molded in door rest. He'd bought the Bel Air in '55 almost ten years ago now, but even then they'd had optional air conditioning, and now he was regretting he hadn't given in to the salesman's exhortations. He glanced down at the clutter on the dash shelf and spotted a half-empty pack of Salems. Six months ago it would never have occurred to him that he'd wind up smoking menthol cigarettes, but now they were all he could take, and no more than five or six a day now, instead of two packs of Chesterfields, or three if it was a long day or a booze night out with the guys. He switched hands on the wheel and poked the right button for KRLD on the radio. Some guy with a whining voice was telling the world that "Big Girls Don't Cry" but Ray really didn't give a damn, as long as it stopped him thinking about what was wrong with him and what was going to happen.

The first hint had been impossibly small, so small that he overlooked it completely. Standing in the shower one day in May he'd vaguely been aware that the water striking the tops of his feet was slightly painful, as though the skin had been sunburned. That was followed by swollen ankles, which he put down to spending too much time on his feet, a decreasing appetite with a strange inverse increase in his weight, and most of all, an odd lack of energy. Idiotically, what tipped the scales and sent him to Dr. Ragland at the Medical Arts Building was the fact that the morning erections he'd had since puberty slowly but surely waned as the weeks went by and finally disappeared altogether. By then he'd put on so much weight that the pad of flesh around his groin had almost completely swallowed up his flaccid organ.

After three minutes in Ragland's examination room the doctor's diagnosis was clear as a bell and tolling an almost certain death knell for Ray Duval. He had congestive heart failure and it was killing him.

"You mean I had a heart attack?" Ray asked.

"A heart attack would have been better. Hearts heal after an attack."

"So what are you talking about?"

"For some reason your heart's enlarged. Scarlet fever used to cause it, but nobody get's that now with penicillin around."

"So, my heart's enlarged. What exactly does that mean?"

"Your heart gets bigger so it has to work harder pumping blood through your body. Your circulatory system starts to shut down to compensate. That's why your ankles and legs are swelling up and why you've developed that big belly. It's called edema. You're retaining water. Lots of it. The more water you retain the weaker your heart gets. Eventually water starts to collect in your lungs. You drown in your own fluids because there's no way to drain it out of your lungs fast enough."

"Jesus," said Ray. "What's the whatchamacallit? The prognosis?"

"Not good."

"How 'not good'?"

"They've developed some new diuretics—drugs that get water off you—but that might not be enough. The best you can do really is keep off your feet and try not to do too much of anything."

"How long?"

"Hard to say. I'll get you into Parkland and onto the diuretics. We'll see after that."

"How long?" Ray insisted.

Ragland sighed, stripped off his stethoscope and stuffed it into the pocket of his white coat. "Even with the diuretics probably no more than a year or two, and that's if you stop working. Keep going and you'll be dead in twelve months."

Ray looked out through the windshield at the gray, scudding sky. Bad weather coming in off the Gulf. It looked like it was going to rain on President Kennedy's parade.

Twelve months, half of them gone. He saw the entrance to the dump up ahead, a county black-and-white Ford Custom parked by the gate, its roof cherry blipping around and a lanky deputy leaning on the front fender smoking a cigarette. Ray switched off the radio. Big boys didn't cry either.

The deputy flicked his cigarette away and stepped forward as Ray pulled off onto the gravel shoulder. He walked up to the Bel Air and Ray cranked down the window.

"You Duval?"

"Right."

"Follow me?"

"Sure thing."

The deputy got back into his cruiser, spitting up a bit of gravel and dinging Ray's front end as he took off down the shoulder. City cops and county cops, always pecking at each other like chickens in a yard. Ray had never really understood it and now it seemed like the stupid games he and his brother, Audie, used to play, always competing, always at each other's throats. Nothing but a waste of precious time.

The Dallas City Dump was a half-mile-square scar on the landscape that was getting bigger with every passing day. Bulldozers rumbled up and around the piles of stinking, fuming garbage like giant rattling insects, pushing the refuse into larger and larger piles. There was every color of the rainbow to be seen, but the predominant tint was a speckled gray brown. Smoke rose from some parts of the dump, controlled burns meant to lessen the volume of material as well as provide a quick start to the process of decomposition.

The deputy led Ray along a maze of narrow roadways cut through the piles, finally stopping at a section of the dump that lay along the filth-choked course of Five Mile Creek. This part of the dump had been reserved for salvageable metals—everything from old bedsteads to spools of rusted wire and even the remains of a few old tractors and other agricultural machinery past its day. There were stacks of car batteries, sloped hills of old-fashioned mangle washing machines drifting down into the creek, and hundreds of refrigerators, everything from old-fashioned iceboxes to the thirties' and forties' models with condensers on the top to aerodynamic-styled fridges from the fifties that bore more than a passing resemblance to his Bel Air.

It looked like the story of Ray's life built out of refrigerators. Born with the iceboxes, grew up with the Kelvinator condensers, and now he'd die with his last meal coming out of the enamel-and-chrome smooth-walled Westinghouse he'd had since his wife ran off and got herself killed these ten years gone by.

There was a small shack built beside the creek between a rickrack pile of old car bumpers and a neater arrangement of various lengths of lead pipe. The deputy stopped his car in front of the shack, got out and immediately reached into his back pocket for a handkerchief to cover his nose. Ray climbed slowly out of the Bel Air and followed the deputy into the bedraggled little building.

There was a card table, a filing cabinet, a half-sized refrigerator, two chairs and a very old calendar for H. J. Justin Boots in Fort Worth. The floors were grease-stained planks. There was a scarred old .22 plinking rifle leaning against the tar paper wall in one corner, and the fat man sitting at the card table in his undershirt had a Walther Pistole 38 in a homemade shoulder holster under his left arm. The two windows were so filthy they were almost opaque. The shack smelled of beer and stale farts. The beer probably came from the refrigerator and no doubt the farts came from the fat man with the Walther.

"This is Mr. Janowski. He runs this part of the dump," said the deputy. "He's the one found the body."

"Nice pistol," said Ray. Janowski smiled. About a third of his teeth were missing and the rest were stained almost black from chewing tobacco. Ray wondered if there was a Mrs. Janowski. "War souvenir?"

"Got it off a dead German. Got lots of them."

"Collector?"

"Naw. Just killed a lot of Germans."

"So you found the body?"

"Just like Cyrus here told you."

"Where?"

"With the rest of the refrigerators."

"Show me."

"Glad to."

Janowski picked up the little .22 rifle and led the way out the door. Ray and Cyrus the deputy followed. Overhead Ray could see clouds of gulls up from the Gulf, trying to beat the bad weather and find something to eat. Ray sniffed and smelled burning rubber.

A rat that must have weighed six or seven pounds raced across their path and headed into one of the labyrinthine heaps of discarded metal. Janowski stopped in front of a relatively new-looking General Motors Frigidaire. "In there," he said, pointing with the barrel of the rifle.

"The door was closed like it is now?"

"Yup."

Ray stared at the white enamel coffin. "How'd you know there was something inside?"

"Rats," Janowski answered. "Dozens of them crawling all over it. They can smell meat through ten feet of concrete."

Ray turned to the deputy. "You called for the medical examiner?"

"Yes sir," said Cyrus. "Just like they asked me." His tongue flicked out and he looked at the closed refrigerator, almost entranced by it. "You want me to open her up?"

"Sure," Ray said. The kid seemed to be enjoying himself.

"Stand back then. Stinks to high heaven." The deputy took out his handkerchief again, covered his nose and mouth with it and approached the fridge. It was leaning back against several other refrigerators, propped up at an angle like a coffin at an Irish wake. Cyrus grabbed the handle, pulled it wide open, then jumped back as though someone was going to leap out and bite him.

The pale, marbled body had been stuffed into the refrigerator with a double fold like a business letter, once at the waist and once at the knees. He was naked and he'd been dead for at least a day or two. Legs, arms and chest were bloated with gas and there were maggots everywhere. The initial report had been correct. The corpse had been dismembered, then reassembled; Ray could see where the galvanized wire used to put Humpty-Dumpty back together again was biting into the distended flesh. Two fingers on the left hand were missing and one on the right. There was a deep indentation on the left wrist that hadn't been caused by the wire. The corpse barely looked human, which was probably a blessing. The only sure thing was the man's color and his sex. There was no sign of any blood at all. The man had not been killed in the refrigerator or anywhere in the general vicinity.

"When did you first notice the refrigerator?"

"Like I said, when I saw the rats."

"When was that?"

"S'morning when I come in."

"What time?"

"Supposed to be here at seven. It was more like six-thirty."

"Why'd you come in early?"

He lifted the gun. "Like to get in some target practice."

"You do it for fun?"

"Sure. No Germans left to kill. Not legal anyway."

"Is there a night watchman?"

"You kidding? What's to steal from a dump?"

"Trouble with kids?"

"No. Sometimes you catch a rag-and-bone man picking over things, but not lately. Caught an antiquator once though."

"Antiquator?"

"You know, one of those guys who gets old junk and polishes it up. Sells it to the rich people along with a bunch of lies about where it comes from."

"An antique dealer?"

"An antiquator, sure, just like I said."

"When was that?"

"Year or two ago."

"You call the police?"

"Took a couple a shots. Ran him off."

"Any idea who he is?" asked Ray, pointing at the body.

"Nope." There was something in Janowski's eyes.

"You lying to me?"

"Why would I do that?"

"Because you look like you're lying." Ray took an educated guess. "You cut off his fingers, didn't you?" Ray asked softly. "He had rings on and you cut off his fingers."

"Did not."

"You make me search you, I'll send you to jail."

"He didn't need them," the man grumbled.

Ray shook his head. It never ceased to amaze him how many truly stupid people there were in the world.

"Wristwatch?" Ray asked. That would account for the deep indentation around the wrist. Like his own leg against the window crank. He shook the thought off. "There was a wristwatch too, right?"

Janowski nodded glumly. "Yeah."

"Get you into very deep shit clipping fingers off a body," Ray said. "Mutilating a corpse, tampering with evidence. Theft."

"I got first crack at anything good comes in here. Always been that way."

"Not bodies," said Ray. "I get first crack at those. Where are the fingers?"

"Threw 'em away."

"The rings? Wristwatch?"

Janowski dug into the pockets of his oversize jeans and pulled out a handful of gleaming metal. Ray took out his handkerchief and held out his hand, palm up. Janowski dropped the jewelry into it. There were three rings: one a plain gold band that might have been a wedding ring, a nugget pinkie and a large oval signet with the initials *JP* scrolled together on the top surface. The wristwatch was a solid-gold Omega Constellation; it looked almost new, no more than a few years old. He flipped it over. There was an inscription in Latin on the back and two sets of initials. Another *JP* and a *PF* beside it.

The radio in the deputy's cruiser made a garbled crackling noise. Cyrus went back to answer it. Ray wrapped the jewelry up in his handkerchief and slid it into the pocket of his sports jacket. His mouth was dry as dust and the diuretics were making his kidneys ache, but there was no way he was going to ask Janowski for one of his beers, or even take a leak behind the shack.

Instead he went back to the Bel Air, took his own Polaroid Land Camera out of the trunk and shot two cartridges of the body in place, waving the prints in the air to dry them, then stuffing them into his jacket pocket along with the wristwatch and jewelry. He'd asked the department to buy one when they first came out but Fritz wouldn't go for it, so Ray'd bought one on his own. He found them useful, and by the time the staff photographer appeared the crime scene was usually a mess. This way Ray got things as fresh as possible. He clambered up behind the fridge and looked at the back. The serial plate had been neatly chiseled off. The fridge would be untraceable. Shit. Ray eased himself back onto solid ground.

Deputy Cyrus came back, took a quick look at the body

and then turned to Ray. "Meat wagon's at the front gate. They want me to guide them in."

"I'll follow you out," said Ray.

"What about him?" asked the deputy, poking his thumb toward Janowski. "We going to arrest him like you said? Mutilating the body and all?"

"He finds the fingers and brings them in to Parkland and I'll think about going easy on him."

"Yes sir."

"Think you can find the fingers?"

"Yes sir."

"Bring them to Parkland? Medical examiner's office."

"Yes sir."

"See that you do."

Ray stumped back to the Bel Air, feeling the weight of his legs. He climbed into the car, lifting his right leg in by gripping below the knee with his hands, then slammed the door. The whole process had left him short of breath again and he could hear his heart in his ears, tripping and stumbling along like a wounded soldier. He lit a Salem and followed the deputy back to the main gate. The black M.E. station wagon was parked on the shoulder. Two men in white lab jackets sat in the front seat smoking. In the back there'd be a collapsible stretcher and a wicker-basket coffin. Ray thought about stopping and telling them to bring the refrigerator along with the body but then he thought again and kept on driving, swinging right, heading back toward Dallas.

He'd had a bad feeling getting up that morning and an even worse feeling when the phone rang and he caught the murder. He had a week to go to his annual physical and he knew there wasn't a chance in hell he was going to get through it. Fritz would have him off the roster before you could spit and any pending cases would be handed over to one of the other white hats in the squad. Ninety percent of homicides involved wives killing husbands or vice versa, with the occasional mob hit thrown in just to spice up the stew, but this one was different and he was damned if he was going to let Fritz take it away from him before he'd gone. A week left in his working life, a week to do his final job and do it well. A week to go out strong before he died weak and useless to everyone in the world including himself. A week to find the killer and bring him down.

Chapter 2

It was only 11:30 A.M. when Ray Duval reached the third floor of police headquarters for the second time that day, but he could already feel the fatigue building. He turned right and stepped into the cramped men's room beside the elevator and spent five minutes there, sighing as he emptied his bladder. Then he went back to the squad room. Everything was pretty much as it had been before, except now Leavelle and Dhority were gone and Perry was the only one left in the room.

"You'd better find something to do or Fritz'll be on your case pretty soon." Ray dropped gratefully down into his old wooden swivel chair.

"Something'll turn up." Perry shrugged. "It's early yet."

"I suppose." To Ray it felt like the middle of the afternoon. He had the bottle of pills they'd given him at the hospital, but he knew if he took another one today he'd be taking a leak every ten minutes instead of just once every half hour, which was bad enough.

Ray emptied the pockets of his sports jacket onto his desk and took off his hat. Perry came over and perched on the desk beside him. "This the stuff from the dump?"

"Yup."

Perry flipped through the Polaroids. "Those cameras are pretty good."

"Useful."

"Is it true you have to be real accurate about pulling off the paper on the back?"

"Not so important as they say," Ray said. "Mind you, I'm not looking for great pictures, just a record of the body in place."

"Could have used one in Seattle last year," said Perry, going through the pictures again, this time more slowly. The previous year Perry had used his vacation to take his wife and his two kids to the World's Fair in Seattle. They'd heard about it for weeks afterward in the squad room, bored to tears by the young detective's predictions about how sure he was a monorail and a space needle were just the things for Dallas. "Ugly," said Perry, dropping the pictures back onto Ray's desk. "Any idea who he is?"

"The kind of man who'd wear three rings on his hands."

"My old man used to tell me that a man wearing more than one wasn't a gentleman."

"Well, this guy had three." He pushed them around on his desk with a pencil.

"No inscriptions?"

"Nope."

"Maybe he was queer," said Perry. "Don't queers wear a lot of jewelry?"

"I don't know," Ray answered. "I don't know any queers." He pushed the rings around on his desk some more and felt a surge of desire for a cigarette. He'd forgotten the Salems on the dashboard of his car and he knew he'd only be able to take a few puffs before his lungs seized up on him and he started gasping. He pushed the feeling down.

"There's gotta be queers in Dallas," Perry offered.

"There's queers everywhere. Like little pink niggers in yellow shirts."

"Maybe I'll start with the watch instead. Omegas aren't cheap, especially solid-gold ones. Somebody should remember an engraved inscription like that." Perry picked up the watch. He flipped it over and read the inscription. *"Tempus Fugit sed Amatus est Infinitus."* He shook his head. " 'Fuck the weather, she said, the mattress is infinite?' Doesn't sound queer."

"I think it means 'Time flies but love is infinite.' "

"Now *that* sounds queer."

Ray heard the sound of a door opening and looked up in time to see Fritz leaving his office with another man. The other man was wearing a dark suit, dark shoes and had close-cropped hair. He had Fed written all over him. They left the bureau, and through the big glass window in the door Ray saw them heading for the main elevators.

"Who's the Fed?"

"Secret Service. Probably another meeting with Curry." Jesse Curry was the owl-eyed and chubby-cheeked chief of police. Like Fritz, Curry had come up through the ranks. Unlike the captain, Curry had kept on going, calling in favors and playing politics, which was never Fritz's style.

"Taking Kennedy's visit pretty seriously."

"Put it this way," said Perry. "He's a long way off his home ground. Better safe than sorry."

"I suppose that's true." Ray pulled open the bottom drawer of his desk and dragged out the Dallas Yellow Pages. He turned to the jewelry section and started making calls. By two in the afternoon he'd given a pass to Perry's invitation to lunch, gone to the can six times, and had a fix on the biggest Omega dealer in Dallas, one of two who carried the Constellation model in solid gold. Once more he headed out into the gloomy day, his legs itching like fury after sitting at his desk for the last two and a half hours. He stopped at the water fountain and tossed down half a dozen aspirin to see if he could make the itch go away, but he doubted it. A few nights before it had been so bad he'd gone to the fridge and packed all the frozen food he could find around his legs to see if he could numb the itch, but all it had done was change the itch to a burn.

Edelson's, the Omega dealer, was on Main Street between Akard and Field just down from the old Praetorian Building. It was in the middle of a fashionable row of smaller stores selling everything from furs to expensive women's shoes. Edelson's itself was quite small, less than twenty feet across and perhaps sixty feet deep. The front window was black with a small square of clear glass showing off a diamond necklace on a flared felt neck stand, spotlit from above in a small beige niche.

Ray went into the store. A woman in her sixties or seventies was having a whispered discussion with a man in an expensive black suit, and a second salesman, younger but dressed the same way as his colleague, was replacing a tray of wristwatches in a glass, waist-high counter. He looked up as Ray approached, taking in the slow walk, the rumpled off-the-rack blue suit and the stained, fawn-colored fedora Ray hadn't taken to be reblocked since he'd picked it up ten years ago. He went back to arranging the tray of watches in the case.

Ray reached the man and stopped, placing his hands flat on the top of the counter. The salesman looked annoyed. He turned and took a cloth and a spray bottle and began spritzing the counter around Ray's large hands. The air filled with the smell of vinegar.

"If you don't mind," said the man.

Ray lifted his hands. The man spritzed and wiped. Ray put his hands down just as they'd been before.

"Sir," said the younger man sternly, "we like to keep our fingerprints off the counter if you don't mind."

"It's not sir," Ray answered. "It's Detective Sergeant."

"I beg your pardon." The kid looked suitably impressed at the title, but he was still giving Ray a dirty look for the way he dressed. Ray reached into his pocket and took out all the jewelry, including the watch.

"Recognize anything?"

"The wristwatch is an Omega Constellation."

"The rings?"

"I don't recognize any of them."

"Flip the watch over."

The young man did as he was told. Ray could see that his hands were shaking a little bit. Hiding something? Or just scared of cops in old hats who didn't take any shit from pretty boys in sharp suits? "The engraving is in Latin."

"You go to private school or something?"

"No, but I recognize it as Latin."

"Can you tell who did the engraving? Was it your store?"

"Edelson's does engraving, yes."

"Did you engrave the watch?"

"It's very difficult to say."

"You keep a record of selling watches like this?"

"Yes."

"And engraving them?"

"Yes."

"Then it shouldn't be too difficult to put the two of them together now, should it?"

"I'll have to ask my superior." The young man cleared his throat. "Mr. Edelson is with a client at the moment." He nodded toward the front of the store. Ray turned and looked over his shoulder. Mr. Edelson was clearly the older man talking to the older woman in the mink coat.

"You want me to get him or do you want to do it yourself?"

The kid looked terrified at the prospect of Ray barging in on the conversation with Madam Mink and his boss. "I'll do it."

"Fine," said Ray. The young man followed the counter around to where Mr. Edelson was standing, waited a few seconds for a lull in the conversation and then put his two cents in. Both Edelson and the old lady stared at Ray. He smiled back at them. Mr. Edelson went back to his conversation with the old woman and the kid trotted back to where Ray was standing.

"Mr. Edelson says if you'll wait until he finishes with Mrs. Saylor he'll be happy to answer any questions you might have."

"Thanks," said Ray.

He scooped up the jewelry and the watch, turned away from the young man and walked back the length of the store. He stopped beside Mrs. Saylor in the mink coat. Mr. Edelson looked up and turned his lips into a puckered little pout of disdain. Ray didn't wait for the man to speak. He took one of the Polaroids of the dead body out of his pocket and placed it on the counter where Mrs. Saylor couldn't miss it. The old lady jerked back as though someone had pulled a chain embedded in the back of her neck.

"My God!" she said.

Edelson looked down at the photograph and blanched.

"It looks a bit like a pig trussed up to have its bristles boiled off, but it's not. It's a man and he's dead and he was wearing an Omega Constellation which he most likely bought here. I'd like you to answer a few questions about it. Now." He turned to Mrs. Saylor. "If you don't mind, that is, ma'am." He tipped his hat to the old woman and she fled from the store.

"Was that absolutely necessary?" asked Edelson, making his little pouty face again.

"Apparently," said Ray. "Your boy back there didn't recognize the engraving on the back of the watch. I thought maybe you might."

Edelson turned the watch over and read the inscription. He nodded. "Yes, this is our work."

"How can you tell?"

"Mr. Vanetti, our engraver, has a particular way with swirls."

"Really?"

"Yes."

"You know who JP is, or PF?"

"The names of our clients are confidential."

"No state secrets in a watch, pal."

"Nevertheless."

Ray dropped the good-old-boy drawl. "Nevertheless, if you don't tell me who JP is, it's obstruction of justice and it gets you put in jail, you pretentious little prick." Ray smiled. "Your memory suitably jogged now?"

"Jennings Price," said Edelson.

"Who is he?"

"He deals in fine editions and manuscripts. He dealt mostly in metaphysics as well as some Texana."

"Texana?"

"Books and documents about Texas. Autographs of well-known Texans. It's become quite a lucrative trade, I hear. There are at least a dozen dealers in Dallas and even more in Houston."

"You seem to know quite a bit about it."

"People who deal in luxury items generally associate with people in like positions."

"Does that mean you knew Jennings Price?"

"Yes. But not well." Edelson paused. "Was that Mr. Price in the photograph?"

"Why do you say that?"

"I assumed it, since you have his wristwatch."

"And his rings. Three of them. Did the Price you knew wear a lot of rings?"

Edelson nodded. "He tended to be a tad ostentatious with his jewelry."

"A tad?"

"Yes."

"You have an address for him?"

"I'm sure he's listed in the telephone directory."

"Save me some time," said Ray.

Edelson nodded curtly and walked back the length of the store. He went through a curtain as black as his suit. Ray looked down through the counter. There were hundreds of rings on display, mostly diamond and sapphire, all of them looking old-fashioned. A discreet card referred to them as "estate jewelry." Stripped off bodies before they were slipped into their coffins or sold to ward off failing fortunes. Every one of them had probably meant something once upon a time and now none of them meant anything. Someone else's bad dream or tragedy. Edelson returned with a card in his hand. He gave it to Ray.

JENNINGS PRICE & CO.

Fine Editions, Manuscripts &
Autographs
Metaphysics, Exotica & Texana
93 Stone Place
Dallas, Texas
Telephone SH8-1555

The top line with Price's name on it was almost unreadable. Stone Place, Ray knew, was a narrow street in the middle of downtown about a block and a half to the east. He'd used it as a shortcut once or twice not so long ago when he walked most places he needed to go downtown and remembered it as lined with high-class stores cheek by jowl in narrow four- and five-story buildings from the last century.

"May I be of any further assistance?" Edelson asked.

"Tell me what you know about Price."

"As I said, I didn't know him very well."

"How well?"

"As business associates."

"A jeweler and a book dealer."

"Sometimes information would come to me that Mr. Price found useful and vice versa."

"You read much?"

"I beg your pardon?"

"You sound like the type of man who reads a fair bit."

"When I can."

"Dickens?"

"Of course."

"*A Christmas Carol*, Scrooge, all that?"

"Certainly."

"That the kind of information you passed back and forth?"

"I'm afraid I don't understand."

"There's a scene in the book where a bunch of servants and the undertaker are selling off Scrooge's stuff to a fence. Bartering. Is that the kind of information you shared?" Ray tapped the glass countertop. "Estate sales. Books, jewelry."

"I resent the analogy."

"Sure you do, but that was the nature of the relationship,

wasn't it? You'd tell him about books from estates you were pawing through and he'd do the same for you. Right?"

"If you wish."

"Make any enemies that way?"

"No."

"Sure?"

"Ours is a somewhat closed community. There is no need for the kind of acrimony you are suggesting."

"So nobody'd kill him for one of his old books."

"I seriously doubt it."

"So what would they kill him for, Mr. Edelson? Sex, revenge, politics, what?"

"As I said, I didn't know him very well."

"Member of any of the same clubs, associations?"

"The chamber of commerce, Rotary."

"Anything else?"

Edelson paused. Ray waited.

"We were both members of the Dallas Gourmet Association."

"Gourmet as in food?"

"Yes. We would invite famous chefs to cook for us."

"How often?"

"Usually once a month."

"You'd go for a meal, have a few drinks and then go home?"

"They were largely social occasions. Sometimes we had guest speakers."

"About food?"

"No. Usually about their own professions, interesting anecdotes, travel tales, that sort of thing."

"Was Price a longtime member?"

"One of the founders actually."

"Any enemies there?"

"None that I can think of."

"Well, he obviously had at least one enemy who really, really didn't like him, Mr. Edelson, so why don't you think on that fact and I'll get back to y'all later."

"Certainly."

"Thanks for your cooperation." Ray tipped his hat and left the store. Something behind the man's eyes said there was more but Ray knew better than to pull on a weed too hard in case you broke it off before you got to the root. He had dandelions in his front yard like that. He'd let Edelson off the hook for a while and then come back at him.

Ray had parked the car in front of a hydrant a hundred yards away, the sun visor down to show off the DPD emblem and keep away traffic cops. He was a little tired by the time he climbed behind the wheel, but the aspirins seemed to have put the itch down to a dull roar. He could feel his feet swelling hard inside his foam-lined Roblees, but even that didn't seem to be bothering him too much today.

He put the key in the ignition but he didn't start the car. Instead he just sat there, leaning back against the vinyl seat, staring at the roof liner and seeing nothing, listening to the unsteady beat of his heart. He found himself thinking about the hospital and how strange it had been, lying in a bed in a ward at Parkland, one tube in his arm pushing in the diuretic and another tube up his Johnson draining out an endless stream of piss as his legs and feet and belly went back to normal.

The guys from the bureau had somehow found an old Dahlberg pillow radio with a detachable speaker you stuck under your pillow so you didn't disturb the people around you. Instead of listening to the sounds of the people dying all around him he'd listened to classical music that came in perfectly on the white, sausage-shaped Dahlberg. Sometimes he knew that he was hallucinating because the soft-voiced host on the broadcasts was speaking directly to him, but it didn't matter because it lifted him up and took him away from where he really was, and that was all that mattered.

The radio turned the hospital into a dream that remained dreamlike even when he was well enough to be up and around, dragging his intravenous pole around the ward and then around the entire wing of the hospital, always knowing that any time he wanted he could go back to the bed and lie down and listen to his pillow and the sounds of Mozart and Chopin and a hundred others he'd never heard of but learned to love.

When they finally let him out of Parkland after two weeks of bringing him back to life he plugged in the Dahlberg at home, but he could never find the classical station that had come in so well over the airwaves while he was in the hospital. Sometimes he wondered if he'd hallucinated all of it and the music had never been there at all.

The whole city was like that for him now, a dream so vivid it had more reality than his waking, breathing day. Always, he was apart from it by the slightest of degrees, a captive in time, often a blurred split second ahead, at other times decades gone by. Sometimes he'd be swept away on a deep, almost religious wave of sadness that never seemed to have a source, but usually presented him with some tiny fragment from the past he hadn't thought about in years, the images clear enough to be frightening and wrenching enough to make him catch his breath in his throat and bring tears to his eyes.

It was exactly 6:39 A.M. on Omaha Charlie. They'd gone up a crevice in the cliff by using their daggers while behind them anyone stupid enough or cowardly enough was getting

*picked off by enfilading fire from a forward bunker high
above them to their left. Ray knew it was exactly 6:39 because he'd seen the mud-spattered face of Lieutenant Norman D. Belcher's Gruen and that's what it said. Belcher got
to the top of the cliff first, with Ray a few seconds behind.
When he came over the cliff, there was Belcher's Gruen, still
on Belcher's wrist, but it was just his hand and there was
nothing left of the rest of his body except some bloody rags
and entrails. Ray just lay there in the mud above Omaha
Charlie and watched the second hand of the Gruen ticking
off seconds that didn't mean a damn thing anymore, because
there was no Lieutenant Norman Belcher anymore, there
was just good old Pfc. Ray Duval and the Gruen. He'd taken
the Gruen off the wrist and put it on his own, not to steal it,
but somehow feeling that as long as he wore it a little bit of
Lieutenant Belcher was still ticking away, like a pulse. Like
a heartbeat.*

Sitting in the car, staring out the windshield, Ray could
feel the hot sting in his eyes. He'd worn the Gruen for the
rest of the war and then he'd come home and taken it off and
put it in a drawer, where it ran down and stopped, surrounded by cuff links and tie tacks and a few loose buttons.
And *that* was the memory that could bring tears to his eyes:
not the death of Lieutenant Belcher, but letting the Gruen
stop without even noticing it, letting Belcher come to his
final end in a dusty drawer.

"Ah, screw it," he said. He wiped his eyes quickly. His
legs hurt but walking a block or so there and the same back
wouldn't kill him and he needed the cooling air and the
smell of rain and at least the illusion that he was alive and
all was well. He decided to go for broke and reached out for
the pack of Salems on the dash. He lit one with his old

Rangers Zippo, the same one he'd had going up that cliff on Omaha Charlie.

Careful not to drag any of the smoke into his lungs until he was ready, he pushed open the driver's-side door of the Chevy, climbing out by swinging his legs out first and boosting the rest of his body out by levering forward with his arms. He slammed the door, locked it and slipped in between his and another car to reach the sidewalk.

He leaned against the passenger-side fender of the Chevy to catch his breath and took a short drag on the stale Salem, feeling the menthol bite hard into his throat but holding back the cough that came automatically. To hell with all of it. Today he would smoke a few cigarettes and do his job as well as he could and enjoy one of his numbered days no matter what it gave him and where it took him. When the day was done he'd go home and pour himself two inches of Maker's Mark in a big glass with two cubes of ice, settle into his big chair and maybe watch *The Beverly Hillbillies* for a while.

Ray pushed himself off the fender, flipped away the half-smoked cigarette and headed slowly down the sidewalk back down Main Street to Stone Place.

Chapter 3

Stone Place was pretty much as Ray remembered: high-class stores occupying the main and sometimes the second floor of four-story stone and brick buildings. They had been rich people's city homes in the late nineteenth and early twentieth centuries. Number 93 was almost in the middle of the long block between Elm and Main. It was four steps up to the tall, black-painted front door and a discreet brass plaque riveted to the wall beside it said only:

JENNINGS PRICE & CO.

ANTIQUARIA

Ray turned the big brass knob and pushed open the heavy door. He found himself in a short, marble-floored vestibule that had a real elephant's-foot umbrella stand with a pair of walking sticks in it. Beyond the vestibule was a large room with a high, patterned tin ceiling and narrow-plank pegged cherry floors. The walls were covered with floor-to-ceiling bookcases except for niches containing display cases every ten feet or so. Down the sides of the room there were more bookcases, head high, and dead center in a long line there was a trio of display cases with glass tops. All the display cases and bookcases had been stained to match the floors. At the end of the row of display cases there was a huge, ornate mahogany Chippendale Revival desk from the 1920s with tapering legs and claw-and-ball feet. A man in his early thirties, fair hair fading away in a widow's peak, sat behind the desk in a gray, high-backed upholstered chair, circling things in a catalogue of some kind. He barely looked up when Ray came through the door, then went back to his work.

Ray decided to hold off revealing himself for the moment. Instead he started browsing the stock, beginning with the bookcases in the alcoves on either side of the vestibule. The books were all old and were arranged in alphabetical order by author: E. B. Fleming, *Early History of Hopkins County Texas*; Henry Stuart Foote, *Texas and the Texans*, two volumes; Grant Foreman, *Indian Removal*; W. A. Ganoe, *A History of the United States Army*; Pat Garrett, *The Authentic Life of Billy the Kid*. Ray pulled that one down and opened it to the flyleaf. It was listed as "fine—$150." It was a paperback, published in Santa Fe in 1882. About 20 to 30 percent of the books had something to do with Texas, and most of them were histories of some kind.

He slowly made his way along the line of large display cases in the center of the room. There were some books, a few objects and a lot of documents of one kind and another, each one identified by a small card: *Texas Declaration of Independence, 1836; William Barret Travis' "Victory or Death" Letter from the Alamo*; a collection of Texas currency; and half a dozen Davy Crockett letters as well as a copy of *Davy Crockett's Almanack of Wild Sports of the West and Life in the Backwoods*.

Ray went and stood in front of the reproduction Chippendale desk and waited for the man with the widow's peak to notice him. It was like Edelson all over again. The fair-haired man paid no attention to him at all. He continued to circle things in the catalogue. From where Ray was standing he could now see that it was a listing of books. Widow's Peak was circling possibles for his master's perusal, no doubt. Except the master was on a slab at Parkland Hospital by now with Dr. Earl Rose cutting him open for a look inside. Ray smiled at that, wondering how Earl would deal with a man in as many pieces as Jennings. His legs had started to itch again and the Salem had made the inside of his mouth dry, another side effect of the diuretic pills. In a few minutes he was going to need a toilet too.

Ray rapped a knuckle on the desk, just outside the red leather insert that covered most of the top. He was in the perfect frame of mind to question the little snot behind the desk.

"Yes?" said Widow's Peak.

Ray decided to keep it simple for the moment, see how the snot reacted when the other shoe dropped. "The boss in?"

"Mr. Price, you mean?"

"Is he the boss?"

"Yes."

"Is he in?"

"No."

"Is he usually in around this time?"

"Not on Wednesdays."

"His day off?"

"You might say that."

Interesting, thought Ray. Whoever killed him would have an extra day before he was missed.

"Perhaps I can help you?" said Widow's Peak. The look on his face said he doubted it very much.

"I need a bathroom."

"We don't have public toilet facilities."

"I'm not the public," said Ray. He reached into his back pocket and took out his buzzer. He flipped open the leather case and showed Widow's Peak. "By the way, what's your name?"

"Errol Timmins."

"How about it, Errol? You have a bathroom hidden away somewhere?"

Errol hesitated, then nodded. He half turned in his chair. "At the back. The last set of shelves against the back wall is faux."

"Faux?"

"The books are trompe l'oeil."

"You lost me."

Errol sighed. "They're painted on."

"It's a door," said Ray.

"That's right."

"Why didn't y'all just say so?" He smiled down at Errol. "What else you got hidden behind the faux door and the trompe l'oeil books?"

"The stairs and the freight elevator."

"Which go where?"

"To the upper floors. Storage on the second floor. Mr. Price's private apartments on the third and fourth."

"Elevator need a key?"

"No."

"Mr. Price's apartment, though, you need a key to get into that."

"Yes."

"You got it?"

"As a matter of fact I do."

"Thought you might. Let's go." Ray made a sweeping gesture with his hands.

"I'm afraid I'm going to have to ask what this is all about," said Errol.

"Don't be afraid to ask," said Ray. "It's about the fact that I have to take a leak real bad and it's about the other fact that someone hacked your boss into little pieces and then stuck him in a fridge and took him out to the dump."

Errol went pale and his hands reached out to grab the edge of the desk. He swallowed hard. Ray noticed the man's fingernails looked as though they'd been polished. He'd never seen a man with a manicure before.

"The key."

"Don't you . . ." Errol's voice turned into cotton wadding. He swallowed and tried again. "Don't you need a warrant?"

"He's a victim, not a suspect. You don't need a warrant to look over a crime scene."

"Crime scene?"

"Could be." Ray shrugged. "He might have been butchered upstairs for all I know. Blood splashed every-where, maybe some guts and brains and who knows what all." He felt his kidneys cramp hard. "But first I really do have to use the bathroom, Errol, so why don't you show me the way and then we'll go on up to Mr. Price's apartment, how's that?"

Ray took his leak and then he and Errol went up an ancient, creaking slat-front Otis to the third floor. Errol pushed up the gate when they thumped to a halt. In front of them was a small foyer wallpapered in gold fleurs-de-lis against a powder-blue background. Dead ahead was a cherry-stained door. Errol made no move to leave the elevator.

"Maybe I should stay here."

"I don't think so, Errol. I'll be needing a tour guide, after all."

"I know very little about Mr. Price's private affairs."

Already getting as far away from Price as he could. Nothing like distancing yourself from the dead. "Who said anything about his affairs? I just want to look around his apartment." Ray smiled. "You have been up here before, haven't you?"

"Once or twice."

"Or more?"

"I can't remember exactly."

"Come on," said Ray. He put his hand in the middle of Errol's back and gave him a little shove. Errol stumbled out of the elevator.

"You never gave me the key," said Ray.

Errol reached into his pocket, pulled out a ring of keys and held them out to Ray. "You do it," said Ray.

Errol looked terrified and sweat was beading up along the edge of his widow's peak. "I'd rather not."

"I don't give a shit. Open the goddamned door."

Errol fumbled with the ring, found the right key and opened the door. He stood aside so Ray could go first. Ray put his hand on Errol's back again and nudged him through the doorway. "Just in case the killer's still in there with a machete or something — he'll hack you up first."

Ray followed Errol into the apartment. It was full of furniture, all of it old. The door led into a short hall stuffed with half a dozen varieties of small table, the walls above them crammed with gold-leaf Middle European icons and as many Victorian miniatures, landscapes and portraits, arranged in no particular way or order. The walls were the same pale blue as the wallpaper in the foyer off the elevator.

Halfway down the hall there was a doorway leading into a modern kitchen complete with fridge, stove, a small freezer unit and Dutch-tiled counters. The floor was done in alternating black and white linoleum tiles. A door on the other side of the hall led into a sparely furnished office with a pair of telephones—one red, one white—and a lot of ledgers. There was an adding machine on one side of the metal desk and a new-looking IBM Executive Electric typewriter in the same powder blue as everything else in the place.

"He like blue a lot?" asked Ray as they headed down the hall.

"It's his favorite color," said Errol.

"Better than red." Ray smiled.

They stepped into the dining room. It was dominated by a wide Regency mahogany extending table with two double gate legs. Ray counted all the legs and came up with a total of fourteen. There was enough room to seat twenty in comfortable Hepplewhite mahogany reproductions with silk-upholstered seats in a thin alternating blue and white stripe that matched the wallpaper.

"Interesting," said Ray.

"Yes?"

"The table's an original but the chairs are fakes."

"Reproductions."

"If something's not real it's a fake."

"You know something about antiques, then?"

"I grew up with them all around me." That and oil wells, Ray thought.

The rugs on the cherry floors were all authentic. Dagestan prayer rugs, Shirvan kilims and Kubas in every color of the rainbow, with blues predominating, of course, including a pale blue Chajli that must have cost Price a fortune.

"He have money or was he born with it?"

"His parents were quite wealthy."

"Oil?"

"Cotton, I believe. Mr. Price was born in Atlanta."

"Now isn't that interesting." Ray nodded, even though it wasn't very interesting at all. "How old was he?"

"Forty-two," said Errol.

"Not married, I take it?"

"No," Errol answered stiffly.

Ray pulled open a pair of pocket doors and they stepped into the living room.

It was full of furniture, most of it antique, none of it matching, but all of it somehow fitting together as though it belonged. There was a huge corduroy modern sectional that took up one wall and half of the next, a marble coffee table on spindly metal legs, occasional tables, end tables, side tables, Windsor chairs, side arm chairs, club chairs and wing chairs, the giant sectional balanced by a massive Steinway grand kitty-corner to it. The rugs were like the ones in the dining room, only larger. Every horizontal surface was covered with something—lamps, clocks, vases, a pair of Gouda ceramic decanters, a Wedgewood bowl, a Derby vase with penguins on it, busts on pedestals. There were paintings that looked as though they were by Old Masters but weren't quite, lots of other paintings, mostly landscapes, framed in heavy gilt, and a pair of authentic-looking Remingtons—*Indian Trapper* and *White Trapper*—and an N. C. Wyeth called *The Silent Fisherman*. There was also a tall glass display case filled with firearms. Ray recognized a Winchester 73, a Frontier Colt, a Spenser carbine in an original saddle holster and a Smith & Wesson .44. Looking closely at that one, Ray saw that the butt had been inscribed: *Texas Jack Cottonwood, Spring 1872.*

"Bedroom must be a treat," said Ray.

"I wouldn't know," Errol answered, but his face was flushed with embarrassment.

"Your boss was a collector."

"Yes."

"All sorts of things."

"Yes."

"Big piano over there. Mr. Price play anything? Dixie maybe?"

"I never heard him play."

"A lot of this stuff looks expensive, the Remingtons and the Wyeth in particular." Errol seemed surprised that Ray had the slightest idea of what he was looking at and who the artists were. "Some of it might even be worth killing for, you think?" Of course in Little Mexico on the edge of the business district you could get somebody killed for a double sawbuck, but Price hadn't died a twenty-dollar death.

"I don't know," Errol answered.

"Anything missing?"

Errol looked around, his eyes doing a machine-gun inventory that said a lot about how often he'd been in the room.

"There doesn't appear to be."

"Any recent pictures of Mr. Price around?"

"I think I could find one."

"Why don't you just do that," said Ray. He eased down on the sectional couch. "I'll just wait for you here if you don't mind."

"No, not at all."

"And while you're at it, you better get me any legal papers of his you know about—wills, insurance policies, that kind of thing—and the name of his lawyer."

"Certainly."

"Mr. Price have any close relatives living nearby?"

"No, sir, none that I know of."

"Too bad."

"Oh?"

"Umm," said Ray from the depths of the sectional. "Means y'all are going to have to come down to Parkland and identify the body for me."

"I'd rather not if you don't mind." Errol looked as though he was going to be sick.

"I don't mind, but someone's got to do it. That's the law. He does look pretty bad, I must say, all puffed up like that. Understandable you wouldn't want to see him that way." Ray shrugged. "But like I said, it's the law."

"Couldn't you find someone else?"

"Why don't you sit down for a minute," said Ray, patting the sofa cushion beside him. "You're looking a bit on the pale side."

"Thank you," said Errol. He sat down, closing his eyes for a moment. His tongue came out and licked his thin, too-red lips.

"Enemies," said Ray.

"What?"

"We were talking about them before."

"No, we weren't," Errol said, frowning as he opened his eyes. There was a gold cigarette case on the marble coffee table in front of them and a silver table lighter to go with it. The engraved initials on the lighter were *TMD,* not *PF* like the watch. There were no initials on the cigarette case.

"You want to smoke, go right ahead," Ray offered. Errol almost lunged for the case. He opened it and Ray saw a photograph inset in the top. "Looks like Marlene Dietrich," he said.

"It is," Errol answered, picking up the lighter and flicking it on. He lit the cigarette. Errol handed Ray the case. It was full of Chesterfields, his old brand. The picture really was of Marlene Dietrich, and signed.

"How'd he get it?" asked Ray, snapping the case shut and putting it back on the coffee table.

"Private sale."

"What does that mean?"

"It never came on the open market. A friend of Mr. Price offered it to him."

"How'd the friend get it?"

"I have no idea."

Ray nodded. Four or five years back he remembered reading about Dietrich's apartment in New York being burgled. The case was probably part of the haul.

"Your boss do a lot of that?"

"What?" asked Errol, puffing on the cigarette, holding it between his second and third fingers rather than the first and second.

"Receive stolen goods."

"I don't understand."

"Sure you do. Miss Dietrich doesn't go around selling her cigarette cases 'cause she can't pay the rent. The case was stolen."

"Surely you're not suggesting Mr. Price is a thief?"

"It would be a burglar, and no. It's like I said, he knowingly received the box as stolen goods. Not that it matters, since he's dead, but it is interesting."

"Why?"

"Because it means he wasn't above that kind of thing. It means he was willing to bend the law. Farther you bend it, more likely you are to get hit with it on the rebound. Enemies?"

"He didn't have any that I know of."

"Lovers?"

"I wasn't privy to his love life."

"You're beginning to sound like one."

"What?"

"A privy, son. So why don't you give me the straight stuff for a minute and I'll figure out a way you don't have to go down to the autopsy room at Parkland and see your boss with his brains on the scale and his liver in a jar."

"I really don't know anything about his love life."

"Everything here says he was queer. That a good guess?"

"Are you asking me if Mr. Price was a homosexual?"

"Yes, that's what I'm asking. And maybe I'm asking if you're one as well. Maybe this was some fairy thing."

"Homosexuality is against the law in Texas."

"I know that," said Ray. "As far as I know it's against the law almost everywhere."

"You're asking me to admit to breaking the law. If I said yes I could go to jail."

"I'm a homicide detective, Errol, not a vice detective. You ask me, the guys who work vice are as bad as the people they go after. I don't care if your boss wore yellow on Thursdays or liked poking little boys in the ass, I'm trying to find out who killed him. You know what they say, equal justice under the law and all that. You think because he was queer I'm going to say, oh, too bad for him, he was a queer, so I'm just going to forget all about who butchered him?" Ray shrugged again. "Some cops might think that way, but not me, Errol." And he meant it.

"I don't see how his sexual inclinations are relevant, or mine for that matter."

"Shows how much you know about homicide. Murder is always about sex, money, revenge, or all three in any combination. But I really don't care shit from shinola about who he was screwing, okay? Just play along, okay? You with me here?"

"Yes."

"Good. Go back a page. Who was he screwing?"

"No one. Not recently anyway. Not seriously."

"What's recently?"

"More than a year. Ever since . . ." Errol ran a manicured hand through the widow's peak and looked as though he was going to cry.

"Don't dangle me, Errol, or we head for Parkland right now."

"For most of last year he had a . . . relationship with Mr. Valentine."

"Valentine?"

"Mr. Douglas Foster Valentine."

"You sound as though I should know who he is."

"Mr. Valentine is very well known in the field."

Ray sighed. "And what field would that be?"

"Texana," said Errol.

"Books as well?"

"Just ones about Texas. Furniture, documents, paintings, ephemera."

"There's a real market for this stuff?"

"Growing by leaps and bounds."

"Leaps and bounds, you say." Ray stared at the box with Marlene Dietrich inside and thought about Chesterfields, and then thought better about them. "What do you know about this Valentine?"

"As I said, he's very prominent."

"Store?"

"On Harwood, near Pacific."

The artsy neighborhood. Galleries and antique stores within a hop and a skip from the big Negro slums just a bit farther north. He wondered for a second if the President was going to run his motorcade through there. Probably not, but give it a few years and it would all be artsy stores and then business towers and the black people would get shuffled off somewhere else.

"What else can you tell me about Valentine?"

"He's very sophisticated. He went to a design school in New York. He may even be from there."

"Were they openly lovers?"

"I'm not sure I know what you mean."

"Did everyone else know?"

"Anyone who counted." Errol flushed again. "It's a pretty small community."

"Queers or people interested in this Texana?"

"Both."

"How many dealers other than Valentine and Price?"

"A dozen or so in Dallas. Several in Fort Worth. Twenty in Houston."

"What about collectors?"

"Serious ones? Perhaps a hundred in the whole state. There are several eastern universities with an interest in the subject as well. Harvard, for one."

"You don't say."

"Yes."

"They were together for most of last year?"

"Not literally. But they were . . . seeing each other."

"And then they stopped . . . seeing each other."

"Yes."

"Why? They quarrel? Fight? Beat each other up?"

"Of course not."

"Then what?"

"They had differences."

"Differences?"

"They disagreed about some business things. Mr. Valentine wanted to join forces."

"Valentine and Price?"

"Price and Valentine." Errol smiled for the first time.

"So they did fight."

"More like bickering. Nothing serious."

"Not serious enough to kill over, you mean?"

"Yes."

"They were sleeping together and they had business problems. So far we've got sex and money, Errol. What about jealousy? Any of that?"

Errol took a deep breath. "Mr. Price accused Mr. Valentine of selling forged documents." Errol suddenly looked greatly relieved. He butted the Chesterfield into a silver bowl decorated with irises that stood beside the lighter.

"Any documents in particular?"

"A number of them, including the broadside of the Texas Declaration of Independence on parchment and the Victory or Death letter from the Alamo on vellum."

"What's the difference?"

"Parchment is made from the skin of sheep, calves or goats. Vellum is finer. It comes from kids, lambs and calves, baby animals."

"And these documents?"

"There are perhaps half a dozen or so of each still in existence. Mr. Price's has a pristine provenance."

"A pristine provenance."

"It means—"

"I know what it means." Ray smiled. "I was just interested in your turn of phrase."

Errol flushed again. "That's what Mr. Price used to say."

"And he said Valentine's was a fake?"

"Yes."

"Worth a lot?"

"Fifteen to twenty thousand dollars at auction. The governor owns one. So does the Dallas Public Library."

"And that's what they had their falling out about?"

"Yes. Mr. Price refused to authenticate Mr. Valentine's copy. He started spreading rumors about Mr. Price. There was talk of a lawsuit."

"Well, you see, Errol, now we're getting down to it. Ex-lovers quarreling over money. Rivals, you might say."

"I don't think Mr. Valentine is the type to . . ."

"Sure he is," said Ray. "We all are." He levered himself upright, away from the tangy smell of the cigarette so close. His legs were like stone. "You go get that photograph and those papers, Errol. Then we'll be on our way."

"But you said . . ."

"Y'all should finish your sentences, Errol. Be decisive—that's what they say about getting ahead in the world. And I didn't say anything except a lot of mights and maybes, so get along and find me that photograph and the rest of the stuff I asked for and then we'll get this thing done and you can take the rest of the day off if you want."

Chapter 4

Since Errol didn't have a car, they drove to Parkland in Ray's Chevy, taking Elm to North Akard, then onto Harry Hines Boulevard and the hospital. Ray parked in the doctors' lot at the back of the low cream-colored building and went through one of the rear doors, guiding Errol down a flight of stairs and along a gloomy cinder-block corridor to the morgue.

"You'll be just fine," said Ray, patting him on the back and simultaneously pushing open one of the doors. He gently eased Errol into the room. There were four chipped ceramic tables in the room, but only one of them was occupied. Doc Rose, the Chief Medical Examiner for Dallas County, had let a lot of the gas out of his subject but the room still reeked of decaying flesh despite the whirling vent fans in the ceiling. Ray guided a nervous Errol over to a nearby counter and offered him a deep sniff from the open plastic bottle of Clorox, then took a dose for himself, the odor of the bleach stunning his sense of smell into submission for the moment. When that was done Ray took Errol by the elbow and brought him to the table. Errol took one look at the wrinkled thing on the table, then turned and vomited forcefully into the stainless-steel liver bowl Ray had ready and waiting.

"That him?"

"Yes."

"His name?"

"Jennings Price." Errol swallowed bile and looked as though he was going to puke again. "Christ, can I go now?"

"Sure thing," said Ray. "Usually you can catch a cab at the Emergency entrance."

"You're not driving me back?"

"Not unless you want to wait around here 'til I'm done with your ex-boss and Dr. Rose here."

Errol swallowed hard again, trying not to look at the thing on the white enamel table. "I'll catch a cab."

"Wise."

Errol vanished.

Ray turned back to the medical examiner. Earl Rose was heavyset, pale, and freckle-faced. He had thinning red hair, and behind the thick lenses of his black-framed spectacles he was slightly walleyed. He was known for his arrogance, his intelligence and his absolute skill as a pathologist. When he talked it was like listening to an overbearing schoolmaster, but Ray and the good doctor had been friends for a long time.

"You bring me disgusting things, Detective Duval."

"Something to make your day more interesting, Doc."

"Do we know who he is?"

"Jennings Price. According to his friend he's forty-two years old."

"Wrong tense, Ray. He *was* forty-two. Time clock's stopped for this poor soul."

"When do you think that might have been?"

Rose poked around in the now-empty body cavity. He

plucked something that looked like part of a translucent spider up between two rubber-gloved fingers. The spider was pink and covered in something yellow that dripped off its back into the open belly. "Had a meal of some kind of bouillabaisse with crawfish in it." The doctor peered into the belly again. "Clams, several kinds of fish." He sniffed. "White wine as well. A gourmet."

"I'll check with young Errol," said Ray, taking out his notebook and jotting in it. "Maybe he had some favorite restaurant."

"Not much digestion," said Rose. He reached between the corpse's legs and pulled a long thermometer out of the man's rectum. "Distended belly and bloating. Rigor's come and gone. He was killed no more than an hour or so after he ate that meal, thirty-six hours ago at the outside."

"Cause of death?"

"Somebody cut his head off," said the medical examiner.

"Slit his throat?"

"I didn't say that, now did I, Ray? I said somebody cut his head off and that's what I meant. Decapitation. From the back and while he was lying on his belly. Tied down to something. Ligature marks on his wrist and ankles. Wire." He wiped the long thermometer on his apron and then set it aside in a jar of alcohol. "You know your friend here was a homosexual?"

"It had occurred to me."

"I can guarantee it. Anal sphincter is loose and keratinized."

"A lovers' quarrel? Tied down to a bed?"

"I don't think so." Rose took off his glasses for a moment and squeezed the bridge of his nose. He'd been wearing glasses so long they'd left a permanent red indentation. "The blow came straight down on the back of his neck and kept on going right through the first cervical vertebra and right on through the common carotid and the jugular. Went from left to right by the depth of the initial cut."

"Not a knife?"

"Not even a cleaver. If this was France I'd say it was a small-scale guillotine."

"It's not France, so what is it that I'd find in Texas?"

"At a guess I'd say a very sharp sword. Maybe Japanese. War souvenir."

"I've got a killer running around cutting people's heads off with Jap swords." Ray shook his head. "I've got a heart condition, you know. I'd like something a little bit less sensational if you don't mind."

"Speaking of which, how are you feeling?" the pathologist asked.

"Just peachy," Ray answered.

"I'm asking a serious question." Rose scowled. "How are you feeling?"

"Better than him." Ray jerked his chin down at the mangled corpse on the table. "But not by much." Rose dropped the subject with a nod. "Anything else you can tell me?"

"Looks like the rest of the dismembering was done with the same weapon."

"Consistent?"

"Apparently so."

"What about those big raw patches?"

"Four of them on the back. Two on the buttocks. Two on the upper thighs. The skin right down through the dermis and the subcutaneous fat layer has been removed in large rectangles. Basically the skin has been flensed like blubber on a whale. Very precisely and very neatly."

"Before or after death?"

"Postmortem, without a doubt. At a guess I'd say he was

bled out completely after the head was removed. A bucket or large basin. Anything big enough to hold half a gallon or so."

"Eight pints."

"Umm."

"Maybe our killer is a butcher."

"A butcher uses a butcher's tools. This is almost like surgery."

"Maybe he's a surgeon," Ray said pointedly.

Rose looked up and smiled. "I said almost."

"You think he did that to make the rest of it easier, less messy?"

"I have no idea what the murderer thought, Ray. I can only tell you what he did. From all appearances the best I can tell you is that this was not a crime done in the heat of passion. There is a contusion on the back of the head. A blunt instrument."

"Sap?"

"Perhaps. There was enough force to knock the man unconscious. While in that state he had his head removed with a single swift cut. There are no hesitation marks. Death would be instantaneous, of course."

"Painless."

"The French authorities seem to think so. There is no empirical evidence I know of to prove or disprove the point."

"What I mean is, it was entirely premeditated."

"Certainly. It could hardly be otherwise." Rose raised an eyebrow over the black plastic frames of his glasses.

Ray looked down at the lump of flesh on the table. Like every other dead person he'd ever seen, it was completely lacking in personality. In his experience, no matter what their condition, corpses exhibited no character. Maybe there really was such a thing as a soul, animating people in life and leaving them in death. "Which do you think is better, cremation or embalming?"

Rose raised the other eyebrow. "How does that relate to the case at hand?"

"It doesn't. It's personal."

"You're asking about yourself?"

"That's it."

"A fairly macabre question to ask a medical examiner."

"I've been staring at you over dead bodies for a long time, Doc. None of this bothers me much anymore except the smell a little bit."

"Usually these things are set out in a man's will, or his next of kin deal with it."

"I don't think I want my brother or my father burying me somehow. I don't have a family of my own. No wife or children."

"Personally, I favor embalming," Dr. Rose answered after a moment. "It seems more in keeping with the way of things."

"The Bible, you mean."

"I suppose so."

"I think so too," said Ray. "I can't imagine getting my body burnt to a cinder." He smiled. "Especially my pecker. Makes me a bit queasy thinking about it."

"Please," muttered Rose. But Ray could see he was thinking about it as well.

"Sorry," said Ray, but he was still smiling.

The medical examiner rummaged around inside Price's chest cavity for a moment. "Why are you asking me all of this now?" he said finally.

"Going to McSeveney's after I leave here."

"The funeral people?"

"Yessir."

"Making your own arrangements?"

"Seems like the smart thing to do. Don't leave a burden on anyone else."

"Funerals can be expensive."

"Why would I care? Can't take it with me."

"You could give it to me," said Rose. And they both laughed, smiling at each other fondly over the marionette remains of Jennings Price.

McSeveney's was located on Madison, just off W. Jefferson Boulevard in Oak Cliff, Ray's own neighborhood. Leaving Parkland, he bypassed downtown, turned onto Zang and went south down to W. Jefferson. He angle parked in front of the Texas Theatre, which had a bad double feature running, *War is Hell*, a Korean War action flick introduced by Audie Murphy, and *Cry of Battle*, a World War II pic set in the Philippines and starring Van Heflin and Rita Moreno. Ray had seen both two nights before; neither had anything to do with any war he'd ever fought in. He walked down to Madison, turned left and went down a few yards to McSeveney's, a dusty two-story brick building with white columns out front and shuttered windows. The front doors were dark wood with brass kickplates. There was a modest black-and-white sign on the narrow strip of lawn outside, discreetly announcing what went on behind the brick walls and the shutters.

A young man in a well-cut black suit took Ray to Thomas McSeveney's office and sat him down in a comfortable brown leather armchair then withdrew. The armchair stood in front of a huge Edwardian-style oak desk with carved legs. The desk was clear except for a gold-and-marble pen set and a red leather-bound ledger set squarely in the middle of the desk. There was another brown leather armchair and behind that an oak credenza, on which sat a row of magazines between a pair of lion-headed stone bookends. Ray leaned forward to read the titles. Most of them were catalogues: Practical Burial Footwear, Ray Funeral Supplies— which seemed appropriate—Boyertown Casket Company, Sealtite Caskets, Major Casket Company, Batesville Casket Company, and then several slipcased editions of *Mortuary Management Magazine*.

Thomas Ian Andrew McSeveney was a tall man, thick in the waist, with a jeweled face, five o'clock shadow and dark hair he wore swept back with a razor-cut part on the left. His suit was dark blue, his shirt silky white and his tie a calm gray and green stripe. There were traces of talcum powder around his collar. He was smiling as he came into the room, his eyes large, a very pale and watery blue and full of sincerity. He sat down behind his desk and folded his bony-fingered hands together on top of his ledger.

"Mr. Duval. We spoke on the telephone."

"Detective Duval, as a matter of fact."

"You're with the Dallas Police Department?"

"That's right."

"We've worked with Chief Curry on several occasions."

Ray nodded. "I was at Mike Parson's funeral. Got a card from one of your drivers."

"How fortunate," said McSeveney. "I hope we can be of service to you." McSeveney paused and leaned forward slightly. It was getting a little late in the day and the carnation in the man's lapel was looking a little wilted. "As I understand it, the arrangements are for yourself?"

"Right," said Ray briskly. He was beginning to wish he'd never come. He could have left things up to the Police Benevolent Society, or even his brother.

"Few people today have the foresight to preplan their own arrangements."

"I'm dying. My doctor says I'm living on borrowed time."

"Oh dear," said McSeveney, his voice much softer than his size. "I didn't know."

"Of course not," said Ray. "I've only just met you."

"I'm not quite sure how to say this but . . ."

"How long? Six months. Maybe a year. Maybe tomorrow morning. It's not like I've made an appointment I have to keep."

"No, of course not."

"I want something simple. Plain."

"Umm," intoned McSeveney, not willing to commit himself to offering simple and plain without putting up a fight. "Why don't we take a look in the Selection Room." Ray could almost hear the capital letters. He nodded and followed McSeveney out of his office and down a short carpeted hallway. It was interesting; McSeveney was running a business, that was sure enough, but there were no signs of it. Everything was quiet, muted, understated. No clacking typewriters, no laughter over the coffee urn. Nothing.

McSeveney led Ray into a large room painted in a pale green with framed panels of red silk, or maybe it was rayon; there was no real way to tell because the lighting, like everything else, was muted, and there wasn't a lot of reflected light off the beige carpeting. The room was full of coffins, which Ray commented on.

"Caskets, Detective Duval. A casket is something altogether different from a coffin."

Ray wasn't quite sure about the difference but he kept his mouth shut. He was shown several colonial styles, a French Provincial with gold "accents," a Valley Forge from Boyer-

town Burial Casket that looked to Ray more like an Early
American cupboard than a place to put a body, and finally a
medium-priced casket from Major Casket that offered
something called a Beautyrama Adjustable Soft Foam bed.
According to McSeveney all the beds were made with Sealy
innerspring mattresses, which was the same brand Ray had
on his bed. He settled for that one and then asked about embalming.

"How long does it really last?"

"That depends on conditions," McSeveney answered.
The mortician was sweating like a purse snatcher.

Ray smiled. "Conditions?"

"Weather, soil porosity and the like."

"So one way or the other the worms are going to get at
me eventually."

"I wouldn't put it quite that way, Detective."

"No, I guess y'all wouldn't." Ray decided to let him off
the hook; he'd had as much of the place as he could take.
They went back to the office and Ray wrote a check for the
price of the coffin and a pickup in one of McSeveney's Ford
meat wagons, which the undertaker called a "service vehicle"—a station wagon rather than a hearse.

"Interment?" McSeveney asked, fountain pen poised
over the sheet in the ledger he was filling in with Ray's information.

"You mean where am I going to be buried?"

"Yes."

"I haven't decided." There were half a dozen cemeteries
in Dallas and at least that many more in Fort Worth. There
was even the family plot in Burkburnett for that matter. "Is
that going to be a problem?"

"Not at all," said McSeveney. "We have affiliates all over

the state and we are in touch with establishments such as our own all over the country."

We can plant you anywhere, Ray thought.

"We'll need some time to make those arrangements, however," said McSeveney.

"How much time?"

"The sooner the better." The mortician had given up and opted to echo Ray's practical style. "Flowers?"

"People want to bring some they can, but I'm not paying for any extra if that's what you mean."

"No flowers." McSeveney pursed his lips and made a little tick in the ledger. "And how long would you wish to remain in the Slumber Room?"

"Slumber Room? I'll be dead, not sleeping."

McSeveney sighed. "The Slumber Room is where the client remains on display so his friends can pay their last respects."

"Costs more, right?"

"No more than a good motel. Roughly fifty dollars per day with a three-day minimum."

"Come with TV and a pool?"

McSeveney didn't so much as crack a smile. "I'm afraid not, Detective."

"I don't have that many friends," said Ray, "and those I do have I hope will come and visit me in the hospital before I shrug off this mortal coil."

McSeveney smiled. Here was something they could share. "Ah, Wordsworth."

"Shakespeare," Ray corrected. "*Hamlet*. Anyway, no Slumber Room." He stood up and reached out a hand across the desk. "Thanks for your help."

McSeveney stood up and shook Ray's hand. The grip was surprisingly strong and dry, more like a bank manager than what you'd expect from someone who traded in dead bodies and embalming fluid. God only knew what kind of person went into a business like this. Was it by choice?

"I guess the next time I see you, I won't be seeing you at all," Ray commented.

"Quite so," said McSeveney, and that was the end of that. Ray found his own way out of the silent building and stepped out onto the street again.

Chapter 5

A faint spitting rain was beginning to fall. Ray looked at his watch. It was past five. He went back to W. Jefferson, passed under the Texas Theatre marquee, the smell of the popcorn and the hot dogs from inside reminding him that he hadn't eaten in a while. He kept on going down the street to Inky's Restaurant at the far end of the block. He picked up a copy of the *Times Herald* from the box by the door and went inside, choosing a table by the window.

A waitress came by and he ordered a chicken fried steak with some okra on the side and a Tecate. He'd seen the waitress before and liked her, but he'd never found the right way to even ask her name. She was in her thirties and looked tired, but she was pretty in a worn-out way with long blond hair and a good body with good legs. A little less chin and a little more cheek and she would have been beautiful. The beer came first and he emptied out the red can into a glass then sat back against the padded booth and looked at the newspaper.

The whole front page was Kennedy, with a bit of Johnson and Connally thrown in for good measure. The reporting on the presidential visit ran for almost the whole first section, with a sidebar on what a perfect place the Convention Center was going to be for the lunch. When you got right down to it the whole thing was just a laugh and scratch for the assorted peckerwoods in the Democratic Party who'd be shaking hands with the man until his wrist ached and trying to get a closer look down the front of Jackie's dress.

Ray's steak came. He tumped the little dish of okra beside his mashed potatoes and then poured the light-colored milk gravy over everything. He picked up the salt shaker, put it down again, and doused his plate with pepper instead. He'd always been a salt lover but the doctors told him that was part of what was killing him, so he'd laid off over the past month or two. All things considered he was beginning to wonder if it really mattered a whole hell of a lot. He picked up the salt and tapped it over his plate.

Alternating bites of his food with sips of the sweet Mexican beer and glances at the folded paper on the table beside him, Ray let his mind wander over the events of the day. Death was coming up on him quick and dirty and there didn't seem to be any way he could avoid it. Borrowed time was one thing, but you didn't expect the banker to be looking over your shoulder, keeping an eye on his dough all the time. First the dump and Jennings Price, then Doc Rose and finally McSeveney and his caskets-not-coffins. He finished his beer and the waitress came over and asked him if he wanted another one.

"Sure," he said. "That'd be nice."

When she returned with his beer, he gave her a nice smile. "Ask you a question?"

"Long as it's not my phone number or do I think Jackie is just cute as a button."

"No, nothing like that. You know the difference between a coffin and a casket?"

"This some kind of joke?"

"Nope."

"It's a funny question." She poured the Tecate into his empty glass.

"I'm serious."

"I know you are. I'm just thinking here."

Ray took a sip of beer and then a forkful of okra, leaning his chin over the plate to keep the gravy off his shirt. He chewed and swallowed. "Any idea?"

"Yeah," said the waitress. "I think a coffin is one of those things you see in a Vincent Price movie. Kind of like a stretched-out diamond with the top and bottom cut off. It has a shape, you know? Like sort of shoulders. And a casket is what you see at funerals now. Rectangles with the top curved a bit. That sound right?"

"I think that's probably right," said Ray.

"Why you want to know?"

Ray didn't want to tell the woman it was for him so he just gave her another smile. "No reason really. Just curious."

"You always get serious about things like that?"

"I'm a cop," said Ray. "Kind of comes naturally, I guess."

"I guess," said the waitress. She picked up the two empties and wandered off. Ray went back to his steak. Knowing what you were going to die of and approximately when had a few advantages. Walking dead like he was meant you could arrange things the way you liked, and pretty much do as you liked for as long as you had, and then you just kind of sat back and took your medicine.

Doc Rose knew all about other people dying but he didn't have any information about himself; just because he was a pathologist didn't mean he could take a rib spreader to his chest or a Stryker saw to his skull for a little peek inside.

And then there was Jennings Price, the death of the day. According to the medical examiner his head had come off in a single stroke, and from the back. Surely he hadn't seen that coming, had he?

Ray filled his fork with mashed potatoes and knifed a little okra on top. He had to admit to himself he'd never seen anything like it. For him murder was pretty simple: criminals killing each other off or husbands and wives killing each other off, or robbers accidentally killing off the people they were robbing. Detecting that kind of thing was reasonably easy even when it was a mob hit. A few years before when Tincy Eggleston wound up in a Tarrant County cistern, it was easy enough to conclude that the crime boss had been rubbed out by one of his competitors. It took a while, but eventually they got a tip that led to the killer and it was another file closed.

Jennings Price was something else altogether; the only thing Ray had heard about that was even close was the man up north they were calling the Boston Strangler. At last count he'd raped and strangled eleven women in the Boston area, and there didn't seem to be any connection between the victims except their sex. According to Doc Rose, Price had been queer, but sexual contact hadn't been part of the killing.

Ray took another bite of steak, then pushed his plate away. He sipped his beer, eyes closed, his head back against the padded booth. Why do you cut a guy up, put him back together, and just for kicks slice off big chunks of skin? You'd have to be crazy to do that kind of thing, but then again, there seemed to be some feuding going on, so maybe the crazy part of it was just covering up some kind of simple greed.

One thing was sure: He wasn't going to solve the killing

in one day. Tomorrow he'd interview the other Texana dealers in the city, including the ex-lover, Valentine. He pushed himself up and out of the booth with some difficulty, then paid his bill to the waitress, who was standing behind the register.

"Ask you another question?"

"Sure," said the waitress, watching as he shoved two bucks into the tip jar.

"What's your name?"

"Rena," she said and smiled. Ray smiled back.

"Nice name."

"Nice of you to say so," she said. Ray smiled again and handed her the folded newspaper. "Maybe someone else might like to read it." The waitress nodded pleasantly but there wasn't anything extra in it. Ray left the restaurant and walked back to his car. Ten minutes later he was home.

Home was a standard postwar concrete bungalow below Davis on Melba Street, less than a dozen blocks north and west of Inky's Restaurant and McSeveney's Funeral Home. The bungalow was small, about all he could afford after World War II and before Korea.

He'd bought it because Lorraine wanted her own house, but she never stopped complaining about it for the whole time they were together. It had two bedrooms, one for the kid they never got around to having, a living room, a dining room, a kitchen and a bathroom. He'd finished off the basement and made a workshop for himself when he got back from Korea and found out that Lorraine was whoring around, and he'd turned the second bedroom into a study with built-in bookcases he put together in the basement.

He knew Lorraine had run off with a businessman from Houston who told her he had money in oil, but two years later when she died in a car accident in Corpus Christi it turned out he was nothing but a cheap hood named Alvin Bert Krolik fronting for the Stateline mob in Mississippi, but more often making his own way by holding up liquor stores. Ray had drunk a toast to Lorraine's memory and was sad for a week or so, but that was it. When the week was done he felt more relieved than anything else. He'd been with a few women since, but nothing very long and nothing very serious, which bothered him sometimes, but not often enough for him to do anything about it.

Ray parked the Chevy in the driveway, went up the three steps to his enclosed porch one at a time and keyed the lock on the front door. He opened it, stepping directly into the living room. The floors were oak, the varnish gone dark over the years, but he'd brightened up the room with a green braided rug and a whole room full of matching green furniture from Sears, Roebuck. It was five years old now but it looked good as new, mostly because he rarely had anyone over and never used the room himself; but it was nice to see first thing when he opened the door.

There was a fireplace at the end of the room with a bookcase on one side, mostly filled with an Encyclopedia Britannica set he'd bought at a secondhand store. On the wall over the couch there was a framed painting he'd picked up at the same place. It was an old sailing ship, all sails set, running with the wind, waves breaking over her bow and so realistic it almost seemed to jump out of the frame at him. He could even read the name on the bow: *Dawn Treader*.

To the right of the fireplace was the dining room. Lorraine had filled it with dark English-style furniture from the twenties that she thought was antique, but as soon as she'd gone he sold it to the secondhand place where he'd bought the encyclopedias and the picture and then he'd gone to Sears again.

The telephone rattled noisily and he picked it up on the second ring. It was Earl Rose.

"Headquarters said you'd gone home."

"You find something?"

"Of course, or I wouldn't be calling." Earl was clearly in one of his moods so Ray just kept his mouth shut, but that didn't work either. "You don't care what I found out? You think I give this kind of service to anyone who brings me a body? Maybe I should just send you a report in a week or so."

"I'm interested."

"Cause of death."

"You said it was some kind of heavy blade."

"I was wrong. Looking in the wrong place."

"What was the right place?"

"Corner of the right eye. I didn't see it until I had the brain out. Some kind of extremely sharp instrument with a U-shaped blade. A miniature chisel of some kind. Never seen anything like it. Left a four-inch notch right into the front of the brain. He might have gone on breathing for a while afterwards, but he was dead in a second or two. Thought you might like to know."

"What kind of person uses a tool like that?"

"Beats me. At a guess I'd say it's some kind of engraving tool."

Ray thought about the inscription on Price's Omega and Edelson the jeweler. "Like the engraving you'd do on a wristwatch?"

"Not that fine, and I think they use some kind of electric tool for that." The doctor paused. "An artist maybe, that's the only thing I can think of."

"Thanks. I appreciate it." Ray found himself thanking a dial tone.

He turned out of the dining room into the hall and went into the bathroom, which hadn't changed at all since he bought the house. The tub was deep, the toilet had a wooden seat and the floor was black and white tile. He undid his belt, slipping down his pants, and peed sitting down because it was easier. He sat there, leaning his left arm on the edge of the tub for support, feeling the hard pulse of the artery in his neck and trying not to count the beats. He thought about what the doc had said but it just made things more confusing. He stayed sitting, even after he'd finished, knowing that if he stayed too long his legs would go to sleep. He stared at the black and white tiles and smelled the bleach he'd used to clean the tub a few days ago. Clorox, same as the stuff Rose used in the morgue at Parkland.

Why a refrigerator? A cardboard box or an old trunk would have worked as well and been a lot lighter. Why cut him up if all you were going to do was put him back together again with wire? Why cut away squares and rectangles of skin after he was dead and could feel no pain? Why kill him at all? Who the hell used miniature chisels?

There were no answers in the bathroom, only the smell of the bleach. Ray stood, zipped and buckled, then flushed the toilet. He rinsed his hands at the sink, avoiding the mirror, then dried his hands on a towel and went out into the little hall again. Straight ahead was the dining room, and from there the kitchen, but he'd just eaten. Left was the bedroom and a nap he could probably benefit from, and right was his study. He went to the right.

Back when he was with Lorraine the study had been their bedroom, with a nice view out into the little backyard and the trees. It was eleven feet by twelve feet with a closet and a second, smaller window that looked out onto the driveway. He'd taken out the bed and given it away to the Salvation

Army along with everything else in the room since he assumed Krolik had screwed Lorraine in the bed and had his paws on everything else. For a while he'd considered ripping out the sink and toilet but eventually he settled down and figured that was going a bit far.

Initially the room had just been an empty shell, but as time passed it began to fill up with things, mostly books, mostly nonfiction, mostly history, mostly military. For a few years he'd collected toy soldiers, which he kept displayed on top shelves of the bookcases and in a tall glass-fronted cabinet. Most of them were made by a French company called Mignot, and with the exception of fifty or so depicting British and American soldiers from the Revolutionary War, the rest were Civil War, predominantly Confederate. He supposed that some of them were quite valuable by now, but he hadn't thought about them much in a long time.

There was a tweed-covered La-Z-Boy in one corner with a seventeen-inch black-and-white GE television on four brass-bottomed legs directly across from it. There was a small desk and a wooden chair for doing bills under the side window and another braided rug on the floor, this one dark blue. Above the desk and along the wall there were a score of photographs, mostly of war buddies from World War II and Korea.

In each and every one of the framed black-and-white pictures Ray was smiling, which he sometimes thought was a little strange under the circumstances. Most of the war buddies were dead, or gone to fat or boring, and he only kept in touch with one or two of them. In the middle of all the pictures was his Congressional Medal of Honor for the pillbox he'd blown up single-handed in Tunisia. The sad thing of course was that none of it really meant much anymore, not to Ray Duval or to anyone else. Roosevelt had draped the medal around his neck himself, but all Ray could remember was the smell of death and Camel cigarettes on the man's breath and the fact that you could see the bones of his cheeks and jaw underneath this baby-smooth skin that was as thin and brittle as parchment.

Ray went and built himself a drink and brought it back into his study. He put the drink down on the table beside the La-Z-Boy and switched on the television, adjusting the rabbit ears until the reception was as good as it was going to get. He'd expected a mindless hour watching *Rawhide* but there was a news special on Kennedy's visit instead. He switched channels and got *My Three Sons*, which he couldn't stand. He rose and switched off the television and listened to the rain tapping on the roof. It seemed to be coming down a little harder. He sipped his drink slowly, knowing it would eventually put him to sleep, and he hated that. Even if it was just sitting in the dark trying to figure out who'd cut up Jennings Price and stuck his puppet corpse into a fridge it was better than sleeping. Sleeping was too much like listening to your own heartbeat and wondering if you were going to wake up the next morning.

He took another sip of his drink and put the glass down on the side table again. It was dark in the room and outside there was thunder and more rain pounding on the shingles. Too many things rushed into his soul in an instant and he found himself weeping uncontrollably. As the thunder banged over his head and the rain came down, tears coursed down his cheeks and he felt like an utter fool.

After a few moments he pulled himself up out of the chair, and, leaving his drink behind, he went into his bedroom, the room that he'd always thought was going to be a nursery. Now there was a single bed with a square mahogany headboard and footboard to match, the mattress covered in a light blue spread of popcorn chenille. There was only one bedside table and a lamp made from one of those fat little Chianti bottles wrapped in wicker. There was a closet full of brown and blue suits and white shirts and a bureau for his underwear and socks.

Ray took off his jacket and hung it up, then slipped out of his George Lawrence shoulder rig and put it and the big Browning Hi-Power on the bedside table. He'd first used the 9mm automatic during the war, and when he'd returned to the force he'd bought one directly from Browning Arms in St. Louis. Dallas detectives could use their choice of weapons, and with the thirteen rounds in the clip the Hi-Power was a lot more useful than anything else he could find except the much heavier Colt .45. He lay down on the bed, in the darkness, wondering if the bed was more like a coffin or a casket, the tears drying on his cheeks. He turned onto his side, facing the closet, and arranged his head on the pillow so he couldn't hear his heartbeat or feel the jerking pulse in his throat. The rain seemed to be coming down harder and it occurred to him that all the fuss about Kennedy's visit might come to nothing if the weather stayed bad; no one wanted a parade in the rain.

11/21/63
THURSDAY

Chapter 6

The Monster sat at one of the tables in the back of the little Mexican restaurant on McKinney Avenue, working his way through a large bowl of Mike Martinez's hottest chili and taking occasional pulls from his third bottle of Tecate. He kept his back to the wall and his face in the shadows. No one even glanced in his direction and the waiters ignored him; he wasn't quite a regular, but he'd been there often enough to be familiar, and thus invisible. In the kitchen a radio was blaring out a Mariachi Vargas song with plenty of horn. The radio was probably tuned to KCOR, the San Antonio Tex-Mex station.

The restaurant was decorated in garish shades of red, green and yellow, contrasting with the drab work clothing of most of the people eating. Most of the El Fenix patrons were construction and railway workers and almost all of them were men. As usual the Monster was one of the few Caucasians in the restaurant, although it seemed as though more and more were crossing the tracks from downtown to enjoy the Martinez family's offerings. There wasn't a nigger in the place, though, and there probably never would be.

The Monster finished his chili and lit a Camel, leaning

back in his chair and enjoying the hot aftertaste of the spicy food in his belly. He looked out over the restaurant, marveling at how much had changed since he'd last lived in Dallas. Before the war no white man in his right mind would have dared to venture into the dusty barrio of shotgun shacks and unpaved streets beyond the warehouse district above Munger Avenue any more than going for a stroll in Deep Ellum to check out what the niggers were up to. Now coming to a place like El Fenix was a safe adventure on a night out with your best girl. They'd even opened up a second restaurant in Oak Cliff, and Mama Martinez was selling her own salsa in jars at the cash register. *El mejor en la ciudad.* The best in the city. There were nightclubs, restaurants and bars up and down ten blocks of McKinney, and the streets north of the main strip were paved now instead of rutted dirt.

He'd harvested a greaser or two in his time but they weren't as much fun as coons, not to mention the problem of their skin color; niggers came in every shade of brown from cream in your coffee to black as squid ink, most of it small-pored and hairless, especially the young ones. Mex skin was a useless olive shade and he'd rarely seen any that was useful—not to mention the hair. The Monster belched quietly. Bad skin for his business maybe, but they sure could cook.

The Monster tipped forward in his chair and tapped his cigarette on the edge of the tin ashtray in the middle of the table. He looked up as the door opened and saw a young couple step into the crowded room. Exactly the pair he'd been thinking about. They were dressed for a night out and in their twenties. The woman was wearing a maternity dress under her raincoat, swelling out sweetly under something in a tweedy brown. Her husband helped her out of the raincoat and the Monster got a perfect view of her. Under the dress she was wearing a white blouse with a Peter Pan collar. The straps over her shoulders were wide with large cream-colored buttons. Like every pregnant woman he'd ever seen she was dressed to look as innocent as possible, her clothing obscuring the obvious evidence of at least one filthy night with the man at her side, his hot hard cock rooting around between her legs like a rutting boar.

The Monster smiled in the gloom, wondering what she'd do if she knew what was sitting only a dozen feet away, watching her, thinking about the soft wet slit under her pretty little dress, wondering what sex her child would be, how smooth and wonderful the infant's skin would be, smoother than unborn kid or calf. He could feel it against his cheek and felt himself harden.

Reuben, one of the younger Martinez boys, brought the young couple across the room, so close that the Monster could smell her perfume. Something old-fashioned, tickling at the edge of memory. *Bourjois, Evening in Paris*. The woman didn't even glance his way, just an ordinary guy with a bowl of chili and a beer in front of him. Ordinary, that was the key to it all. So ordinary everyone and anyone paid no attention. It had always been like that, even back in the beginning. Lost in the crowd, free to do as he pleased. A missing nigger kid didn't spark much attention; the only problems he'd had came from taking the white kids, and in the end they hadn't been worth it anyway.

The Monster took a sip of his beer and a drag on his cigarette. What was that old saying his father thought was so funny? You can't tell a book by its cover? Not true. Not true at all.

*   *   *

Ray woke up three times during the night, once to go to the bathroom and twice because he was sure he was having a heart attack, even though his doctor had told him that wasn't the way he'd go, except at the very end. He'd lain still as death in the bed both times he'd been awakened by the chest-clenching panic he was so familiar with. He didn't want to call an ambulance or drive up to Parkland himself and then find out it was nothing, which he was sure it was, but at the same time he was sure lots of people had died that way—not taking action because they might look stupid. There was also a third way of looking at it. He woke up with the same choking anxiety every night, so if you assumed that you couldn't be having a heart attack *every* night, you probably weren't having one now.

The third and final time it was getting on for 6:30, so he decided to stay up for good. Wearing nothing but his Fruit of the Looms, he went into the kitchen, had a bowl of Total with milk then went and had a shower. By the time he was dressed and on his way out the door he felt almost normal again and could even make believe that he was perfectly all right. It was still raining when he got into the Bel Air, but not as hard as the night before. He made it to the squad room just after 7:30 and right before the shift change.

John McDonald, one of the old guard who occupied the desk across the aisle from Ray, flipped a piece of paper across to Ray. "Seen this?"

Ray looked down at the piece of paper. It was a badly printed poster about the size of a sheet of typing paper. At the top there were two pictures of the President, one full face, the other left profile like a mug shot. Underneath the pictures, in bold type it said:

WANTED

FOR

TREASON

The text below had seven numbered paragraphs, each one presenting one of Kennedy's "treasonous" activities, ranging from a simple *Betraying the Constitution (which he swore to uphold)* to the more complicated *He has been wrong on innumerable issues affecting the security of the U.S. (United Nations—Berlin Wall—missile removal—Cuba—wheat deals—test ban treaty—etc.)* and the obscure *He has been caught in fantastic lies to the American people, including personal ones (like his previous marriage and divorce).*

"Where'd you find this?" Ray asked.

"They're all over downtown," said McDonald. "Must be a few thousand—telephone poles, walls, on the ground."

"Think it means anything?"

"Naw," said McDonald, shaking his head. "You know what this town is like. Some guy with a printing press and a bee in his bonnet gets his gonch in a wringer and prints these up. Freedom of the press and all that shit."

"Yeah."

"Hear you caught a murder."

"Strange one."

"Stiff in an icebox, right?"

"Yeah."

"Mob?"

"Don't think so. No connection I can find. Something to do with queers maybe."

"Either way you should talk to Jack about it."

"Jack?"

"Ruby, you know, the guy who gives the bulls free drinks

at his bar. The Carousel Club." McDonald pulled a fat, worn-smooth wallet out of the sagging back pocket of his pants and rummaged around in it for a moment. He flipped a small business card onto Ray's desk: *Carousel Club, Continuous shows, Girls! Girls! Girls! Open to two a.m. nightly. Your Host ... Jack Ruby.* There was also an address on Commerce Street and a telephone number. Ray wrote the address and number down in his notebook and underlined the name Jack Ruby. He flipped the card back to McDonald, who put it back in his wallet.

"Used to be Chicago mob or something?"

"So he says."

"Why would he know about queers?"

"He lives with a guy."

"That doesn't make him queer."

"There's been rumors."

Ray shrugged noncommittally, took out his notebook, and flipped back to yesterday's notes and found the name of Price's ex-lover—Douglas Foster Valentine. There was no home number listed but there was a commercial number for Valentine's Rare Books and Art on Harwood, barely two blocks away. It was too early to call so he spent the next hour talking with incoming cops taking over the day shift and read most of the morning edition of the *Times Herald.* He drank three cups of coffee from the big West Ben urn and ate one of the blueberry muffns Runny Ronny from the night shift had left behind. Ron Cope had a wife who baked obsessively and he could always be counted on to leave a few of Amanda's overly sweet gems behind when he headed home for his eight and eight.

At nine o'clock Ray called Valentine's and got the man himself on the phone. The voice was a smooth baritone with a little bit of adenoid in it, making him sound as though he had a perpetual mild cold.

"My name is Ray Duval. I'm a detective."

"A policeman?"

"Yes. I'd like to talk to you about Jennings Price."

"Why? Has he stolen something? Forged a document and tried to sell it?"

"No, nothing like that." Ray paused. "You don't seem to like him very much, Mr. Valentine."

"He's a thief and a liar, among other things."

"Also among other things he's dead," said Ray, and waited. The silence was long enough to make Ray think he might have been cut off. "Mr. Valentine?"

"Sorry, just digesting the information. Presumably since you're a policeman Jennings didn't die of natural causes."

Ray smiled. Valentine was backing away from his anger, using the man's first name. "No, he was murdered. We found him at the dump, inside a refrigerator."

"I'm sure he would have preferred something a little more dignified, but I'm not surprised."

"Why's that?"

"Jennings dealt with some fairly unsavory characters from time to time."

"Business or pleasure?"

"Both. He sold books but he sometimes purchased his favors."

"Is that a fact?"

"Yes. Young ones."

"Maybe we should talk about this in person, Mr. Valentine."

"Feel free. You're at police headquarters? That dreary pile beside the courthouse?"

"That's it."

"Then it won't take you more than a few minutes to get here. I'll put on the coffee."

Ray used the main elevators along the corridor and went out the front door instead of having to walk up the Main Street parking ramp from the basement. The rain had faded to almost nothing and he found himself enjoying the fresh smell of the wet streets and sidewalks as he made his way up Harwood Street to Valentine's store. Unlike the space occupied by Jennings Price, Valentine's Rare Books and Art was an ordinary storefront with a plain sign, gold on black above the double glass doors. There was a wheeled plywood cart full of mildew-damaged books and humidity-bloated paperbacks just at the entrance, and a small sign saying ANY BOOK—10 CENTS. Ray pushed open the door and a little bell tinkled. Old-fashioned; part of the image or a genuine eccentricity?

Valentine's Rare Books and Art was the size of an average shoe store and not half as well lit. There were bookcases against all the walls and an island of bookcases in the center of the store. A dogleg to the right was also crammed with books, and in a completely separate room behind a waist-high counter on the left there were more books, these in bookcases equipped with glass doors and locks. The good stuff. In the back room Ray could also see a pair of old velvet-upholstered armchairs and a side table with an ashtray on it. He smelled coffee, a richer, deeper aroma than the brew in the squad room.

A slim, relatively short man rose from behind the counter. He was in his late forties or early fifties, his hair a little too long, brown with gray at the temples. He wore metal-framed glasses and was dressed in a white shirt, tapered pants with a small blue check and comfortable-looking suede shoes.

Ray held out his hand as the man came around the counter. "Mr. Valentine?"

"You must be Detective Duval." The two men shook. Ray noted that Valentine's grip was firm and dry, and when they shook the other man met his gaze directly. "I've got coffee in the back." He led Ray into the back room. Out of sight from the outer room there was a small table with a coffee urn, a small bottle of cream and an old jam jar that had been turned into a receptacle for sugar. There was one cup with a mismatched saucer and several mugs.

"Mug or cup?"

"Mug."

"How do you take it?"

"Regular, two sugars."

Ray sat down in one of the armchairs. Near the two chairs there was a space of wall between bookcases. There were several photographs in black and white showing a younger Valentine in an army uniform but without any rank insignia. The background of the pictures was all Washington, D.C.

Valentine brought the coffee, put the mug down in front of Ray, then sat down himself. He brought out a package of Marlboros, lit one with a plain steel Zippo, and offered the package to Ray.

"No, thanks. Probably cough up a lung smoking something that strong." He nodded toward the photographs. "You were in the army?"

"That's right. Surprised?"

"Should I be?"

"Some people are."

"Because you're homosexual?"

"Who said I was? And why would it be any of your business?" He sipped his coffee, then took a long drag on the cigarette, the smoke flaring from his nostrils in two long trails.

Ray shrugged. "I'm a detective, Mr. Valentine. Half of what I do is make assumptions, then go around seeing if I assumed right or not. The little popinjay over at Price's place said you and Price were lovers once upon a time. I also assume that there were all sorts of homosexuals in the army and the navy and the air corps, which is fine with me as long as they keep their peckers in their pants and point their guns in the right direction."

"Queers make a lot of assumptions too, Detective. They assume that the general population think they're perverts, so they tend to be a little too defensive."

"What were you in?"

"Monuments and Fine Arts."

"Never heard of it."

"Part of G2."

"Intelligence?"

"Not really. We went into Europe looking for stolen art, tried to protect what was left after almost six years of war."

"No combat then?"

"Some."

"Ever shoot anybody?"

"Once. A looter in Berlin."

"Kill him?"

"Yes. Almost by accident. He came out of a building I was going into. He had a gun, so I shot him."

"Any idea who put Jennings Price into a refrigerator?"

"He had lots of enemies."

"So you suggested on the telephone."

"I can't think of any of them I know personally who hated him enough to kill him."

"You said he was a thief and a liar."

"I meant it."

"Then explain it."

"I suppose in your trade you'd call it receiving stolen goods. Jennings bought documents stolen from local archives, small towns around the state."

"He didn't do it himself, right? He bought them from other people."

"Yes. They're called pickers."

"So these pickers just walk into some small-town museum and steal documents?"

"Not museums. Usually county courthouses. They usually don't have much in the way of staff. It's not hard."

"Sounds like you've done it."

"No. That was Jennings. He was proud of it. Explained how it was done in minute detail."

"You didn't turn him in?"

"We were lovers. Then."

Ray tried not to let himself think about what two men being lovers meant and sipped his coffee. He was also getting a little taste of Valentine's Marlboro secondhand and enjoying it immensely. "Boy over at Price's says it was you doing the stealing and forging."

"Errol? He's Jennings's pet. Was. Anything Jennings told him he'd believe." Valentine raised one hand and gestured around the room. "You've been to Jennings's place, obviously. Which of us appears to be reaping the glorious benefits of the rare-book trade?"

"Right now I'd say Jennings Price was reaping his just desserts in the pits of hell if the Episcopalians are to be believed. And appearances can be deceiving, Mr. Valentine, as y'all know full well."

Valentine laughed. It was a pleasant sound, and once again it sounded natural and unforced. Valentine didn't seem to be nervous or hiding anything. He stood up, went to the left wall and used a small key from his pocket to take two books out of a cabinet. He came back to where Ray was sitting and held both books up the way a model showed you two detergents on television. One of them was a tattered paperback called *My African Journey* by Winston Churchill M.P. It showed a picture of a much younger Churchill than the man who had guided England during World War II standing with a big-bore rifle in his hand and a dead rhinoceros at his feet. The second book was an even more tattered hardcover edition of something called *Corn and Root Crops*.

"Which do you think is more valuable?"

Ray looked from book to book. "The Churchill book."

"In most catalogs, certainly. It's quite rare, while the crop book is not."

"So why is it more valuable?"

"Well, for one thing, you can't tell a book by its cover, but you can sometimes tell by the flyleaf." He handed the book to Ray, who opened it and turned to the first page. "Who is Sam Ealy Johnson?"

"The Vice President's grandfather. He started up the first ranch in Johnson City. Just as an autograph the book is worth more than the Churchill, but the book itself is prime Texana." He smiled again, taking the book back from Ray and locking them both back in the case. "As you said, appearances can be deceiving. Especially among people." He picked up his cup. "More coffee, Detective?"

"That'd be fine, but I would like to use your facilities if you don't mind."

"Not at all. Bear to your left. You'll see a door at the back of the little dogleg."

"Thank you."

The bathroom was neat, tidy and smelled faintly of Murphy's Oil Soap. There was a can of Bowlene on the toilet tank and the toilet paper roll was full. The small window was frosted glass protected by a half dozen steel bars sunk firmly into the concrete sill. Shiny burglar alarm tape ran across the frosted glass and the leads led to a wire in the corner of the small space and then up into the ceiling. Valentine had more than the tinkling bell on the front door to keep him safe. Ray finished up and went back to join Valentine, who was in the process of lighting another cigarette. Ray sat down again.

"Not much business this morning."

"I don't get much walk-in trade."

"What kind of trade do you get then?"

"People who know me, know about the shop. Regulars." He took a drag on his cigarette. "I do a lot of business over the telephone," he added, chewing smoke on his words as he exhaled. Ray watched him, fascinated, remembering when it was that easy to smoke. He had a brief, nightmarishly vivid image of his lungs filling with a slick mucus liquid and he quickly banished it.

"How does that work? Doing business on the telephone."

"After a while you get to know what people want. Sometimes they're very specific. I keep lists. When I find something I know one of my regulars would like I call him on the telephone."

"My good friend Errol says there are about a dozen major dealers in this Texana stuff in Dallas. A hundred collectors in the state."

"That's about right. But there's really only seven or eight dealers you can really count as major."

"How many of the collectors are in Dallas?"

"Maybe half. The rest are in Houston."

"Rich people?"

"Mostly."

"Important people?"

"All rich people are important." Valentine let out a small smile.

"I take your point."

"But what you mean is important as in political, or social."

"Got it in one, sir."

"A few. A judge or two. The governor and some of his people."

"Connally collects this stuff?"

"He does."

"Calls you on the telephone?"

"From time to time."

"I guess that makes you important."

"I wouldn't say so."

"What about the Vice President?"

Valentine's lip curled briefly. "Mr. Johnson collects guns."

Ray paused for a moment. "Who do you think killed Price?"

"I told you, he had contacts with some unsavory people."

"Pimps?"

"Procurers of one kind and another. Sexually as well as in business."

"Anyone in particular?"

"I'd rather not say."

"What about you, Mr. Valentine?"

"What about me?"

"You ever use the services of these . . . unsavory characters you don't want to put a name to?"

"My proclivities aren't . . . weren't as exotic as those of

Jennings. That was one of the reasons we stopped seeing each other."

"You've got me all curious here, Mr. Valentine. About these proclivities."

"Jennings liked to believe that he was avant-garde, ahead of the times."

"I know what avant-garde means. I can even spell it."

"Sorry."

"No need. You were saying?"

"He liked to use drugs. Hashish in particular. He also liked . . . group activities."

"Orgies and such?"

"You might say that. They often included very young boys."

"How young?"

"Thirteen and fourteen. Once or twice even younger."

"You didn't like it?"

"No. Believe it or not, Detective, I'm quite conservative when it comes to my love life."

"So you think one of the people he used to get him his little playmates might have killed him?"

"I think it's possible."

"What about the business side of it?"

"I think that's possible as well."

"You know all the dealers in town?"

"Of course."

"And most of the collectors?"

"If not all."

"Same people Mr. Price knew?"

"Yes."

"Any of them capable of killing him, or have cause to?"

"Possibly."

"How about a for instance."

"Jennings specialized in documents. If he sold a particularly expensive item to someone and they later found out it was stolen or a forgery, and thus effectively worthless . . ."

"I get you. They might get pissed off enough to kill him. Maybe somebody who didn't like the idea he'd been taken advantage of. Word gets out—maybe it makes him look foolish and he can't afford to look foolish."

"You're the detective, Detective. I'm just saying it's a possibility. Make of it what you will."

"Well," said Ray. "It's like I was telling young Errol— it's usually sex or money." He smiled at Valentine. "Sometimes it's both."

"I don't know anything about what motivates murderers."

Ray stood up, wincing, his legs feeling like lead, his feet all pins and needles from sitting too long. "It's a funny thing about murderers," he said. "I've been a cop for a long, long while and it surprises me every time how ordinary murderers seem right up until the time they kill someone."

Chapter 7

Walking back to headquarters from Valentine's shop Ray didn't even bother going back up to the squad room. He called his ex-partner from the desk in the jail office on the City Hall side of the basement parking lot, made sure Ron was home, then climbed into the Chevy. He drove up the parking lot ramp and headed north up to the expressway.

Ray and Ronald Tyrell Odum had known each other since the end of the war, when they'd both enrolled in the Traffic Officer's Training School at the Texas Agricultural and Mechanical College, the next best thing to a police academy at the time. R. T. had been an MP in the Pacific, and with Ray's previous time as a beat cop on the Dallas force before the war, making detective had been a snap. In all the years since, neither man had ever been partnered with anyone else.

The two men came from very different backgrounds. R. T.'s money was about as old as a Texan's money could be, and both the Tyrells and the Odums claimed to have had relatives at the Alamo. Tyrell Oil went back the better part of a hundred years, expanding into cosmetics and pharmaceuticals after the First World War and chemicals and frozen foods following the Second. There weren't too many places you could go in Texas without seeing the Tyrell Red Eagle peering down at you from a gas station, or up at you from the frozen food section of the supermarket. As a child, R. T. had been given the grand tour of Europe and the Holy Land, followed by a round-the-world cruise that lasted more than half a year. Instead of joining the family business, Ron had first become a soldier and then a cop, instantly earning his father's respect and his mother's growing anxieties. By the late forties his mother became progressively more delusional and demented; by the early fifties she had become institutionalized. In 1955 she died of some undiagnosed malaise, leaving R. T., an only child, the sole heir of all his father's holdings, including the big stone house on Vickery in the Highland Park district of Dallas.

Ray's background, on the other hand, had been the essence of nouveau riche. His father had been a farmer up by the Oklahoma border who literally tripped into an oozing pool of tar sand and became an instant millionaire, selling off most of his land to oil development companies for a share in the profits. Half the leases had gone bust, but the other half hadn't, and his old man was one of the lucky ones who cashed in during the Burkburnett oil stampede in 1912.

His father instantly started collecting bad art, while his mother started collecting bad furniture, and bad men on the side. Before the ink on the divorce papers was dry, Ray and his brother, Audie, short for Claudius, had been sent off to a boarding school just outside of Houston called the Hicker Academy—a wretched hole that was one step this side of a reformatory.

Somewhere between then and Ray's eighteenth birthday his father had remarried a woman named Abigail Tasker, who'd been his housekeeper. Ray didn't mind Abbey, but he never forgave his father for sending him away, and he joined the Dallas police almost out of spite, then found out he enjoyed it. Audie had toed the line, gone to law school at Harvard, and, after a little political and maybe even financial greasing by Daddy, was now the chief prosecutor for Wichita County. Somewhere along the line Abigail had fallen by the wayside as well.

Ray drove through the Vickery Place district until he reached R. T.'s newly inherited residence on the corner of Vickery Boulevard and Skillman Street, facing into the long narrow park that ran for a block between Llano and Vanderbilt. The whole area was nothing but turn-of-the-century mansions and R. T.'s was no exception—a monster of a place in gray stone complete with a turret, endless numbers of mullioned windows, an elegant porch leading up to a massive oak door, a curving gravel driveway, and a stone wall completely surrounding the property and sealed off by a pair of high, curving wrought-iron gates. With the gates closed you could see the iron form of the Tyrell Red Eagle, wings spread, one to a gate, one eagle eye glaring at anyone with the temerity to think that he would be allowed through.

Ray turned in off the street, stopped in front of the gates and banged out R. T.'s initials in Morse code on his horn. A few seconds later the gates creaked back, pulled by some mechanism hiding in the shrubbery. Ray drove through and the gates closed behind him. He drove up the lane and parked in front of the house behind R. T.'s brand-new lemon-yellow Sting Ray split-window coup. With a little bit of difficulty Ray managed to lever himself out of the car and into the drizzling rain. R. T. was already on the front porch, a bottle of Jax in each hand.

"Come on in out of the rain, son, your hat's getting wet."

Ray reached the porch and R. T. handed him one of the

bottles. Somewhere along the line the man had fixed on the Louisiana brew as the only beer worth drinking and he had crates of the stuff brought in and stored in his basement. Ray assumed it would be the same in his newly inherited house, except here the basement was a whole hell of a lot bigger than his previous place. R. T. was dressed casually in jeans and a pale blue shirt, his big feet stuffed sockless into a pair of Bass Weejuns. Ray had heard himself described as a con- crete block with a face to match; R. T. was just the oppo- site — slim, narrow faced and with the fingers of a piano player. He was two years older than Ray but looked ten years younger. He had big horsey teeth he didn't mind showing when he smiled, and the only real sign of length- ening middle age was his high domed forehead and thinning thatch of blond hair gone to gray. The only creases on his tanned face were laugh lines and somehow there always seemed to be a twinkle in his light blue eyes.

R. T. led Ray into the house. There was a raised foyer with a checkerboard marble floor and steps leading down into an enormous living room. A door on the right led into the turret and a smaller door directly in front led into a pow- der room. There were plants all over the place and a huge chandelier hanging from a ceiling at least fifteen feet above them.

Ray followed R. T. down the two steps into the living room. It was stuffed with antiques, huge armoires, blanket chests, end tables, side tables and refectory tables. Except for the gloominess of almost every piece of furniture it looked like the inside of Jennings Price's apartment. "Flo likes all this foreign shit," said R. T., waving a hand. "Frankly I don't much care for it." Flo was Florence, his wife, who had changed her first name by deed poll to Flo- rentina the week after she married R. T., an affectation that

never really took except on her checks and invitations to
charity balls. She was po' white trash from somewhere up
north like Floydada or Plainview, and Ray had the sneaking
suspicion she might have been on the stroll before she came
down to Dallas and hooked R. T. a few years back. Not that
he'd ever say anything to his friend, but they both knew Flo
didn't like him very much, which is why he saw less and less
of R. T. as time went on.

They finished up in the kitchen at the back of the house.
It was large, plain, and the cupboards were the original
cream-colored, tongue-and-groove notched V-board. The
floor was green linoleum and the furniture was chrome — a
room Flo hadn't put her hand to so far. They sat down at the
yellow Formica-topped table in the center of the room and
sipped their beers for a few moments without saying anything.

"Feeling any better?"

"Not feeling much worse." Ray shrugged.

"Still alive." R. T. grinned. "Always a good sign."

"I've got a bad one, R. T."

"Guy in the refrigerator making like Pinocchio?"

"Word gets around."

"I keep my ears peeled."

"It's eyes you keep peeled."

"What do you do with ears?"

"Keep one of them to the ground."

"Okay, I keep my ear to the ground. People tell me
things."

"What do they tell you?"

"They tell me the guy was an antique dealer who got cut
into about ten pieces and that he had big slabs of skin taken
off him. Then he gets stuck in a refrigerator and taken to the
dump."

"What do you get from that?"

"Dump says it's the mob," R. T. answered, taking a slug from his bottle of Jax. "Cutting him up, that's maybe mob too, but the chunks of skin, that's something crazy."

"That's what I'm worried about." Ray sighed, sipping his own beer. "I'm worried it's a crazy. According to the doc the guy was skewered with some kind of miniature chisel through the corner of his eye, then cut up with a Samurai sword or something like it." He shook his head. "Goddamn but I hate crazies!"

"Because they never get solved." R. T. nodded.

"Remember the one we found in University Park?"

"Naked as a jay on her hands and knees like she was about to get goat-humped, except her privates were cut out and laid on her back like a saddle. Everybody had an alibi."

"We spent six months on that case off and on. Never even came close."

"Think you've got the same thing here?"

"Maybe." Ray nodded. "Not sure. On the surface it looks like some random crazy, but you don't have to dig too far to find suspects and motives all over the place. Seems like the guy was stealing archive documents and forging them as well as receiving and a bunch of other stuff. Also he's queer, and according to one of his ex-'friends' he was into some hard action."

"Don't like queers," said R. T. "Don't understand them." He got up and fetched another bottle of Jax from the fridge. Ray sipped his first beer and listened to the rain pitter-patter on the window that looked out into the big backyard. R. T. sat down again. "So what do you think of this Kennedy thing?" he asked.

"What Kennedy thing?"

"Him coming here."

"Going to screw up traffic royally, that's all I know."

"My old man thought he was the worst thing that ever happened to this country. A know-nothing with stars in his eyes and too much money. If he wasn't already dead, Kennedy visiting Dallas would have killed him." R. T. smiled broadly and leaned back in the chair. "Mind you, he was a Goldwater Republican. Had a bumper sticker on his Caddy that said 'Vote AuH20 in '64.'"

"Cute," said Ray. He took another sip from the long-necked bottle then set it carefully down on the table.

"Something on your mind?"

"I just don't know if I can finish this," Ray answered.

"The beer? No sweat, pal, I got lots in the basement."

"Not the beer."

"Hey," said R. T. "I know that, I was just trying to lighten the mood, you know?"

"I know."

"So what is it?"

"This murder. I keep on thinking I'm not going to be able to figure it out in time."

"In time?" R. T. paused and then shook his head. "I don't get you."

"I've got my physical next Friday. I won't pass and then that'll be it."

"You want to solve this in a week?"

"I don't want to leave a cold case as my last thing on the Job. Hell of a way to hand in my potsie."

R. T. shrugged. "Then do what you always do. Forget about crazies for now. Concentrate on being a cop. Talk to suspects and witnesses. Talk to yourself. Use that nose of yours. Nine out of ten times when it twitches the way it used to, it was twitching in the right direction."

"I'm not so sure about that. There's something familiar

about this, something right on the edge of my brain, but I can't seem to find the key."

R. T. took a long slug from the Jax, finishing it. He put the empty bottle down beside its mate with a bang. "You will. You always do."

"You realize how pissed I am you're not working this with me?"

"You know how pissed I am you didn't retire the same time I did? We could be out in the piney woods right this second with a cooler full of those new snap-top cans, catching trout and throwin' them back like nobody's business. Why are you still looking for crazies or anyone else this time of your life, Ray? How long you been on the Job, you old fool? Thirty years?"

"Give or take a war or two."

"No wife, no shit to take. I've got more money than I know what to do with, so why aren't we out on a boat on a lake covered in mosquitoes and having a hell of a time?"

Ray smiled. "Because I hate fishing and so do you."

"Well, that's true enough," agreed R. T., "but it's the idea that's important. You need a murder with a chopped-up corpse in a Westinghouse like I need another Flo."

Ray levered himself up from the table. "But you've got Flo and I've got a murder." He leaned down and scratched his leg through the cloth of his trousers, then stood upright again.

"Promise me you'll quit after this?" said R. T., standing up beside his friend, reaching out and touching his shoulder. "It doesn't have to be fishing. I just want to have some fun before . . . you know."

"I know."

"Bowling," suggested R. T. as he accompanied Ray back to the front door. "We could bowl every lane in the state. See how far we got. Something to think about." The two men went out onto the porch. It had stopped raining and water was dripping from the eaves.

"Kennedy gets his parade," said R. T.

"They'll have that bubble-top thing on in case it starts up again. Wouldn't do to have the First Lady get her hat spattered. People are going to be disappointed." Ray went down two steps. R. T.'s voice stopped him and Ray turned to look up at his friend.

"Whoever killed your man must have known him. You have to get close to poke a man in the eye with a screwdriver or a chisel."

"Friends?"

"Not necessarily." R. T. scratched the line of his jaw. "Relative?"

"Queer buddy?"

"No, I wouldn't think so. Those kinds of things are spur-of-the-moment. I'd buy the chisel in the eye, but not the rest of it. Too . . . purposeful, if you know what I mean."

"Somebody he jerked around with? Business?"

"Maybe. He'll be close, though. First or second ring."

Over the years Ray and R. T. had developed a theory about homicide suspects. They charted it out in rings, like the "zones of destruction" they talked about in *Life* articles about A-bombs going off. The First Ring was ground zero. Husbands, wives, jealous lovers, sons and sometimes even daughters. Second Ring was close friends, sworn enemies, business associates with a grudge or something to gain. Third Ring was people from the past with an axe to grind or crooks who were in the wrong place at the wrong time. The Fourth Ring was the random crazy or, on very rare occasions, cases of mistaken identity. Suicides didn't count, but murder for hire did, and the unknown killer usually managed to connect back to Ring One or Ring Two. Over the years there had been very few exceptions.

"Then I better start making a list and checking it out. Find out who's been good and who's been bad."

"Be Christmas before you know it," said R. T., smiling, his eyes crinkling.

Ray gave him a wave and then climbed back into the car. R. T. retreated into the mansion. The gates were already open when Ray reached them. He turned back onto Vickery Boulevard and put himself back on the expressway heading south.

He turned off the expressway at Pacific Avenue and pulled over at the first telephone booth he saw. Using his notebook to retrieve the number, he called Valentine and asked him if he'd be kind enough to write out a list of dealers like himself as well as a list of clients Jennings Price might have been involved with.

"A lot of those people are my clients as well, Detective. I wouldn't want them bothered."

"They won't be bothered, Mr. Valentine, they'll be asked a few questions."

"I'd rather they didn't know where you got their names."

"Cooperate with me, Mr. Valentine, and I'll be pleased to cooperate right back."

"I'll bring the list over myself."

"Just leave it with the desk sergeant on the main floor. He'll see it gets to me."

"Consider it done."

"You're a scholar and a gentleman, sir."

Ray pulled the cradle of the pay phone down and flipped through his notebook to the Jack Ruby notation. He dialed the number—RIchardson 7-2362—and let it ring a dozen times. Finally a thin, male voice answered.

"Carousel Club. Larry Speaking."

"Larry?"

"Crafard. I work here. Club doesn't open 'til nine."

"Is Mr. Ruby there?"

"Who wants to know?"

"Detective Ray Duval of the DPD."

"You a cop?"

"You can assume that, Mr. Craphard."

"Crafard." The voice was thin and weary, with a Yankee flatness to it. Detroit maybe.

"Get Jack Ruby for me."

There was a muffled rustle as Crafard put his hand over the phone and called out, "Hey, Jack, it's for you. Some cop."

An extension was picked up. "Ruby." There was a pause and then Ray heard Crafard hang up his receiver.

"Detective Ray Duval."

All of a sudden Ruby's voice took on a hearty tone. "Detective. What can I do for you?"

"Answer a few questions."

"Anything I can do, I'll do."

"I'm in a phone booth at South Pearl and Pacific."

"Well come on down. Shoot the shit, ask your questions. My pleasure, Detective. My pleasure."

"Ten minutes," Ray answered and hung up. The man sounded like he'd been dipped in grease. Like Craphard there was a northern accent, this one rounder, meaner and recognizable. Chicago.

Ray climbed back into his car and looked at the pack of Salems on the dashboard. He let one hand rub across his chest, wondering what was going on under his fingers. He had a sudden image of the clock ticking inside the Peter Pan crocodile. It was the first movie he'd seen with Lorraine after getting out of the VA hospital after he got back from Korea, and it was the last. He could almost see the alarm clock in his own chest, the two bells, like chrome-plated ears about to ring. He switched on the car, put it in gear and headed for the rough end of Commerce Street down toward Dealey Plaza and the warehouse district.

Ruby's nightclub turned out to be a half street number on the second floor above a barbecue joint. Ray found a parking spot in front of a hydrant, took his DPD Official Business placard out of the glove compartment and tossed it onto the dash. He climbed out of the Chevy and locked it. The smell of barbecue sauce and cooking beef wafted out of the main-floor restaurant. Once upon a time Ray would have stood there taking in the ambrosia of grilled beef and a thick sweet and spicy sauce, but now it was only making his stomach turn. He found the double doors that led to the Carousel, pushed through them and began slowly climbing the long, steep flight of stairs, hanging on to the rail and pausing every few steps to catch his breath. Finally he made it to the top, stopped again so that he wouldn't arrive for his interrogation puffing like a locomotive pulling a hundred freight cars up a mountain. When he felt a little better he pushed through the red vinyl padded door and stopped to let his eyes adjust.

The club was a good size with three circular bars with top surfaces big enough to take a stripper dancing on and two dozen more tables reserved for club members. At the far end of the big room there was a good-sized stage with dark red curtains, the curtain color repeated on the tablecloths. The walls were brown, artificial wood paneling. Knotty pine by the looks of it. The only other decorations were crowns and prancing horses done in cardboard and aluminum foil tacked up on the wall.

A man half stood at one of the tables. He waved. He was barely five feet, potbellied, with slicked-back hair brushed straight back. He had a pile of ledgers with him on the table and an adding machine.

Ray skirted the circular runway bars and headed for the table.

"Siddown, siddown," said Ruby. He slammed the ledger closed while he was talking. A cigar was fuming in a tin ashtray. Ruby saw Ray looking at the ashtray and misinterpreted the look. He reached into the inside pocket of his pinstripe jacket and took out a virgin cigar, still in its plastic wrapper.

"Want one?" said Ruby. He lit the stub of his own with a wooden match. Before Castro, Ray had smoked the occasional Havana delight, but this was something of a different sort.

"No, thanks," said Ray.

"Something to drink?"

"Iced tea might be nice."

"Vera! Iced tea and a scotch rocks."

He didn't even look over his shoulder to see who he was talking to.

"So what did you want to talk about, Detective . . . ?"

"Duval."

"Duval, right."

"People down at the station who know you say you know pretty well everything that's going on in the way of good times in Dallas." Mention queers first thing and he was going to get antsy.

"Depends on how you define good times."

"Clubs, women, booze."

"No secret. This is Chicago down south. You got a dozen clubs in three blocks from the Celebrity to the Texas

Lounge. You got any booze you want, any broad you want, any time you want. You got a stripper like Vera with her tits starting to point at the floor instead of the ceiling and then you got hot new acts like that Jody kid at the Regent Club. Cans on her like a B-52. Tassels go in opposite directions when she gets into her hump-and-grind routine, you know what I mean?"

"No trouble from Vice?"

"No trouble from the cops, period, and you know it as well as I do. No reason for trouble. Stripping's not against the law, neither's selling booze."

"It's against the law if you're selling the booze off premises, and it's against the law if you and your club are just pimping and the strippers are nothing but hookers with good moves."

"Hey. No one's complained so far. You keep it clean, you keep your head down, you comp the right people, everybody's happy." Ruby offered up a wide, fat-lipped smile. "These are modern times, Detective; this is the way the world works now. These days Al Capone would be mayor of Chicago and Frank Nitti would probably be governor."

"You make it sound like you knew them."

"I knew everybody in Chi, Detective. I still do. Just like I know everyone in Big D."

"Boys?"

"What about them?"

"Happen to know anything about what goes on that side of the tracks?"

"Not my thing."

"But you know about it."

"Some."

"Give me a such as, Jack."

"Parties."

"What kind of parties?"

"There's a few bars, one or two clubs, but usually it's parties. Big ones."

"Where?"

"Places change a lot."

"What kind of places?"

"Why you so interested?"

"Murder. Some aspects of it lead me to think queers might be involved."

Ruby nodded and Ray was sure he noted a look of relief on the man's face. The iced tea arrived, complete with a sprig of mint on top. "To cooperation," said Jack, and clinked glasses with Ray.

"Cooperation."

Ray caught a glimpse of a thin man in a windbreaker walking toward the doors leading to the stairs. "Larry?"

"You know him?"

"On the phone he sounded like he came from up north."

"Michigan, I think," Ruby said.

"You're Chicago, right?"

"Right." Ruby took a long swallow of his drink. Ray caught a whiff of the scotch. He tasted his own. Tea and lemon and too much sugar. "You interested in what I know about the queer scene or you interested in me for some reason?"

"Just interested in what you can tell me."

"I did."

"Parties."

"That's right. Say one of them is a real estate agent. He's got a big house somewhere he's trying to sell. He invites all his queer friends to a party in the house. Supposed to be he's trying to attract buyers, but it's really a bumfuckers' ball. You know?"

"There money in it for anyone?"

Ruby smiled. It turned his lips thin as a snake's. "Person who sells the booze and the food."

"You do any of that?"

He shrugged. "Once in a while."

"Ever meet a guy named Jennings Price?"

"Not that I can remember."

"Valentine?"

"No." Too quick with the answer. He knew he could go and dig around in that for a while and Ruby might squirm. He decided to save it for later. "I thought you said this was about a murder."

"It is. Guy we found chopped up in a fridge at the dump."

"Chopped up?"

"Butchered, then put back together with electrical wire."

"Sounds like a lot of trouble. Two in the head is quicker."

"In your neck of the woods."

"In any neck of the woods." Ruby smiled again and returned his fuming cigar to the ashtray. "You're trying to piss me off, aren't you?"

"Why would I want to do that?"

"See how I acted. See if you could get me to say something I shouldn't say."

"You saw right through me, Jack." Ray lifted himself up from the table.

"Talked to a lot of cops in my time. Likeable, most of them."

"I'm not the likeable sort. Been a cop too long."

"I can see that."

Ray gave him a little wave. "Thanks for the help."

"Nothing to it."

As Ray headed back for the stairs he heard the crank and clatter of the adding machine start up again, but when he pushed open the door and took a look back across the club, Ruby was staring right at him. He went out the doors and down the steep stairs to the street, wondering all the way down why Ruby had been relieved when Ray mentioned a murdered homosexual and why Larry had been so eager to leave the Carousel Club in such a rush.

Chapter 8

By the time he got back to the squad room it was almost four in the afternoon. Dhority and Roberts had two Negroes in the interview room accused of knocking over a Sonny Bryan's Smokehouse on Inwood Lane, and Leavelle and Cecil Stringer had a man named Drucker in the interview supply room handcuffed to a pipe and waiting to be taken upstairs to the cells on five for beating his wife to death with a Louisville Slugger and trying to cover up by putting her out with the regular trash.

True to his word, Valentine had sent over a list of clients, sealed in an envelope that Rodney, the desk sergeant, had put in a manila circulating memo envelope. Ray undid the string, stripped open the smaller envelope with a straightened paper clip and sat back in his squeaky old chair to read it. It was broken down into dealers and collectors and neither list was very long:

DEALERS
Eric Dunbar & Associates
Paul Connaught Gallery
Rose Waring Antiquities
Arthur Allenby Archives

<u>COLLECTORS</u>

J. P. Carran
Howard Moresby Case
W. H. Harrison
Alexandra J. Holt
William Parr
Paul Futrelle
Clifford R. Parker
Sen. E. Edward Stanton

Ray didn't recognize any of the dealers, and he hadn't really expected to, but some of the collectors' names were familiar. J. P. Carran was a big-time oil lawyer with a penchant for beating his wives and mistresses, then paying them off; Alexandra Holt gave charity balls and raised money for good causes; Paul Futrelle was the Dallas Supervisor of Schools and Stanton was a redneck state senator who'd bigoted his way into the capitol in Austin on the sheet-tails of the local Klan. Ray couldn't identify the others on the list, but presumably they were among the rich and powerful as well.

He jotted down the names in his notebook along with a badly drawn doodle of Pinocchio and another doodle of an old-fashioned icebox like the one Jackie Gleason had in his apartment on *The Honeymooners*. He wrote down the words *time* and *care* because that's what he'd seen. Whoever killed Jennings Price had taken a great deal of both and that just didn't fit in with any idea about murder he knew.

He wrote out the name *Peter Pan*, underlining it twice and drawing an arrow back up to his crude drawing of Pinocchio. He seriously doubted Walt Disney had come out from California to kill Price, but hell, you never really knew where a murder was going to take you. Pinocchio was obvious, given the state of the man's body, but what did Peter

Pan have to do with anything except the image of a ticking clock in his chest earlier that afternoon and the fact that the picture had been the last thing he'd seen with Lorraine? He lifted his pencil and was about to scribble out the Peter Pan notation when his phone rang at him. He picked it up and hit the blinking button on the line panel.

"Duval."

"It's your brother."

"Audie?"

"How are you?"

"Fair to middling."

"That's no answer, Ray."

"You sound like the Old Man, except he'd call me Horatio and he'd call you Claudius. And it's the only answer I'm willing to give because it's the only one you deserve."

"Why do you always have to be such a prick about things, Ray?"

"Lack of a formal education, I suppose. You went to Harvard Law and screwed girls, I went to France and got shot at. Now I'm dying from some kind of heart thing that probably runs in the family."

"You could have gone to any university you wanted. Not like money was lacking."

"The Old Man wanted you to become a lawyer and then he wanted you to become county prosecutor, and now he wants you to run for governor, and maybe after that take a run at the White House. Dreams of glory. So far you're halfway up the ladder. Wichita County prosecutor. The Old Man didn't have any dreams of glory for me."

"We going to go into one of these 'Daddy didn't love me' routines?"

"Daddy loved me all right. Every once in a while he'd remember he had two sons and he'd say—'What chew up to these days, Ho-Ra-Ti-O.' And I'd tell him and he'd say something like, 'Now don't that just beat all!' "

"I really don't need to listen to this asswipe, Ray."

"I got the Congressional Medal of Honor from FDR's own hands and that's what the Old Man said. 'Now don't that just beat all.' I got out of the VA with enough screws in my legs to open a hardware store and I come home and you two are playing backgammon on the sun porch, and I give him the picture they took of me and the president in the Rose Garden at the White House. I thought he might want to frame it or something. Hang it up somewhere where he'd point it out to his friends, but he just looked at it and then he looked at me and then he told me it was a good thing I'd come home because I looked too skinny in the picture and what I needed was fattening up. Then he gave me back the picture. He gave it *back* to me, Audie." Ray tried to control the flood of thoughts coming into his head, feeling his heartbeat begin to accelerate, every once in a while one of the beats like someone thumping his chest with a fist.

"You always took the Old Man too personally."

He tried to speak calmly, staying in control. "Damn right I took it personally, Audie, since that's how it was meant, or actually, impersonal's probably a better description of me and Daddy."

"It's his birthday today. His seventy-fifth."

"Now don't that just beat all!"

"He wants to see you, Ray. We're having a party and he wants to see you."

"Why?"

"Because he's afraid he won't ever see you again. He's afraid you're going to die and that he's going to outlive you and it's making him sick to his heart."

"Not as sick as mine."

"Put away the jokes, Ray. It's not the time."

"Who's joking?"

There was a long silence. Then Ray heard a sigh that made him see his brother's drawn face and hound-dog eyes. "Why do we always fight this way, Ray?"

"You know why."

"No, Ray, I surely do not."

Ray sighed and wished he could still smoke properly. "Because we don't know each other, Audie. We've got nothing in common except the past and nothing in the past is worth remembering. We're brothers by blood but we don't think the same, or hope the same or anything else the same. You want to be governor. I want to solve the murder I'm working on. You like things complicated, that's why you're a politician. I like things simple, so I guess that's why I'm a cop."

Another long silence, and then Ray's brother spoke again. "I checked. There's a Southern Aviation flight at seven. I'll meet it if you want."

Ray looked at his watch. Ten past four. Just like his brother to forget how much he hated flying. It was a two-and-a-half-hour drive and he could probably beat that if he tried. Cyn would be there, of course, which might make it worthwhile, or it might make it so hard he'd stop breathing. "I'll drive up, Audie," he said, and gently hung up the phone without saying anything more. He spent ten minutes just sitting there, waiting for calm to come in a room full of crimes and criminals. Eventually it did. He took out the Gem Junior razor he kept in his desk drawer along with a jar of Burma-Shave and a toothbrush he kept there for late nights or early mornings on the job.

Normally he would have signed out with the captain but Fritz was off at another Secret Service meeting with Chief

Curry and had taken his secretary with him, so Ray checked himself out on the chalkboard screwed to the back wall of the jail elevator without any information about when he'd be back. Not that Fritz would care; his head was full of cotton wool with all the Kennedy visit hoopdeedoo, and concern for Ray's whereabouts would probably revolve around whether he was dead or not.

The detective retrieved his car, drove west almost to Fort Worth and put himself into the heavy evening traffic on U.S. 81. By the time he reached the little farm town of Rhome the traffic was thinning out and it was dark enough for him to pull the knob for the lights, creating a comforting tunnel of light as he headed for home. He finally gave in, pushed in the lighter and fired up one of the Salems, taking small drags every once in a while, like sipping wine, but mostly letting it just hang in his mouth, letting a little smoke trickle back into his nose, pushed by the stream of air from the half-open vent window. After all, it was a celebration, wasn't it? The Old Man was seventy-five years old.

Ray stared down the double cones of light, a faint moon shining on the patchwork of endless fields and low hills in the distance that never seemed to come any closer. He'd always liked driving at night, and sight was just about the only thing unaffected by what was killing him. He kept his foot heavy on the gas, keeping the big needle on the fan-shaped speedometer at a steady seventy-five to keep up with the Old Man.

Most people, he knew, thought about what was going to happen in the future, about things they were going to do, or places they'd go, women they'd sleep with, children they'd have, or millions they'd make before they reached a certain age. Not long ago he'd felt the same way, putting most things out of his mind except the Job and his radio hobby—

not happy, but maybe content, which was probably the best you could expect at that age after two wars and an ex-wife like Lorraine.

Now he lived on memories, flipping through them like a deck of cards with girlie pictures on them, pausing once in a while to examine one in particular, then moving on, moving back and forth, trying to find the scheme of it all, but inevitably failing, because it wasn't just days and nights and people, it was fragments, small pieces of vision, snippets of sound, faint aromas, good and bad that triggered his mind.

"Rolling up a Persian carpet," he said out loud around the dangling cigarette. Because that's what it was. Rolling up his life like a carpet. Setting himself aside in some basement storage room. Years ago, decades ago, he'd read an article about Persian carpets in a *National Geographic* magazine at the Edwards Public Library on West Gilbert Street in Henrietta. How many stitches in a nine-by-twelve carpet? How many memories in a dying man's head? Both were created by little children, except the little Persian boys and Turks went blind and all he was doing was feeling sorry for himself because he was dying and going home.

It wasn't really home, of course, any more than boarding school had been. Sometimes he thought to himself that he'd never had one. In Burkburnett after the oil came in and the Old Man sold off his ranch in leases the place got too rowdy, so the Old Man moved them all down to Henrietta and bought one of the old mansions that had been abandoned during the Indian Wars. He'd always thought it strange that there were so many mansions there, but they'd been built by men who'd gotten fat selling horses and cattle to the army at Fort Sill just up the way, or shipped them out from the big railhead to Fort Worth and the slaughterhouses.

Ray'd hated everything about the place and hated it still.

Small-town Texas at its worst, women putting on airs and graces while they spent their free time fucking each other's husbands while their sons and daughters fucked each other under the bleachers at Tex Rickard Stadium during football games and sometimes during the annual Clay County Pioneer Reunion and Rodeo. Rickard had been born and raised in Henrietta, but he'd escaped and gone on to be the first boxing promoter to put a fight together with a million-dollar purse. He'd even named his own hockey team after himself up in New York, Tex's Rangers. He'd been one of the lucky ones; most people born in Henrietta died there as well.

The sex was always fumbling and desperate, a substitute for getting out of town that often ended with the couple staying for the rest of their lives for that brief unprotected fit of passion while the Henrietta Hurricanes battled with every other high school in Clay County. It was one of the few useful pieces of advice his father had given him: "Once your tallywhacker's out there's no stopping him, so bind the sumbitch up like Holy Moses in his swaddling clothes before you poke her. Remember, son, you marry the woman, you marry the family, and there's no families in this town I want sitting down at my Thanksgiving table for turkey and sweets."

The admonition had two sides to it, of course: the Old Man didn't want him bringing any big-bellied white trash home to share his turkey and the wealth of his oil leases. He also didn't want his son Horatio to live any kind of life where the city limits of Henrietta or even Clay County were his only universe. Phillipus Lee Duval knew perfectly well he was a short-mouthed farmer from the dry-as-dust northern boondocks of the state with no whit of a chance to be something other than rich, but he thought he could start a dynasty like the Roosevelts or the Rockefellers and fully intended to have both his sons college graduates, preferably from somewhere in the Yankee north that blowtorched off the edge of their good ol' boy accents.

Ray balked at all of it. Without a by-your-leave on his eighteenth birthday he'd left a note for his old man telling him his intentions and then took the Greyhound into Dallas and joined the cops. For the first few years he tried to keep something going with the Old Man, visiting now and again, but pretty soon he realized that his father was pinning all his hopes on Audie, and Audie was responding in the approved manner.

From then on Ray was never more than a sidebar to his brother's life. Even when he came home wounded from the war with the highest military decoration in the land, it was Audie's first murder trial that stole the conversation around the dinner table that night. Even that far back there had been talk of the Old Man's political ambitions for his son, ways and means of pushing his career from county prosecutor to a position on the bench or a state senator's slot before he made the hop, skip and one-two jump to governor to congressman to senator and finally to the White House. The Old Man had the money and the connections to make much of it come true, but Ray had never liked the look on his younger brother's face as his daddy spun tales of his son's future, listening like a little boy while the Old Man spun fairy tales. They were P. Lee Duval's dreams, and Audie was shrugging them on like someone else's coat while the Old Man stood behind him pulling in the fabric and adjusting the sleeves to make the dreams fit.

Ray took his left hand off the wheel and tipped the butt of the Salem out the vent window, flecks of the long ash blowing back onto his jacket. He felt a thousand years old and tired down to his bones, and not for the first time he found himself almost welcoming the thought of death, letting it come over him like a cool green blanket, taking him down to a dark world without thought or dreams or anything else, the world not changing one little bit because he was gone, not feeling his absence, not caring for his passing in any way at all. Oddly, he was beginning to find the thought almost comforting. A soul moving through time, there for a moment, then gone in the wink of an eye.

At Bowie, roughly halfway home, Ray turned off the main highway and into the town. Once upon a time Bowie was known best for the fried chicken sandwiches you could buy there when the Dallas to Wichita Falls train pulled in, but the poultry industry was almost shut down now, replaced by big natural gas storage tanks scattered across the landscape like giant golf balls, while the spaces in between were filled in by dreary-looking, small manufacturing companies.

He pulled the Chevy up to the pumps at a Texaco station on the outskirts of town and went into the Dine-A-Mite next door. He put down a quarter for the new *Life* magazine and then sat down at the counter. He ordered coffee and pie and a second coffee to take with him. As he ate and drank he flipped through the *Life* issue. Some Broadway unknown named Elizabeth Ashley was on the cover and the inside wasn't much better. Two editorials, one about the Bobby Baker scandal in Congress, the other about a new military government in Vietnam. He read a brief article about a sheriff in California killed by a boy out in the desert that didn't amount to much except a couple of dead people shot for no reason, and the rest of the magazine was full of things he wasn't much interested in, particularly the beginning of a series on the First World War.

He drank his coffee and ate his pie. Bobby Baker lining his own pockets as secretary to the Senate majority leader was just good ol' boy politics and nothing new, but the paragraph about Vietnam was a telling thing, an omen that most people probably just overlooked because pronouncing names like Ngo Dinh Diem and Duong Van Minh was too hard. After fighting in two of them Ray could smell war coming like the tang of electricity you got in your nose when a storm was on the way. Nobody saw Pearl Harbor, nobody saw Korea, and nobody was seeing this. He closed the magazine and finished his pie. The only good thing was, he wouldn't be around to see it.

He picked up his Dixie of coffee, left it black and added three sugars to give him some extra energy. He paid for the two coffees and the pie, went back to the Texaco and paid for his gas. He set out again, dropping the glove compartment door and jamming the Dixie into the opening. Ray settled back in his seat and drove through town, most of which was shut down for the night even though it was only just past six.

He turned off at Mission Street and headed along Old State 59 for less than a mile, thinking about Audie and how he'd missed joining up, first for World War II because he was still in law school at Harvard and had a deferment, and then for Korea, because by then his eyes were bad enough to get him a 4F. It also didn't hurt that by then he was living back in Texas and the Old Man was serving on his local Selective Service Board. Ray had enlisted both times, which either made him a fool or an idiot or perhaps both.

Sometimes, even back then, he had wondered if he hadn't been born to be a warrior plain and simple, and that the Job was just a poor excuse. As a child he'd had a recurring nightmare about running through the fog and the skeleton trees of Belleau Wood, firing an empty horse pistol at ghostly German soldiers, weeping because there was no end to the forest or the fog or the Germans and he knew that inevitably he was going to tire and fall and die.

He'd been obsessed with the battle and everything about it, spending all his time after school looking through the pages of what few books on the subject there were to be had, realizing that his dream was no dream, that it was accurate down to the sight of a marine with lieutenant's tabs decapitated in front of a German machine-gun nest.

In his dream the man had no name but in the pages of the *Henrietta Independent* for June 26, 1917, his name was William Heiser and he came from Petrolia, Texas, not many miles away. He told his father about the dream, and about the dead man's name, but his father had told him never to speak of such things again and that it was all foolish superstition, and Ray never had. Even so, and even now Lieutenant Heiser and those ghostly woods came back to him, leaving him nine years old again, alone and in the dark.

Ray reached East Barker Street and slowed almost to a stop, staring at what remained of the old Alamo Plaza Tourist Court, gone now, like the real Alamo, crumbled away to some rain-filled holes and a few arches of masonry and stucco rotting away to nothing year by year.

It was more than an hour's drive from home, but still barely far enough to calm Cyn's holy-Jesus terror that her father the reverend might burst in on them in the throes of passion after the prom that night. She was nineteen and graduating high school and he was twenty-eight, back for Homecoming. It had been the sweetest moment of his life and he had never forgotten a single detail of it, from the taffeta and chiffon bouffant dress that crinkled and whispered as she stepped out of it on the floor of the motel room to the instant when he'd entered her and found her so ready.

He spent as much time with her as he could, coming up

from Dallas on his off-shift days, spending his vacation days with her and any other holidays he managed to get off. At first the difference in their ages was a bother to both the Old Man and the reverend, but they got over it eventually and everything seemed to be going perfectly. The only thing that got in the way was the Second World War. He spent three months in training, sixteen months in combat and six months in the VA hospital in Virginia. A month over two years, with lots of letters and never a hint of anything wrong, but when he got back she was already married to his brother and was pregnant with their first child, his nephew, Leonard. He'd talked to her about it once, then never again. He moved back to Dallas and spent another two months taking physicals for the DPD, until he was finally reinstated as a detective sergeant.

He gave the remains of the old Alamo Plaza Tourist Court one last look, and smiled because he knew that the only way to get through what was happening to him was to seize each memory for what it was. No matter what came after, that night was still the greatest moment of his life, when he was young enough and alive enough to still think anything was possible.

Chapter 9

Ray drove on for another hour. The interstate had long cut Henrietta off and he passed by without thinking too much about it. He drove around Jolly and Raymond, and when he reached the Clay County line he turned off the interstate and went around the bottom of Wichita Falls heading south on old 79, finally turning onto the Ranch Road that skirted Lake Wichita. At 7:00 P.M. on the dot he reached Old Lake Road and headed for Triple Ridge.

Ten years ago, when Audie joined the County Prosecutor's Office, he and Cyn had moved out of Henrietta and into Wichita Falls, since living in Clay County while you were a junior prosecutor in Wichita County wasn't politically very smart. Not to be undone, the Old Man had followed suit, sold the rambling old house in Henrietta and bought a two-hundred-acre ranch on the shores of Lake Wichita. The previous owner called the place Oak Farm, which the Old Man thought was stupid since there wasn't but half a dozen oak trees on the place, so as soon as money was laid down he changed it to Triple Ridge Ranch, which was reasonable, since there *were* three ridges and you could see all of them from the main house.

The ranch was on the other side of the road from the lake itself, but the property had lots of water of its own, including a natural pool, a trout stream that fed down to the lake, a second, larger pond and a big heated swimming pool the Old Man put in when he heard that swimming in the winter was good for your arthritis. There were barns, sheds, workshops, a cabin that was easily a hundred years old nestling at the base of one of the ridges and Rose Cottage, a two-room guest house on the trout stream just before it went under the road and into Lake Wichita. There were enough stands of trees scattered around to make it private, but mostly the two hundred acres were given over to feed hay the Old Man let his next-door neighbor, Charlie Warren, harvest. In the middle of it all, reached by a long driveway, was the house itself, a concrete-and-stucco monster that looked like a Bavarian farmhouse built into the side of a low hill, facing the lake for the view.

He turned into the driveway and took his foot off the gas, feeling his stomach clench at the thought of dealing with his father, and worse, of sitting through dinner with Cyn. Audie had almost certainly told her about his condition, and the last thing he wanted to do was spend the evening with her across the table, her brown eyes half filled with tears for him, her face soft with pity.

He parked beside his father's brand-new aspen-white Cadillac Eldorado Biarritz and his brother's dark green Studebaker Avanti on the paved lot at the side of the house. He took a deep breath and let it out slowly, telling himself that this was a necessary thing, that it would take his mind off the killing of Jennings Price for a while, and that it was almost sure to be the last time he ever laid eyes on any of the people there.

He went around to the other side of the building and

climbed a short flight of steps up to the second-floor kitchen, which stood at the top of the slope. He let himself in and the first thing he saw was Cuquita, the maid and cook his old man had kept since shortly after his mother left. She had made a pot of coffee in the big silver pot the Old Man used, and was getting cups and saucers together on a big wooden tray with bone handles. Spotting Ray, she stopped what she was doing and came across the room, giving him one of her five-foot-tall bear hugs with plump little arms that didn't connect around his back.

"Dinner is finished, Mr. Ray. They are having cake and now coffee on the dining balcony."

"How's the Old Man?"

"Seventy-five years old. Cranky." She shook her head. "I can do nothing with him. He is a goat and he drinks too much."

"I'll second that." Ray smiled. Ever since he'd known what sex was he'd been pretty sure that Cuquita and his father were sleeping together, but he'd never known for sure and he'd never had the balls to ask either one of them. Maybe if she was still up when he left, he'd finally ask her.

"You want coffee too, Mr. Ray?"

"Sure."

Cuquita got another cup and saucer, fully loading the tray. Ray tried to edge around her and pick it up himself but she slapped him hard on the back of his hand. "Go away. Go see your family and let me do my job!"

"You go first."

"All right." She patted Ray softly on the cheek. "It is good to see you again, Horalito," she said gently, using the pet name she'd given him decades before.

"You too," Ray answered.

Cuquita picked up the tray and turned to use her broad

fanny to push open the swinging door that led out to the dining balcony that loomed above the first-floor living room. Ray was right behind her.

The Old Man was seated at the head of the long table, his back to the floor-to-ceiling display case of stuffed birds and smaller animals he'd shot over the years. The living room walls downstairs were filled with the heads of larger creatures, while the floors were adorned with rugs made out of a bear, a mountain lion, a zebra and a tiger. According to the Old Man he'd killed something in every country of the world except the communist ones, and fished in every ocean at one time or another. It was the kind of place Ernest Hemingway would have liked.

Audie and Cyn were seated across from each other close to the Old Man. Audie was cutting himself another slice of the big chocolate birthday cake and Cyn was using her fork to push hers into smaller and smaller pieces. The only choice he had was to sit down next to his brother or to Cyn and he didn't want to do either. Cuquita made the decision for him, taking the place setting beside Audie and sliding it down to the far end of the table facing his father. She put the coffee down between Ray and Cynthia and served Ray first, adding cream and two sugars, just the way he liked it. When he had his cup in front of him Cuquita began serving everyone else.

"I thought I was the goddamn guest of honor and I don't even get my coffee served first?"

"Ray's the guest, Daddy," said Cynthia. Hearing her calling his father Daddy was almost more than Ray could bear. He sipped his coffee and stole a glance in her direction. She'd added no more than five pounds over the years and her hair was still the glorious reddish brown he remembered.

She'd be forty-one or forty-two now, but she hadn't aged so much as she'd grown into herself somehow.

His brother, on the other hand, now had a bowling-ball belly and the beginning of dewlaps hanging from his cheeks. His hair was thinning and going gray, and he was wearing glasses. The Old Man didn't look particularly good either. He still smoked and his face bore the evidence in leathery skin and deep-cut grooves and lines, running here and there without much pattern except for the three deep notches in his deeply tanned forehead and the spread of chicken tracks leading away from the corners of his dark blue eyes. There was a wineglass on the table a quarter full of something honey colored, like sherry, and there was the ruins of another drink beside it, this one in a cut-crystal whiskey sour glass.

"You're late," said the Old Man, looking down the table at him.

"Couldn't be helped."

"Coulda left earlier."

"Working."

"Work too much. Should have been a man of leisure like me." The Old Man was slurring a little, but he still had his head screwed on straight. Just because he'd been drinking didn't mean he was drunk.

"I didn't strike oil like you did."

"'Came a cop, didn't you? All that homicide shit. No wonder you caught a sickness in your chest."

"Daddy!" scolded Cyn, but she was looking at Ray.

"I'm supposed to pussyfoot around all of this?"

Ray laughed. "No P. L., pussyfooting just isn't in your nature, is it?"

"Have you heard any more from your doctors?" asked Audie.

"Haven't been to one in a while."

"You sure that's wise?"

"I'm not sure of very much anymore, Aud."

"What do they have you doing?" said the Old Man. "Light duty, I'd guess." He didn't even wait for an answer. "Audie here's forming a committee to look into running for the Senate. We're thinking, what the hell, state senator's the long way around, whyn't we just shoot for the bull's-eye, see if we can get our boy and girl all the way to Washington the first go-round."

Ray looked at his brother. "Think you can pull it off, Audie?"

"Hard to say. Daddy thinks I can do it."

"Of course I do, or I wouldn't be pouring all this money into it."

Ray turned to Cyn. "What do you think about all this?"

"I don't really understand much of it."

"You do what the sumbitch Kennedy did. Or at least his father. You spend money getting his face shown and his good points pointed up and his bad points disappeared altogether." The Old Man laughed, the laugh turning to a cough and then a rough caw of phlegm, which he hawked discreetly into his napkin, folding the linen and putting it down neatly beside his plate. "It was money that got that Northern smart-ass into the White House and it'll be money that keeps him there along with that pretty wife of his."

"You don't think any of his programs are valid?" asked Cyn.

The Old Man looked at her like she'd dropped out of the sky from Mars. "Programs? You mean all this civil rights crap he's pushing for? It's shit and no amount of glue's going to make it stick. He's not talking to a bunch of old ladies in Boston at that Trade Mart tomorrow, he's talking to businessmen whose daddies were Klan and whose daddies before them were Klan." He looked down the table at his elder son. "You know what I mean, don't you, Horatio?"

"I suppose I do."

"How many Klan you think still in the police in Big D?"

"Never counted the pointy hats, but there's at least a few."

"Bet your Texas ass, boy. And we're not just talking beat cops, are we?"

"No, I guess you're right."

Audie interrupted, trying to change the subject and distance himself a little from a father who knew far too much about the Klan and its members. "What exactly are you working on, Ray?"

"Homicide," he answered. "A local antique dealer."

"Somebody shoot him during a robbery?" Audie asked.

Ray shook his head. "I wish it was that easy. No. He was found at the dump inside a refrigerator. Cut up and wired back together like a puppet." Out of the corner of his eye he saw Cyn's features screw up with distaste.

The Old Man looked thoughtful as Cuquita came and cleared away the last of the dessert and coffee dishes. Audie took out a pack of Luckies and lit one with an expensive-looking lighter. Ray stared down the table at him, biting back a twitch of envy at his easy, thoughtless inhaling of the smoke. Then the Old Man spoke up.

"The little nigger girl in Oklaunion. Now I remember."

"Little nigger girl?" Audie said.

"That's right," said the Old Man. "The funny thing is she wasn't from Oklaunion at all, she was from Haynesville. Wasn't quite all nigger either. Some said there was some Kikapoo in her's well."

"What little nigger girl?" Audie asked, getting a cool

look from Cyn on the other side of the table. He gave her a look back that said it was him echoing his father's word, not using it himself, but she wasn't quite buying it. Ray smiled to himself and waited for the end of the story.

"Little girl, maybe ten years old. Pretty as a picture, little ribbons in her pigtails like they used to do back in the old times."

And sat out on the lawn singing spirituals while Massah and Massah's wife rocked on the front porch and sipped juleps, thought Ray, except those times ended long before the Old Man was born.

"What about the little girl?" Cyn prompted, putting her hand out and touching the Old Man's wrist. Once again Ray felt an ache in his chest.

"Well, for one thing, she was murdered. Summer 1936 or '37, I think. Can't remember exactly. You were in law school and Horatio was already in Dallas. You wouldn't remember."

"Sure I do," said Ray suddenly, amazed at himself for not remembering sooner. Was that the Peter Pan he'd written in his notebook? "They found her chopped up in an old ice-box."

"That's right," said the Old Man, nodding so deeply his chin almost touched his chest. He jerked back his head and reached out for his drink.

"At first they didn't know who she was," Ray went on, remembering some of the details. "All they knew was she wasn't from Oklaunion, because there was no one missing there. Took a while to put a name to her."

"Wasn't much easier with the others," the Old Man said.

"Were they all nig—Negroes?" asked Audie.

"First three, as I recall. No one really gave it much thought. I mean they were niggers after all and we all figured it was a nigger thing, you know. Between them, so it didn't make any sense getting involved."

"How many all told?" Ray asked.

"Can't remember," said the Old Man. "Seven?" He nodded. "Sounds right. Anyway, after the first three they were white. Trash, mind you, but still white."

"Kids?"

"Yup."

"Pieces cut out of them? Squares and rectangles?"

"Seem to remember something like that."

"Anything ever done about it?" Ray's father had been a justice of the peace back then and he would have known.

"Not much. Nothing about the nigger kids. Jurisdiction problem too. Some of the kids were killed in Clay, some in Wichita, some in Archer."

"What about that, Audie? Would that make a difference?"

"Not now. Back then maybe. Complicate things."

"Would you have files on the killings?"

"Probably. Buried in the basement somewhere."

"I need to see them."

"Now?"

"Now would be good, but I guess I can wait until tomorrow."

"You really think there's some kind of connection? Those cases have gone pretty cold, Ray."

"Kids killed, chopped up, put back together again like puppets and hidden in iceboxes with chunks cut out of them. Pretty distinct M.O."

"A long time ago," offered Cyn.

"Twenty-five years." Audie nodded.

"People go away," said Ray quietly, looking at Cyn. "They come back too."

"You really think this is important?"

"Yes."

"Then let's go now and get it over with," said Audie. "Cyn and I are supposed to be in Big D at the Trade Mart tomorrow for the President's luncheon speech."

"Sounds like you're flying high, brother."

"Connally offered the invite," said the Old Man, giving off a choking little laugh. "Been kissing ass since he found out we were taking the short route to Washington and not going after the governor's spot next go-round."

Ray glanced at his watch. It was almost nine. His brother saw the look.

"Come on," said Audie, standing up, obviously a little liquid on his legs. "Get you those files if we can find them."

"Why don't we take my car?" said Ray. "No sense in taking yours too."

"I wouldn't be caught dead with you in that old heap. We'll take mine."

"Whatever you say, Aud, but let me drive."

"Fuck you, Ray. You think I'm drunk?"

"Audie!" said Cyn, color rising into her cheeks.

"Yeah, I think you're drunk. Give me the keys."

"Fuck you," Audie grumbled. He put one hand out, fingers splayed on the edge of the table to keep himself balanced.

The Old Man rapped the table with his knuckles. "Give him the keys, Claudius." Grumbling, Ray's brother dug into his pants pocket and tossed him the keys to the Avanti.

"I'll get him back as soon as I can," Ray said, looking toward Cynthia.

"We were going to stay here overnight anyway," she answered. "Get an early start in the morning."

"You do the same. No way you're driving back to Dallas

tonight," the Old Man ordered Ray. "Know where the key to Rose Cottage is?"

"Over the door."

"Put it back when you're done."

"Will do."

Sitting behind the wheel of the Avanti, Ray found his way back onto Highway 79 and headed north into the city of Wichita Falls. The car was a wonder of design, the interior laid out like the cockpit of an airplane, the main switches on a console overhead. It seemed to be padded everywhere and Ray didn't have any of the pains behind the knees he had in the Chevy, or the sense that his blood was being cut off. Beside him, his brother leaned against the side of the door, eyes half closed.

"Know why I'm doing this for you, don't you?"

"Sure," said Ray. "You wanted to keep me away from Cyn."

"Becher ass," Audie muttered. "Strangest thing. Better I do, the more she doesn't like me. Maybe she never got over her crush on you."

"It wasn't a crush, Aud."

"Whatever you want to call it. But I tell you something, I saved you a lot of grief, brother. A whole lot of grief."

"Why is that?"

"'Cause she's a bitch, Ray, and we were both too stupid to see it. Difference is, Adolf Fucking Hitler got in the way for you and saved your bacon."

"You're drunk, Aud. You want to have a hangover at lunch tomorrow?"

"Cyn's a true-blue bitch. She'd've fucked half the coordinating committee to get us chairs for that lunch. She'd've fucked the fucking governor himself."

"Shut up, Aud. You sound like a fool when you talk that way."

"Courthouse is Sixth and Lamar. Wake me up when we get there." He let his head fall back against the molded headrest of the seat and was snoring almost instantly. Ray kept driving, both hands on the wheel, trying not to think about what his brother had said, trying to believe that it was just the liquor in him talking.

Not believing it.

Chapter 10

When the Wichita County Courthouse was built in 1919, it looked like every other blockhouse-style judicial building being erected at the time. Last year the building had been completely renovated and now looked more like a modern art gallery or an airplane hangar than a courthouse.

Ray parked the Avanti in a spot right out front, then shook his brother awake. Together they went up to the glassed-in lobby, where Audie tapped on the door, showed his identity card and was let in by a suspicious guard in a uniform a couple of sizes too large for him. When the guard realized that the slightly drunk man smelling of Wild Turkey was actually his boss, he became falling-over helpful and guided both Ray and Audie down the fire stairs to the basement records room. It was divided into two areas — a small outer office that was filled with cards indexes like a Carnegie Library, and then, behind a second door, the cavernous file room itself that filled a good half of the building's basement.

The door guard left them and Audie sunk down at a swivel chair behind a gray metal desk. "How is this stuff organized?" Ray asked.

"Year, date, prosecution number. Homicides are on yellow cards with red tabs. That should give you a box aisle and row number."

"What year did the Old Man say these killings happened?"

"Summer 1937, '38, he said. Wasn't too sure." Audie was barely awake, leaning dangerously far back in the chair. Ray got him turned around with his head down on the desk, and then went back to the index cards. He riffled through 1937 looking for the telltale red tabs and came upon quite a number, but none of them was what he was looking for. He went on to 1938 and found his first match halfway through the drawer. It was the first of the white killings, July 17, 1938, a Sunday. The card said the victim was Mary Lou Mitchell, aged ten. There was an investigation number, and thankfully it was cross-indexed with numbers for the rest of the killings, nine in all. Three of the investigation numbers carried the prefix "[neg]," meaning Negro.

Ray left his brother sleeping and went through the steel mesh door into the file room itself. With the numbers in hand it took him the better part of two hours to collect all the files together, but he finally managed it. He found an empty file box on a table beside the door and dumped all the string-bound files into it. He carried the files into the outer room and roused his brother.

"Time is it?"

"Ten."

"Better get back to Daddy's."

"Come on then."

Audie raked his hands through his hair, yawned and got up from the desk. "Want me to carry that?" he asked, nodding at the box.

Ray shook his head. "I can manage."

They headed back to the lobby, this time using the elevator. "Should show you my office." Audie belched discreetly. "Nicest one in the place. Corner on the top floor. Big shots only." He grinned.

"I don't qualify."

"No, but you're my bro, bro, and that qualifies you, and besides, you're dyin', so you deserve to see what you missed."

"Didn't miss anything," Ray answered. The elevator doors slid open and they stepped out into the lobby. The same security guard was waiting.

"Like to sign that material out, sir?" he asked.

Audie snorted. "My big brother here will do it."

"Afraid it has to be you, Mr. Duval. I mean, he's your brother and all but you're the county prosecutor."

"Who knows?" Audie grinned, signing the ledger. Ray stepped up and added the file numbers. "Maybe the next time you see me I'll be president of the United States, so what do you think of that?"

"Be great, Mr. Duval. Could use a Texan in the White House." The man was clearly willing to say anything just to get the obviously drunk county prosecutor out of the building. People who witnessed their ultimate bosses three sheets to the wind might lose their jobs.

"Sooner'n you think," said Audie.

"Come on, bro, let's get you home." Ray shifted the box under one arm, grabbed his brother by the elbow and led him out of the building, letting the security guard lock up behind them. He eased Audie down the long flight of steps to the street, then poured him into the passenger seat and dumped the file box in back. Half an hour later he brought Audie back to Triple Ridge and put him into Cuquita's efficient hands.

"There is a daybed in the den. I put him there."

"The Old Man asleep?"

Cuquita smiled. "As drunk as his son."

"Mrs. Duval?"

"I give her hot milk and honey. Don't worry. I tell her where her husband is sleeping it off."

"Good. Good night, Cuquita."

"You too, Mr. Ray. You sleep good, I hope. You going early or you come up to the house for pancakes?"

"Leaving early, I'm afraid."

"Too bad. You always like my pancakes." She paused. "Maybe next time, Mr. Ray."

"Sure," said Ray. "Next time." And they both knew there wouldn't be one.

He took the file box to his car, drove back up the long driveway, then out onto the Old Lake Road again, traveling for less than two hundred yards before he reached an open gate and a short drive around an old hawthorn thicket to Rose Cottage.

The cottage was just a bedroom and a bathroom with two windows and a narrow porch, but it was just what he wanted—a soft bed and some distance from the Old Man. Dessert was all he could have taken and he was glad enough to be quit of his brother as well. From the way it sounded, Audie's marriage was coming apart at the seams and Ray'd had about as much of his brother's bad-mouthing of Cynthia as he could stand. He wanted to scrub the whole evening out of his mind, and with the box of files he had the means to do it.

He found the key and opened up the cottage. It had a musty smell to it so he put a wooden stop under the door to keep it open and freshen the place. He switched on the overhead light and looked around. Nothing had changed since he'd stayed here after coming back from Korea. An iron bed with a footlocker. A writing table under the window with an old candlestick telephone on it with a cloth-covered cord and a rag rug on the painted wooden floor. Over the bed was a painting done by his father. It was amateurish but realistic enough for Ray to see what it was—a rowboat with a little outboard on the back being launched at the end of the sand road that led down from their little cabin at Lake Arrowhead, a few miles south of Henrietta. There was a roughly painted-in small boy in the bow, looking out over the lake while a man pushed off, poised to jump into the boat and start the engine. A single line of darker paint arced up from the young boy's hand. A fishing rod. The little inscription at the bottom had the Old Man's initials and the date, 1930. Ray was already in the cops then, Audie twelve years old. It was Audie in the boat, and the Old Man pushing off. A day on Lake Arrowhead fishing.

Ray turned away from the painting, searching for a memory to match it, coming up with nothing very close. He went back out to the Chevy, brought in the files and dumped them on the bed.

He spent a few minutes putting the files in chronological order, beginning with the first [neg] file, a twelve-year-old girl named Lucille Edmonds. Lucille's father, Titus, had worked in the ice plant in Haynesville and her mother had worked as a day maid for a family in Wichita Falls, commuting by bus on the weekends. According to the file she had been deceased for a year prior to the murder of her daughter. There was no cause of death listed. Originally the case had been investigated by a Wilbarger County sheriff's deputy named Dulane, but it had eventually been handed over to the Wichita Falls Police Department and a detective sergeant named Ed Finney.

On Sunday, April 24, the young girl had been found in the town dump in the town of Oklaunion a few miles on the other side of the line in Wilbarger County, hence, the sheriff's deputy. Finney immediately latched on to the girl's father as the likely suspect since he was alone with the child all week, but there was no real motive, and by the third of the Negro killings he was obviously out of contention.

Since the dead girl was a Negro, only a visual autopsy was done, by a pathologist at the state hospital, but that was enough. Lucille had been sexually assaulted orally, anally and vaginally and a substance (presumably semen) had been rubbed into her eyes so roughly the eyes had burst open. Her sexual organs and rectum had been removed by a sharp instrument and placed in the belly cavity, which had been punctured just above the navel. A large area of skin had been removed from the belly above the navel and smaller pieces removed from the thighs, the buttocks and either side of the spine. The body had then been carved into twelve separate pieces and rejoined. The pathologist noted that the cutting up of the body appeared to have been done postmortem.

According to the doctor the girl had been dead for less than twenty-four hours before she was found, which was odd, since she had disappeared from her home three days previously, probably on her way home from school. A brief note at the end of the investigative report by Finney presumed that "the colored girl" had been killed in Haynesville, dismembered in a second location (unknown) and placed in the icebox at that time.

Two witnesses had been interviewed, Titus Edmonds and the caretaker at the dump, James P. Dunnagen. Their names were only noted with the term *N.O.I.* scrawled beside them. It took Ray a few moments to figure out what the letters meant but he finally assumed they stood for Nothing Of Importance, since there were no statements. There were also no photographs, either of the crime scene or the body. All in all it was one of the sloppiest, shoddiest and vaguest homicide reports he'd ever seen. On the other hand, it had been written in 1938, twenty-five years ago, and the murder victim was a Negro child.

He shuffled through the files until he reached the first white killing, Mary Lou Mitchell, age ten, discovered on July 17, 1938, Sunday again. Mary Lou had been taken three days previously while walking home from school in the small town of Kamay, on the southern edge of the county.

Like the Negro girl she had been moved, this time deposited in the garbage dump in Mankins, another small town no more than half a dozen miles from her home. Although she was the first white child in the list of those murdered and assaulted, there had been three before her, beginning with Lucille Edmonds in April, Tilly Chambers in May and Lillian Berry in June, all found on Sundays, all disappearing three days earlier and all raped, assaulted, eviscerated and mangled like Mary Lou Mitchell.

In Mary Lou's case the file was ten times thicker than those for the three Negro girls and contained a wealth of crime scene and autopsy photographs. The pictures were grisly, but they proved one thing to Ray: even though the antique dealer was an adult, and had not been sexually interfered with, Jennings Price had been butchered identical to the way the girls had been killed, right down to the single, razor-sharp cut to the neck resulting in decapitation and a small chisel cut into the brain through the orbit of the eye.

By this time the investigation into the multiple murders had been taken over by two Texas Ranger detectives working on the case full-time out of Wichita Falls — Detective Sergeant Robert Moran and Detective Sergeant Harry

Durkin. Both men interviewed more than a dozen people but neither man came up with anything. Frustration increased when another corpse turned up at the dump in Electra, a mining town no more than three or four miles from Haynesville, the town where Lucille came from. Titus Edmonds was interviewed again, this time with a full statement, but once again the man was definitively cleared. At this point in the file Moran noted that Titus Edmonds had a burning cross set alight in his front garden a week after the discovery of the second white corpse, that of thirteen-year-old Helen Reeb. Three days later he was beaten with a six-foot length of braided wire nailed onto the end of a baseball bat and then lynched in front of his own house. No arrests were made, although there was a small penciled note in the margin that said "*contact James at the Kl.*" *Kl* obviously stood for Klavern, but James, whoever he had been, was lost in the mists of time. The rest of the young girls — Sally Wells, eleven, Anna May Johannsen, ten, Mona Cutleaf, twelve, and Maybelle Killeen, thirteen — had been kidnapped respectively in September, October, November and December, always three days before the Sunday they were discovered and always in a town dump several miles and sometimes more from the town where they lived.

Shortly after the Maybelle Killeen incident local deputies were guarding town dumps in more than twenty communities across four counties, but the killings seemed to have run their course. By New Year's Day there had been nine bodies buried and not a clue as to who had killed them so horribly. Detectives Moran and Durkin had gathered an enormous amount of information by that time, including dozens of supposed eyewitness accounts of the girls being kidnapped that all came to nothing, as well as scores of newspaper clippings and offers of supernatural aid, but all they could really do was wait for the murder that would come in January.

It never did. Nor was there a killing in February, March or April of 1939. By May the killings had dropped out of the public eye, and by July, with no new killings, the people of Texas, and in particular those in Wichita Falls, turned their attention to the war that seemed to be brewing in Europe and to the twin World's Fairs in San Francisco and New York. With all that, the murders of nine nigger and white-trash Texas children were all but forgotten.

By January of 1940 the files were officially listed as "pending" and put into storage. Durkin and Moran had been sent back to regular duties months before that when it became clear that the strange killings had ended, much to everyone's relief.

It was hot and stuffy in the cottage. Ray stacked up the files and put them on the table by the window. He cracked a window for some more air, then stripped down to his boxers and lay down on the metal-frame bed, both pillows propped up behind him. Usually now, it was the only way to sleep. If he put his head too low and his ear to the pillow he could hear the wet rattle of fluid in his lungs and the straining beat of his heart in the pulse under his jaw.

He closed his eyes and thought about the first of the children to die, Lucille Edmonds. According to the brief file her birthday had been in the first week of April, so she was just twelve. When he was that age the only things on his mind were baseball and fishing and what to do about the constant and insistent erection that never seemed to go away, or when it did, reappeared at the most inappropriate moments, like standing to answer a question in geography class.

To him the Negro kids in Henrietta went to the black school and that was just the way it was and had nothing to do with him. Negroes were niggers, because that's what the Old Man called them, and that's what everyone else called them.

The Klan was a strange secret society like the Masons, but nobody paid much attention because everyone knew that Carl Bean, who ran the hardware store, was a member, and so was Freddy Corbett and his twin brother, Artemis, who ran one of the cotton gins in town.

It all seemed innocent enough and ordinary enough, but meanwhile little kids, some of them nigger little kids, were being raped and tortured and almost skinned alive before their heads were chopped off their bodies. And what that meant was that it hadn't been safe at all. It never was and it never would be. His small happy world had been a lie, just like the lies that later sent him across the Atlantic Ocean to watch his friends die all around him, and God help us all, it had been that way for every generation that had come before and would come after.

He stared at the pile of old dusty files in their old pale folders bound with pink ribbon that had once upon a time been red. Lucille Edmonds would be in her late thirties now if someone hadn't fouled and destroyed her. The life she would have had might not have been a very good one, perhaps no better than the one her mother or her father led, but she would have seen time pass, perhaps borne a child, and that was something, however small, that had been stolen from the world.

He thought about his own life and wondered idly if it had really amounted to very much, any more than Lucille Edmonds's would if she'd had a life to live. Probably not. There'd be few to mourn his passing, few to miss him in their hearts if any. Long before he'd come down with his sickness he'd wondered about things like that, staring down at a murder victim, sometimes so freshly killed the body was still warm, so recently slipped from life by a bullet or a knife that the illusion of being alive remained. It was an illusion that never lasted long and then the day continued, minus this one soul, and nothing of it remained, and except on rare occasions there was no one or nothing to mark the person's passing. It had been the same in his wars, like Lieutenant Belcher and the Gruen wristwatch he wore. He died, the watch lived on and no one really cared.

Ray took a breath and let it out slowly. He'd always been a morbid bastard, which was probably a good thing considering his job and his present condition, but as his ex-partner, Ron Odum, had once pointed out, death was a state of being, not a state of mind. He heard the sound of gravel crunching on the driveway outside and his eyes flickered automatically to his old tweed jacket hanging over the chair, the shoulder rig and the Browning rolled together on the seat. Then he settled back against the pillows. It was too far to get to and whoever was out there probably wasn't someone intent on blowing his brains out. He waited and a few seconds later Cynthia stepped through the open door, wrapped up in a dark blue silk robe with huge orchids on it. As she stepped inside the cottage she instinctively pulled the knot on the thin belt a little tighter at her waist. Outside he could hear a quick gust of wind creaking through the old hawthorns. A car drove fast down the Old Lake Road, or maybe it was a truck, because there was a lot of gearing down and rattling as it hit the curve just past the cottage.

"Aren't you a sight?" She smiled.

"I could cover up if I'm causing offense."

"No, don't do that. I like boxer shorts."

He looked down at himself. They were plain, light blue. "Nothing special. Just Fruit of the Loom. Cotton."

She sat down on the edge of the bed. She put her thumb and forefinger around the hem of one leg. Her touch made his skin quiver. "I thought they might be silk."

"I'm not the type to wear silk boxers."

"No. Always the practical one."

"Audie sleeping?"

She curled her lip. "Passed out."

"The Old Man?"

"Went to bed hours ago." She looked at the tiny gold watch on her wrist. "It's late. Past one."

"I'm surprised you're still up. You should be asleep yourself."

"Speak for yourself. You being sick and all and here you are up and working. Can't be good for you."

"Difference is I don't much care anymore," Ray said. "And I like to work. Makes me feel like I'm doing something."

"All I've ever been is a wife." She paused. "Or a girl-friend. I never even got to be a mother."

"You or Audie?"

"Neither one of us, though he never got checked. Just . . . it didn't work out. Wouldn't have been good for the job." There was an awkward pause.

She moved her hand so that it lay flat in the center of Ray's boxers. She started to move her hand back and forth in small motions, then grabbed him through the fabric, milking his foreskin back and forth the way she had years ago.

"You don't have to do this, Cyn. You shouldn't do it."

"I want to." He started to thicken, which was a surprise, because the last thing on his mind these days was sex; death had a way of dampening his urges, not to mention the effect of his failing heart.

"What about Audie?" he asked.

"I don't owe him anything."

"He said you played around."

"I do."

"Why?"

"Because he doesn't want me or he doesn't need me, or maybe he just doesn't care either way." She pulled at his shorts and his half erection slithered out.

"Then get a divorce. It should be easy enough."

"Real easy." She leaned over and took him into her mouth briefly, something she'd never done back when they were together. She brought up her head and it made a wet little popping noise. "Trouble is, it would be bad for his career."

"What do you care about his career?"

"If he's going to be a senator, then I'm going to be the fucking senator's wife. If he's going to be the governor, even better." Another shock, he'd never heard her say fuck before, and he began to understand that he'd never really known her at all. She started sucking at him again but he reached down and pulled her away.

"Enough."

"I want you to come. I want to do it for you." She paused and he thought he saw tears forming in the corners of her eyes but he didn't believe her for a minute. "I wanted to because you're . . ."

"Sick? Dying?"

"Yes."

He sighed, because he was a professional when it came to knowing a lie from the truth, even when the lie was halfway plausible like this one. "No, Cyn, you want to do it for yourself. You want to screw your husband's brother again so you can betray him just like you betrayed me." He pushed her away. She sat back and Ray pulled up his boxers and swung his legs over the side of the bed.

"I never betrayed anyone. You were gone and he was there. I didn't know if you were coming back from the war."

"You could have waited to find out."

"I had a life to live."

"You married my brother for the money you knew he was going to get. You married him for the power you thought he might have. I was a cop, and I was always going to be a cop, and you didn't like the idea of being a cop's wife. You would have dropped me even without the war."

She raised her hand to slap him but he caught her wrist. "You go on now, Cyn," he said softly. "You go on and leave now." He let go of her arm. She stood up and gave him a long look. "I hope it works out for you and Audie. I hope he takes you as far as you wanted to go."

She made a little face and looked down at the still-visible evidence of her ministrations. "That's all you are, all of you. Pale white cocks. Fat worms. You think that's all women want." She turned away, and as she did so Ray could see that the tears were flowing freely now, but they were from anger, not compassion. She reached the door and he stopped her.

"Cyn?"

She turned around. "What? Changed your mind?"

"You tell Audie what you did here, or lie to him about it and he won't believe you, understand?"

"I could make him believe me. I could make him think I screwed you all night long."

"You know something, Cyn, I don't think he'd really give a good goddamn one way or the other. You'd just wind up making things harder on yourself."

"Fuck you, Ray Duval." She went out, slamming the door hard. Ray stood up and went to the desk, picked up the gun and rig and looped it over the back of the chair. He sat down and riffled through the files again until he got to the slim folder given over to the Lucille Edmonds investigation, what little of it there was.

He opened the folder and read through it again, and saw what he'd missed the first time. Lucille was taken walking home from school. After a war or two and twenty-five years, Finney, Moran and Durkin might be dead and gone, but what about Lucille's friends? They would have been walking home from school just like her, and some of them, at least, would almost certainly still be around. He picked up the phone, dialed 0 for operator and asked for Haynesville information. Haynesville didn't have its own exchange but Electra did, and the operator there gave him what he wanted: the number for the black elementary school in the area as well as a number for its principal, Miss Amanda Pinkers. He jotted down the numbers in his pad and went outside to take a last breath of air before trying to sleep. Outside, the crickets were chirping as though it was summer and overhead there wasn't a cloud to be seen. It was a beautiful night and strangely warm for so late in the year.

Standing there, smelling the pine and the hawthorn and the air still sweet with a hint of rain in it, he suddenly knew exactly where he belonged in the world and what it had all come to in the end. A few weeks before he'd been watching the Disney show on a Sunday, which might have been an omen if he believed in omens, and there'd been a part about time-lapse photography. He'd watched plants grow like magic and buildings rise in seconds from basement to topping off. He'd been entranced by it all, especially the time-altered opening of a bloodred rose from nothing but a dew-sprinkled bud at first light to a brilliant full-blown flower by midday. To most it would just be a camera trick, but for Ray it had been a haunting epiphany of what time's essence really was, and standing in the doorway of the cottage, Rose Cottage, he understood that whatever length of borrowed time remained to him, his purpose was to reach back through the years and solve the savage killings of Lucille Edmonds and all the rest, which in turn would give him whoever had killed Jennings Price in the here and now. A small thing in the universe perhaps, but something to hang on to as he drifted to the grave: I did this one thing, if nothing else, and there need be nothing more to ease me to my death.

11/22/63
FRIDAY

Chapter 11

Ray was up at six, shaved and showered by six-thirty. He thought about taking his water pill, then decided against it; the last thing he needed was to be pissing like a racehorse all day, and missing a dose wasn't really going to make that much of a difference in the long run. He laughed, nicking himself with the razor; he didn't really *have* a long run according to the doctors.

He put on his shoulder rig, slipped into his jacket, scooped up the old file folders and headed out the door. He had a quick, lucidly erotic memory of Cynthia and pushed it away, ashamed enough for both of them. He climbed into the Chevy, wound up the dashboard clock as usual, setting the time from his wristwatch, then threw the files in the backseat and drove away.

Reaching the end of the Old Lake Road he turned onto Highway 79 and headed north. He could still see the image of the blossoming rose in his mind and for the first time in weeks he felt interest and energy flowing through him. It was like that old spiritual he used to hear sometimes when he was a boy, "May the Circle Be Unbroken." He began humming it under his breath as he drove, slipping onto 287, heading northwest toward Iowa Park and then to Haynesville, where it all began.

At ten past eight he reached Electra and swung off the highway onto old State 25, a strip of two-lane blacktop that had been patched so often there was barely any of the original road left. The land was mostly scrub brush and small farms, half of them looking deserted. He reached Haynesville a few minutes later, barely recognizable as a town except for an old general store, a Gulf station and a liquor joint. There were half a dozen other buildings in varying states of repair clustered around the crossroads at the intersection of State 25 and County 240. A weathered sign said the population was sixty, which looked about right. He parked the Chevy and went up the worn, parched steps to the porch of the general store. The day had turned bright and strangely hot for November. Kennedy would have near perfect weather for his parade.

There was a big red Coca-Cola cooler beside the screen door and Ray paused, pushed open the top and pulled a bottle out of the water-ice inside. He used the opener on the front of the cooler, then went into the store through the screen door. The place was small, two aisles and a counter, with wood plank floors that had lost their varnish half a century ago. A tall thin man in his late fifties or early sixties wearing bib overalls was leaning on the inner side of the counter. He had a hand-rolled cigarette fuming in his mouth and a copy of the *Wichita Falls Times Record News* in his hands. Kennedy's visit was all over the front page, just like it was on every other newspaper in Texas. Ray dug a nickel and a penny out of his pocket and put them on the counter in front of the man. He ignored the coins. Ray dug his wallet out of his back pocket and pulled out a dollar.

"Package of King Sanos."

The man in the bib overalls didn't look up from his paper. "You see them up there?"

Ray looked over the man's shoulder at the rack of cigarettes against the wall. There were no King Sanos. "Can't see them."

"'S because they eren't there."

"Newports then."

"Eren't there neither," said the man. He pushed his newspaper off to one side, picked up the nickel and the penny and slipped them into the front pocket of the bib overalls. "You gonna rob me or something, or you really want cigarettes?"

"Do I look like I'm going to rob y'all?"

"Look like you've got a gun under your jacket, one of them fancy holsters like you see on that *Naked City* story on television. Man comes into a store, asks for cigarettes eren't there and has a gun might be thinking about robbing. Wouldn't be a smart thing to do though."

"Why's that?"

"Been robbed before. Didn't like it."

"Understandable."

"You look old enough for the war. You in it?"

"Europe. Rangers. Korea."

"Then you know what a trench gun is."

Ray nodded. "Sure do. Military shotgun. Winchester. Army used it in both World Wars. Korea as well."

"Cut down the stock and bolt it under the counter, stops you getting robbed too. Put a big hole in the side o' the counter I'd have to fix, but put a big hole in y'all too. Right about where you keep your ladypoker from where I'm standing."

"I'm a police officer."

"Not a Texas Ranger. Not County Sheriff neither. I'd know."

"Dallas PD."

"What do you want here?"

"You live here long?"

"Never left except for the war. Born, growed, got old, all in the one place."

"Ever hear of a little girl named Lucille Edmonds?"

The man stared at Ray as though he'd seen a ghost. "Shee-it!" he whispered. "Not heard that name since I was a little-bitty boy."

"So you knew her?"

"She wasn't no playmate of mine. I mean she was a nigger an' all. But she shopped in this store when my daddy owned it, and so did her daddy too. What was his name?"

"Titus."

"Right. I remember now."

"They lynched him."

The man in the bib overalls nodded. "That's right, that's right," he said. "Like to ripped his head right off his shoulders."

"You saw it?"

"'Course I saw it. My daddy took me. Said he figured it was just about my last chanst to see something like that. He was right too. Never saw another."

"You know a woman named Amanda Pinkers?"

"Sign out there says population sixty. More like fifty-two or three. I know them all."

"Know where she lives?"

"Sure. Mile north 'til you get to the turning. Go right on East Lalk 'til you cross China Creek. She's got the house beside the school."

"Thanks." Ray drained off his Coca-Cola, then put the bottle on the counter. He turned and left the store.

"You got two cents on that bottle comin'," the man in the bib overalls called out.

"Keep it," Ray answered without turning back.

He drove up Highway 25, turning away from the blacktop as it headed west, following a gravel road east. With the window open for a breeze he could smell the sharp tang of the Red River less than a mile or so away, the border between Texas and Oklahoma. He crossed a plain concrete bridge with a little sign before it that said CHINA CREEK, and he was there, a plain white house with a groomed lawn that went down to the creek, and a larger building beside it with a row of small windows on one paint-peeling wall. The building had a tiny belfry like a church and Ray could see an old rusty bell inside it.

He pulled onto a rutted drive beside the house and got out of the car. The smell of the creek was thick and dark as peat, overwhelming the more distant tooth of the river. There was a porch facing the road, with an old-fashioned glider on one side and a screen door on the other. He tapped on the frame of the door and a few moments later he heard the sounds of shuffling footsteps. A small, bent woman appeared at the door, skin black and wrinkled, eyes blinking behind wire-frame glasses and hair shining white, bound back with a rubber band in a little knot at the back. She had to be at least eighty or eighty-five. Her dress was long and printed with small blue flowers. She looked a little startled to see a white man on her porch, and a little afraid. He hoped a little corn pone and some manners would make her less so.

Ray took off his hat. "Morning, Mrs. Pinkers. My name's Ray Duval. I'm a detective from down in Dallas."

"Duval?"

"Yes, ma'am."

"Relation to Claudius Duval, the county prosecutor?"

"Yes, ma'am. He's my brother."

"What do you want with an old black lady this time of the morning?"

"Wanted to ask you some questions if I could."

"I do something wrong?" She smiled thinly. "Rob a bank? Murder someone? Memory's not what it was."

"No, ma'am. This is about something that happened a long time ago."

"Lucille Edmonds?" said the little old lady without a hitch or pause to take a breath. "Or Titus, her father?"

"How'd you know that?"

"I'm old. You get old, you either get stupid or you get wise. Nothing else happened in Haynesville since they paved Highway 25 and Henry Haynes built the General Store. Luci Edmonds was murdered and so was her father."

"He was lynched."

"That's murder in my book." She paused. "How 'bout yours?"

"Murder in my book too."

"Why you coming around after so long? Twenty-five years now."

"I think there may be a connection to a case I'm working on."

"That the only reason?"

"At first. Then I saw how badly Lucille's case had been investigated and I thought it deserved another look."

"Well, good for you, son." She pointed to the glider. "You sit down and I'll get us some iced tea. You like it with lemon and sugar?"

"Sure, that'd be fine."

"Sweet or sour?"

"Little on the sour side." He paused. "What about the school?"

"Gave the children a day off. They'll be coming in at noon to watch Mr. Kennedy's procession on the television. Chance for them to see a white man who has a care for the Negro race doesn't come too often. Him and the Reverend Mr. King, except they don't seem to give him as many parades."

Ray ducked his head and looked toward the school building. Sure enough there was a large television aerial at the back of the roof peak. Principal Pinkers ran a progressive school.

Ray sat down on the glider and wiggled his toes inside his shoes. Even when he took the water pills the toes were squeezed together and his instep bulged. Another few weeks and he'd have to go up a size or move away from the loafers he favored and buy some lace-ups he could keep loose.

Principal Pinkers appeared a moment later with two tall glasses of iced tea, each one with a slice of lemon tucked down among the chips of ice. She handed a glass to Ray and then sat down beside him. He took a sip of his drink and was surprised to find that it had been made perfectly, tart sweet, just the way he liked it.

"Good?"

"Perfect."

"I'm not one of those old ladies who likes everything sweet. Not my nature."

"How long have you been teaching at the school?" Ray asked.

"Forty-five years this July. Started after my husband was killed in the war. Didn't have any children of my own, didn't have any desire to marry again, so this was just fine." She sipped her tea. "So what do you want to know about Lucille?"

"Who her friends were."

"Everybody in the school. Always twenty or thirty in the class. Only black school for quite a way around. Even sneaked in a few from Wilbarger. Kept them the week in my own house. Their mommas or their daddies would come and get them for the weekends."

"The ones who didn't stay, they generally walked home?"

"Anybody close. Mile or two. Rest would get picked up, usually a bunch all going the same way and one of the fathers with a hay wagon or a pickup."

"But Lucille walked."

"Every day except Tuesday."

"What happened Tuesdays?"

"Bobby Clay drove the Co'-Cola truck up from the Haynesville store. Last stop on his deliveries. He'd use 240 to get back to Burkburnett and drop off the kids on the way."

"He take any special interest in Lucille?"

"I know where you're going, Officer Duval, but you can just turn around and come back. Bobby Clay had three kids of his own and played Santa Claus at the school every Christmas. Always brought a couple of crates of Co'-Cola with him to give to the kids."

"Still alive?"

"Heart attack. 'Fifty-four. Sugar diabetes too. All that Co'-Cola, I guess. Cut off both his legs but it didn't do any good. Smoked as well. Wasn't even fifty years old."

Ray took a long draft of the iced tea. "Lucille have any special friends?"

"They were all special. I remember that class as clear as day. They were all close." She took a sighing breath. "Just an old woman feeling the grave, but I always thought they knew."

"Knew about Lucille?"

"No. Knew that they were doomed, a lot of them."

"Doomed? Dark word."

"Dark times." She eased herself up from the glider, taking her now-empty glass with her. "More?" she asked, nodding at Ray's glass.

"I'm fine."

She disappeared for a moment and then came back out onto the porch, her glass filled again and a framed photograph in her hand. She handed the photograph to Ray and then sat down again.

"Lucille's front row, exactly in the middle."

There were three rows of ten and one row of five. The girl in the middle had a broad smile on her face, her hair done in braids, wearing a gingham dress and sandals. Not especially pretty, but happy-looking. Ray stared at the image for a long moment, then looking more closely saw that a lot of the males' faces had small, inked X's beside them.

"The X's?"

"Like I said, I think God must have put shadows over them right from the start. Most of them in that picture are no more than thirteen or fourteen. One or two were a little older. We had all classes in the school, up to high school. In 'forty-one they all joined up, every man jack of them. They all joined the army infantry. An all-black combat unit. The ones there with the X's never came back."

"More than half," Ray said quietly. He looked more closely at the photograph. The boy directly behind Lucille seemed to have his hand on her shoulder. Ray commented on it.

"That's her brother. Marcus."

"Were they close?"

"He was fourteen, she was twelve. He blamed himself for

her murder. Usually he walked home with her, but that day he stayed back to play some baseball with his friends."

"Whoever took her might have taken him as well."

"I know that, but he still feels it, even today."

"He lives around here?"

"When he came back from the army he rebuilt the old place. Still lives there. Farms an acre or two, few chickens for eggs. Pays for the rest with his veteran's pension."

"Close by?"

"Mile or two. Down to Moeller Road, then south to the first bend. Big oak tree where they did Titus is still there. Same place Lucille was heading for that afternoon." She sighed again. "I think he feels close to her there, and the cemetery's not too far. He goes every Sunday. I've seen him there. I go there too, to think about my Carl."

"Your husband."

"Yes. There's a headstone, but Carl's somewhere in France. Never buried, just ground into the mud in some place I never heard of, some place I'll never go." She shook her head. "When I'm gone there won't be anyone to re-member him. Half the graves in Carla Cemetery are like that. Old, overgrown, untended. Sad."

Ray let a moment pass, staring out over the porch to the sun-drenched field and the road.

"Who do you think killed Lucille?" he asked finally.

"God," she answered immediately. "Same as my Carl. I spent a lot of my life believing that God was God and Jesus was my Savior, but all that went away when Carl died. A monster killed Lucille, stole her perfect innocence, fouled her, threw her in a garbage dump. That's God's work. His wonders to perform." She was crying freely now, the tears running down the seams of her old face. She shook her head. "My Carl wasn't taken up to heaven on a golden chariot. He was blown into blood and bone, then ground underfoot. Lucille was torn apart like an animal's prey. God's work, all of it."

"A monster?"

"Not someone from around here," she said, regaining her composure, wiping at her tears with a curled arthritic finger. "That kind of a thing in your mind you can't keep secret from your friends. It would have come out. And he moved on, like Lucille and those other two Negro girls were practice for the white ones. He came from hell and then he went back and I don't think you're going to find out anything after all this time."

"Maybe not," said Ray. "But I think it's important to try."

"Why? Going to bring her back, or her daddy?"

"Maybe," said Ray. "Maybe in a few people's hearts it will bring them both back."

"You truly think that? A white man?"

"I truly think that, Mrs. Pinkers. I truly do."

"Then you go on, son. You go on and give it your best."

Ray thanked the old woman for her help, then climbed back into the Bel Air and headed down the road. It took him less than five minutes to reach his destination.

The Monster flicked on the light switch just inside the doorway then came down the basement steps, his bare feet padding lightly on the stairs as he descended. He'd chosen the Oak Cliff rancher because the garage led straight into the kitchen and was high enough to accommodate his van, and the full-height basement that ran the length of the house gave him plenty of room to work in and plenty of privacy.

The basement was divided into three distinct spaces: the furnace room and service area at the foot of the stairs, a normal-enough-looking workshop in what had once been the recreation room, and finally, hidden behind a floor-to-ceiling hinged sheet of peg-board for his tools, a third room for his little captives. The room was windowless, the walls covered with narrow mattresses, the space between the rafters in the ceiling stuffed with rolls of insulation. The room had once been a laundry and it still had an extremely useful drain in the middle of the floor, a pair of cement sinks and a copper-tub Maytag washing machine from the thirties. He'd installed a big turquoise Hotpoint fridge that was only a couple of years old. Across from the appliances there was an old metal bedstead with a thin mattress. So far he'd only used it once since his return, but he knew it would give him a great deal of pleasure in the months, or perhaps even years, ahead.

Standing perfectly still at the foot of the stairs he reached down and touched himself lightly, feeling himself beginning to respond, either from expectations for the future or from memories of past enjoyment. He wasn't an old man by any means, but recently he'd begun to notice that he was living more and more in the past, and sometimes he wondered if that was a sign of something wrong within him, an omen. On the other hand he enjoyed his memories almost as much as each new conquest, the way you'd enjoy a favorite book, or the taste of a familiar wine on your tongue.

He still remembered the first one. The police always thought it was the Edmonds girl, but they were wrong. He'd taken a girl from school out to Eagle Flat in the old man's truck but everything went wrong. She wasn't too bright and not too pretty, but she'd been easy enough, which is why he'd taken her to the Flat in the first place, but when he tried to do it all he could see was his father's face and all he could hear was his mother's voice and he hadn't been able to do anything. She'd laughed at him and in the end she did him with her hand, but it hadn't been enough. The rage had been like a living thing inside him, but he caught himself before he did anything more than slap the girl around. He took her home then drove fifty miles to Vernon and the nigger cribs on the edge of town on the road to Paradise Creek. He waited for hours in the darkness and finally his opportunity came. A young, pretty little whore, no more than eighteen or so, had come out of one of the one-room tin-roof shacks and started walking toward town. He'd pulled up beside her in the truck and offered her a lift and that was the beginning of it all.

When he was done he drove out to the dump, which he knew well enough, chopped her into pieces with the old man's kindling hatchet and stuffed the pieces into an old icebox he found. He never even knew her name and apparently no one else did either. She'd never been missed or discovered, or at least there was no news of her. The power of his secret had lasted him for almost a year before he struck again.

Standing at the foot of the stairs he saw that he was fully aroused, and naked he walked toward the little room. He slid his worktable to one side, pulled on one of the empty pegboard hooks and opened his hidden door. So far the child had only known the fear of being bound up in the darkness; now he would show her the way to Paradise. He stepped into the little soundproofed cell and closed the peg-board door behind him.

The big oak tree was there, just like the old woman said, and Ray could see an old scar where a thick branch had once overhung the short dirt drive that led to the house. The house itself looked a lot like Mrs. Pinkers's, one story, shingle roof with a porch in front, in this case screened rather than open.

Behind the house was a chicken coop with an enclosed run and a shed hung with a dozen or more frames holding stretched muskrat skins. Behind the shed there was an outhouse.

Ray parked the car and got out. Also hanging from the shed wall he could see three or four big jackrabbits and a pair of quail. He slammed the car door to announce himself, and thirty seconds later a man appeared on the porch. It was the boy he'd seen in the photograph grown to manhood and into middle age. He was half bald and what hair remained was shot with gray. He opened the screen door and came down two steps, stiff on the left leg. Ray took a few steps forward, then stopped, keeping his distance for the moment.

"You Marcus Edmonds?"

"Who wants to know?"

"My name is Ray Duval. I'm with the Dallas Police Department. Mrs. Pinkers at the school sent me over."

"Why?"

"To talk about your sister."

"Lucille's been gone for twenty-five years."

"I'm trying to find out who killed her."

"Why? She was just another nigga then, so what's changed?"

"A man in Dallas was recently killed the same way."

"Was he raped and sodomized?"

"No."

"They find jism in his mouth and all the way down his throat?"

"No."

"Then he wasn't killed the same way as my sister."

"He was torn apart just like Lucille, then put back together again. He had his genital organs cut off and stuffed into his mouth. He was crammed into a refrigerator and left at the Dallas dump. That sound familiar, Mr. Edmonds?"

The man stared at him for a long moment. "You'd best come inside," he said finally. He reached down with both hands and turned the left leg, then went back up the two steps, swinging that leg wide. Ray suddenly realized that it was artificial. He reached the top step, opened the screen door and disappeared. Ray followed.

The inside of the house was spare and clean. It was basically a single room. To the right there was a kitchen area with an old wood stove and an ancient icebox beside it. Shelves beside the icebox formed a pantry. Still on the kitchen side there was an old table with four plain chairs, and beyond that a braided rag rug in an oval shape. There was a worn, green-painted stand-up cupboard against the far wall, a reasonably new-looking La-Z-Boy recliner with a cane laid across the arms. Behind the chair, pinned within a cloth-lined shadow box, there were half a dozen military decorations. Against the side wall there was a metal bed with a small, homemade side table. There was a coal-oil lamp on the side table and two more hanging from the rafters. Against the front wall, below a large window, there was a plain wooden desk and another kitchen chair. To the left of the desk there was a handmade floor-to-ceiling bookcase full to overflowing, a portable radio crammed in among the books. Ray noticed it was a 1941 Zenith portable, cloth-covered and powered by a six-volt dry cell. Looking at the radio and the hurricane lamps it was obvious that Marcus Edmonds didn't use electricity.

The black man took the cane off the La-Z-Boy and eased himself down. He used the cane to point at the desk chair. He leaned back, then used both hands to pull his left leg up onto the wide footrest. "You know the story about how my sister died then?" The man had none of the country bump-kin in him. His voice was clear and educated.

"I know what's in the files."

"Not much, I'll bet."

"No. Not much," Ray agreed. "There's not even a men-tion of her having a brother." He paused. "No one ever talked to you?"

"No." He put on a po'boy accent. "Just anotha no-'count nigga." He shook his head. "Just like Lucille. Just like my father. They lynched him, you know. From that oak tree out-side."

"I saw the missing limb."

"I sawed it off when I got back from the war. Used the wood in that stove over there. My father would have appre-ciated the fact that I put it to good use."

"Is that how you lost the leg?" Ray asked.

The man smiled. "Sawing off the limb and sawed off my own?"

"In the war."

"Take a look in the case," he said, jerking his thumb over his shoulder.

Ray got to his feet, shocked at how heavy his legs were feeling without the water pills, and walked stiffly across the room to the framed medals. The case was divided into two sections. On the top there was the Buffalo insignia of the 369th Infantry Division and below it three medals, the Dis-tinguished Service Cross, the French Croix de Guerre and the French Legion of Honor. The second line had the Black Panther "Come Out Fighting" insignia of the 371st Tank Battalion, and below it the Purple Heart, the Distinguished Service Cross and the Bronze Star.

"Top ones are my father's, the bottom ones are mine. My father's reward was getting lynched by his white neighbors and mine was getting my leg shot off when one of our own shells hung fire and then went off before I could get out of the tank."

"You sound bitter."

"I lost my family. I lost my leg, and all of it useless. Of course I'm bitter."

"Why'd you come back here after the war?"

"I didn't right away. I went to Columbia University on the G.I. Bill. My father took us to New York just after Luci was born. Bound for glory in the big migration after the first war. My mother died in a tenement and my father couldn't find any work better than shining shoes. So we came back." Marcus Edmonds made a snorting sound under his breath. "I tried the same thing, even got a degree, but it was no better for me than it had been for my father. So I came back too, and here I am. Sure I'm bitter."

"Mrs. Pinkers thinks you came back so you could be close to your sister's grave."

"And my father's. It seems right."

"I can find out who killed Lucille. He's like you, I think; he came back as well."

"I doubt you can find him."

"Let me try. Tell me what you know."

"Nothing to tell. You drove from Mrs. Pinkers's, you drove the route Lucille would have taken that day."

"Then so did the killer. Maybe you saw him. Maybe you just don't remember."

"I remember playing ball with my friends. I remember Luci coming up to me and telling me it was time to get on home and I'd probably get a spanking from Daddy if I didn't come right then, but I ignored her and she walked away and I never saw my sister again. That's what I remember."

"What time did you go home?"

"Half an hour later."

"What time would that have been?"

"School was out at three. I played for half an hour or so. Call it three-thirty, quarter of four."

"See any cars or trucks, either direction?"

"Not that I recall."

"Think. Maybe it was familiar."

Marcus Edmonds closed his eyes and lay back in the chair, the cane across his lap like a sword. "Nothing comes to mind. Not much traffic back in those days. Easier ways to get to Burkburnett even then. Just regular stuff. Locals."

"Like who?"

"On that particular day?"

"Yes."

"Remember the ice man came for Mrs. Pinkers. Always used to give us big chips of ice to suck on. We'd have to wipe off the sawdust."

"Who was he?"

"Think his name was Bacon. Family lived by the big ice-house he kept at the end of Highway 25 on Adama Creek. That's where he cut his ice in the wintertime. Froze up solid. Used to blast it out."

"What time did his truck go by?"

"Around noon."

"Where would he have been at three?"

"No idea."

Ray nodded to the icebox in the corner. "Were you on his route?"

"Sure. But on Mondays. He did this whole side of the county pretty well. Different routes on different days."

"You see anyone else?"

"Delivery truck from the store, junk man, sheriff's car a

couple of times, making his rounds, hearse from Todmorden's coming back from Clara."

"Todmorden's?"

"Funeral parlor in Electra. Most people used them because they're close."

"Negro or white?" Ray asked bluntly.

"They'd take money from anyone. Had a new hearse for whites, an old one for black people. Different drivers too. Back then it was Deuteronomy Dupree. I fought in the war with his son Gabriel."

"Which hearse did you see that day, do you remember?"

"The nigger bus. Everybody called it that. It had glass sides so you could see the coffin inside. The other one just looked like an old station wagon with curtains."

Ray wasn't quite ready to give up on it. Something was nagging. "Which way was it coming, to or from the cemetery?"

Marcus Edmonds closed his eyes again, his hands gripping the cane hard, his forehead slashed with lines as he concentrated. He opened his eyes. "From. I can see it clear as day. All the kids watched when Deuteronomy went by. It was before Luci went home. He was heading back to Electra. He must have been because there was no coffin inside the hearse, you could see right in."

Ray was running out of questions. He looked at his watch. It was just past ten. Still early. It was a two-hour drive back to Dallas; if he was lucky he'd miss the Kennedy parade.

"One more thing, if you don't mind."

"Sure. I'm not going anywhere."

"I know it's this way for me so it's probably the same for you, Mr. Edmonds, but after all these years is there something that sticks out, a detail, a thought, maybe something as simple as how something smelled or looked?"

"The day Lucille was taken?"

"That afternoon," said Ray, pulling it in. "That moment." The detective waited. It wasn't the first time he'd asked that question of a witness. Sometimes they didn't know what he was talking about and sometimes they did. He wasn't looking for something as melodramatic as a clue, but just a sense, a feeling that could put him there.

"I can hear her voice. Clear as anything," said Marcus Edmonds, a faint look of shock on his face as though he wasn't expecting the memory to be so distinct. "She had her books done up with one of my father's old belts and she told me she'd seen an old lamp that day with a fringe on the shade and she asked me if I thought we'd ever get electricity so we could have a lamp just like the one she'd seen." He paused and Ray saw that his eyes were wet. "And then she told me to come along home with her and I didn't and she died."

Chapter 12

To give himself a little more time to think Ray decided to go back to Dallas by way of Gainesville to the east, and then straight down the interstate into the city. Just before leaving 82 and getting onto the interstate he pulled over at a truck-stop, sat down in a booth by the window and ordered himself a proper breakfast. Getting out his notebook, he opened it and used his pencil to jot down the date at the top of the page, 11/22/63, and then started doodling out the information he'd learned on his trip home. By the time his ham and eggs arrived he'd polished off two cups of coffee and had a diagram that spread out over two pages of his notebook.

1938

Negro	*White*
Lucille Edmonds	Mary Lou Mitchell
Tilly Chambers	Helen Reeb
Lillian Berry	Sally Wells
	Anna May Johannsen
	Mona Cutleaf
	Maybelle Killeen

1963
Jennings Price
18–20 in 1938 + 25 = 43–45 yrs old.

Ray was sure that he was on fairly solid ground with the age of the killer. If the monster who'd killed little Lucille Edmonds had been in his thirties or forties back then, he'd be in his sixties or early seventies now. Price had been no prizefighter but he'd probably been capable of defending himself against an old man, and the very violence of the crime didn't seem possible for a sexagenarian or perhaps even older man. No. The killer had been young in 1938, just starting out on his horrible spree, practicing. Which would put him in his forties now.

The difficulty of course was in finding a connection between the killings of Lucille and the others and the murder of Jennings Price twenty-five years later. He flipped back through his notebook and jotted down the previous list of words he'd jotted down over the past few days.

PINOCCHIO
TIME
CARE
PETER PAN

Pinocchio still ran through all the killings like the wire the murderer used to reconstruct his victims. *Time* and *Care* seemed to fit the earlier murders as well. The killer hadn't just taken Lucille or any of the others randomly. Ray was sure of that. He'd seen them all before, marked them as potential victims and then taken them at an opportune, planned moment. He added another word to the list:

PLANNED

And then one more, only because it had seemed important to Marcus Edmonds, the thing that had brought tears to his eyes.

OLD LAMP

He put them all together in a single list now.

PINOCCHIO
TIME
CARE
PETER PAN
PLANNED
OLD LAMP

None of which really added up to much. A careful young man in 1938 who planned nine savage murders and got away with all of them. He put away his notebook for the moment and addressed the breakfast on the plate in front of him. He'd been hungry when he pulled into the truckstop but now his appetite seemed to have left him. He slipped one of his fried eggs onto a piece of toast and forced himself to eat it.

Behind the counter the waitress switched on the radio. A breathless news reporter on KRLD was telling the world that Air Force Two, carrying Vice President Johnson and Mrs. Johnson, had just landed at Love Field, and Air Force One, carrying the President, was expected to land within a minute or two. Ray looked at his watch. It was 11:35. He sopped up the yolk from his second egg with the other piece of toast and chased it with the last of his coffee.

The waitress appeared with a new pot and filled the cup before he had a chance to stop her. She was nothing like

Rena at Inky's, the restaurant down the street from the Texas Theatre. He thought about her for a moment, enjoying the memory and wondering if he had the guts to ask her out on a date, wondering if there was any point. Who wanted to go out with an aging cop with a bum ticker?

KRLD was announcing Kennedy's arrival now, complete with a long boring description of Jackie's pink suit. He tuned it out, sipping his coffee and trying to concentrate on the Jennings Price killing, letting his thoughts flow freely, looking for some connection that made sense. Of all the material he'd read the only thing that really struck him was the actual cause of death in Price's murder: some sort of fine chisel. All of the nine girls had been killed that way, and according to the files they'd been held for some time, perhaps as much as two or three days, while they were brutalized and then strangled with the same kind of wire that would be used later to turn their corpses into puppets.

The majority of homicides Ray dealt with were simple and straightforward—people killing other people for a good reason, at least in their minds, and generally using the usual prosaic weaponry of violent death: guns, knives and blunt instruments of one kind or another. No strange miniature chisels that didn't fit any occupation he knew about, no giant blades like some kind of monster shears, no bodies turned into Pinocchios. This was a job for a headshrinker, not a cop. He thought about that for a few minutes, wondering if a shrink might be able to throw some light on the problem, but then he dismissed the idea; most of the psychiatrists he'd ever seen or heard about seemed to be crazy, and as far as he knew there weren't any around that knew the first thing about what made killers tick.

Ray looked down at his notebook, reading the words, putting them together like puzzle pieces. The radio announcer was describing the motorcade as it left Love Field and headed toward downtown, talking as though Dallas had never seen a president before, or had a parade. The sound of the radio and the clatter of dishes faded away to nothing as the first bright spark of intuition jerked through Ray's mind and he suddenly knew that motive was going to be the key to finding out who killed Jennnings Price.

Luci Edmonds and the others had been killed for what they were: objects to be raped and violated, their skin harvested like some kind of gruesome talisman or trophy. Something in the killer's sick mind had made him kill out of some unfathomable, twisted desire. The murder of Jennings Price had been methodical and carefully planned, either for gain or some other purpose, the method masking the meaning.

Ray closed the notebook and pulled a couple of crumpled dollar bills out of his pocket, tucking them under the edge of his cup. His brain was starting to freeze up and he knew he was making connections that might not even be there. For all he knew there was nothing to link the old murders with Jennings Price except happenstance. To get anywhere he'd need to keep his focus on the present, not the past.

He stood up, went back outside and slipped into one of the phone booths beside the toilets. He dialed the operator, gave her his badge number, and she put him through to headquarters. He asked the switchboard for 351, and Gerry Henslee, the sergeant handling channel 2 dispatch, picked up on the second ring.

"Henslee."

"It's Duval." In the background he could hear a torrent of radio chatter. "Anything going on?"

The dispatcher was almost out of breath. "The Kennedy parade is driving me crazy. Leavelle and Brown are picking up some armed robbery suspect, everybody else is downstairs waiting for Jackie, and they found another body at the dump."

"Shit. When?"

"Early. Six, six-thirty. No one could get hold of you. Fritz is a little pissed, by the way."

"I'm half an hour out. I'll go right to the scene."

"Forget it. Fritz is already out at the Trade Mart lining up for his filet mignon with the rest of the high hats and the M.E.'s already got her on a slab."

"Her?"

"Yeah. A kid. Ten, eleven." The radio traffic in the background was getting frantic. "Look, I gotta get back to it, some guy just had a seizure in Dealey Plaza."

"Anyone asks, I'll be at Parkland."

"Ten-four." The phone clicked in the detective's ear as the dispatcher hung up abruptly. Ray stood in the booth for a moment, then dropped the receiver back onto its hook. He stepped out of the booth and stood in the bright sunlight, squinting at the late-morning traffic heading in and out of the city, waiting for the ruptured hammering of his broken heart to steady before he climbed back into his car and drove away from the truckstop. He glanced at the clock on the dashboard. It was twelve noon exactly.

Reaching the low-slung shape of Parkland Hospital, Ray parked in one of the rear lots. He took the Polaroid camera out of the trunk and made his way down to the morgue. The dispatcher was right. Doc Rose already had her on the table. She was black, eleven or twelve and cut to pieces like the others. Scattered over her body were dark red, perfectly regular patches where sheets of skin had been removed. Rose was using the hose attached to the long, stainless-steel autopsy table to wash the little girl down.

"This makes two," said Rose, looking up as Ray came into the room.

"No. It makes eleven," Ray answered. He took out his notebook and reeled off the names. "Lucille Edmonds, Tilly Chambers, Lillian Berry, Mary Lou Mitchell, Helen Reeb, Sally Wells, Anna May Johannsen, Mona Cutleaf, and Maybelle Killeen. He paused. "Edmonds, Chambers and Berry were Negro, the rest were white. All from rural communities, all between ten and thirteen years old. All killed the same way."

"I don't believe it," said Rose. He shut off the nozzle on the hose. A little bit of pink water and some small pieces of discarded tissue went swirling down the drain hole directly below the little girl's buttocks. Ray noticed a half-moon-shaped scar on her left hip. "Nine little kids. I would have heard about it."

"The killings all took place in a nine-month period in 1938. The Negro kids didn't make a ripple in the pond and the white girls came from trash families. Took place in four or five different counties, which muddied the investigative waters as well."

"Christ on a crutch," said Rose. "Nineteen thirty-eight isn't that long ago. They had goddamn telephones. They could have talked to each other."

"Appears they didn't."

"How'd you find all this out?"

"Went home to my daddy's for his birthday. He mentioned something about an old case. Made the connection and did some checking around." He looked down at the child on the table. Her eyes had been brown but they were clouded over now, and patches of her skin had darkened from lividity. "Anything new here?"

"Found in the dump again."

"Refrigerator?"

"Old icebox. Almost an antique."

"Rats find it again?"

"No. Janowski, the caretaker. He went looking this time."

"Anything different about her?"

"Different from what? The guy who came in yesterday? Yeah, plenty. She's been raped half a dozen times in each hole in her body. It looks like whoever killed her had her tied up long enough to give her ligature marks on her wrists and ankles."

"So he kept her for a couple of days?"

"I'd say more like three or four from what I can tell."

"The skin removed the same?"

Rose nodded. "Uh-huh. Sixteen by ten from the back. Eight by five from the belly area, four by two and a half from each of the thighs."

Ray thought about it for a moment as he opened up the Polaroid. "All the measurements are divisible by two from the larger ones."

"So the killer likes symmetry. Maybe he's a math teacher."

Ray set the flash and took several shots of the dead girl, including one of the scar on her thigh. "I think it means something. The skin he takes."

"Of course it means something," Rose answered sourly. Ray stripped the backing off the shots and began fanning the air with them. "It means the man's out of his mind." He paused. "Those other children. Back in 'thirty-eight? They had patches of skin taken off as well?"

"Yes."

"Same size as these?"

"Files didn't say," Ray answered. "Guess they didn't think it was important back then, but I think it's a good bet."

"A link anyway." The medical examiner let out a long-suffering sigh and pulled off his rubber gloves. He tossed them onto the edge of the sink, then reached under his rubber apron and pulled out a package of Camels. He lit one with a shiny gold Ronson and stood back from the table, blowing a cloud of smoke up at the low ceiling. "Glad I just cut 'em and shut 'em." He stared owlishly across the mutilated corpse. "'Cause I don't think you've got a chance in hell of finding out who did this."

"Why's that?" said Ray, folding up the camera again.

"This one, the one yesterday, all those others. Mutilation, rape, sodomy. Whatever motive the killer has is in his head, nothing normal, nothing real." He took another puff on the Camel. "One for my headshrinker friends in the Psycho Ward."

"You might be right," Ray answered, sliding the Polaroid back into its leatherette carrying bag.

The overhead P.A. system crackled. "Dr. Tom Shires, please report to Trauma Room One, stat."

The doc frowned. "Why would they want Shires in Trauma?"

"Who is he?"

"Chief of surgery. I think he's in Galveston today."

The call came again, this time more urgently. "Dr. Shires to Trauma One, *stat*."

Ray couldn't have cared less about what was going on in Trauma Room One; he was trying to make sense of dates and times. "Was there anything to show that Jennings Price had been held for a period of time before he was killed?"

"Who?"

"The guy from yesterday."

"No. He was still in rigor. He was found twelve to twenty-four hours postmortem."

"So whoever did the killing already had the little Jane Doe here when he killed Price."

"If the same person killed them both."

The P.A. crackled again and a very nervous sounding nurse began rhyming off a list of doctors. *"Dr. Richard Dulaney, Dr. Gene Akin, Dr. Kent Clark, Dr. Giesecke, Dr. Jack Hunt, Dr. Kenneth Salyer, Dr. Seldin, Dr. Shaw, Dr. White, Dr. Peters. Please report to Trauma Room One and Trauma Room Two, stat."*

"What the hell is going on?" said Rose. "That's half the staff of the hospital. The only people they didn't call was Ben Casey and Dr. Zorba."

"Traffic accident maybe." Ray shrugged. He looked down at the girl on the table again. He noticed that everywhere she'd been cut the top of the wound looked crushed, while the wound itself as it cut down through flesh and muscle and bone was razor sharp.

He asked Rose, who pointed at the slice just above the left knee. "Normally I'd say it was just the result of a blade broader at the top than at the bottom. In this case very wide, like an axe, or a hatchet."

"Normally?"

"There's not a hatchet or axe made accurate enough or with a honed blade sharp enough to do this, or the other fellow."

"So what was it?"

"Beats me," said Rose. "Whatever did it is on a hinge, I can tell you that much. Cut begins at the left and follows through to the right in one stroke."

"What kind of hinge?"

"You remember that movie a few years back? Guy's on a boat and he gets sprayed by radioactive mist?"

"The Incredible Shrinking Man."

"That's the one. There's a scene where he tries to defend himself with a pair of huge scissors. Imagine he cut his legs off instead—that kind of hinge."

"Thanks, Doc. I'll go tell Fritz that my two victims were cut apart by monster scissors and my best suspect is Allison Hayes."

"Who?"

"She was the star of *Attack of the Fifty Foot Woman.*"

"You got any useful information inside that big head?"

"Stretchers to Emergency, please. Outpatients, please leave the corridors immediately. This is a police order. Clear the corridors immediately and proceed to the Emergency area."

"For Christ's sake." Rose turned off the water and hung up the hose. He flipped the butt of his cigarette into the sink and stripped off his apron.

"You're not going to finish up?"

"Not until I find out what's going on up there."

Tossing his apron onto a hook the medical examiner banged out through the double doors and headed down the ceramic-tiled corridor. Ray slung the camera bag over his shoulder and followed. They went down several more corridors, then up a flight of steps that led them to the Minor Medicine area. The corridor beyond the door was filled with orderlies, patients in wheelchairs and white-uniformed nurses. Rose grabbed a Negro orderly who was parking a man in a wheelchair out of the way.

"What's happening?"

Ray stared; the orderly's face was wet, eyes full of tears. "Say the man's been shot. Governor too."

"Man?"

"President man, don't you know nothing?"

"Out of the way."

Rose cut a path through the milling swarm of patients and personnel, then turned right down the Obstetrics corridor toward the two trauma rooms and the curtained emergency booths. Two nurses at the station on the left were working the telephones. Both of them were in tears like the orderly. President of what, and why were they crying?

Ray slowed down. There were two or three empty stretchers up against the walls, some more people in wheelchairs and two very frightened-looking children, both wearing casts. Looking down Ray saw that the checkerboard floor was splattered with brains and blood. He saw something gleaming dully on the floor under one of the wheeled stretchers and with some difficulty bent to pick it up.

It was a bullet. From a rifle by the looks of it, and a large caliber. He slipped it into the pocket of his jacket and continued to follow Doc Rose down the hall, losing him in the milling crowd. There were cops everywhere, uniforms, detectives, state troopers and dark-suited Feds. One of the Feds stepped forward and tried to block his way by putting a flat hand on his chest.

"Nobody gets any farther than this."

"Who the fuck are you?" Ray asked, removing the hand.

The hand went inside the man's jacket. "Who the fuck am I? I'm the fucking Secret Service and you don't go any farther, farm boy."

"Detective Sergeant farm boy, asshole." Ray pushed him out of the way, bouncing him off the wall. He took a few steps forward. Left and right there were little curtained booths. Directly in front of him, like a sad terrible dream, sitting on a brown chair on the right, her jacket and her skirt heavy with blood, sat Jackie Kennedy, the President's wife, a blank, slightly angry look on her face. Directly across from her, also in pink but not as bloody, sat Governor Connally's wife, Nellie. The two women were staring at each other across the narrow little passage. From behind Mrs. Kennedy in the trauma room, Ray could hear low voices and the clatter of equipment. From the other side, Mrs. Connally's side, he could hear the governor groaning in pain.

Dazed, not quite sure of what he was witnessing, Ray stepped aside as two priests appeared, one older, one younger. The older man was carrying a small black bag. Mrs. Kennedy stood up and went into the trauma room and the two priests followed her. The door closed softly behind them. Doc Rose had disappeared.

"The poor woman," whispered Governor Connally's wife.

"The President was shot?"

The dark-haired woman plucked at something on her jacket and dropped it onto the floor. "His brains were blown out of his head. I watched as the top of his skull came off and there was his brain and it exploded all over us."

The conversation was inconceivable, the information being offered like something insane. "And the governor, ma'am?"

The woman smiled faintly. "The doctors say he'll be all right."

"That's a good thing, ma'am." What else did you say to the governor's wife when you met her bloody in a hospital corridor? "That's a good thing."

"Yes, isn't it?" She paused and the smile flickered again. "This means Lyndon's president now."

"Yes, ma'am, I suppose it does."

The door behind Ray opened and he turned. The two

priests came out and behind them Ray saw Jackie bent over the sheet-covered body of her husband, as though she was kissing him. Two Secret Service men came out of nowhere and one of them took the elder priest by the elbow.

"You don't know anything, understand?"

"Yes," said the priest, and the two men in their vestments walked slowly away. The Secret Service man who'd spoken to the priest turned to Ray just as Mrs. Kennedy reappeared.

"This is a restricted area."

"I'm waiting for Dr. Rose."

"I don't know about any Dr. Rose. Was he working on the President?"

"He's the chief medical examiner for the county," Ray answered. "If the President was shot and killed that makes it a homicide. I'm a homicide detective and every murder in Dallas requires that the victim be autopsied by the medical examiner's office."

The Secret Service man glanced at Mrs. Kennedy, then grabbed Ray by the arm and led him down the hallway a few steps. "Not this time, pal. No crackerjack county coroner is touching President Kennedy. He's going back to Washington now. Understand?"

"Tell that to Doc Rose." Ray thought about the bullet he'd found and wondered about giving it up to the arrogant Secret Service agent. He kept it in his pocket. A last pair of doctors left the trauma room where the President was lying. As the door swung closed again Ray saw that he was being tended to by a single nurse now.

Ray stood in the corridor and let it all whirl around him like some mad dream. It was as though the air itself had cleared to something almost crystalline, and each sound was clear and bright and painful in his ears. A black man in some sort of purple churchlike robe appeared and was turned away by the two Secret Service men standing by the door to Trauma Room One. The door to Trauma Room Two opened and a stretcher and several doctors appeared, turning left and then right, headed for surgery, with Nellie Connally running to keep up.

A moment later a huge bronze casket was wheeled down the corridor by two more Secret Service men. They had a hard time maneuvering it into Trauma Room One. Jackie tried to follow it into the room but she was stopped by the man who appeared to be the senior Secret Service agent.

A nurse appeared and went to a supply cupboard nearby. Ray watched as she rummaged around in the cupboard and came up with a folded plastic sheet. He figured it out quickly enough and so did Mrs. Kennedy, who went a little paler, if that was possible. Ray had seen brains on the floor and the nurse was probably going to use the plastic sheet to wrap around Kennedy's head to keep more from spilling out onto the satin liner of the casket.

Finally Doc Rose appeared, elbowing his way through the crowd of doctors, cops and Secret Service people crowding the main corridor and the short passage down to the trauma rooms. Rose stopped and looked at Ray.

"Who are these two?" he asked, pointing at the men on either side of the door to Trauma Room One. Jackie Kennedy gave the medical examiner a short look, then stood and went into the room where her husband was being lowered into the casket. From where he was standing Ray could see that the body was naked, wrapped in sheets, and as he'd thought, the head was wrapped in plastic that was already smeared on the inside with blood and gray matter, obscuring the face of the dead man. The door closed.

Doc Rose stepped up to the taller of the two Secret Service agents. "My name is Dr. Earl Rose. I'm the medical examiner for Dallas County."

"Roy Kellerman, Secret Service."

"There's been a homicide here. You won't be able to remove the body. We'll be taking it down to the morgue for an autopsy."

Ray thought about that for a moment, visualizing the naked body of the President of the United States. His head blown off, lying beside the dismembered corpse of the unknown victim. Both just as dead.

"Nobody touches the body," said Kellerman. "It goes back to Washington."

"We have a law here," Rose answered. He pushed his glasses farther back up his nose. "And you have to comply with it, president or no president."

A balding man a little older than Ray and wearing a dark suit and horn-rims appeared, striding purposefully down the narrow corridor. He stopped in front of Kellerman. "What's going on?"

"This man is from some health unit in town, Doctor. He tells me we can't remove the body." Kellerman almost smirked when he said it.

The doctor in the dark suit raised his voice, spittle flying in Doc Rose's direction. "We are removing the body."

"Who the fuck are you?"

"I beg your pardon?"

"I said who the fuck are you? I'm Earl Rose, Chief Medical Examiner for the County and City of Dallas. Who the fuck are you?"

"Dr. George Burkley, the President's personal physician."

"No, you're not. President Kennedy is dead. You're not his doctor anymore. I am, by law."

Burkley sputtered, "But this is the President of the United States."

"Was," Doc Rose answered.

Kellerman spoke up. "We're taking the body, sir, whether you like it or not. I'm not leaving Mrs. Kennedy in there with a coffin with her husband in it just because of some stupid city ordinance you have."

"This happened in Dallas County. A homicide. A homicide in Dallas County requires an autopsy by my office."

"I'm going to need someone bigger than you to tell me that," Kellerman answered.

"Then I'll get somebody bigger," Rose answered. He stomped away. As soon as he turned out of sight Kellerman gestured to the Secret Service men strung down the corridor. He turned to Bill Greer, the Secret Service man who had driven the President's limousine. "Let's get out of here."

Ray turned away, knowing that no matter what Doc Rose tried with these people, the body in the casket with its brains held in by a plastic bag was going back to Washington one way or the other and sooner rather than later. He walked down the corridor, heading toward the Emergency entrance and the ambulance bays. Just before he reached the doors he saw another swarm of Secret Service agents hustling a tall, long-nosed figure out of a room on the left. Lyndon Johnson, the new president. Following the group Ray went out through the swing doors and blinked in the sudden splash of bright sunlight.

He'd never seen anything even approaching it. There were cars and ambulances and limousines littered everywhere, and on the grass and the pavement, standing alone or in little clusters, there were hundreds of people, almost all of them crying except for the news reporters and their cameramen, who were filming the people crying. Two Secret Service men were putting a clear plastic bubble top on the big Lincoln limousine that was parked, slewed by the Emergency doors a few feet away. And what was Jack Ruby doing, talking to a uniformed cop at the edge of the parking lot? The two Secret Service men snapped down the clips on the bubble top, securing it, and all Ray could think about was barn doors closing after the horse ran off.

Ray felt no grief; perhaps because he was in shock, but more likely because he was so close to death himself. And he suddenly realized what he was observing, this first tear of sorrow that would ripple out until the anguish and the pain took over the entire nation, if only for a few days, or perhaps weeks, but long enough to ensure that there would be no equality for the little black girl who lay forgotten on the cold steel table in the basement behind him, her death overwhelmed by another, the chances of discovering her killer fading with each passing hour. No justice for all those other little girls, so many years ago.

"Well, to hell with that," he said under his breath, and went to find his car.

Chapter 13

Ray left Parkland, threading his way through the litter of station wagons and panel trucks from the TV stations that were strewn around the Emergency entrance, then made his way onto Stemmons Freeway and headed back into town. He took the cloverleaf at the triple underpass, but Dealey Plaza was closed off with sawhorse barricades, so he had to zigzag his way back to the Police and Courts Building using half a dozen side streets. It was another dream; wandering, scattered crowds of people on the sidewalks, looking dazed, or crying, or simply standing still, staring into space, moving traffic almost nonexistent, cars double-parked or stopped at intersections, drivers and passengers bent over dashboards, straining to hear their radios. An empty Marsalis Street bus, abandoned, the driver staring into the window of a TV store watching a dozen blinking, shifting screens. Not a single honking horn. The end of the world, like that movie he'd seen a year or so ago at the Texas.

He came up Commerce Street, turned down the ramp, then swung right into the parking garage. There was a crowd of people around the desk in front of the jail elevator, most of them with microphones or notepads in their hands, badgering Sid Able, one of the jail clerks manning the intake desk. More reporters. Ray parked, then switched off the engine. He reached for the Salems on the dashboard then drew back his hand. He leaned against the vinyl and closed his eyes. The end of the world, fucking Nikita with his finger on the button, a thousand times worse than Castro and his missiles, and here he was worrying about a death that meant nothing to anybody. Except him.

Ray roused himself and climbed out of the car, wondering if the wave of dizziness that made him pause in the darkness was his ailing heart or just the last hour catching up with him at last. He blinked, seeing the rusty stain across the thigh of the First Lady's nubby pink suit again, wondering if she'd try and wash it out, stifling a crazy laugh when he realized she'd be destroying evidence in a homicide. As if she'd ever want to wear *that* outfit again. He pushed himself away from the side of the car, his legs as heavy as tree trunks. Doc Rose really was going to be pissed.

There were a few more reporters on the third floor but the squad room was empty except for Len Graves, one of the eight-to-four-shift detectives, and Ewell, the captain's secretary. Graves was on the phone and so was Ewell. There were other extensions ringing, but no one to answer them. Graves gave Ray a nod, then hung up his phone. He ignored the blinking buttons below the dial.

"It's bad, Ray. Really bad," said Graves. He rubbed his forehead. "We killed him. We killed the G.D. President of the United States." His voice was hollow and there was a sheen of sweat on his face even though the office was air conditioned. The detective looked as dazed as the people Ray had seen driving into downtown.

"We?" Ray eased himself down into a chair.

"Big D." Graves shook his head. "It happened here. You think that doesn't mean something?"

"I was at Parkland," Ray answered, looking for something to say.

"It's going to take a hundred years before anybody forgets it happened here. Maybe never."

"Where's the crew?" Ray asked, looking around the empty room.

"Fritz called in all three shifts. Everybody's down at the Plaza."

"I guess that's where it happened."

Graves looked at him as though he was insane. "You don't know?"

"I told you, I was at Parkland. An autopsy."

"It was the Book Depository."

"The Hertz Building?"

"What?" Graves looked confused.

"The place with the big Hertz billboard on the roof? The one gives you the time?"

"Yeah, yeah, that's the place."

"What about it?"

"They say that's where the shots came from. Maybe from somewhere in the railyards back there. No one knows anything much yet."

"How many shots?" asked Ray, suddenly remembering the bullet in his pocket. He didn't mention it to Graves.

"Nobody knows that either. Three, four."

"They hit the governor."

"Christ! He's dead too?"

"No. I talked to his wife. He's going to be all right. That's what the doctors told her anyway."

"Connally's wife?"

"Umm," said Ray. "They were across from each other. Mrs. Kennedy and the governor's wife."

"You saw Mrs. Kennedy?" Like she was a movie star.

"She had blood all over her suit."

"Christ!"

The two men sat silently together for a moment, surrounded by the ringing telephones. Ewell finished his conversation and hung up. He looked over at Graves and Ray and then looked away. There were tears staining his cheeks. He got up quickly and left the squad room. Ray swung around in the swivel chair and stared up at the big clicking IBM clock on the wall. It was two o'clock; the whole world turned upside down in ninety minutes. He levered himself up out of the chair and left Graves by himself in the squad room.

Ray went down the hall and glanced into the press room that overlooked Main Street. There were at least a dozen reporters in the small room, and lineups for the three telephones. A square-jawed reporter with smart eyes was heading out of the room. Ray thought he looked vaguely familiar. The press pass on his tweedy sports jacket said D. Rather.

"You somebody I should be talking to? Somebody important?"

"Not so's you'd notice," said Ray. D. Rather made an irritated noise in his throat and slipped out through the doorway. He turned away from the open door and went into the Juvenile Bureau. Like Homicide-Robbery, the JB offices were almost empty. Millie Toombs, the fat, black bureau receptionist, was listening to a radio perched on top of a row of filing cabinets. She was wearing a billowing flower-print dress that seemed terribly out of place. Like Ewell, there were tears on her cheeks. She turned to Ray as he entered the long narrow room.

"Isn't it awful, Ray?! Just so awful!"

"Yes, it is."

"I was downstairs on the steps when they went by. She was so beautiful and he was so handsome. Smiling and all and waving."

"I need some help, Millie."

She blinked at him, not understanding. "What?"

"I need some help. Files."

"Files?" She blinked again and this time lifted one hand and wiped at her face, the smeared makeup smearing even more, her eyes like a raccoon's. It really was like a dream that he'd stepped into, out of place with everyone else.

"Negro children. Runaways or just missing. Eleven to thirteen, say, three, four days back."

"Negro children? What do you want with Negro children?" The receptionist was looking at him as though he was speaking some foreign language.

"A homicide," Ray said flatly. "I'm trying to identify the victim." The voice on the radio began to talk excitedly about a policeman who'd just been found shot beside his squad car in Oak Cliff. "Shit," said Ray, not quite believing what he was hearing.

"Oh God," Millie moaned. Ray listened for a moment. There was no information on who the cop was, or whether he'd been killed or not. Shot cops and governors, murdered presidents. Blood and brains in the hospital corridors, a little girl on a metal table, unbearably naked and torn.

He tried to focus on what he was doing and touched Millie lightly on the arm. "What now!?" She turned on him, her face flushed red, her eyes angry, as though he was intruding on some private space around her. Then she remembered and waved her hand at an overflowing wire basket on a desk beside the door. On top of the pile there was a magenta expanding file tied shut with the word *CURRENT* printed in large black letters on its side. "There!" Millie said, and turned her attention back to the radio. Ray thanked her even though she wasn't listening, went to the desk and picked up the bulging file. He stood for a moment, listening to the newsman on the radio going back and forth between the assassination of President Kennedy and the shooting of the police officer. According to the man on the radio Johnson was now being sworn in as the new president of the United States and would soon arrive in Washington in Air Force One, Kennedy's body and Mrs. Kennedy with him.

Putting the file folder under his arm, Ray left the JB and headed back down the hall toward Homicide-Robbery. Just before he reached the door a crowd of Stetson-wearing detectives and uniformed cops poured out into the corridor from the direction of the jail elevator and more people came around the corner from the main elevator lobby, pouring toward Ray like a thundering human flood. In the center of it all he picked out two detectives, Charlie Walker and Gerry Hill, escorting a battered-looking man in khakis and a torn, mud-colored shirt. Behind Ray, the press room was suddenly emptying out and he heard someone say, "They got him! They got the son of a bitch!"

The corridor was now completely filled up and Ray was pushed off to one side, hanging on to the thick file, pressing it up against his chest to avoid having it torn from his hands. Walker and Hill managed to bully their way to the door of Homicide-Robbery, pushing away the reporters. They slammed the door behind them, leaving a pair of hefty-looking uniforms to block the path of anyone not authorized entrance. Realizing that getting to his desk was going to be almost impossible, Ray tried to think of somewhere he could go to consult the Juvenile file. He remembered a supply room on the far side of the main lobby and pushed his way toward it.

As he crossed in front of the stairs another crowd surged upward toward him, most of them carrying camera equipment or toting microphones. The elevator doors opened and Captain Fritz appeared, half a dozen uniforms and detectives trailing behind him. The narrow hall to Homicide-Robbery was still choked with people and the captain was brought up short. Questions were being thrown at him from all directions and suddenly there were flashbulbs popping everywhere.

"Is this man a suspect in the assassination of President Kennedy?"

"Now y'all don't go saying that!" Fritz barked. "He hasn't been charged with that! He's only being questioned about the police officer who was shot!"

"What's the policeman's name?"

"We're not saying until his next of kin has been informed. Now if y'all will excuse me!"

Scowling, Fritz pushed his heavy glasses up on his nose and elbowed his way down the corridor to his own office. With the tide of people heading in the opposite direction, Ray crossed to the supply room and slipped inside.

There was a rubber doorstop on the floor and he kicked it into place at the base of the door, sealing himself in. He looked around. There were shelves on three sides filled with stationery and a sink against the back wall with a pail and squeeze mop beside it. There was a step stool in front of him and Ray sank down onto it gratefully. He slid the file onto one of the shelves and put a hand to his chest, resting for a moment before he did any more.

He caught his breath, ignoring the faint tightness in his

chest, and unwound the loop of string on the file. He opened the folder on his lap and began flipping quickly through the individual files, most of them consisting of no more than the standard single-page mimeographed Missing Persons report. Some of them had photographs stapled to them, most did not. There had been seventeen juvenile runaways since the beginning of the week, eight Negroes, three Mex and six white. Of the eight Negroes only two were possibles, Alice Jane Watkiss, fourteen, and Martha Ellen Caddo, twelve. Neither report had a picture of the child in question. There was no mention of a scar in either report.

Ray compared the two reports. The girl he'd seen this afternoon had been flat-chested and slim-hipped, the pubic area, what was left of it, bare. At fourteen, Alice Watkiss was probably more developed than that. Ray checked the name of the detective who'd taken the call. Patrick Haddon, working the four-to-midnight, and not someone Ray had ever seen, at least not to his knowledge. He thought about going back to the JB and getting Haddon's number from Millie, but then he decided against it. This was going to be a felonious freebie in Big D—nobody was going to be working on anything but Kennedy, and even if they were off duty no one was going to be following up leads. Dallas, like the rest of the country, was going to be spending the night and the next few days in front of the television.

Ray took out his notebook and pencil, then jotted down Martha Ellen Caddo's particulars. The report was bare bones, listing name, address and lack of phone number— the initial contact had been made from a neighbor's place. Apparently Martha Ellen had disappeared on her way home from the Paul Lawrence Dunbar Library on the downtown end of Thomas Avenue. Ray looked at the home address: Hugo Street and Woodside, which put it just off of Hall

Street Park, deep in the Negro district, and a good ten blocks from the library branch. A lot of distractions in those ten blocks, including a slew of bars and nightclubs and three Negro movie theaters—and that was if she'd really been headed home. If she'd turned south instead of north she would have been downtown in five minutes. Or what if she'd taken a bus?

"She's a victim, not the killer," said Ron Odum, sitting in his kitchen. "All these what-if's you've got don't matter." He shrugged. "Whether she took a bus or not makes no never mind." There were no bottles of Jax on the table between them this time, only coffee. Real, not like the instant Ray made for himself. The rich smell of it wafting up from the percolator sitting on the stove filled the room.

R. T. unfolded himself from his chair and went to fill his cup again. He came back, sat down and lit a cigarette. "I'm surprised you're still at it."

"Because of the President?"

"Kind of overwhelming, don't you think?" Ray's ex-partner took a sip of coffee, looking across the table, smiling faintly. "Not your everyday run-of-the-mill Big D homicide."

Ray shook his head. "People are going to make a big thing about it, but it could have been anywhere."

"Could have been," said Odum. "But it wasn't. Just like your little girl and the bus. It happened here. It happened for a reason."

"And if this Martha Caddo turns out to be the girl I saw at Parkland today, is there a reason for that?"

"Sure," said Odum easily. "She's a little nigger kid. According to what you found out your killer likes chopping up young girls, especially nigger girls. The man who killed

Kennedy wanted to kill the president of the United States. The president of the United States happened to be in Dallas today."

"Then he was stupid," said Ray.

"How so?"

"It was supposed to be raining today. If it'd been raining they would have had that bubble-top thing on the limousine. I saw them putting it back on at Parkland. Not much at forward planning, this assassin."

"Well, there you go," Odum answered. "You're probably right, which tells you something about your man, doesn't it?"

"Such as?"

"He's not stupid. By your count he's killed eleven people and so far, at least until my old good friend Horatio Duval comes around, he's got away with it. Smart."

"Lucky?"

"Smart. No one has good luck that long." Odum tipped ash into his saucer. "We're back to what-ifs and coulda-beens again. If you hadn't gone home for your daddy's birthday you wouldn't have found out about those other cases, now would you? Like I said, his luck ran out."

"Like the cop who got killed today."

"Officer J. D. Tippit."

"You know him?"

"Twelve hundred cops on the DPD? No." He took a last drag on the cigarette and butted it. "But you can bet your ass the guy they picked up gets charged with the President as well."

"Why?"

"Probably don't know yet. Just before you got here. They were shuffling the guy up to the cells and some reporter asked—turns out the guy worked at the School Book Depository. Half hour after the assassination he kills a cop in Oak Cliff who maybe just got his description from dispatch. Too much for coincidence."

"The guy I saw didn't look like he could kill a roach with a size-twelve boot," said Ray. "Five-foot fuck all with skinny little arms and legs and pale as a mushroom."

"Lee Oswald," said Odum.

"That's his name?"

"According to the TV." Odum nodded. "Lee Harvey Oswald." He paused and made a little sound in the back of his throat. "Strangest thing, Ray, they're not running any commercials. Radio as well, from what I can tell. Damnedest thing."

"What do they know about this fellow?"

"Not much, I don't think. Not yet anyway."

"Well, this Lee Harvey Oswald isn't going to help me find out who killed Jennings Price and all those little girls."

"Now that's the part that really does stick in my craw," said Odum. "Last time you were here, it's this Price character, so you think one way. Some kind of crazy queer killer, maybe this ex-boyfriend. Now you got all those girls upstate from all that time ago, and you've got a fresh one they find not too far from the queer. Hard to make up a story to go along with that."

"I already thought of that," Ray said wearily.

"And?"

"You've got someone killing little girls up north twenty-five years ago. The killing stops, maybe the guy gets put into the loony bin, maybe he's in jail, maybe he just moves away, or maybe it's like they used to say about Jack the Ripper. He was the son of somebody in the royal family, or a cousin or something."

"No kings in Texas." Odum grinned. "Louisiana maybe, but not Texas."

"You know what I mean. Big shot. Governor, state senator. Someone who could cover things up. It doesn't really matter."

"Keep going."

"Okay, so he's out of the picture, at least in Texas. Twenty-five years goes by. He comes back, or thinks enough water's gone under the bridge to make it safe."

"So he kidnaps this little pickaninny and Jennings Price finds out?"

"Doesn't even have to be the girl I saw at Parkland. What if Price already knew, had found out about the old cases and was maybe blackmailing our killer? The killer gets fed up and turns him into chop suey."

"Which puts you back with the queers, which isn't too strange when you think about it."

"I've got to go back and talk to Ruby again."

"Jack Ruby?" Odum frowned.

"You know him?"

"Of him." Odum kept frowning. "You've already seen him? When was that?"

"Just after I talked to you last time."

"He tell you anything?"

"Not a lot. He said a lot of queers meet each other at parties people set up for them in empty houses."

"Why would he know anything about it?"

"He lives with a guy, for one thing."

"Doesn't prove anything."

"No, but it gets you leaning in that direction."

"Who told you about Jack Ruby?"

"McDonald."

"That old fart."

"He used to work Vice. Ruby's got a nightclub. I can see him supplying queer parties. Looks like a money-grubber."

"He's a Jew," said Odum. "What do you expect?" He picked up his cigarettes and tapped the package against the table. "I was you I'd steer clear."

"That's about all I have to go on." He sighed again. "It's going to be a nightmare if I go back to the connection between Jennings Price and this whole antique thing. Talking to anyone in this town's going to be screwed now."

"What about the pickaninny's family? You talked to any of them yet?"

Ray looked at his watch. Almost five. He glanced out the window over the sink that looked onto Ron Odum's rear garden. It was already dark. "Next on my list," he said. There was a long silence. Odum broke it finally, his voice distant.

"You remember what it was like, Ray? You remember what it was like to have a target come to you? Palm-of-your-hand stuff, solid gold, couldn't fail if you tried."

"Sure," said Ray.

They'd gone hunting on a deer stand his daddy had rented not far from Lake Kiowa. No one was having any luck and Audie was particularly pissed since the Old Man had given him a brand-new rifle for his thirteenth birthday complete with a telescopic sight and a monogrammed leather case and all. Ray was using the old Garand and standing off a little to one side when he caught movement out of the corner of his eye and turned.

The buck was close to two hundred yards away, carefully lifting its hooves as it stepped like some kind of dainty dancer through the brush and trees, and then it stopped and turned a second or two after Ray did, turning its head, big eyes staring at him. There was no shot at that range and too

*many trees between them but Ray knew the deer was his as
surely as a sacrifice from Bible times. He lifted the Garand
to his shoulder and his cheek and watched the deer take
three steps to outline itself against a small rise bare of trees.
It turned slowly, offering up its flank, and Ray fired, squeezing the trigger, keeping the rifle steady and watching as the
buck tumbled down, first to its knees and then sideways as it
died, the feet pointing toward him.*

*"That was mine!" Audie screamed, his face red, the big
gleaming gun in his hands, sunlight winking off the glass eye
of the scope. "That deer was mine!" But Ray knew it wasn't
true, knew that the deer had been his to kill long before
they'd even come to the stand. Later in your life you might
call it nothing more than luck or coincidence, but back then
Ray knew better, knew that it was magic and superstition
rolled into one, destiny maybe, or fate. No matter how you
looked at it, the deer had come to him, and him alone.*

"They're already saying on the news that maybe there
was more than one shooter involved," said Odum. "But I
don't think so. Dallas didn't kill the President, this Lee Oswald character did. He didn't think about it, he looked at the
newspaper and he saw the motorcade was going right by the
place he worked and he took a gun and he fired because he
was *there* and Kennedy was *there* and that was all she
wrote."

Ray clambered to his feet. "Maybe," he said. "One way
or the other I guess he'll have his day in court and then we'll
know."

"We'll never know what really happened," said Odum,
starkly, his eyes out of focus, seeing somewhere, something
else. He stood himself to walk Ray out to his car. "You can
bet on it."

Chapter 14

The Monster wept as he sat on the sagging old couch and stared blankly at the television set on the far side of the almost-unfurnished room. He'd known about the assassination almost from the time it happened. The radio he kept at the shop was always on and always tuned to KLIF so he could listen to Russ Knight, his favorite disc jockey, and Joe Long, who did the news. At a little after twelve-thirty in the afternoon there'd been a flurry of unsubstantiated reports about shots being fired at the motorcade, and then, shortly after one, Joe Long, already at Parkland, reported that the President was dead and that Lyndon Johnson was being sworn in aboard Air Force One at that very moment.

The Monster left his shop at four, returning home through a city that appeared to be in shock. The streets and sidewalks were virtually deserted and most of the stores he passed had already closed, hastily scrawled signs announcing their corporate grief. Once home the Monster made a brief check of what was left of his prisoner, then went upstairs, made himself a watery bourbon and switched on the television.

What he saw was as confused as the radio reports he'd heard, both from the radio in his shop and the transistor he kept on the littered dashboard of the van. He'd seen the same shots of Chief Curry going from his office down the hall to the Homicide Department, refusing to answer any questions, a blurry sequence of images of the alleged killer, and for the last half hour, the arrival of Air Force One in Washington, half-lit scenes of the coffin coming down to the ground, Jackie climbing into an ambulance with her husband, Lyndon Johnson's bloodhound face asking for the nation's help and God's, none of it really meaning anything at all.

Chaos.

The Monster picked up his glass from the end table and drained away the ice-cube water, wetting his dry tongue and mouth. He felt the rage mounting in him, making him shake, his mind desperately casting around for something to think about that would distract him, even for a few seconds. The president of the United States, his president, was dead and there was nothing he could do about it, nothing to defuse his anger, nothing to hold back the terrible memories of his impotence in the face of events, and the terrors that had consumed him so often in the past. He stared at the television, watching the world repeat itself again and again, ricocheting in flashing bursts, noon to five p.m. and back again, Walter Cronkite in shirtsleeves, taking off his glasses, eyes wet with tears as he lurched out the announcement that the President was dead, and coming from the hangdog face, for the first time the world knew that it was true.

The Monster felt his breath coming in short sharp gasps, his heart racing and spasms of electricity in his limbs, jerking his arms and legs like the subtle twitching of a puppet, the wires at his joints forcing him into the dance from which he knew there would only be one result. He fought as hard as he could, his teeth clenched, and then, so horribly, someone chose to run something that looked like a home movie of the President in a ratty sweater, on the beach with his son, his little son with his glowing face, a child with the complexion of an angel, and the Monster could control himself no longer.

"Too soon," he whispered. "It's too soon for another one." But he couldn't hear his own warning, or if he could, he ignored it. He pulled himself up, the glass tumbling out of his hand, bouncing heavily on the filthy carpeting on the floor. "Too soon." But it was for the President, the terrible anger. It was for John-John, the perfect golden child. The Monster headed through the kitchen, swept his keys off the counter by the double sink full of overflowing dirty dishes, and pulled open the door leading to the garage. "Too soon," he moaned again, then went through the door, slamming it behind him.

Martha Ellen Caddo's address on Hugo Street was second from the end in a row of two-story brick houses that probably dated back to the turn of the century. There were no setbacks from the cracked and broken sidewalk, no grass and nothing in the way of a stoop except three cement steps without railings. The steps had probably been added on when the original wood steps rotted away. They were a little skewed, sitting an inch or so away from the front door. Paint on the window frames was cracked and peeling and the curtains over the windows themselves were old and faded. Cars parked by the curb were all older than Ray's and three or four of them were up on blocks. There were no streetlights here, and even though it was almost fully dark, a few kids were trying to get in a last inning of stickball on the street just past Martha Ellen's house. The kids were all black, which was to be expected in this area, the original

Irish immigrants long gone on to bigger and better and richer things. He was right in the middle of what a lot of his colleagues on the DPD called Niggertown.

Ray parked the car and climbed out. Seeing him, the stickball players disappeared as though they'd never been there, melting silently into the darkness. Ray smiled. Not only was he white, but even in the dark those kids knew for a certainty that he was a flatfoot. He locked the car, crossed the sidewalk and went up the off-kilter cement steps. Like all the houses in the row the only spot of color was the front door, in this case a startling yellow. There was no bell or knocker so Ray used his knuckles. A few moments later Ray saw a twitch at the curtains on his left, and then the door opened. He was surprised to see a man standing there instead of a woman. He was even more surprised to see that the man was dressed in a suit and tie, the suit old-fashioned but well cut, the tie a plain dark blue. The man in the suit was the color of coffee with a bit too little cream in it, his eyes a darker brown. He looked to be in his middle thirties or maybe older. Ray always found age a hard thing to pin down with Negroes.

"Yes?" There was no fear in the man's voice, no panic or guilt. Something though. Resignation?

"I'm looking for Mrs. Caddo, Martha Ellen Caddo's mother."

"Gone."

"Will she be back soon?"

The black man in the suit smiled. "No, sir, you misunderstand. She's dead. Died when Mar'Ellen was born." He made the name into a single word.

"I see."

"I'm Mar'Ellen's father, Danny Coulthart. Her mother and I were never married but I gave Mar'Ellen the name. It seemed like the thing to do, give her a reason to remember her mother. Something to take her on." He stared at Ray. "You're from the police?"

"Yes. My name's Duval, Ray Duval."

"I guess this is about Mar'Ellen. You haven't found her, have you?" It was almost a plea. Until she was found there was still a chance she was alive.

"We're not sure," said Ray. He took a little step forward and Coulthart backed up, opening the door wider.

"You'd better come in."

Ray stepped over the sill and into the front room of the little house. It was neat and tidy even if it wasn't very much. A front room with an old broken-back couch that had a patterned piece of fabric spread over the back. A table and three chairs, a dark blue rag rug on the floor, a crucifix over the door leading into a back kitchen and a television in the corner with a worn-out, green velvet La-Z-Boy in front of it.

The set was on with the sound turned down. Ray could see Walter Cronkite, his heavy black glasses in one hand, staring mournfully into the camera, his mouth barely moving under his mustache as he talked to the nation. Taking a few steps forward and looking around, Ray saw an open hardcase for a guitar on the floor beside the couch.

Inside it was a classic-looking wood-body Dobro resonating guitar with a gleaming, portholed silver dish. It was one of the old models with an eight-legged "Spider" bridge support that went right across the dish. The last time Ray Duval had seen one was at a black-and-tan piney woods speakeasy when he was seventeen or so and doing things he shouldn't have been with people he shouldn't have been seeing, at least by his father's lights. The same night he'd seen the Dobro he'd also heard Alger Alexander and Blind Lemon Jefferson and he'd been a blues convert ever since, not that he got to hear it much; there was no such thing as a black-and-tan in Dallas, and even if there was he'd have been too self-conscious to spend any time in one.

"You play that?"

"I do. Have done for a while. It's my trade."

"A beautiful instrument."

Coulthart crossed the room and knelt down before the hardcase. He picked up the guitar carefully and sat down on the arm of the La-Z-Boy. A moment later the room was filled with sound as he laid out the first few bars of "Shotgun Blues," a Lightning Hopkins hit from a decade before. He stopped suddenly, his eyes turning to the television screen. On it they were showing the arrival of Kennedy's body coming out of Air Force One. A few moments later Lyndon Johnson was speaking from a podium. Without saying anything Coulthart got up from the chair and put the guitar back in its case.

"Antoinette," he said quietly. "That's what I call her. After Mar'Ellen's mother."

"Pretty name."

"She was a pretty woman." Coulthart swung the La-Z-Boy around and gestured to it. Ray sank down into the chair and Coulthart eased himself down on the couch. "I didn't expect to hear from anyone, not today, with all this going on." He waved a hand toward the television.

"It's not my case," said Ray. "The world doesn't stop just because the President dies."

"World doesn't stop when my twelve-year-old girl slips out of sight."

"True enough." Ray paused, trying to plan out what he was going to say. He didn't even know what Mar'Ellen looked like. "There was no picture with the report," he said finally.

"I play the weekends at the Lights Are Blue down on Thomas Street, get some session work from time to time." He shook his head. "Not much left over for pictures, sir."

"Call me Ray."

"I don't think so."

There was a rough, embarrassed silence that dragged on for a long moment. Coulthart broke it finally, leaning forward on the couch, hands on the shiny knees of his dark trousers. "Mr. Duval, if you've got something to tell me about Mar'Ellen, why don't you just tell me. She's been gone almost a week and I'm not a fool, Mr. Duval. Cop doesn't pay a personal call in Niggertown for no reason."

"No," Ray answered. "You're right, and there is a reason."

"You found her?"

"No."

"Then what?"

"Look," said Ray. "I'm not even assigned to Juvenile. Your daughter's name came up in relation to something else. Something I'm working on."

"I see." He sat back against the couch and nodded. "So it's not about Mar'Ellen at all."

Ray was starting to feel sick about what he was doing. If he was honest about things he'd tell this man they'd found a little girl butchered and then strung together with baling wire, raped and sodomized and every hellish thing you could think of. Kennedy had his brains blown out, all that power and promise blinked out in a second. Whatever pain he'd felt, whatever fear, was nothing to the terror and the torturous pain and the foul indignity of what happened to that little girl.

"I'm not sure," Ray said finally. "All I know, anything you can tell me about what might have happened to your daughter might just help her, and might help some other people too."

"Mr. Duval, you can forgive me but all I care about right now is my Mar'Ellen. I've got her and I've got my job but that's all, Mr. Duval."

"So help me."

"How?"

Ray took out his notebook. Just above the address was a little sketch of the half-moon scar on the dead girl's thigh. He ignored it for the moment, flipping the page over. He wrote down Coulthart's name and underlined it.

"The report says your daughter was last seen on Monday, after school."

"That's right. She and some of her friends went to the library."

"That's Thomas Street and Boll roughly, isn't it?"

"Right."

"What was she doing at the library?"

"She liked books, Mr. Duval." The words were spoken politely enough but Ray sensed a bit of iron behind them.

"Who was with her?"

"I told you. Friends."

"Any friends in particular?"

"No."

"Did she have a lot of friends?"

"Seemed to. Everybody liked her."

"A best friend?"

"Not that she ever said anything about."

"She bring any of her friends home?"

"Once in a while. She knew better, though. Most of the time I'm not here."

"Oh?"

"Either doing work or looking for it, Mr. Duval. She

knew how to get along on her own. She had a key, knew where I kept whatever money we had for groceries. Made her own dinner lots, made mine most nights. She's a good girl, Mr. Duval."

"When did you realize she was missing?"

"There's only one bedroom, Mr. Duval. She sleeps there. I sleep on the couch. Makes sense, getting in late like I do. The house was all locked up, kitchen was clean, everything looked like it was supposed to. Sometimes I'd come home and I'd go upstairs and look in on her, but not that night. I was too tired. It was three, four in the morning. I just went to sleep right where I was."

"So you didn't realize until next morning?"

"Next afternoon. I didn't get up until past noon. She wasn't here, but I thought she was in school."

"And?"

"There was no money missing from the jar."

"I don't get you."

"There's a jar in the cupboard. I needed some cigarettes and I went to it and I saw that there was still three dimes in it, and two dollar bills."

"So?"

"It was the same amount that'd been there last time I looked. Three dimes, that was the problem."

"Why was it a problem?"

"Every day Mar'Ellen takes a dime for milk at school. She likes it with her lunch and it's good for her, so I don't mind."

"So she hadn't taken a dime for lunch that day?"

"No. I knew something was off. Looked like the bread hadn't been touched and we had a few slices of ham in the refrigerator, and that was still closed up in paper. I went upstairs to her bedroom and it just didn't feel right. She wasn't there and it didn't look as though she'd been there."

"Was there anything wrong? Anything out of place?"

"No, nothing like that. It was just . . . bad."

"And?"

"I went next door and used their telephone and called the school. They said Mar'Ellen hadn't been there since the day before." He shook his head. "I went down but they didn't say much more to me than that. Principal was polite enough but . . ."

"Any reason you can think of, Mr. Coulthart, that she'd run away in the first place?"

"No."

"You were on good terms?"

"Yes."

"No big fights or arguments recently?"

"I told you, Mr. Duval, she's a good girl. She never makes any trouble for me or anyone else. Does her homework and all, gets good grades." A faint smile flickered across his features. "She was proud of me," he said quietly.

"Proud of you?"

"Proud of me being able to play Antoinette. She always asked me what records I'd played on and who I'd played with, and she sometimes even went down to buy them at Polly Dee's."

"Polly Dee's?"

"Record store."

"Where is it?"

"Thomas Street, between Routh and Fairmont."

"Toward downtown."

"I suppose you could say that."

"But still in . . ." Ray hesitated.

"Still in Niggertown, yeah."

"Could she have gone there?"

"I went. Polly said she hadn't been."

"Polly a friend?"

"I know him, he knows me." There was a long, flat silence that Ray left alone. Coulthart finally picked up on it. "I don't think so, Mr. Duval. Polly's not that kind. He's married and he's got kids of his own."

"Anywhere else she might have gone? Places she liked?"

"I don't think so. Not like there's a lot of toy stores on Thomas Street."

"What about the movies?"

"If she didn't have any money, how was she going to get into a movie?"

"Sneak in?" Ray offered. "I used to do it all the time."

"I don't think there's much on that would have interested her."

Ray agreed. He'd seen two out of the three marquees for the theaters on Thomas Street. One was showing *55 Days at Peking* and the other was showing *Under the Yum Yum Tree*. "Could have gone in with a boy she liked. Maybe he paid as well."

"She's twelve years old, Mr. Duval. She didn't even like boys."

"Kids can fool you."

"Not Mar'Ellen." He was firm here, probably too firm, but Ray was pretty sure it wasn't a lead worth following up.

"You ever walk her home from school?"

"When she was younger, if I could be there when it let out."

"She have any particular route she liked to follow?"

"I always told her, come straight home. Stick to Thomas Street until you get to Hugo, then come right on down."

"Lots of distractions on Thomas Street, Mr. Coulthart. Not all of them too . . . savory."

"Maybe that depends on who you are," the black man answered. "Unsavory to you might not be unsavory to me or my friends or to Mar'Ellen. She grew up here. She knew the neighborhood. Some dives, some clubs, some places a man like you even might not be too smart to go into, but this is broad daylight, Mr. Duval. This is a little girl in broad daylight walking down a familiar street."

"Who would she go off with?"

"No one. She knew better than to talk to strangers."

"Someone who wasn't a stranger then. A friend, someone she knew?"

"I know a lot of people, Detective."

"Any you can think of who might take her, for whatever reason?"

"No."

"All those dives and places you talked about . . ."

"Yes?"

"Any of those she might have stopped into?"

"Maybe Pop Mercier's, but like I said, she didn't have any money."

"All three dimes."

"That's it, Detective."

"Who's this Pop Mercier?"

"Louisiana fellow. Been here since time began. Runs a candy store."

"A book?"

"No, sir. Like I said, a candy store. Lots of candy behind a big curved glass case. Cold drinks, cigarettes, tobacco, that kind of thing. You know that ice cream you buy in a paper roll, jam it into a cone?"

"Mel-o Rolls," Ray said.

"That's the one. Pink ones what Mar'Ellen liked. Supposed to be strawberry but tasted . . . pink. Looked like bubble gum. Fat old man and his fat old wife sold them."

"Where?"

"Just past Allen Street. East side. Little joint. Between a butcher shop and some place on the corner. Pool hall, I think."

"She go in there a lot?"

"Some. With me. Little money to spare we go there for ice cream or some of those green leaf things. Licorice whips and such."

"What if someone had money and took her in there? Would she go?"

"She might. A friend of hers maybe, but she was pretty proud about not having money. Neither one of us is of a mind to take charity."

"What if she found a penny on the street?"

"Sounds like you're trying to convince yourself, not me, Detective. I just want my daughter back, not tales about finding pennies and if she went into Pop Mercier's or not."

Ray nodded and looked down at his notebook. He had enough, more than enough perhaps, but he thought he'd fly something else past this Danny Coulthart. "Know a man named Ruby? Jack Ruby?"

"Owns the Carousel Club," said the black man. "Sure, I know him to nod to him. Why?"

"Ever work for him?"

"No. Carousel's a strip club, Mr. Duval. I don't work strip clubs." He paused. "Or whorehouses neither. Not anymore."

"So how do you know Ruby?"

"Jack Ruby knows everyone. Came to the Lights Are Blue one night and started talking big about record deals and how he had people he knew in Chicago and Detroit could do us a lot of good."

"He ever come through with anything?"

"Lot of people talk, Mr. Duval, not very many come through with anything." The remark was obviously pointed in his direction. Ray pulled himself up out of the La-Z-Boy with some effort. He tried not to breathe too hard as a wave of dizziness swept over him.

"You okay?" asked Coulthart, getting up from the couch.

Ray nodded. "Haven't eaten enough today." He snapped the notebook closed and slipped it back into his pocket. "One more question."

"Sure."

Ray tried not to imagine the growing fan of Polaroid pictures in his other pocket, tried not to think of the graying thing he'd seen on the table at Parkland, or the flecks of hardening tissue fusing with the blood on Jackie Kennedy's suit. "Does Mar'Ellen have any scars, any distinguishing marks?"

Coulthart gave him a strange look, his eyes becoming wary and apprehensive again. "Matter of fact, she does. A scar on her thigh. Not where you can see it. Scar like a little half-moon. In the schoolyard two, three years ago. Playing horseshoes and she fell on the piece of pipe, cut right through her dress."

"A half-moon scar." Ray nodded. He could taste bile at the back of his throat. He turned toward the door.

"You'll let me know if you hear something?"

"Of course," said Ray. Coulthart opened the door and Ray stepped out into the darkness. He went down the steps and back to the car. He stood in the darkness for a moment, and just before he opened the door to the Bel Air he thought he could hear the sound of Coulthart's guitar coming, faded, toward him in the mournful evening. Even after all these years Ray could still remember the words, especially the last verse.

> *Run, get me my shotgun,*
> *Put two shells in my hand.*
> *Please run get my shotgun,*
> *Put two shells in my hand.*
> *I'm gonna kill my baby*
> *And blast and blast her fancy man.*

He drove down Commerce Street and pulled over at the Carousel Club. There was a badly painted sign on a piece of shirt cardboard stuck into one of the street-level display cases that simply said CLOSED TONIGHT. It was easy driving; there was almost no one on the streets, and by the time he reached it the triple underpass was open again. Everything was dark and silent except for the lights still burning on the sixth floor of the Texas School Book Depository. The lights flashing on the Hertz billboard said it was 7:10. He took the Houston Street Viaduct to Zang, and then Zang down to Jefferson. By the time he parked in front of Inky's it was 7:30. Like Ruby's place, he'd expected the restaurant to be closed, but the lights were still on and he could see Rena at the counter by the cash register, smoking, a newspaper spread out in front of her. All the booths and the tables down the middle of the restaurant were empty and none of the counter stools were occupied.

Ray stepped into the restaurant, letting the door swing closed behind him. Rena looked up and recognized him and smiled.

"Guess you can pick your own spot," she said.

Ray sat down in the same booth he'd taken before, right

in the front window, looking out onto the street. Rena folded up her paper, grabbed a menu from the stack by the register and came over to him.

"Your regular?" she said. She had a way of cocking her hip while she stood that Ray found attractive.

"I didn't know I had one," he said.

"Sure you do," said Rena. "Chicken fried steak with some okra on the side and a Tecate."

"You remember what everybody orders?"

"Just some people." She smiled. "You want the beer now, or with your dinner?"

"With dinner if that's okay."

"I don't mind long as you're willing to eat my cooking. There's no chef. Boss said he could go home early because of the assassination. He said I could go too if there weren't any customers. I was about to close up."

Ray made a little movement to stand up. "Hey, I can go somewhere else if you're in a hurry."

Rena put a hand on his shoulder. "I'm in no hurry. You just stay where you are." She moved away and Ray watched her back as she moved. There was a little swing to her hips but nothing out of line, like she was trying to make a point with her ass or something. The last time he'd seen her the blond hair had been swinging long and free but now it was done up in some kind of twist and held there with a pair of combs. She went through the doors into the kitchen and disappeared. Ray looked out the window, not seeing much except his own reflection.

The water pills had certainly worked on his face. The meat of his cheeks and jowels were gone, leaving him looking haggard, his eyes starting to sink into his head. He gave himself a weak smile in the glass. Whatever thoughts he'd entertained about Rena could be flushed down the crapper with a face like that. Not that he'd really expected much beyond the smile he'd already gotten and maybe some talk if there was time enough to get to know her better.

A few minutes later she came back with the steak and the okra and the Tecate and put them down in front of Ray. She reached into her pocket and took out a paper napkin with cutlery rolled into it and laid it down neatly beside the plate.

"There you go," she said. She seemed to hesitate.

Ray unrolled his cutlery and used the fork to point to the seat on the other side of the booth. "Sit down if you'd like."

"Really?" she said, obviously pleased.

"Really," said Ray. "Unless you've got some pressing duties elsewhere."

"I'll get my coffee." She went back to the counter, picked up a Corey pot and topped off her cup, then brought it over to the booth. She put it down on the table and then slid into the seat. "Inky'd have a fit if he saw me doing this."

"Not supposed to fraternize with the customers?"

"Something like that."

"Maybe he'd make an exception today," said Ray. He sliced off a piece of steak and forced himself to eat it, most of his appetite gone somehow. He followed it with a slug of beer.

"Such a terrible thing," said Rena. "Just a big hurt, nothing else."

"Meaning?"

"The President gets killed but what does it really do?" There's another president now. Everything goes on, not much changes, except Caroline and John-John and Jackie have to be full of grief, to live with it."

"Murder's not about changing things," said Ray, thinking out loud. "Murder's not about the person who dies, that's just incidental. It's about the person who does the killing.

Shows he has power over the victim, and when the victim's dead, the killer's won, because he's still alive, even if he knows he's going to get hung or go to the electric chair. All this stuff going on and just about the only person who doesn't give a damn is President Kennedy. He stopped caring a split second after the bullet hit. Like a curtain going down. For him it's over."

"You think about this kind of thing a lot, or is it just today?" Rena asked. "Little morbid, don't you think?"

"I'm a homicide cop," he said and smiled. "They pay me to think about those kinds of things."

"No kidding. I'd never have thought."

"What did you think?"

"I didn't."

"But you remembered my regular."

"I didn't mean I didn't think about you, I just meant I never thought about what you did for a living." She made a little blowing noise, her cheeks going red. "You're getting me all tangled up."

"Sorry. I took advantage of you."

"Oh yeah?"

"Sure. I knew I thought you were pretty and I liked your name and I already knew you were a waitress at Inky's Restaurant on Jefferson Boulevard."

"Charm boy. What do you do for an encore, sing a Bobby Vinton song?"

"Maybe Perry Como." He smiled.

"You really are a cop."

"Yup. For a long time."

"The guy they picked up at the Texas. You think he killed the President?"

"Not my case."

"You're not interested? This is the crime of the century!"

"Maybe, but it's not mine."

"You have a case?"

"Yes."

"Interesting?"

"To me."

"Murder, I guess."

"That's right. Two of them in the last couple of days. Nine others that go back to the thirties."

"And you think they're connected?"

"Yup."

"You do anything else other than being a cop?"

"Work you mean?"

"Hobby more like. When I get a little time, holidays, I like to sew, make clothes."

"I collect old radios. Try to fix them so they work again."

"So you think about things other than dead bodies?"

Ray reached into his pocket and touched the Polaroids again. He took his hand away and put it flat on the cracked vinyl seat beside him. "Yeah. I think of other things once in a while."

"Married?"

"Nope."

"Ever married? You look like the kind of guy who'd be married."

"Years ago. She ran off with a crook and got herself killed."

"More murder?"

"Automobile accident." He paused. "Now you're the one who's sounding like a cop."

"Just like to get things straight before . . ."

"What?"

"In case you hadn't noticed women have to make the moral decisions because the guys don't know how."

"All guys?"

"Most of them in my experience."

"What moral decision are we talking about?"

"The one where I justify that because the President got shot we're all in shock, and tonight we all need someone to be with . . . that moral decision."

"We don't even know each other."

"But we want to. I want to, and I think you do."

"I've never had a conversation like this."

"Me neither. Only happens in empty restaurants just after the president of the United States has been assassinated."

"The headshrinkers probably have a name for it."

"Probably." Rena reached out with one hand and covered Ray's with it. For somebody who worked as a waitress all day it was remarkably smooth. She didn't move the hand or the fingers, just lay them on top of his.

"I should tell you something," Ray said.

"Is it important?"

"Maybe."

"Then tell me."

"I'm dying, Rena."

"You look okay to me."

"It's called congestive heart failure."

"Is there some kind of cure?"

"You die, that's the only cure."

"It's true you have this, it's not some kind of joke? Because if it is, it's a pretty sick line, especially on a day like today."

"No joke."

"How long?"

"I don't know exactly. Six months. A year, maybe less."

"How long have you known?"

"Couple of months."

"Jeez."

"I just didn't want you to say anything or do anything you might regret. I'm not very good boyfriend material, if you know what I mean. I'm pretty sure it's going to come out at my physical next week and then I'm probably going to be out of a job."

She let her fingers run between the knuckles of his hand, rubbing lightly. She smiled. "Why don't we see how things go along and just leave it at that."

"Okay."

"Time to go," Rena said, sliding out of the booth. "I've got to close up."

"I'll drive you home."

"No need," she said. She picked up Ray's plate and headed through the kitchen. She was back out a moment later, wiping her hands on her apron. "You can walk me. I only live around the corner."

11/23/63
SATURDAY

Chapter 15

Ray woke up to the sounds of someone else making coffee and for some reason he found it embarrassing; in fact he felt almost everything about the situation he was now in embarrassing. An older man with a much younger woman and he doesn't even have the decency to tiptoe out of bed after they're done so they can avoid the inevitable embarrassed conversations. He took a deep breath and let it out slowly.

The bedroom was relatively dark, located at the back of the apartment. From what he'd seen the night before it was a living room/dining room combination at the front overlooking Zang, a tiny galley kitchen, a bathroom and then the bedroom, all running off a central passage. Everything looked neat and tidy, if a little poor. The chest of drawers in the corner looked as though it came from another age and the dark green velvet curtains on the back window looked like they came from a church or a funeral home.

Ray heard Rena coming down the hallway, spoons and cups clattering on a tray, and pulled the sheet up higher around his chest. He felt stupid doing it since they'd been naked as jaybirds the night before, but it made him feel a little better to be covered.

She appeared carrying a tray of coffee things, which she set down on the edge of the bed. She was wearing Ray's shirt with nothing else under it and when she knelt down on the edge of the bed to pour the coffee he could see the firm round shape of her ass and the furry cleaving between it.

"You peeking?" she asked, looking over her shoulder.

"You bet."

"Good. Girl likes to be appreciated."

"Believe it, Rena, you're appreciated more than you know."

"Well, so are you then, Ray. I had a very nice time last night, I must say." She squirreled around, handed him a cup of coffee and took one for herself, sitting cross-legged on the bed, the tail of the shirt the only thing covering her.

He sat up straighter on the bed, pushing a pillow up so he didn't get a Brylcreem stain on the wallpaper. He felt his breathing ease and wondered if it was his heart or the fact that he could see right up between her legs to the soft bush of hair between them. He smiled a little because he couldn't remember a single time he'd been with Lorraine when she hadn't been covered, at least part of that time.

"You're smiling. That's nice. I bet you don't smile a lot."

"Probably not."

"So, a penny for your thoughts."

"Just thinking it's nice here. Feeling a little embarrassed."

"Too late for that, Ray."

"Some of the things we did last night when I couldn't get . . . couldn't get . . ."

"Hard?"

"Yeah. I've never done those before."

"Tonight you're going to do some of those things to me."

"Tonight?"

"You think we were just going to do this once?"

"I thought that's all it would take," said Ray.

"What's that supposed to mean?"

"We'd go it once, you'd get a good laugh and that would be that. You got to admit, Rena, I wasn't very good."

"Good enough for me and bound to get better."

"Nowhere to go but up?"

"There you go, putting yourself down again."

"I don't have much experience at this kind of thing."

"Most men in your place would've got up in the middle of the night and tiptoed away."

"Why? You're a nice person."

"Maybe they didn't want a person. Maybe they just want to get laid."

"That's not my way."

"I know that, stupid. You may have a bad heart, but you've got a good one."

"Didn't know you can find both in the same people."

"Oh, shut up and drink your coffee."

"Doctor says it should be decaffeinated."

"Sanka? Stuff tastes like mud." Rena watched as Ray took a long sip of the strong aromatic brew she'd brought to the bed. "That's my man. Live dangerously."

Ray sat back against the pillows, the cup and saucer in his lap, feeling a little rivulet of contentment coursing through him. Last night had been a great gift, even if there had been a moment or two when he thought his heart was going to tear in two like some old piece of cloth washed too many times; the hard, drumbeat hammering had kept on long after they'd done. But it had been wonderful.

Rena finished her own coffee quickly, then came up from the end of the bed and sat beside Ray, one hand coming out to lie across his chest, her long slim fingers threading through the thick patch of silver and black hair that ran between his nipples. "You've got a mane like a lion," she said.

"Old lion maybe."

Rena gave him a mock slap across his equally hairy stomach. "Stop with all this talk about being old."

"How old are you?"

"Something you never ask a lady." She smiled back.

"Come on."

"Thirty-two."

"And you can't find anyone your own age?"

"Who says I want someone my own age?" She made a little snorting sound. "Who says I want anybody at any age?"

"Don't mind me," said Ray, smiling. He reached out and put the tips of his fingers on her bare knee. "I'm just surprised anybody wants someone like me at all. Especially an old worn-out me without too much time left on the clock."

"I'm no virgin, you know that."

"Really?" said Ray, grinning. "I never would have known."

"First time is so long ago all I can remember is his first name, Dougie, and the fact that we did it in his parents' root cellar. Never been able to abide turnips ever since. I guess everyone thought I was racy, or a slut or something, but I always liked it and I never made excuses like I'm so drunk, or I'm in love or anything. I used to tell jokes to my friends about how I figured that the secret of eternal youth could be found on the heads of the pricks of young boys. I don't think so anymore."

"Why not?"

"Pricks as hard as a piece of wood are nice except when that's all they are, and not for too long. It took me a while but I finally figured out I wanted to be with a man who led his prick, not followed it. Few and far between, believe me."

"Woman as pretty as you are, you'd think you'd have all kinds of dates."

"Not so many. Lots of men are afraid of pretty women. I spent a lot of Friday nights at home when I was in high school."

"I would have asked you out," Ray said softly.

She smiled. "I'll bet you would." She leaned forward and took his face in her hands and kissed him firmly on the lips. She sat back again. "You are some man, Ray Duval."

He threw his legs out over the side of the bed. "Some man who's running out of time to catch a crazy person."

"On a Saturday?"

"I think so."

"Not many people are going to be around. Not with Kennedy. A lot of people are just going to be watching TV."

"What about you?"

"Inky'll be opening up, not until noon, though. Early closing."

"What time?"

"Seven."

"You really want to see me again?"

"I want to see you tonight."

"You want to come to my place? I might be late."

"That's okay."

"Key's under the flowerpot to the right of the door."

"Some cop."

Ray stood up, naked beside the bed, looking around on the floor for his clothes. Rena stepped up to him, shrugging off his shirt and letting it fall to the floor around her feet. She wrapped her arms around Ray, the top of her head barely coming to his chin.

"Not a lion," she said, squeezing. "My great big hairy bear."

"I didn't think women liked body hair."

"Then they don't know what they're missing."

"Why don't you give me my shirt?"

She reached down between them, squeezing, then milking his foreskin back and forth until she felt him thickening in her hand.

"Why don't we go back to bed for a little while."

"Pretend we're sleeping in?"

"Something like that."

"Okay."

Ray drove into Niggertown again, the streets as dead as Sunday. Rena was right; almost everything was closed and somehow Ray knew it wasn't because they wanted to be so much as they knew it was expected of them. They would lose a lot of business if they didn't close out of respect for the fallen man.

Pop Mercier's was open, though, with a big Coca-Cola sign over the front door and window, lights on inside the dark, narrow space. Ray parked the car, took out his notebook and wrote out the date on a fresh page: 11/23/63. He locked the car and went up the four steep concrete steps. He opened the door and a bell on a spring tinkled above him. The floors were wood; flypaper hung down from the rafters, the curling varnished traps smelling like summer, still with a few trophies of desiccated bugs hanging overhead. To the right was a huge, curving glass display case full of every candy any child could want, from licorice bull's-eyes, to all-sorts, to green leaves, twisters, jawbreakers, blackballs and bubble gum. Next to the candy case was a two-doored ice cream freezer with *PUR* in scrolled letters on one door and

ITY in scrolled letters on the other. On the wall behind was a dispenser for sugar cones.

Off to the right, behind the big candy display case, were shelves loaded down with cigarettes, chewing tobacco, cans of tobacco and a clip rack of Zig-Zag cigarette papers. Opposite there was a big Coca-Cola cooler full of soft drinks in ice water with rack after rack of novelties above. The bottom shelves sold everything from dishwashing soap to toilet paper and mousetraps.

The ringing of the little bell on the door brought Pop himself out from behind a curtain at the end of the store. For a second before the curtain swung shut again, Ray caught a glimpse of a large, fat woman, knitting in her lap, watching a flickering television with a pair of bent rabbit ears on top.

"Hep you, Officer?" Pop Mercier was immense, over six feet, his huge, almost completely bald head resting on a thick fat neck over broad shoulders and a massive belly cloaked in a spotless apron that fell from his chin to his knees. Pop looked out at the world through thick, black plastic-rimmed glasses that looked a lot like the ones Walter Cronkite had been holding in his hands the night before. He sat down on a tall stool with a worn red corduroy cushion attached to it with fabric tapes.

"You know a man named Danny Coulthart?"

"Sure."

"His daughter?"

"Mar'Ellen."

"That's right."

"I know just about every kid along here, Officer." He opened his mouth and grinned expansively, his entire face taking on the expression of a clown in a circus. He could have been anywhere from fifty to ninety. The man's hair was white as snow and so were the flecks of beard against his coal-black skin. "My job to spoil them rotten and rot their teeth all at the same time."

Ray looked beyond the old man to the counter behind him. There were three or four open packages of cigarettes there. "You sell cigarettes to the young ones too?" he asked. "Two for a nickel maybe?"

"I sell cigarettes to their parents, two for a nickel, Officer. I don't sell cigarettes to kids until they old enough to smoke."

"How old's that?"

"Sixteen."

"Good enough."

"That's what I think."

"Mar'Ellen come in here a lot?"

"Most every day."

"Her daddy told me she only ever had a dime for milk."

"Cost you a dime for a pint of milk in here, Officer, in the school it's just a nickel, so she usually had money left over."

"What did she buy?"

"Whatever she wanted. Changed. Green leaves mostly. Sometimes she'd take a Co'-Cola and drink it standing right here. She'd give me the nickel, and when she was finished she'd give me the empty bottle and I'd keep the two-cent return. Smart as a whip."

"She's disappeared."

"I know that."

"When did you see her last?"

"Week ago."

"What day?"

"Monday. Day she went off."

"She alone?"

"Had one of her little friends with her."

"Who?"

"One of the Kimberly twins. Tina or Tana, I can't remember which."

"They friends?"

"Not really. The Kimberly girl just came in and asked Mar'Ellen if she could have a penny and Mar'Ellen gave her one. She bought some mint leaves, then scooted out."

"They didn't leave together?"

"No."

"How long was Mar'Ellen in the store?"

"Couple or three minutes."

"Talk about anything?"

"Told me about her daddy playing at the Lights Are Blue. Liked to talk about her daddy lots."

"Proud of him?"

"You bet."

"No problems between them?"

"'Bout doing her homework or not, but that's about it."

"Any ideas yourself?"

"About what happened to her?"

Mrs. Mercier came lumbering out of the back, pushing the curtains aside. She stood beside her husband, put one hand on his shoulder. Her arm was as big around as a prize-fighter's. "She went up in smoke, Officer. She turned into nothing overnight and you or nobody else is going to find her."

"Why's that?"

"Because you don't give no never mind 'bout some nigger kid who wanders off on Ross Street and never gets seen again, that's why."

"If I didn't mind to it, Mrs. Mercier, I wouldn't be here, would I?"

"I'm sure you got your reasons, sir, but they aren't my reasons and they ain't the reasons of this community."

"Now Charlotte, don't you carry on."

"Don't you 'now Charlotte' me, you fat old man. You know what I'm saying is true. Niggers in this town is good for porters and elevator operators and warehouse workers and truck farmers and such and if they real smart they might get to go to college so they can get to be nigger doctors who only work on other niggers, or maybe to bury them, and now the one man who might have done something to change that gets his head blown off, and guess where that happens, it happens in this town, where niggers aren't even shit on your shoes."

"Charlotte!"

"To hell with that, it's true. Mexican gets more respect in this town than a nigger."

"I don't know about that, Mrs. Mercier."

"Do you know about all the other little pickaninny kids vanished?"

"Tell me."

"Happens all the time. Sometimes they old enough to head up north to De-troit or Chicago, make their way there, maybe a year later you get a postcard or a letter or sometimes a telephone call asking for money, but then there's the little ones. Ten years old, eleven, twelve. Children. Just up and gone and you never see them again or hear from them again. Mar'Ellen's not the first. Won't be the last. Now you tell me where they've gone, Mr. Policeman."

"How long would you say this has been going on?"

"We come down from Muleshoe in 'thirty-six when my momma died and opened up this store less than a year later. Beginning it was nice an' peaceful here, but even so you always knew it wasn't safe. Children, little girls especially."

"Charlotte, you're making too much of this."

"Then get the man to check. Get the man to go back

through the years and tell me how many of the nigger girls who just wandered off and disappeared were boys, not girls." The old woman shook her head. "Something bad's been going on here for a long, long time, Detective, and no one's ever done anything about it."

"Reports must have been made."

"Sure they were. Reports no one paid any attention to." She smiled at Ray coldly. "How many niggers on the Dallas Police force right now, sir?"

"A few."

"How many detectives?"

"None."

"How many patrolmen, say, after the war ended?"

"None."

"There you go. Some black woman comes along, says my baby's gone, how much attention you think some white cop with little white babies gone is going to pay? No attention at all, that's how much."

Horribly, she was probably right, and if his killer was responsible for even a few of those disappearances and was careful not to have their bodies found, then it was a whole new ball game. "Any of these children you're telling me about ever found? Any of them appear again?"

"Couple, few. Sometimes they turned out to be running away from something bad at home, or got lost, or drunk too much with a boyfriend. Sometimes dead."

"Dead? The police must have been involved then."

"Only dead one I ever heard of was Betty Shoemaker. Found her all wrapped up in a plastic bag in a ditch. She was from around here."

"When was this?"

"Eight, nine years ago."

"Where was the ditch?"

"Just outside a little place called Joshua."

"Johnson County?"

"That's right," said Mrs. Mercier. "Never would have heard about it if it wasn't for my cousin."

"You remember how old the girl was?"

"Ten."

Ray closed his notebook and shoved it back into his pocket.

"You've been a help."

"To who, Mar'Ellen Caddo and her daddy?"

"Maybe."

Mrs. Mercier looked at him, beads of fat sweat rolling into the faint down of sideburn on her cheeks. Her eyes were like cold blue chips of some impossibly hard stone behind her gold-framed glasses. The lines around her lips turned her into old leather. She had the look of someone who'd seen more in her life than she'd ever imagined, or wanted to.

"She's dead, isn't she?" the old woman asked.

"I never said that."

"You look it, though. You look as though you know for sure the person you're looking for is already dead."

"I don't have enough information yet to be sure of that," Ray lied. The half-moon scar was enough and he knew it.

"If she's dead now, none of those questions mean anything."

"Sometimes the dead can help the living."

"Help you," said the old woman. "Help you figure out what you need to figure out, and that ain't got nothing to do with any feelings Mar'Ellen might have had."

"I'm a homicide detective, Mrs. Mercier. It's what I do."

"You told Mar'Ellen's father yet? Told him she's dead?"

"No."

"Keep it that way as long as you can," said the old woman, her voice softening.

"It may hurt less if he knows."

"It may hurt less if he dreams for a little while longer."

"I'll think about it."

"You do that."

"And I really do thank you for your help. Both of you."

"If we did help, then do something with it."

"Charlotte!"

"I'll try my best, Mrs. Mercier. That's all I can promise."

Ray said good-bye and left the store. Standing outside he looked around at the broken, empty street. There was a book bindery across from him, the windows boarded over, a pool hall, a transient hotel, a garage and a box store. What kind of world was this for children, what kind of gauntlet to walk through each and every day coming home from school?

Or hadn't he been paying attention when the old woman had warned him? Maybe the killer hadn't really left the jungle at all—he'd just changed his hunting ground a little. Killing little girls up in the north country would get you noticed, even if the victims were black, but down here would it really make any difference?

How many little kids could be listed as missing down here without anyone really taking much notice at all? A smart animal only killed what he could eat; maybe the killer only took enough to keep himself satisfied and no more, except now his appetite was getting stronger.

He climbed into the Chevy, took the Salems off the dashboard and lit one, coughing with the first breath, but forcing himself to drag again. He thought about the big march to Washington a few months back and those sit-downs in that Woolworth's in Atlanta. Sidney Poitier might be a rich black movie actor but that wasn't going to get him a room at the Adolphus, no way, no how.

And any chance for that was gone now; that's what Mrs. Mercier was thinking, and Danny Coulthart, and Amanda Pinkers and Titus Edmonds. All of them. Any chance or hope of justice or redress died the day before in those red and gray trickles he'd seen splashed on the checkerboard tiles in the corridor of Parkland Hospital.

Foolishness, of course, because no one man was going to change the country, but maybe it would have been a start, something to tack a little more hope on to, like building a ladder. Ray started up the car. More likely a tower of Babel.

So here he was, sitting in Niggertown of a Saturday, with the president of the United States murdered and more murders of his own than he knew what to do with. He had a pocket full of Polaroid pictures and less than seven days to turn the puzzle into a finished piece.

So what do you do? he thought. You go back to first principles, that's what you do. Instead of sitting on your fat spreading ass thinking about your own death you go right back to where it started and look at the puzzle parts and make sure you've got them fitted together right. In this case that meant taking another run at Douglas Foster Valentine.

Chapter 16

Ray Duval was surprised to find Valentine's shop open; everything else from Neiman Marcus on down was shuttered up tight with signs edged in black on the doors. The bell on Valentine's door made its tinkling noise, just like the one on Pop Mercier's door, and Valentine, sitting on one of the big chairs in the small back room, looked a little startled to find a policeman in his store. He got up out of his chair and came into the front room, standing by the counter, close to the cash register.

"Detective Duval, isn't it?"

"That's right."

"You received the list I sent over to you?"

"I did."

"And now you'd like to talk about it, I presume."

"Among other things."

"Still no luck in finding out who killed Price?"

"There's been another killing."

"Good Christ," said Valentine.

"None of your bunch," said Ray.

"My bunch? You mean the queer bunch?"

"The antique dealer bunch."

"Who?"

"A twelve-year-old girl. Negro."

"And you think it's the same killer?"

"They were killed in exactly the same way, detail for detail."

"I don't see the connection."

"Neither do I," said Ray, "which is why I'm here talking to you."

"Doesn't seem right somehow."

"That someone else has been murdered?"

"No, I mean, with this Kennedy thing."

"They're both just as dead."

"It's hard to concentrate on anything else, that's all I'm saying, Detective. The president of the United States is assassinated and it affects just about everyone on the planet. A lot of people are worried about a war."

"Too late," said Ray. "If Khrushchev was going to start lobbing H-bombs our way, he missed his chance."

"I suppose so . . . still."

"Your store's open for business; you can't be grieving that deeply."

"My store is open because I'm not a hypocrite like most of the other people in this hick town. One day they're taking out ads in the *Times Herald* calling the poor bastard a traitor and the next day they're sobbing and crying and beating their breasts because they got exactly what they wanted. I don't know why anyone's surprised. Big D isn't Big D Democratic. Give it enough time and every cracker lunatic winds up getting off the Greyhound on Lamar."

"You sound pretty hot under the collar."

"Excuse me for having an opinion."

"You're not a local boy, are you?"

"Dallas?"

"Texas."

"No. Atlanta."

Ray pulled out his notebook and flipped back a few pages. He nodded to himself. "I believe Mr. Price was born in Atlanta as well."

"That's right."

"You knew each other there?"

"We grew up together there. Went to the same high school."

"Is that a fact?"

"We had shared interests."

"Such as?"

"Art, for one."

"Young boys?"

"Just each other."

"You were lovers then?"

"For a time. Long enough to know that we liked it better with each other than we liked it with girls."

"Anybody know?"

"I doubt it."

"Then what happened?"

"J. P.'s father had a lot of money back then. He went to Harvard."

"You?"

"Emory."

"Never heard of it."

"Neither has anybody else," said Valentine with a laugh. "It's about twenty minutes outside Atlanta in the Druid Hills. I had a full scholarship. Class of 'forty-one."

"And then right into the army?"

He nodded.

"Rank?"

"Captain. You got your bachelor's, you were a captain, you had your master's, you were a major."

"Price?"

"Master's in art history. He was a major. Came out a colonel, just like the chicken fellow."

"You were both in the same outfit?"

"I applied. Jennings had the pull, like I said."

"So you spent time together in Europe?"

"We met up from time to time. We were all over the place. He had a lot of things going on as well."

"Like what?"

"I don't think I want to speak ill of the dead."

"Little late for that."

"One of the things he did was catalogue artifacts for repatriation."

"Try that again."

"The Nazis had whole platoons of SS going around and confiscating art. We confiscated it back. The OSS had a looting team as well, so we worked together. There were four or five big 'collection centers' behind the front lines. The paintings, jewelry—everything was taken to these collection centers and catalogued. J. P. was in charge of one of them. Wiesbaden."

"So?"

"So if it wasn't catalogued it didn't exist. If it didn't exist, nobody went looking for it."

"You're telling me he stole things?"

"I wasn't in a position to know. I was just a lowly captain running around trying to save things from looters, and making sure things that had already been saved weren't destroyed or 'liberated.'"

"Liberated by who?"

"You name it. The Russians had a whole division that did

nothing but swipe things and send them back to Russia. Our own people did it, so did the French, the Poles, the Brits. Everyone wanted a piece of the pie."

"Big operation?"

"Big enough. Some of the stuff you could just slip into your pocket and then stuff into your duffel bag. It wasn't like customs was going to go through your underwear when you got off the *Queen Mary*."

"Bigger stuff?"

"Shipped by air. Usually as something else, or with forged clearances."

"You're making it sound pretty organized."

"It was. That's what J. P. was all about. Organization."

"So what was his part in it?"

"You saw his place?"

"Yes?"

"His old man had money, but not that much money."

"So he smuggled things into the country after the war."

"Too smart for that. Never got his hands dirty. He just helped other people. Made a lot of friends with the big-time types, the ones who were going back to the States to become museum curators."

"How did it work?"

"Lots of corrupt art dealers at the end of the war, name any country, but France was big, so was Italy. J. P. would get things sent to his pals, who'd sit on them for a while, and then 'discover' it with a cute story and a forged provenance. A legit dealer or museum would acquire it and everyone was happy except the original owners, and most of them were dead anyway."

"He did this by himself?"

"He had help. He bribed people."

"Any particular help? You, for instance?"

Valentine looked pained. "Detective, a man walks in here with cow shit on his shoes and puts down a nice little leather-bound diary I open up and discover is one of Galileo's lost journals, I'm going to offer him ten dollars and send him on his way, then turn around and sell it at Sotheby's for ten thousand dollars, but that doesn't make me a thief."

"Just a cheat."

"Are you trying to get me angry, Detective, maybe because if I was angry I might say something useful?"

"Crossed my mind."

"Sure I cheat. It's the nature of the business. Picker cheats the person selling, junkman cheats the picker, dealer cheats the junkman, dealer cheats the final buyer, buyer cheats on his income tax, calls it a business expense."

"Okay, there's always a bigger fish in the sea, but who was helping Price?"

"He had a clerk. Another local boy."

Ray took out his notebook and pencil. "Who?"

"Schwager. Dick Schwager. He was about twenty-two or twenty-three then. My sense is they were fucking each other at the time."

"Any idea where he is now?"

"I can tell you exactly. He lives with his sister in a little town called Blackstone, about forty miles north of here off Highway 75."

"How do you know his whereabouts?"

"He came back from the war pretty well set up. Presumably by J. P. He opened his own little antique store in his hometown. Keeps an apartment here as well for his romantic liaisons. I occasionally buy from him, so do a few other dealers. He keeps his eyes out."

"Call him," said Ray. "I think we should pay him a visit."

"We?" asked Valentine, looking vaguely horrified at the suggestion.

"I need someone to ask the right questions."

"I thought I was a suspect."

"You may be," said Ray. "That doesn't mean you can't cooperate with your friendly Dallas Police, does it?"

"I'll have to close the shop."

"You won't be selling anything for the next few days unless it's got a picture of JFK or Jackie on it."

"I suppose you're right." He pursed his lips for a moment. "What kind of automobile do you drive, Detective?"

"A 'fifty-seven Chevy."

"Oh dear."

"What's that supposed to mean?"

"Nothing. I don't suppose you'd mind going in mine."

"And what would that be?"

"A 1964 T-Bird."

"Business must be good."

"Good enough."

"I'm still not entirely sure what you're hoping to accomplish," said Valentine, sitting behind the wheel. The interior was white leather to match the outside but with black trim. Everything was sparkling. Ray let himself sink back in the bucket seat on the passenger side of the console, enjoying the sensation of being a passenger instead of a driver. The car was smooth as glass on the road and the interior was almost perfectly soundproofed. Outside the sky was the color of pewter, the overcast low and oppressive.

"There's some kind of kids' puppet show with a car like this in it," said Ray. He reached out and ran his hand across the sharply defined dashboard. "I saw it one Saturday morning, last month. *Fireball XL-5* I think it was called."

"You didn't answer my question," said Valentine, glancing over at Ray and giving him a strange look.

"Sorry, I get distracted sometimes these days. I'm not quite myself."

Ray went into the pocket of his jacket, flipped through the Polaroids and handed the one of Mar'Ellen Caddo across to him. Valentine glanced at the picture and almost drove off the road. Luckily there was virtually no traffic, north or south.

"Jesus Christ!" He threw the picture back into Ray's lap.

"Just thought I'd get your reaction."

"But how can Jennings—"

"During the spring and summer of 1938 there were nine little girls raped and murdered in several counties upstate. Each one of them was dismembered and then wired together like a puppet, like your friend and your onetime lover, Jennings Price. I've done a lot of thinking about this, Mr. Valentine, and I've come to the conclusion that the solution to all of this is somewhere in the past. Your past maybe, or Mr. Price's past. This man Dick Schwager is from the past. That could make him important."

"What about that list of dealers and clients I sent over to you?"

"If nothing pans out here I'll have to try it. But you don't chop a man into pieces and rape little girls because someone owes you money or vice versa. It's important I jump a few squares on the board here."

"You on some kind of schedule, Detective?"

"You might say that."

They drove on in silence. Finally Valentine spoke, keeping his eyes glued to the road ahead. "In 1938 I was twenty years old and living in Atlanta, Mr. Duval. J. P. would have been twenty-one. At Harvard. You've got to know we had nothing to do with those killings."

"Already figured that out," said Ray, smiling quietly. "But your friend was murdered, and he was murdered in the same way as those little girls, so there *is* something he has in common with the killer. Perhaps you as well."

"I can't see how that's possible."

"Me neither," Ray answered. "But that's what being a detective is all about. Making connections. Seeing links when other people don't."

"What about lovers?"

Ray turned to Valentine, staring hard. "Someone on that list was Price's lover?"

"Who knows?"

"You might."

"Jennings didn't have lovers, he had sex. With a lot of people."

"Yourself included."

"Half the queers in Dallas included and a few from Fort Worth besides."

"You think one of them might have killed him?"

"You're the detective, not me," said Valentine. "And whatever you think, Mr. Duval, homosexuals aren't particularly homicidal by nature. The only thing they are by nature is homosexual."

"I wouldn't know," said Ray, starting to feel a little uncomfortable.

"No, I don't suppose you would."

Ray tried to think it through; his intuition told him that any lover, Valentine included, almost certainly had nothing to do with murders committed twenty-five years ago— which in turn probably meant they weren't involved in the disappearance and death of Mar'Ellen Caddo.

* * *

Blackstone, Texas, stood within a hundred yards of the Grayson/Fanin County line about sixty miles north of Dallas. The town was named after a Boston entrepreneur, Henry G. Blackstone, who purchased a tract of land directly in the path of the Missouri, Kansas and Texas Railroad. With a combination of rail access and excellent farmland, Blackstone soon attracted plenty of settlers and businesses to the area. Henry Blackstone got rich and headed back to Boston, leaving nothing behind but his name. While cotton was king, Blackstone flourished, both as a place to grow it and a place to ship it, but as the years rolled by Blackstone languished, its businesses closing and moving to larger centers nearby.

Reaching the small city of McKinney, they turned onto Texas 69 and continued north, eventually reaching Blackstone a little more than an hour after leaving Dallas. Valentine guided the T-Bird down an empty Main Street, every single business closed except for the Mobil station, then turned up a numbered farm road on the eastern edge of town. They drove north again, leaving the town behind them, then turned a second time, stopping in front of a yellow clapboard farmhouse directly across the country road from a walled cemetery. There was a gate with a wooden sign on it that said Willow Hills Cemetery. There were no hills that Ray could see, but there were plenty of willows, a number of them around the yellow farmhouse.

To the right of the farmhouse and connected to it by a makeshift addition was something that had either once been a small barn or a large garage. It was painted a deep red color, and like the cemetery it also had a sign: RICHARD M. SCHWAGER ANTIQUES.

"Could just as easily say 'Junk,'" Valentine commented, getting out of the car. Ray followed him, noticing for the first time that behind the house there was an extensive greenhouse, and beyond that a small apple orchard. With the slamming of the car doors a retriever came bounding out of the open door of the large garage and raced toward Ray and Valentine, tail wagging, tangle foot, its tongue lolling out of its mouth in a ridiculous grin. A harsh voice brought it up short and a woman the size of a small tank appeared, dressed in a blossoming parachute-style dress with short sleeves barely able to contain the immense biceps within. She had her hair up in pink curlers and the curlers covered by a lime-green kerchief. She had a cigarette lodged directly in the center of her small, heavily lipsticked mouth.

"It's you," said the woman, staring at Valentine, talking around the cigarette.

"Yes, it is, Mrs. Schwager."

"Nice car," she said, looking beyond him.

"Yes, it is."

"Who's your friend?" asked the fat woman. She peered closely at Ray. "He looks sick."

"He's a police detective. From Dallas."

"Zat right?" She let out a coughing laugh and delicately removed the cigarette from her mouth before she spat down on a patch of brown, burnt-out grass. "Come to interview me about killing the President?" She shook her head. "Dumb sumbitch, you ask me. Teeth were just too good to be true."

"We came to talk to Dick."

"Dick's dying, why don't you leave him be?" Ray's eyebrows went up.

"I'm aware of Richard's condition, Mrs. Schwager, and I promise you I won't upset your brother more than necessary."

"This about those papers people are saying he stoled?"

Ray broke in. "It's about a murder, Mrs. Schwager."

The immense woman stared at Ray. She put the cigarette back into her mouth and drew on it heavily, then swallowed the smoke, eating it the way he used to do himself. She let the smoke trickle slowly out through her nostrils. "My brother never killed anyone but a few Germans during the war."

"He's not a suspect, Mrs. Schwager. I just want to ask him a few questions."

"About what?"

"Jennings Price."

"That queer boy!"

"Yes, ma'am."

"He's in the greenhouse with his stupid roses," she said. She slammed a meaty hand onto a meatier thigh. "Come on, Delilah." She turned and the dog followed her back to the garage. Ray watched them go.

"The dog's male."

"She's like that."

"If *his* name is Schwager and *her* name is Schwager, and they're brother and sister, how come she calls herself Mrs.?" Ray asked.

"I suppose no one would marry her, so she married herself."

"It sounds like she doesn't know her brother is a homosexual."

"Some people can make themselves believe just about anything, Detective."

Ray thought about Delilah, with nuts the size of swinging tennis balls. "I suppose you're right," he said.

Chapter 17

They came around the back of the house and Ray saw that the greenhouse ran the full width of the building and sixty or seventy feet back toward the orchard. A light rain was beginning to spit down from the gunmetal sky, tinkling on the glass panes in the greenhouse roof and making a harsher banging sound against the areas on the side walls that had been replaced with heavy plastic.

Valentine pulled open a lightweight door and Ray followed him into a small room walled with chipboard that was set out with shelves full of terra-cotta pots of all sizes, small gardening implements on peg-board racks and bags of potting soil stacked up on the floor. A second door led into the greenhouse proper, but even in the little potting shed Ray could feel the damp, cloying heat and taste the overpowering smell of tea roses in his nostrils, almost worse than anything he'd experienced in the autopsy room at Parkland.

They went into the greenhouse and Ray was suddenly faced with a sea of roses in orderly ranks, wave after wave of color heading toward the rear of the wood-and-glass enclosure. There were Coventry Cathedrals, Granadas, City of Leeds, Liverpool Echo and Grace Abounding. Tiffanys,

Honor, Tequila and Don Juan, First Love and Madame Butterfly. Thousands of them in every shade of red, pink, yellow, white, and even a tawny gold. In the middle of it all, a brightly polished brass spritzer in his hand, was Dick Schwager.

According to Valentine, Richard Schwager was in his mid-forties but he looked at least twenty years older than that. He was wearing expensive-looking gray trousers, a red-and-blue-striped silk shirt and what appeared to be a blond shoulder-length woman's wig. His eyes were sunken behind heavy tortoiseshell plastic glasses and Ray could see every bone in the man's face. His skin had a faintly blue cast and on his hands Ray could see the man's veins, like thick, pale worms. The man's nails were a little too long and shiny and his lips looked as though he'd used a touch of lipstick, but it wasn't enough to cover up the fact that some terrible disease was eating him alive.

"Cancer," said Schwager, reading Ray's mind. "Leukemia." Almost as though he was proud of it. He smiled and Ray could see that the man's small teeth were stained and in very bad shape. "I suppose you're here to talk to me about J. P." He gave Valentine a short, bitter look as though the antiquarian book dealer had betrayed some kind of trust. He turned to Ray. "And you would be?"

"Ray Duval. I'm the detective investigating Mr. Price's murder."

"Dear me, investigating the death of an aging fruit like J. P. I'd have thought you'd have your hands full with poor Mr. Kennedy's passing." The strange man made a small giggling sound and spritzed a large bush loaded with pale, creamy blossoms. Overhead, real raindrops hammered on the glass and the plastic.

"The only thing that gives me any pleasure now," he said,

sighing melodramatically like some Southern belle and smiling at Ray again. "And it's lovely and warm in here. Come along."

He turned on his heel and walked down the long aisle to an open area about halfway down the greenhouse. A small area had been cleared and set out with white wrought-iron furniture: two chairs, a love seat and a round, glass-topped table. On the table there was a large pitcher of iced tea and several glasses set on a silver-edged tray. Ray wondered how the man had known they were coming, and once again, eerily, it seemed as though Schwager read his mind.

"You never know when guests are going to drop in. It's only polite to have refreshments ready."

"They come for the roses?" asked Valentine, sitting down in one of the chairs.

Schwager let out a little squeaking laugh as he carefully lowered himself onto the love seat. "Well, they certainly aren't coming for me anymore, dear." He waved a hand at the tray on the table. "Help yourself and pour me a glass while you're at it, won't you?"

Valentine did the honors, pouring three glasses of iced tea. It was perfectly brewed, not too sweet, tart with a little lemon. It was all Ray could do to stop himself from draining the glass and asking for a refill. Amanda Pinkers had a rival.

"It's very neat and tidy, isn't it?" asked Schwager. For a moment Ray thought he was talking about the greenhouse, but then he realized Schwager was still thinking about the Kennedy assassination. "The man is killed, his assailant runs, is captured, and the story's ended, all in a few minutes. I always thought murders were messy things that took ages to solve, like in mystery stories. Or like poor old Jennings." Schwager made his little giggling noise again and took a small sip of his iced tea. He lifted his legs up onto the love seat and crossed them at the ankles. Ray noticed he was wearing pale gray leather slippers that matched his trousers perfectly.

"Murders usually are messy," said Ray, taking a careful sip from his own glass.

"I seriously doubt there was only one assassin," said Schwager. "They're talking about seeing someone firing from that little knoll by the railway tracks."

"I hadn't heard that," said Ray, only faintly interested.

"Oh yes, it's been on television."

"I don't watch television. Not very much."

"Neither do I," Schwager said. "Certainly not the news programs. I've problems enough of my own." He paused. "I do like the *Gary Moore Show*, and sometimes I watch *Have Gun, Will Travel*." Schwager touched the open collar of his shirt as though he'd suddenly been chilled. "Wire Paladin, San Francisco."

Ray kept looking at the man over the rim of his glass. He was like something out of a sick fairy tale—literally—and he wondered how a man like that could survive in a town like Blackstone, or anywhere else for that matter.

"Did you know I was an art teacher for simply ages?" he said, staring back at Ray through the tortoiseshell glasses. "In Taos, New Mexico, after I got out of West Texas State."

"When was that?"

"West Texas State?"

"Yes."

"Nineteen thirty-eight. I spent a year or so teaching in high school but it was just too tempting. Taos was different. You could let your hair down." He reached up and patted his wig carefully, as though he was afraid it might tip off. "So to speak." He giggled.

"Did you know Mr. Price?"

"No. You might say we didn't travel in the same circles back then."

"But you were a clerk for him in the army," put in Valentine. Ray was grateful for the push; he didn't need Schwager's life history.

The wigged man gave a small mock salute, his hand shaking slightly. "I wasn't really a clerk, more like his assistant. And I didn't start out that way."

"How did you start out?"

"I enlisted. As a private. In the army. I had a friend at the time who thought he'd do better in the navy."

"But you were a college graduate," said Ray. "You could have been an officer."

"I knew that. I was accepted as an officer candidate. I went to the artillery school at Fort Sills and trained as an FO."

Ray looked curiously at the husk of a man across from him, pansified to an almost ridiculous degree. Being a Forward Observer was one of the most dangerous jobs in the army, involving sneaking up to the battlefront to observe enemy positions and direct fire for the big guns using a radio. FOs had just about the shortest life expectancy for combat soldiers; either they died from their own friendly fire when it fell short or they were picked off by enemy snipers.

"Not a pleasant occupation."

"Cannon fodder," said a nodding Schwager, his wig bobbing.

"Who were you with?"

"Eighty-seventh Armored Field Artillery Battalion."

"Big unit, small?"

"Small for what it was expected to do. Five hundred men,

sixteen officers. We had a few tanks but mostly they were priests. Eighteen of them."

"Priests?" asked Valentine.

"Howitzers, 105mm, mounted on tank chassis," Schwager explained, warming to the subject. "We could level a small city in three or four minutes."

"Where did you meet up with Price and Mr. Valentine here?"

"I met J. P. at a place called Quedlinburg in the Harz Mountains. I didn't run into Douglas until Wiesbaden."

"What happened when you met Price?"

"We both recognized each other as queer, that was the first thing."

"How?" It was something Ray had wondered about from time to time.

"Just looks, a feeling. Something you wouldn't understand."

Ray was perfectly willing to stipulate to that. "You became lovers?"

"Not immediately. This was March of 'forty-five, you've got to remember. The war in Europe was almost over and everyone knew it. J. P. had more pressing matters at hand."

"Such as?"

"Quedlinburg was like Ali Baba's cave, almost literally. A fairy-tale town with half-timbered houses and a castle, cobbled streets. Never a shot fired in anger; it was the center of the German floral industry; they did a roaring business in funerals and parades right up until the end of the war."

"Ali Baba's cave," said Ray, getting Schwager back on track.

"Oh yes. Well, it was also Heinrich Himmler's favorite spot. It was the place where German kings and queens were historically crowned, so it was full of treasure, especially the religious kind. Jeweled Gospels, reliquaries. Apparently Himmler liked to have all sorts of secret SS rituals there. When the war started everything was moved to a bank vault, and later on to something they called a *Champignonzuchterei*. A mushroom-growing cave."

"Ali Baba's cave."

"Which is where J. P. found it."

"And removed it?"

"That's right. I was the one who found the place originally, and when he showed up with his Monuments and Fine Arts team it was like an omen. I told him about what I'd found. Supposedly he logged it into one of his ledgers, packed the stuff up, and me with it."

"The treasures were never registered?"

"No," said Valentine. "That's how the game worked. Art objects would come into the collection center and anything Price wanted he simply left off the books. Most of it was books and documents."

"Why?"

Valentine answered. "It was his area of expertise, and books and documents were easy to smuggle. Jeweled crosses, Leonardo paintings and bags of gold bullion attract attention. Old books and papers don't."

"That's how it began," said Schwager. "And then he got into the forgeries."

"Why forgeries?"

"Cheap to produce," Valentine answered.

"If you find yourself in possession of one drawing by Hans Holbein, why not make yourself another five or six and sell them as originals?" Schwager shrugged. "I had enough art training to be a reasonably good copyist and we had all sorts of processes for aging paper and leather bindings. Smoking, coffee marking, that kind of thing."

"Coffee marking?"

"It worked best with the instant coffee powder they gave you in your rations. You dampened the paper then took a teaspoon of coffee powder and threw it up in the air. Where it landed it made beautiful 'foxing' marks—old iron deposits. Smoking darkened the paper. The longer you smoked it over green wood the 'older' the paper got."

"And you actually made money doing this?"

"Lots," said Schwager. "J. P., Douglas over there, me and Koop."

"Koop? What did he do?"

Valentine nodded. "I remember him. Another local boy. J. P. liked to keep it in the family, so to speak. He apprenticed to his father as a bookbinder or a papermaker or something. He could fix bindings, fake them, age paper, anything to do with books or documents and he could do it. When Jennings met him he was a picker."

"Picker?"

"J. P. had a 'friend,' so to speak, who owned an antiquarian bookstore. Koop sometimes brought him books he'd found and sometimes Jennings's 'friend' gave Koop books to fix."

"I thought Price was from Atlanta?"

"He was. He spent the summers here. An uncle or what have you. That's how he got started. If you know what I mean." Schwager leered.

Ray contemplated the unsavory image for a moment, then brought his thoughts back to his investigation. "So what happened after the war?"

"I mustered out first," said Valentine. Lived in New York for several years. By the time I got back here J. P. was already in business."

"Forging?"

"Not at first," said Schwager.

"You were working for him?"

"With him is how I like to think of it."

"A business arrangement?"

"Yes." Schwager giggled again. "The bloom had gone off the romantic rose." He reached behind him and let his skeletal fingers caress a drooping yellow bloom at his shoulder. "We spent almost a decade simply working our way through the material we'd spirited away from the Wiesbaden collection center. It wasn't like there was any lack of shady dealers to sell it to. J. P. used the money to expand his own legitimate business." Schwager allowed himself a small smile. "I spent my ill-gotten gains on other things."

"The forgeries," Ray prompted.

"Just the last few years or so. J. P. was getting into debt. He decided to do for Texana what he'd done for the Third Reich."

"He used pickers to walk into county archives and just walk out with historic documents, then forged other things," said Valentine.

"He had a Crockett letter on vellum supposedly from the Alamo. We must have made and sold fifty copies of the same letter."

"This is with Koop's help?"

Schwager shook his head. "No, no. Koop disappeared somewhere into Germany. Berlin, 'forty-six or 'forty-seven. Nasty place then." He laughed. "Probably had his throat slit by some table-girl's pimp on the Kudamm."

"You sound like you know something about it."

"I dabbled," said Schwager. "Sugar lickers and wild boys."

"Sugar lickers?"

"You figure it out." Schwager giggled again and made his

mouth into a small O and stuck his tongue out, waggling it back and forth. Ray turned away for a moment, feeling his face flush.

"This Koop wasn't a homosexual then?"

"I don't think so."

"Any sense that he could be violent? Anything strange about him?"

Schwager thought for a moment. "He used to disappear for days at a time. He'd get this tense look in his eye and he'd go all quiet and then he'd disappear. People were getting killed all the time, whores, pimps, black-market types. He could have been doing anything and you'd never have heard about it. Lots of places to hide bodies too."

"Were you involved in any of the forging after the war?" Ray asked, turning to Valentine.

"I didn't have to be. I had a little money put aside, I'd put together good contacts in New York and elsewhere. Jennings was always a risk taker. I had a better sense of self-preservation, I suppose. The police would have caught up with him eventually."

"I agree," said Schwager, poking gently at his wig. "When people in the business started telling tales out of school, I knew it was time for us to part company. I mean, he was selling things to the *governor* for pity sake! It was getting a little too warm in the kitchen."

"What about lovers?" said Ray, just to see what the response would be. There was a quick look that passed between Schwager and Valentine and some kind of quick acknowledgment of something but Ray decided not to pursue it.

Schwager let out a long braying laugh that eventually turned into a painful-sounding cough. He gathered himself together, took a long drink from his iced tea and let out a sigh. "You're a riot, Detective, a regular riot."

"What's so funny?"

"J. P. was born to be a slut, Detective. He used people, then tossed them out like a teenager's cummy Kleenexes."

"I think the word Richard is looking for is promiscuous," said Valentine. "But he's right. In terms of being an actual lover, no one took Jennings seriously." It was essentially the same answer he'd been given by Valentine before. Another look telegraphed from Schwager across the table. Once again Ray decided to let it lie, at least for the moment.

"What about business enemies?" Ray asked. It was a long shot and an unlikely solution, but it was a necessary question.

"Every dealer in town," said Valentine.

"Every dealer in Texas," said Schwager, laughing.

"But not enough to kill him?"

"I doubt it," offered Valentine. "He was a cheat, a liar and a thief and everyone knew it."

"But they still did business with him?"

"Great stock," said Schwager. "J. P. always had the best and paid the least for it. If you had a client who wanted something specific that you didn't have, you'd go to J. P. He'd stiff you, but you'd get the item."

"When I was there I saw something that was clearly stolen. A robbery in New York."

"The Marlene Dietrich cigarette case?"

"That's right," said Ray, surprised.

"It's a come along," said Valentine.

"Explain."

"It's like crows," said Schwager. "They go after anything shiny. The Dietrich case is just to get you interested. You never actually get to buy the case because eventually you'd find out that it was on some police force's hot sheet, but in the meantime it would establish the dealer's bona fides, and also his ability to bend the law, sell you something with a wink and a nod."

"A con."

"Crudely put, but accurate."

"Did Price have any connections with the mob?" asked Ray, thinking about Ruby again.

"Possibly." Another look passed between Valentine and Schwager.

"Either one of you know Jack Ruby?"

"The name is familiar," said Valentine. But his eyes shifted.

Schwager was a better liar but not by much. "Not to me." He shook his head.

Ray could smell the lie even through the reek of the roses all around him. He sighed. It was beginning to sound as though Jennings Price had lots of people with potential motive, but none of it seemed to fit the murders of the little girls.

"A cat," said Schwager, draining the last of his iced tea. "That's what Jennings was."

"How so?"

"Curiosity and all that. It's probably what killed him. Always had to know everything, have his finger in every pie, his nose in everyone else's business. A cat."

"I guess he ran out of lives," said Valentine.

"Guess so," Schwager said. He stood and picked up a pair of shears from the shelf behind him. He studied the roses immediately in front of him and chose a large, pale pink blossom on a long stem. He handed it across to Ray. "I think this is appropriate. It's a Rhum von Steinforth, a cross between a German Frau Karl Druschki and an American

General McArthur." He smiled, showing his bad teeth again. "You can dry it out and throw it on the coffin at my funeral."

Zinnia Brant lay on the filthy bed, too tired and too frightened to cry anymore. Too terrified to make a sound beyond the ragged whisper of her breathing. The room was windowless and dark and she had no idea how much time had passed; only that she was very hungry and ashamed. He had touched her everywhere, even tried to put his finger inside her, but it had hurt and she had screamed. He'd smeared something slippery on her the next time and lain on top of her, almost smothering her, pushing his thing between her legs, hard as a piece of root and bigger than any she'd seen on the boys she knew, but that hadn't worked either and he'd given up. But he was only beginning and somehow she knew that. She knew as well that if he ever really did it that it would split her in half like a piece of fruit and she'd die, right here in this horrible place, and maybe she'd go to heaven and maybe she wouldn't, but either way she didn't want to go, not right away, no matter what her mother and old Grammy said about Jesus and God and flaming chariots of retribution like the reverend talked about every Sunday. For now she was alive, even though she'd peed and pooped herself, and that was shameful too, but for the time being it seemed to be keeping the Monster away from her.

It had happened so quickly. She'd gone to the 7-Eleven and she'd done just what her mother told her to do, buying a loaf of bread and a German's bar for her treat, hardly spending any time at all looking at the comic books. Her favorite was *Magnus, Robot Fighter, 4000 A.D.*, but she didn't have twelve cents to buy it for herself, even though it looked pretty good this month, what with Leeja being trapped in some kind of submarine with her feet stuck in something that looked like nose boog, while Magnus came to her rescue wearing fins, a shark bigger than he was sneaking in behind. Leeja was blond and Magnus was white as well but it wasn't the kind of thing Zinnie thought about too much, since the whole world was white and there was no such thing as a nigger Lone Ranger. The closest she'd ever seen was Turok, or maybe Tonto, but Indians didn't count and neither did wets. She giggled, thinking about a Mex superhero, like that would ever happen!

She'd taken another bite of chocolate bar, put the comic book back in the rack, and picked up her bag with the loaf of Mrs. Baird's in it. She stepped out into the cool darkness, the boom and rumble of the traffic on the expressway echoing down from above. Directly in front of her there were half a dozen teenagers, all white, lounging on the hoods of a couple of old jalopies, smoking cigarettes and talking loudly to each other. Her mother had told her about something she called "discretion was the better part of valor," and that meant when she saw a bunch of white people, grown or kids, she was supposed to keep a smile on her face and put wings on her shoes, and *that* meant she was supposed to keep out of their way and if she got into any trouble she was supposed to run like hell.

Instead of going down the parking area to the sidewalk Zinnie walked along in front of the store, then down between a white van and the wall of the building next door. She took another bite of the German's bar and out of the corner of her eye she had a split second of horrible realization when she noticed that the side door of the van was open and that she was in big trouble.

It all happened so fast. A hand reached out and grabbed her by the hair and then she was off her feet and inside the van. He let go of her and like the big stupid she was she swung the bag of bread as though that was going to hurt anyone and then there was a big square of something sticky over her eyes and mouth and one hand around her throat, choking the screams in her throat, stillborn. More tape around her ankles, her hands dragged behind her back and bound with more tape and then she was pushed down onto the floor of the van, falling onto something prickly and soft. Burlap bags or a rough blanket of some kind. A few seconds later she heard the van start up, the rumble of the engine vibrating through the floor, and then the crash and clatter of gears as the Monster put it into reverse and backed up out of the 7-Eleven parking lot.

They didn't go very far, no more than a hundred yards or so, and then the nightmare started up again. The engine died and then the Monster was on her again. He ripped off her clothes, broke her glasses clawing at her like an animal, and when his fingers hooked under her underpants she knew that her mother had been right about everything and she whipped her head back and forth, chewing at the tape across her mouth, the screams of unbridled dread and terror drowned out by the thundering noises coming from directly above her.

She knew this place. The dark hole of nothing right under the expressway. Even in daylight it was no place to be and Zinnie felt her bladder open and drain into the blanket under her naked skin. For the first time in the brief passage of her life Zinnia Brant understood that death wasn't some vague thing that only happened when you were very old and that it turned on a simple twist of fate, like heads or tails on a spinning dime, even for little girls.

Chapter 18

Ray stood at one of the urinals in the third-floor men's room completing another of his seemingly interminable drainings when John McDonald, the ex-Vice cop, came lumbering into the room and stepped up to the urinals next to Ray. He unzipped and let out a small groan of satisfaction as his bladder began to empty.

"Too much fucking coffee," he said.

"Amen."

"Still a zoo out there. I met a reporter from Frankfurt for Christ's sake! Germany if you can believe it."

"How come you're here at all?" Ray asked. "This isn't your shift, is it?"

"Naw," said McDonald. "But I wouldn't miss this shit for the world. Kind of thing you tell your grandchildren about." He turned his head to Ray. "You got grandkids, Ray?"

"Don't even have kids."

"Too bad."

"I guess so."

"Two boys and a girl and six little ones between them. Makes life worth living. Anyway, like I said, I wouldn't miss any of this."

"They still questioning this Oswald character?"

"Off and on. He comes up and down from the cells like a yo-yo. Still no lawyer."

"He hasn't asked for one?"

McDonald laughed. "Oh, he's asked all right. Curry and Fritz just don't seem to be hearing him too good." McDonald shook himself a couple of times, tucked himself back into his trousers and zipped up. He went over to the chipped enamel sink in one corner of the room and gave his hands a cursory wash. "'Member I mentioned Jack Ruby to you?"

"Sure," Ray said, still standing at the urinal.

"He was here last night."

"What?"

"Midnight look-see. Sort of a press conference. You shoulda been here."

"I saw Ruby at Parkland."

"That right?" McDonald hauled down a relatively fresh section of roller towel. "Anyway, Jack's there with all these foreign correspondent types, making like he's some kind of reporter, and the D.A. makes some comment that Oswald's a commie, that he was on some kind of Cuba Committee, but Wade gets the name wrong and Jack actually corrected him, gave him the right name." McDonald snorted, grabbed a piece of paper towel off a roll balanced on the back of the sink and blew his nose loudly. "It was the funniest damn thing you ever saw, Ray. All these reporters and it's Jack fucking Ruby giving them the goods and embarrassing the hell out of the D.A."

"Funny," said Ray.

McDonald gave a little wave. "Well, back to it." He turned and left the bathroom, leaving Ray still at the urinal. He finally finished the chore, picked up the fat folding file from Juvenile and went down the hall, cutting his way through the press of photographers and reporters who seemed permanently camped outside Homicide-Robbery. None of them paid him the slightest attention. At the end of the hall the press room door was wide open and someone had dragged in a couple more tables. There were at least a dozen more reporters, photographers and cameramen crammed into the room, all of them talking either to each other or on the few phones in the room. Turning, Ray stepped into the relative calm of the Juvenile office.

He dropped the big magenta expanding file of missing persons back into the wire basket he'd taken it from the day before. Millie Toombs gave him a nasty look from behind her desk. "I said you could look at it, not take it."

"Sorry," Ray apologized. "I didn't think you'd miss it."

"Bad joke, Detective Duval. My ass would have been in some sling if that file had disappeared."

"Such language." Ray smiled. Up on the filing cabinets the radio was still on, but turned down now so that it was barely audible. The only thing worse than the President being killed would be a nuclear war, and you wouldn't need the radio to find out about that. Today it was nothing but background noise.

Millie looked up from an open file on her desk. "Just got another one."

"What?"

"Little Negro girl run off." She glanced down at the report on the desk. "Like you were looking for."

"Tell me."

"Name, Zinnia Brant, like the flower. Twelve years old. Address on Virgil Street."

"Deep Ellum?"

"That's right."

"What happened?"

"Her momma sent her out to the 7-Eleven store to get some bread for the next day's breakfast. She never came back."

Ray nodded. He could remember when the 7-Elevens used to be called Tote'm stores, because you had to tote the stuff home in bags. "How late she go out?"

"Just before nine."

"Already dark. Where's the store in relation to the home?"

"Three blocks. The 7-Eleven's right there by the expressway."

"Not a nice neighborhood."

"Depends on your color, Detective."

"Safe for her?"

"Shoulda been."

"Who called it in?"

"The mother. Eileen Brant. Leaned pretty hard on the Mrs. part. And she brought it in. Picture as well." Millie unclipped a photograph from the report. It looked like it had been taken at a fifty-cent photo booth like the kind they had at the bus station. The girl was plain, her hair done in braids, wearing black plastic eyeglasses, her skin fairly light.

"Anybody check it out?"

"Not so far."

"Nobody went and talked to the 7-Eleven staff?"

"All I got is the incident report. She disappeared last night, nobody's seen her since." Ray could see a couple of dicks, Stetsons on their desks at the back of the long room, doing nothing but smoking and talking.

Ray took out his notebook. "Give me whatever numbers you've got."

Millie did as she was asked, then she sat back in her creaking old chair, the full weight of her broad beam tilting the chair back to a dangerous angle. "Now how come a homicide detective is suddenly interested in little nigger girls running off, which is something nobody in this department really pays much attention to."

"That's why," said Ray.

"I'm just a dumb old receptionist," said Millie. "Why don't you explain that to me?"

"A smart man who wants to get away with murder kills people nobody cares about. Nobody on the DPD or in the press cares about little Negro girls from Deep Ellum, or up country."

"That is a fact."

"But it's still murder. Homicide is color blind."

Millie snorted loudly. "Tell that to your Captain Fritz; bet your white ass he's got a few bedsheets in the family tree, or better yet, you go and look it up in your files, how many Negro murders got solved in Big D last year."

"You be careful how loud you say that kind of thing, Millie, and who to."

"That a threat, Ray Duval?"

"No, Millie Toombs, that's just good sense." Ray could see that her eyes were wet as she looked up at him and he knew she was thinking about Kennedy being killed and thinking that with a native son like Lyndon Baines Johnson in the big chair there wasn't going to be much chance for civil rights until at least the end of that man's term.

"I'm sorry, Millie."

"No need to be sorry," she said. "I'm used to things the way they are; just going to have to get used to it again." She took a little breath.

"You make me a mimeograph of the report?" asked Ray.

"Called a photocopy machine, Ray. We've had one for a couple of years now."

"I'm a bit behind on things like that, Mill."

Millie took the report, disappeared into one of the small rooms at the back of the office and came back a few moments later with a copy of the report. Ray folded it in half lengthwise and slipped it into his inside jacket pocket.

"Thanks, Millie."

"You go find her, Ray. Find her quick."

"Do my best." He gave her a smile but it faded away as soon as he left Juvenile and stepped back into the hall. If this little girl had been taken by the same man who took Mar'Ellen Caddo he had two or three days at the most before the child was finally murdered.

It was dark by the time he pulled the Chevy up the Commerce Street ramp and darker still by the time he wound his way across the bands of railway track and into the depths of the Deep Ellum district. Ignoring the girl's home address he drove directly to the 7-Eleven store, tucked up beside the expressway on an unmarked street that formed a narrow, almost invisible underpass. There was garbage strewn everywhere and when Ray stepped out of the car he could smell the exhaust from the cars up above him and hear the sounds of tires singing on the pavement.

He stood beside his car for a moment, listening and tasting the air. He had one of those maudlin images that had been haunting his thoughts ever since the doctors had given him his death sentence. All the people in his hearing, everyone in this city alive today, in the whole country, would be dead and buried in seventy or eighty years, even the little kids like John-John Kennedy and his sister. All of them would be dust and none of it would mean anything, because by then they'd all be replaced. Life went on so amazingly easily when you died, even if you were the president of the United States.

He went up the narrow paved area to the front door of the scrappy-looking store. There was a stringy-looking white man behind the main counter wearing a short green smock and a white and green fatigue-style cap on his head. His pocket said 7-11 and his name tag said DWAYNE, and below that, MANAGER. Dwayne had an Adam's apple like a Ping-Pong ball, pale skin and reddish hair. He looked as though he was about thirty-five but his skin was broken out in acne sores like that of a teenager.

The store had five narrow aisles loaded down with pack-aged food, a few necessities like toilet paper and frozen food in a freezer along the back. There was a soft drink cooler just beyond the counter. Tucked in behind the cooler was a photo booth with the word *AMAZING* on the side and a slot for quarters. Probably where Zinnia Brant had her picture taken.

Ray went to the soda pop cooler and took out a bottle of Big Red. He popped the cap on the cooler opener and took a sip. It tasted like nothing else in the world, a bit of lemon, a lot of fizz and the sweet sick sense that you were drinking ice-cold liquid bubble gum. He took it over to where Dwayne was looking through a copy of *Handguns* maga-zine. There was a picture of an automatic on the cover and a Police Special, but the big illustration was a close-up of some cowboy type quick drawing a Colt single-action Army in presentation brass and steel that would probably blow up in your hand if you ever really tried to fire it.

"Like guns, Dwayne?"

"Who wants to know?" Dwayne asked, looking up briefly.

Ray took another sip of the Big Red, then put the bottle down on the counter. He reached into his back pocket, took out his ID wallet and showed Dwayne his badge. "I do."

"Sure. I like guns. I keep one under the counter."

"Can I see it?"

"'Course." Dwayne put the magazine faceup on the counter and reached down. He came up with a shiny Colt Trooper, bored as a .357 Magnum. He laid it on the counter beside the magazine.

"Big gun."

"Big enough."

"Ever use it?"

"Flashed it a couple of times, kids trying to take a five-finger discount. They don't do it again."

"Keep it loaded, Dwayne?"

"Wouldn't be much use empty."

"Got a permit?"

"'Course."

"Company get it for you?"

"Naw. They say you get stuck up, just hand over the cash."

"Smart."

"Yeah, well."

"Anybody ever try to hold you up?"

"Not so far."

"How long you worked here?"

"Four months."

"Know this girl?" He took out the picture of Zinnia.

"Nigger girl."

"Negro."

"Yeah, well, I see a lot of nig— Negroes in here. It's a Negro neighborhood, isn't it?"

"Just look at the picture. She's got braids, she's twelve years old. She came in here last night around nine. Maybe bought a loaf of bread. You were here last night?"

"Till eleven, just like the name says."

"Remember her?"

"I'd be lying if I said I did, Officer. I sell a little bit of everything to a little bit of everybody, if you know what I mean. People going to work, people coming home and everything in between. White trash, niggers and wets. Once in a while I even get a Chink. Don't remember any of them. Go crazy if I tried. Color blind too."

"Okay, you don't remember her. What do you remember, say, between eight and when you closed up?"

"Eight to nine it was pretty busy, mostly cigarettes and pop."

"Kids?"

"Yeah, but older, with cars, you know? High school boys."

"No problems?"

"Noise, swearing. Talking about Kennedy, what they'd been doing, who'd been in school, who'd been watching and such. More excited than anything. Lot of bullshit going on."

"What kind of bullshit?"

"One of them said he'd been right there, saw the whole thing, but no one believed him when he said it was a colored looking out the window with the gun."

"A Negro?"

"So he said." Dwayne let out a hog laugh that seemed too big for him. "Funny thing is, the other boys called him Amos Lee."

"So?"

"Lee. Don't you get it? Lee like in Lee Harvey Oswald."

"I see. That the only thing a little bit odd?"

"The Corvan."

"Corvan?"

"It's a Corvair van. White. Parked out front for better part of half an hour. Empty. It was getting me a little pissed. Only people supposed to park out front are customers."

"See the owner?"

"No. Lots of times people come in here, ask to use the bathroom, and then I tell them we don't got one so they sometimes go and take a leak, even take a shit under the expressway. Pretty dark under there, even during the day."

"Get the license number?"

"I was going outside to get it, call the tow truck to haul sumbitch off, but when I looked out he was gone."

"What time was that?"

"Nine-thirty, about."

"White?"

"That's it."

Ray thanked the man, put down a dime for the Big Red and headed for the door. There was an upturned wooden milk crate on the left and there were still a few copies of the *Dallas Morning News* piled up on it with the headline KENNEDY SLAIN ON DALLAS STREET. There was a smudged-looking picture of Johnson on the left and a larger one of Kennedy on the right. Strangely, the Kennedy picture was a line drawing, not a photograph. Ray thought about buying one, knowing that it would quickly become a collector's item, but then he realized how stupid *that* was. He stepped out the door, still carrying the Big Red. He looked to the right. The underpass was like the entrance to a cave. He took a swallow of the soda then balanced it on the roof of the Bel Air. He unlocked the car, unlocked the glove compartment and took out his big, rubber-covered police Eveready. He locked up the car, picked up the bottle and headed down the narrow extension of the street that ran below the expressway. He flipped on the flashlight, holding it a little away from himself and moved the beam back and forth.

The street extension dead-ended with a concrete barrier

that looked as though it had been put together when the expressway was being built. To the left and right there was nothing but garbage-strewn muddy ground. A derelict car had been turned on its side, the stuffing of its seats torn out, the windshield and the windows smashed and the hood missing. There was also a rusted fifty-gallon drum covered in soot a few feet away from one of the concrete overpass abutments. Probably a makeshift fireplace for bums when the weather got bad.

Ray lowered the beam of the flashlight, playing it across the waste ground directly at his feet. This was the logical place for his kidnapper-killer to knock out or gag his victim without being seen, but so far he hadn't seen any evidence of a struggle. Or had the child struggled, had the man somehow lured her here? He also kept his eye out for fresh tire tracks; the 7-Eleven manager's description of the white Corvair van was interesting. Had his man parked it, then headed into the welcoming shadows of the underpass to somehow "prepare" for his victim? And how did he know she'd be coming at all? Or maybe it was just a crime of opportunity, picking his spot then waiting for a victim to fall into his trap. Too many things to check, too many people to talk to for too little information.

He went deeper into the darkness, wheeling around with the flashlight. He remembered Chief Curry giving some kind of speech a few years back, quoting some big-shot detective, probably a Fed, who'd said that a criminal always brings something to a crime, and always leaves something behind. It was meant to be profound, but if you thought about it, the idea was pretty stupid. So what if he leaves something behind? Unless it had his name and address on it, what use was it to a cop like Ray? Fingerprints, hair samples, even blood samples were no good to you if you had nothing to compare them with. Even the van was probably a red herring, nothing more than what Dwayne the manager had said—some poor guy who needed to take a leak or drop a load real bad and didn't want to do it in public.

He'd gone twenty yards under the expressway and come up empty. A few feet ahead of him was the dead-end street on the opposite side. He turned around and headed back toward the 7-Eleven. On a whim he stepped over to the fifty-gallon drum and pointed the beam of the flashlight down into it. His heart sank. Clothes, and not old and worn rags either. He took the copy of Millie's incident report out of his pocket and put the light on it. According to the report, Zinnia Brant had been wearing a tartan skirt, a white blouse with a green sweater over it, white ankle socks and navy-blue-and-white saddle shoes. He shone the light back into the drum. Resting on some half-burned trash there was everything on the list as well as a pair of soiled white underpants that smelled strongly of urine. He couldn't see any blood anywhere. The shoes were on top of the pile. He took a pencil out of his inside pocket and used it to lift the saddle shoe up where he could shine the light on the scuffed leather sole. There was no mud or any other evidence that the girl had crossed the muddy ground beneath the expressway.

Ray carefully put the shoe back in the drum and retraced his steps to the parking lot of the 7-Eleven. Using the pay phone at the end of the building he called in to Homicide for a couple of specialists to come out and handle the evidence for him. The dispatcher picked up on the fifth ring and told Ray there was no one available since all the technicians were handling the Kennedy evidence, bagging and boxing it for shipment to the FBI lab in Washington.

"So what am I supposed to do?"

"Bag it and box it yourself, Detective."

"Jesus," Ray whispered and hung up the phone. He went back into the 7-Eleven and Dwayne gave him an empty Lay's Potato Chip box with the "Betcha Can't Eat Just One" slogan on the side. He also convinced Dwayne to hand over a dozen sack-lunch-sized bags as well.

Ray went to the rack of housewares hanging on a peg-board by the freezer and found a pair of corn tongs and a pair of dishwashing gloves in a plastic bag. He brought both items to the front counter.

"You'll have to pay for those."

"Fine. Just give me a receipt."

Dwayne totaled it up on the cash register. Ray paid out of his own pocket and put Dwayne's receipt for the items in his wallet.

"I guess you found something," said Dwayne.

"Yeah."

"No body?"

"No." Ray dropped the tongs, the bags and the rubber gloves into the potato chip box.

"Nothing to do with Mr. Kennedy, I suppose," Dwayne said. "Now that would be something."

"No," Ray answered, heading for the door with the box in his arms. "But stick around, I've got some more questions."

"Not going anywhere until eleven." Dwayne smiled. "Just like the name says."

"Good." Ray went outside and back into the underpass. He put on the gloves and, using the tongs, lifted the various pieces of clothing into the box. He bagged the stained underwear and each shoe, then took the box back to his car and put it into the trunk, locking it carefully. He put the flashlight back into the glove compartment and went back into the store.

He spoke to Dwayne again. "This Corvan or whatever you call it, where was it parked?"

"On the right, and that had me a little pissed too. He was parked so you couldn't get another car in beside him."

"He was hogging an extra space?"

"That's right."

Ray took out his notebook and his pencil and made a quick sketch.

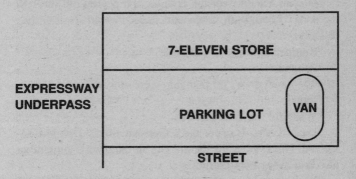

"That about right?" he asked, showing the sketch to Dwayne.

The 7-Eleven manager nodded. "Except there were more cars in the lot."

"The high school kids?"

"Yeah."

"You know anything about these vans?"

"Sure."

"Windows?"

"No. The model with windows is called something else. Greenwood, or Greenbrier or something."

"Panel doors?"

"Yeah."

"Left or right?"

"I think both sides. That's one of the features."

"Double or single?"

"Not sure. Double, I think." He nodded. "Yeah, I'm pretty sure they're double."

"Slide or do they hinge?"

"Hinge."

"How much could you see of the van from the counter?"

Dwayne leaned over the counter and peered out through the door. "I could tell it was still there. I could see the driver's side."

"Bumpers chrome or painted?"

"Painted."

"The panel doors on that side were closed?"

"Yup."

"What did the little girl buy?"

"Loaf of Mrs. Baird's and a German's bar," Dwayne answered. His eyes went wide. "I'll be damned. I remember her clear as anything now."

"Sometimes works like that," said Ray. "Memory trick." He waited for a moment. "Anything else you remember? Her coming in, her leaving?"

"You're right, she had braids. Talked a little quiet. Knew how to count her change."

"What'd she give you?"

"Dollar bill."

"What did she do with the change?"

"Held it in her hand, bag with the bread and the chocolate in the other arm."

"How soon after she left did you go out and check on the van?"

"'Bout five minutes after."

"How often you sweep up out in the parking lot?"

"Whenever it needs it."

"When did it need it last?"

"Couple days ago."

"No cleaning up since last night."

"Nuh-uh."

"All right. You've been a help."

"Glad to be of service," said Dwayne. Ray let himself out of the store, cursing under his breath. Here were the first pieces of hard evidence he'd had in the case since the death of Jennings Price. He took out his notebook again and made a few quick adjustments to his sketch. If the child was heading home with her bag of shopping she'd probably avoid cutting down through the cars belonging to the teenagers and would instead go as far along as she could and turn down between the brick wall of the housing row next door to the 7-Eleven and the apparently empty white van. With both of the panel doors opened Zinnia Brant would be hidden from view for the few vital seconds it would take for her assailant to pounce. Once he had her inside the van the rest would be easy.

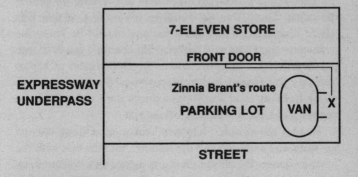

A quick grab at the girl, a hand over her mouth and drag her into the van, unnoticed from the street or the store, and that would be that. Maybe some sort of gag or chemical to knock her out. He could strip off her clothes, take them to the drum under the expressway and be gone within moments without leaving a trace.

Ray followed his hypothetical track until he stood at approximately the point where he thought the little girl might have been taken. There were half a dozen old oil stains on the ground but nothing else. Between the brick wall of the building next door and the parking lot there was a two-foot-wide strip of earth that might have once been intended as a bordering garden, but it had long since gone to weeds. There was also a scattering of paper garbage, including a Baby Ruth wrapper and the wax-paper wrapper for a package of Bazooka Bubble Gum. Halfway down the border strip there was a torn triangle of paper with a brown outer wrapper— the top of a German's chocolate bar. Ray looked in the dirt and grime on the edge of the border and spotted two pennies and a half-buried nickel and a half-buried dime. Zinnia's change. He found a crumpled Kleenex in his back pocket, unfolded it and picked up the shreds of evidence, including the coins. There was no doubt in his mind that this was where Zinnia Brant had been kidnapped, but he knew the evidence was effectively useless. He couldn't get even one police technician to come down, the Department of Motor Vehicles was closed and tomorrow was Sunday, so it was going to be at least forty-eight hours until he could even begin to look for the white Corvair van.

He took the refolded Kleenex back to the Chevy, opened the trunk and carefully put the Kleenex into the box with the other evidence. He closed the trunk again, then walked back to the phone booth. He looked up the number he wanted in the Yellow Pages, then dialed. It was answered on the first ring.

"Friendly Chevrolet." A buttery woman's voice.

"Billy Harcourt there?"

"Sure is. Who's calling?"

"Ray Duval."

"Hold on." There was a clunking noise as the receiver was put down and then the receding sound of high heels on linoleum. Ray leaned back against the booth, fatigue finally catching up to him. What he really wanted to do was take a run by Inky's, pick up Rena and a bag of food, and go home, but he still had a lot to do.

"Bill Harcourt." Hale and hearty with a cigarette and coffee grate.

"Ray Duval."

"The Bel Air."

"That's me. I'm surprised you're open; no one else is."

"I'm a Republican."

"Oh."

"So what can I do for you, Ray? Trading-in time? We've got some sweet deals."

"More like a favor."

"Such as?"

"Do you sell Corvair vans?"

"Corvans or Greenbriers?"

"Corvans."

"Not many."

"I need to find out the name of everyone who's bought a white Corvan in the Dallas–Fort Worth area."

"You kidding?" Harcourt laughed. "Corvan's have been on the market for a couple of years now."

"There can't have been that many white ones."

"Be surprised, Ray."

"Can you ask around?"

"Yeah, I suppose I can do that. When do you need to know?"

"As soon as possible."

"This doesn't have anything to do with Kennedy, does it?"

"No."

"Good. I don't want anything to do with that shit. Give me a phone number, I'll see what I can find out."

"I owe you one."

"That you do. Trade in your old heap to anyone else and your name is mud, sir."

"Mud it is," said Ray. "I promise you'll get it, one way or the other." He read off both his office and home phone numbers and then hung up and went back to his car. He sat behind the wheel, rubbing a hand across his chest and waiting for his breathing to slow. Every day now, less and less activity caused more and more tiredness. The water pills were turning his kidneys into tight, hot wedges of agony in the small of his back. The wet, rustling sound was there each time he drew breath now. He forced himself to keep his eyes open, pushed the cold, true thoughts out of his mind and concentrated on the job at hand. He took out his notebook, checked Jack Ruby's home address and started up the car.

Chapter 19

Number 223 South Ewing Street was a run-down, colored brick two-story apartment building called Marsala Place. It was built around a concrete courtyard with a swimming pool in the center. It was also less than half a dozen blocks from the location at 10th and Patton where Oswald had supposedly shot Tippit, the uniformed cop, the day before, twenty minutes or so after the Kennedy killing.

Jack Ruby's apartment was on the second floor, forcing Ray to climb the long set of white-painted fire-escape-style steps bolted to the side of the building. He paused at the top of the stairs, holding on to the rust-nubbled railing waiting to catch his wet, rasping breath and for his heart to slow down.

When he could breathe again and the wheezing, whistling sound receded, he went down the open second-floor balcony until he reached number 207, at the far corner. He could hear music coming from inside, and the sound of voices. Sounded like something scratchy by Benny Goodman. The voices were muted. Ray took a couple of deep breaths and rapped on the door, hard.

The music stopped so quickly it sounded as though

someone had been waiting with his finger over the phonograph needle. The voices dropped away almost as fast. He could hear padded footsteps, as though someone was walking over wall-to-wall carpeting. The door opened a foot. It wasn't Ruby. Instead he was facing a red-faced man with a crew cut wearing a soiled pair of khakis and an undershirt. His fat cheeks and double chin were bristly from not shaving and his eyes were as red as his cheeks.

"What?"

"My name is Ray Duval. I'm a detective. I'd like to speak to Jack Ruby."

"Wait."

The man turned away from the door and for a moment Ray could see beyond him into the living room. The television was on. It should have been the new Phil Silvers show or *The Defenders*, but it was just more Kennedy footage. There were half a dozen men in the room, one of whom got up quickly, turning away as though he had to use the bathroom. If Ray hadn't known better he would have sworn it was his old partner, Ron Odum.

He did recognize two of the men sitting on the scrappy couch in front of a coffee table loaded with beer bottles and bowls of snacks: Joey Civello, the man rumored to be head of the mob in Dallas, and Charlie Sansone, a fellow DPD detective working out of Narcotics.

Suddenly Ruby was in the doorway and stepping out onto the landing, pulling the door shut behind him. "Detective Duval," he said with a smile. "You dropped by my humble home."

"Sorry to interrupt. Looks like you're having a party."

"Just a few friends over for drinks." He paused, taking Ray's elbow and leading him away from the door. "So what can I help you with?" He paused again. "Unless this is a social call."

"No, it's not a social call."

"Then why don't we go down and talk by the pool."

Ray wasn't about to insist on barging into Ruby's apartment, but Civello and a Dallas narcotics dick was an odd combination. Sansone was too well known to be working undercover.

Ruby led the way down a flight of steps in the middle of the landing that went down to the concrete courtyard surrounding the pool. He pulled up a couple of aluminum and plastic-webbed garden chairs, facing each other, a foot or so from the edge of the water. Ray sat down, glad enough to be outside in the cool of the evening, but feeling the heavily chlorinated pool water stinging his nose and eyes.

Ruby slapped his hands down on his knees and smiled, the spread lips fattening his cheeks like a squirrel. "So then, Ray, what's your mind?"

"It's Detective Duval, Mr. Ruby."

"Fine." Ruby's lips closed in a surprisingly effeminate moue of hurt feeling.

Ray took out his notebook and flipped through the pages. He came to the transcribed list he'd been given by Valentine. He handed the open notebook across to Ruby, who looked down at the page.

"What's this?"

"A list of people."

"I can see that, Detective."

"I've got reason to believe that one of those people was involved with Jennings Price, the murdered man found in the dump."

"And you think I know which one it is?"

"I'm sure of it. Your name keeps on coming up, Mr. Ruby. In some unlikely places with some unlikely people."

"Who?"

"Dick Schwager?"

"Never heard of him."

From the street Ray could hear the sound of a powerful engine starting up. He looked up toward Ruby's apartment. A staircase just like the one he'd used led down to ground level and the street. He wondered if Civello was beating feet.

"Let's do a little deal, Mr. Ruby. You try and remember what you know about the people on that list and I'll try to forget the people I saw in your living room just now."

Ruby hesitated for a long moment, then nodded. He looked down at the notebook again and then back up at Ray. "Only name that rings a bell is Paul Futrelle." He smiled. "Hey, I'm a poet and didn't know it."

"What kind of bell?"

"The queer kind."

"Paul Futrelle is married. He's got kids. Try again, Mr. Ruby."

"God's truth, Detective. Lots of married queers around. It's like camouflage. They lead double lives."

"He's a school supervisor."

"So he is." Ruby handed back the notebook. His eyes flickered up to the second-floor door of his apartment, then down again.

Ray studied the name in the notebook. He flipped back several pages. The inscription on the Jennings Price Omega Constellation read *"Tempus Fugit sed Amatus est Infinitus."* "P. F. to J. P." The J. P. was Jennings Price, the P. F. was Paul Futrelle.

"Aw shit." He should have seen it as soon as Valentine gave him the list. Or maybe he hadn't wanted to see it.

"You want to know if he was fucking Price, well, he was. Too many people knew it."

"What are you saying?"

"I'm not saying nothing." Ruby shrugged. "But some people are gonna make some unavoidable conclusions. Like Paul Futrelle had a secret he'd do anything to keep and Jennings Price had a mouth on him like Howdy Doody." Ruby reached over and put a small pudgy hand on Ray's knee. "Now Supervisor Futrelle may be queer, but he's got some powerful friends, Detective Duval. I'm not sure I'd like to be the cop who broke the news to Dallas that Paul Futrelle was fruit salad."

"Sounds like a threat." He lifted Ruby's hand away from his knee. The man's skin felt a little oily, as though he'd rubbed his fingers through the Brylcreem he used to grease back the hair on the sides of his head. Ruby wasn't offended by the gesture, and pulled a package of Newports and a lighter out of his pocket. He offered the package to Ray, who shook his head. Ruby lit one for himself, then slipped the package and the lighter back into his pocket again.

"No threat, just the straight goods, Detective. It's just like what you might think you saw upstairs in my living room; a little bit too hot to handle for a small-time dick."

"I'm not interested in what I saw in your living room," Ray lied.

"That's good."

"Not for the reasons you think, Jack. It's just that I've got other things on my mind these days."

"Whatever way you want to play it, Detective."

"Maybe you should get back to your party."

"Maybe I should at that." Ruby flicked his cigarette into

the air, a red arc that was snuffed out as it hit the pool. "Take care now." The pudgy little man with the thinning hair got up and went back to the stairs. He went up them two at a time, walked down to the door of 207 and went inside.

Ray levered himself up and headed back to the car. He checked his watch. Five after nine. Ten minutes since he'd arrived. He started the car and headed north to Jefferson, his face and his hands green in the lights from the dashboard. He glanced at himself in the rearview and for the first time a dead man stared back at him and for the first time the thought started rolling through his head that he was afraid of dying. He looked away from the mirror and concentrated on his driving, pulling to a stop as carefully as a little old lady when he reached the intersection at Jefferson. There were too many terrible thoughts in his head now, all fighting for dominance, this new fear of dying uppermost; but not far behind was the glimpse of the man he'd seen in Jack Ruby's apartment.

He waited for the traffic to clear, then swung the Chevy left, heading west down Jefferson to the Texaco at the corner of Cameron. There was a phone booth beside the toilets and he parked beside it. The telephone book in the booth was so much scrap paper so he dropped in a quarter, got his change and dialed information. Futrelle turned out to have an unlisted number so he put in a call to Betty Finch, his diminutive contact at the phone company. She got him the number in less time than it took to spell Futrelle's name. According to Betty he lived in Kessler Park, a ten-minute drive north and west.

"I owe you one," said Ray.

"You owe me about a thousand by now," said a laughing Betty and then she clicked off the line.

Ray scribbled the address and phone number down in his notebook, then hung up. Getting his dime back he scooped it out of the change holder and put it back in the slot. He looked at his watch. Twenty minutes now since he'd been at Jack Ruby's apartment. He dialed Ron Odum's number from memory and let it ring ten times without an answer. There would have been barely enough time for R. T. to make it back to his place from Ruby's if he'd been there at all. He banged the phone down, calling himself a dozen different names, and concentrated on the job at hand. This time he dialed Paul Futrelle's number. Someone picked up on the third ring.

"Futrelle residence." Sounded like a butler or something like it. The man was speaking through his nose.

"I'd like to speak to Mr. Futrelle, please."

"Mr. Futrelle has retired for the evening, I'm afraid."

"This is important."

"Perhaps if I might enquire what this is about."

"Tell him it's about a friend of his."

"And which friend would that be, sir?"

"Mr. Jennings Price."

"And your name, sir?"

"My name doesn't matter."

"Yes, sir. Please hold the line."

There was a faint clunking sound as the person on the other end put the receiver down. A long, echoing minute passed and then a second voice came on to the phone, the voice hollow.

"Who is this?"

"Mr. Futrelle?"

"Yes." The voice had the snap and impatience of authority but there was a trickle of fear running through it. The hollow sound was still there on the line.

"You need your extension hung up."

"Andrews?"

"Yes, sir?" The butler's voice.

"Hang up."

"Of course, sir." There was a click and the line cleared.

"You always let your butler listen in on your telephone calls?"

"Andrews isn't my butler, he's my personal assistant. He looks after my interests."

"Which sometimes involves eavesdropping?"

"From time to time. Now who are you?"

"My name is Duval, Mr. Futrelle. Detective Ray Duval. Dallas PD."

"Why didn't you say so in the first place? Chief Curry and I are good friends."

"I'm sure. I was simply being discreet."

"In regards to what?"

"Jennings Price."

"Mr. Price is an antique dealer. He specializes in documents and rare books."

"I'm aware of that. It's your relationship with him that interests me."

"I have no relationship with him other than the purchase of several volumes of Texas history."

"Purchase anything recently?"

"Yes, as a matter of fact. Eugene Barker's *The Life of Stephen F. Austin* and Frederick Olmsted's *A Journey Through Texas, 1857.* Mr. Price was going to have the latter volume rebound for me."

"You're aware of his murder?"

The voice was stiff. "I have been advised of his demise, yes."

"You don't sound very torn up about it, Mr. Futrelle."

"Why should I be? He was a business acquaintance, barely that. In fact, I'm not entirely sure why I should be having this conversation, especially at this time of night."

"Because you bought Mr. Price a wristwatch, Mr. Futrelle. An Omega Constellation with the inscription *Tempus Fugit sed Amatus est Infinitus*. Time is fleeting but love is infinite. P. F. to J. P. The P. F. stands for Paul Futrelle, the J. P. for Jennings Price."

"That's absurd. I barely knew the man, why would I buy him an expensive watch?"

It was time to take the plunge. "Because you were homosexual lovers, Mr. Futrelle."

There was an excruciatingly long pause. Futrelle finally spoke. When he did his voice was level and without inflection. "As I said, Detective, I'm good friends with Chief Curry. I'm not sure he'd appreciate his people going around slandering innocent citizens."

"It's no slander, Mr. Futrelle. I've had the information corroborated by more than one person." It wasn't quite true but both Valentine and Schwager had hinted broadly enough at Jack Ruby. Ray decided to dig his own hole a little deeper. "I have other evidence as well."

There was another long pause. "Presumably this is some kind of shakedown, I think you call it."

"No, sir. I'm simply investigating Mr. Price's murder. Your name has come up in connection with that murder. I have no desire to defame or embarrass you."

"What do you propose, Detective?"

"That we meet."

"When?"

"Now, if possible. I'm running out of time."

"It's almost ten o'clock at night. What am I supposed to tell my wife?"

"An emergency meeting of some kind."

"Where?"

"Drive down to the end of Kessler Lake Drive and walk into Kidd Springs Park. I'll be on one of the benches."

"How will I recognize you?"

"I look like a cop," said Ray. "A cop in a tweed sports coat and no Stetson."

"And what do you expect me to tell you?"

"Whatever you can, Mr. Futrelle." He hung up the telephone. He tried R. T.'s number again, but there was still no answer. He hung the phone up a second time and went back to the car. He had the driver's-side door open when a man in a brown Texaco uniform came around the corner and into the drift of reddish light thrown by the sign on the pole a few yards away.

"You can't just park here and not buy gas, you know," said the man.

"I was using the telephone. Sorry."

"You come into a gas station, you're supposed to buy gas."

"I'm a cop. It was an official call."

The man in the uniform stopped and stared at Ray. "This is about the jacket, I guess."

"What jacket?"

"Oswald's jacket." The man in the uniform pointed to an empty parking lot behind the gas station. "That's where they found it."

"I didn't know that," said Ray.

The man in the uniform looked disappointed. "I thought it might be about the jacket."

"No."

"Well, you should have bought gas then."

"Next time," Ray answered. He climbed into the car, groaning with the effort as he pulled the door shut. He started the engine, pulled the light switch and drove out of the gas station.

Chapter 20

Kessler Park was the jewel of the Oak Cliff neighborhoods, a mix of eccentric mansions built along Coombs Creek, and south of Colorado Boulevard composed of well-maintained Tudor houses. Ignored by city planners until the twenties because of its densely forested, craggy terrain, it eventually became one of the city's most sought after residential districts. Having found a secluded area of unique terrain, most residents never left, which explained its stability while other, older Dallas areas deteriorated. At the foot of the hilly neighborhood, and protectively surrounded by it, was Kidd Springs Park, a large lagoonlike pond in its center, the last spring-fed lake in the city.

Ray came at the park from the east, parking at the end of 5th Street, then walking into the dark, moonlit park, skirting the edge of the lagoon, following the paths north to where he expected Futrelle to appear. It was quiet, any traffic sounds smothered by the trees that edged the pathways. The loudest sounds were the watery splashing of the swans and ducks swimming in the lagoon behind him and the faint chittering noises of a light breeze moving through the leaves.

On the ground there was a faint, ghostly mist that wet Ray's cheeks and hair with dew. If it wasn't for his errand, Ray realized he might find the darkness and the quiet relaxing. He'd only visited the park once or twice, and that was years ago, which was ironic considering that his own house lay only a dozen blocks to the south in the old Dallas Land and Loan district on the other side of Davis Avenue. He found himself thinking about Rena and wondered if it would be a nice thing to bring her here, maybe on her day off. After his physical next week he'd be having quite a few of those himself.

He slowly climbed up the path leading to the Kessler Lake Drive entrance to the park and spotted a dark form already occupying one of the green wooden benches. The man was elegantly dressed in a topcoat over a dark suit and tie. He was tall, well built and had little flares of gray at the temples of his otherwise dark, thick hair. As Ray approached the man stood up. He wasn't Ray's idea of what a queer should look like, but thinking about it for a second he realized that he didn't *have* an idea of what a queer should look like. Limp wrist and a lisp, swiveling hips and a mincing walk in shoes that were too tight?

"Detective Duval?"

"Yes."

"I'm Paul Futrelle." Ray held out his hand for the man to shake but Futrelle ignored it.

"You didn't have to get dressed up," said Ray.

"I didn't," Futrelle answered. "I'm supposed to be attending an emergency meeting, remember?"

"Sorry."

"No, you're not. You're enjoying this, Detective. You think you've got some kind of tiger by the tail and you're going to hold on hard and see what it gets you."

"I told you this wasn't a shakedown, Mr. Futrelle. I meant it."

"One way or another it's a shakedown. You want something and you think I can give it to you, and you're dangling a secret over my head like some kind of sword of Damocles."

"I'm no Dionysus out to teach you a lesson, Mr. Futrelle. I'm just a cop looking for information."

Futrelle sneered. "Astounding, a member of the Dallas Police Department who's read Cicero."

"Actually, it was a kids' book on Greek and Roman myths and legends I read while I was getting over the measles." Ray smiled. "Next best thing to a Classics Illustrated Comic."

Futrelle took Ray by the elbow and turned him back the way he'd come. "I'd feel better if we walked as we talked."

"Whatever you like." Ray shook off the hand on his elbow. They headed back down the web of pathways toward the lagoon.

"What exactly do you wish to know? Presumably I'm not a suspect in Jennings's murder?"

"You were a lover scorned," said Ray. "One of the oldest motives around."

"I'd like to think that I'm above that sort of thing."

"Most people would, Mr. Futrelle. Unfortunately that's not the case."

"Do I need some sort of alibi?"

"The time of death is too vague. From what the medical examiner tells me he died sometime earlier in the week. Monday or Tuesday."

"The last time I saw Jennings was on Monday afternoon."

"Where?"

"I'd rather not say."

"His place?"

"No."

"Not yours."

"Of course not."

"So where was it?"

"I told you, I'd rather not say. I have no right to involve other people in my affairs."

"You do if it involves murder."

"You're telling me that I have to answer you."

"If you don't I'll have to formally charge you."

"Would you really dare to do that, Detective Duval?"

They had reached the lagoon and paused to watch the pale white forms of the swans gliding through the mist. When the Rangers had been stationed in Ireland just before being mobilized, Ray had gone down into the Republic and visited the city of Cork. A grayer, gloomier place he'd never seen, full of gray and gloomy people. There'd been a swan pool there as well but with none of the gentle magic he felt here.

Ray turned to the dapper man beside him. "Yes, Mr. Futrelle. I'd formally charge you. I'll be leaving the department in the near future so I've got little or nothing to lose and I'd like to wrap this up before I go."

"If I wanted to I could cause difficulties with your pension, Detective. You must know that."

"Now who's dangling the sword?" Ray asked.

"You're a stubborn man, Detective."

"I'm a dying man, Mr. Futrelle, and I'm losing my patience. Time is something I have very little of left and you're wasting it."

"I'm protecting my own interests."

"Leave that to me. Now where did you meet with Jennings Price?"

"A mutual friend has a small apartment up above University Park."

"Who's the mutual friend?" Ray asked. "And don't tell me you'd rather not say."

"Ricky Schwager."

"The rose fancier?"

"You know him?"

"We've met."

Futrelle looked shocked. "He told you about me?"

"Never said a word. Neither did his friend Valentine."

"Then how did you know?"

"I'm a detective, Mr. Futrelle. I detect. I asked Valentine for a list of Price's major clients. Your name was on it. I took it from there."

"So he did tell you."

"No. Like Schwager. Not a word."

"Nice to know there's one or two people you can trust."

"Unlike Price?"

"Jennings was Peter Pan and Tinker Bell all rolled into one. You could never tell what he was going to say, or to whom, or where he was going to land when he started flitting around town."

"What was the meeting about on Monday?"

"Nothing in particular. I just wanted to see him."

"You have a key to this place?"

"Yes."

"Did Price?"

"Yes."

"Ricky sounds like a generous fellow."

"I'm not sure, but I think Jennings was paying the rent. He'd let Ricky know he was using the apartment and he'd stay away. Ricky only really used it on weekends anyway, Thursday to Sunday usually."

"What did Price use the place for, other than the obvious? Or was it just a love nest?"

"He sometimes took potential buyers there. He had it decorated with some very nice pieces."

"What kind of buyers?"

"The less-respectable sort, I suppose you'd call them."

"People who didn't particularly care where the goods came from?"

"Yes."

"Sellers too?"

"Presumably."

"You ever meet any of them?"

"No." Futrelle let out a long breath, the air fogging in front of him. "I only knew of them through Jennings."

"What time did Price leave the apartment on Monday?"

"Just after six."

"Any idea where he was going?"

"No."

"Did he have anything with him?"

"Several books."

"The ones you mentioned to me?"

"No. They were older. The bindings were cracked and one of them had a broken spine."

"Were they valuable?"

"Perhaps, but they were in very bad condition."

"Nothing else with him?"

"A manila envelope."

"Know what was in it?"

"No."

"Was he sending it or getting it?"

"Getting it. The flap had been torn open."

"Do you know where it was from?"

"I could see the seal."

"And?"

"It was from the U.S. Army Records Center in St. Louis."

"No idea what it was about?"

"No."

"Price didn't tell you?"

"No."

"The key to this place. You have it with you?"

"I beg your pardon?"

"The key. To the love nest."

"Yes."

"Give it to me."

"I don't understand."

"I want to go there, look around."

"Now?"

"Now," said Ray. "Why? You want to come with me?"

"Good Christ, no." He paused. "Don't you need a warrant?"

"Not if you give me permission. And the key."

Futrelle reached into his topcoat and took out a ring of keys on a leather holder. The enameled crest on the holder said CADILLAC. The school supervisor slid the keys around on the ring to a pair of brass Yales on a separate, short piece of wire. As he slipped the keys off the ring Ray noticed that the man's hand was shaking. Futrelle handed over the keys.

"One key's for the main door, the other's for the apartment. It's the Willowbrook complex on East University Boulevard. Building two, apartment 211."

"Just off 75."

"That's it." Futrelle nodded. Ray dropped the key into the pocket of his jacket. That close to the interstate it would be a snap for Schwager to get down for weekends. "Ricky might be there, you know," Futrelle added.

"I doubt it," Ray answered. "I think he's in mourning."

There was a pause. Futrelle jammed his hands into the pockets of his topcoat. "Is that it? Are you finished with me, Detective?"

"Unless I find out you really are a suspect in this thing, yeah, I'm finished with you, Mr. Futrelle."

"I can be assured of your discretion?"

"As much as you can be assured of anything in this world."

"Thank you."

This time it was Futrelle who held out his hand, and this time it was Ray who ignored it. "Good-bye, Mr. Futrelle." Ray turned and followed the path back toward his car. He turned once to look back and Futrelle was still standing there, staring out over the lagoon, watching the pale shapes of the swans glide back and forth across the dark water.

Ray picked up the car and found his way up through Kessler Park and Regent Park, its not-so-opulent neighbor, eventually finding an on-ramp for Interstate 30, which in turn took him back across the greenbelt and up onto Highway 75. From there it was only ten minutes up to Schwager's love nest on University Boulevard.

The buildings in the Willowbrook complex were low, modern structures, flat-roofed, with modern, angular bay windows. In many ways they were a newer, updated and considerably better maintained version of Ruby's building. Ray parked the car in front of Schwager's place, used one of the brass keys to let himself in through the glass-and-aluminum front door, then took the small elevator up to the second floor. The carpet in the corridors smelled of artificial pine scent heavy enough to make Ray sneeze. He reached

211 and let himself in without knocking. All the lights were off and there was no sign of Schwager or anyone else.

Ray switched on the lights and took a tour of the apartment. It quickly became clear that this was not the place Jennings Price had been murdered and dismembered in. The apartment was immaculate—one bedroom, floors done in glowing cherry and carpeted with antique Persian rugs. The walls were white except for the living room, which was done in robin's-egg blue. It had recently been painted, judging from the faint smell that wafted through the air. It was this room that had the large, jutting bay window. In the window, arranged on several small tables, were bouquets of multicolored roses in bloom. Touching them Ray discovered that they were artificial—silk that needed dusting rather than watering.

Half the wall space in the living room was arranged with vitrines—Victorian glass-fronted cabinets for showing off small pieces of bric-a-brac, a collection of hand-blown glass paperweights and several very expensive-looking gold and ivory reliquaries studded with small gems or pieces of colored glass.

There were two floor-to-ceiling cherry wood bookcases on the opposite wall bracketing a large oil painting of an old man in a straw hat framed in ornate gilt. A small brass plaque on the frame identified the painting as PORTRAIT OF PATIENCE ESCALIER BY VINCENT VAN GOGH–1883. Ray didn't have the faintest idea who Patience Escalier was but he knew the name van Gogh and was astounded to find a painting by him hanging in an anonymous one-bedroom apartment in north Dallas, three blocks off the freeway.

The wall facing the window was covered in smaller framed items, and taking a closer look Ray saw that they were mostly autographs and letters. Oliver Wendell Holmes to a woman named Eliza Leslie, dated December 25, 1839; a much-scratched-out letter from Thomas Jefferson recommending his friend James Monroe, dated October 5, 1781; and a long frame with three cut-out mattes holding what was identified as a complete letter on vellum from Davey Crockett to a man named John O. Cannon, dated January 20, 1834. It was all fascinating, but it wasn't what he was there for.

Ray turned back to the bookcases. Almost all the books were bound in either brown or black leather, their spines and titles engraved and decorated with gold leaf. Almost all of them were titles having to do with witchcraft or the occult, like the majority of the volumes in Price's collection. It suddenly occurred to Ray that he might have missed a lead; could the murders have something to do with the occult, some kind of voodoo/witchcraft thing? Ray took down a book called *Influenza del Magnetismo Sulla Vitae Animale.*

The leather cover, clearly not the original, was buttery smooth and soft, the title elegantly engraved in flowing script in rich gold. He ran his hand over the cover again, enjoying the warm, smooth feel of the leather, then slid it carefully back into its place on the shelf. There might be a lot of the devil's work going on in Dallas, but the thought of witches' covens and human sacrifices going back twenty-five years was a little hard to swallow.

On the other hand, a richly laid out little apartment like Schwager's, underwritten by someone like Jennings Price, could have a variety of uses; not only was it convenient for bringing "unsavory" buyers and sellers of high-end antiquities of less-than-stellar provenance, but the antiquities and art on display—like the gem-studded gold and ivory reliquaries, the van Gogh and all the rest—might be just the thing for impressing potential young conquests.

Ray went into the bedroom. It was small, with several nondescript landscapes on the walls, a chest of drawers, a bed, a reading chair and a mirror-doored cupboard that faced the bed. Opening the sliding doors he found two dozen open-necked silk shirts of every stripe and color, half a dozen pairs of neatly hung expensive knit trousers and four identical chalk-stripe suits. The floor of the cupboard was filled with a line of shoes, most of them black and some of them almost feminine-looking.

Going through the chest of drawers Ray found a jewelry box full of gold chains, intricately worked gold bracelets and several gold rings, one set with diamonds, the other two with tigereye. There were three watches, an 18k Rolex Date-just, an oversized Lange German officer's watch and another Omega Constellation, this one on 18k solid-gold Grand Luxe, one model above the one worn by Jennings Price. Out of curiosity Ray checked the back of the watch and found no inscription.

Ray went back into the living room and went to the bay window. Looking out he could see a line of fast-food restaurants and bars running down a mile-long strip of Greenville Avenue, parallel to the freeway. Schwager wouldn't have had to go far for food or liquor and god knows what else. For all he knew the whole building here was filled with queers, and maybe the bars were too.

He turned and went back to the middle of the room. In all probability this was the last place Jennings Price had been before he went off to meet his death, and unhappily, Paul Futrelle was probably the last person to see him alive.

It was easy enough to cast Futrelle as the jilted lover, as good a motive for murder as any, and it was equally easy to cast Valentine as either another jilted lover or someone bilked out of money with a forgery. Jealousy from Futrelle, revenge from Valentine, or maybe even a mob killing; Jack Ruby seemed to have threaded his way through almost every step of Ray's investigation, so maybe the seedy-looking club owner had ordered a hit for some past slight to the local bosses, like Civello and his friends. Dope maybe, or gambling debts? Who knew? All of it fit, but at the same time none of it fit at all, because none of his suspects, if that's what they really were, had anything to do with the killings from a quarter century ago, or the most recent murder of Mar'Ellen Caddo and the disappearance of little Zinnia Brant.

He suddenly decided he'd had enough for one night and headed for the front door of the apartment. He stopped at the telephone table. There was a small notepad and pencil beside the phone, but the pad was blank and there wasn't the slightest impression on the top page. He opened the drawer. Inside was a Dallas/Fort Worth phonebook. He pulled it out of the drawer, prepared to flip through it for numbers scrawled in the margins, when he saw an address book underneath it. The book had a leatherette cover with the word *Address* stamped on it in gold ink, and a tab index on the side. He flipped through it and saw that every page and line was filled with names, addresses and numbers. Some light reading over breakfast maybe. He half folded the address book and stuffed it into the pocket of his jacket and let himself out of the apartment, no farther ahead than he'd been before he dragged Paul Futrelle out of his happily married home.

He drove back the way he'd come, following Highway 75 back into the city through almost nonexistent traffic. As he got closer to the city he saw that most of the bright lights were dark, including the spotlights on the forty-foot revolving Pegasus on top of the Magnolia Building. The city was in mourning for a dead president, or maybe ashamed of his murder and hiding from his ghost.

Ray had so little energy left his eyes were drooping as he drove, but he knew he had one last errand to run before he found his rest. He took the Webb Street exit and made his way across to Vickery Boulevard and R. T.'s place. He pulled up across the street and checked his watch. Just past eleven. He got out of the car, crossed the street and looked in through the gate. R. T.'s Corvette was parked in front of the main door. Ray found the intercom button for the gate and pressed it, repeating R. T.'s initials in Morse code. A long minute later the gates swung open. Ray walked up the walk and casually put his hand on the Corvette's hood as he went by. Not hot, but definitely warm. He eased himself up the steps, using the handrail to keep his woody legs from betraying him. By the time he reached the door R. T. had it open. He was wearing slippers, a dark red silk dressing gown, smoking a cigarette and had a bottle of Jax in his hand.

"That for me?" Ray asked.

"My nightcap. Helps me to sleep."

"Since when did you need booze to help you get to sleep?" Ray smiled as sincerely as he could. "What's the matter, guilty conscience or something?"

"The only thing I feel guilty about is using beer to help me get to sleep. This is the sixties. I should be using that Valium stuff *Time* magazine had that article on a while back." He stepped away from the door. "Come on in."

"No, thanks. Just came by to make sure you were all right."

"Why wouldn't I be all right, Ray?"

"I called. There was no answer."

"A guy can't go out on the town without his friends worrying?"

"Is that where you were, out on the town?"

"As a matter of fact, no, Ray, I was right here, drinking beer, reading a new book."

"What book was that, R. T.?"

"It's called *One Day in the Life of Ivan Denisovich* by a guy named Alexander Solzhenitsyn."

"Russian?"

"That's right, Ray, I'm a secret commie." He took a drag on his cigarette. "What's with the interrogation?"

"I told you, I was worried."

"Well, I'm fine. You can go to bed knowing that your friend spent a quiet evening with a book, not getting himself into trouble, which is probably more than I can say for you, since you look like complete shit."

"Just a little tired."

His friend spoke gently. "Then go to bed, Ray, or come in and have a couple of beers, and sleep it off in the guest room."

"Maybe I'll drop by tomorrow, we can have a proper visit."

"Won't be here tomorrow."

"Where you going?"

"Piney woods, the bottoms. Crack of dawn. Just like I said you and I should do. Taking my own good advice."

"How long you be gone?"

"As long as it takes, Ray." He smiled. "Now go to bed."

"All right," said Ray. "Good night, R. T."

"'Night, Ray."

Odum closed the door and Ray went back down the steps to the gate. He went through, then crossed the street to his car. His friend had lied to him about going out, and that probably meant it was him that Ray had seen at Ruby's, but for the life of him Ray couldn't see why. He slid in behind the wheel of the Chevy and started the engine. It was late, his brain was turning to porridge and it felt as though he didn't know about anything anymore. He swung the car into a U-turn, heading back to the freeway and home.

She was asleep in his bed when he got there.

"How did you get in?"

"Some detective. You told me where the key was, re-member?"

He didn't, but it didn't matter. It only mattered that she was there.

"I've just got to go to the bathroom," he said.

She smiled up at him and put her hands behind her head. "That's okay, I'm not going anywhere."

He smiled back, took off his jacket and hung it over the chair and then went into the bathroom. He tried not to look at himself in the mirror, bending over the sink and splashing cold water on his face. He brushed his teeth and then unbuttoned his shirt. He opened the medicine chest and took out a can of Redi-Spray, but then he remembered that it stung his armpits so he splashed on some bay rum instead. He ran his fingers through his hair, smoothing it back, then rubbed a palm across his cheek and chin. Bristled, but not too badly; another side effect of the disease that was killing him—his beard grew at half the speed it had before.

He went back into the bedroom, hung his shoulder rig over the chair, then took off his shirt and pants, sitting on the edge of the bed. He stripped off his socks and dropped back onto the bed beside her.

She put a hand on his chest and sniffed delicately at the armpit closest to her. "My hairy teddy bear has become a fruity teddy bear."

"Oh jeez, don't talk to me about fruits. I spent the whole day with them."

"Okay, no fruits."

"I didn't expect to see you."

"I knew I'd see you eventually if I played Goldilocks and climbed into your bed."

"I'm glad you did."

"Long day?"

"Confusing day."

"Nobody's talking about anything else except Kennedy," said Rena. "It's spooky. You walk down the street and pick up these little bits of conversation and it's always about Kennedy, or Jackie, or Oswald. It's like it's not over. It's like it's never going to be over."

"A curse on Dallas."

"Something like that."

There was a small silence and then Ray spoke tightly. "I feel like I'm in the middle of something I don't understand."

"I don't get it," Rena answered. She let her fingers trail down the thick line of hair on Ray's belly to the elastic waistband of his Jockeys.

"I'm sick. I'm dying, remember I told you?"

"Yes."

"I haven't said anything about this to anyone."

"You don't have to say anything to me if you don't want to. You hardly know me."

"No," said Ray. "I want to tell you."

"So tell."

"I'm dying, and it's like I see things very clearly, the individual parts, the colors, the shapes, but it's like I'm not seeing the whole thing. I can't put it together."

"You mean this case you were telling me about, the little girls?"

"That's part of it, but it's my whole life, everything. I keep on trying to figure out how I fit into it all, and I can't quite see." He was talking quickly now and he couldn't stop himself. "It's like I knew all of this was going to happen, I even knew the Kennedy thing was going to happen, but I didn't believe it because I couldn't do anything about it, and I can't do anything about those little girls either. I thought I was afraid of dying, but it's not that, it's that I'm afraid I'm going to die and when I do, if I haven't figured it all out, all those souls are going to die with me. As though they're all my responsibility. It's as if I can see it all, but it's all too late. Like second sight that serves no purpose." He shrugged. "I'm not the superstitious type, but lately it's the way I've been feeling, way deep under things. I guess it sounds stupid to you."

"It doesn't sound stupid," said Rena. She pushed her head under his chin. "My momma even had a name for it, that feeling people have when they're close to dying. She called it the wisdom of the bones."

"Now you're the one starting to sound spooky."

"Maybe I can do something about that." Rena pushed her fingers under the elastic and into the tangle of his pubic hair.

"I'm not making any promises," Ray warned.

"I'm not asking for any," she said and turned and kissed him softly on the mouth.

That night he dreamed about the painting that hung in Rose Cottage but in his dream he was actually standing in the painting itself, the feel of the sandy loam of the roadway down to the water hot between his toes. His little brother was already in the boat with his fishing rod and Daddy was pushing off and no matter how loudly Ray called out to them, he couldn't make his father wait. Finally, the Old Man pushed the boat away from the ragged shore, started up the outboard and headed down the lake, his back to Ray, deaf to his desperate cries.

11/24/63
SUNDAY

Chapter 21

When Ray woke up the following morning Rena was gone, having left a note taped to the refrigerator asking him to give her a call, either at home or at Inky's later in the day. She'd left him a percolator full of coffee on the back burner of the stove, and after a half cup standing over the sink he headed for the bathroom and a shower. Instead of just his feet, the needle spray of the shower stung almost everywhere it landed now.

Stepping out of the cubicle he toweled off and hazily saw himself full length in the mirror on the back of the door. He stared at himself, transfixed. Usually the thickness of his legs seemed to be at its least noticeable first thing in the morning, but this time it hadn't receded at all. His belly was sagging as well, his navel pulled down to an obscene little slit nestled among his thick black body hair.

He stepped closer to the mirror, rubbing away the haze with the palm of his hand, and looked at the rising worm of his carotid artery, raised and visible now almost up to the bottom of his earlobe. His doctor had told him that the carotid was like a thermometer—the higher it went, the closer you were to absolute heart failure. For the first time

Ray dared to actually put his second finger onto the twisted cord of his flesh, feeling the rapid, stuttering pulse as his racing heart took him beat by beat toward his grave. He pushed the towel over his face, breathing hot breath into it, reminding himself that for now at least he was a living, breathing human being.

Throwing the towel over the shower curtain bar, Ray picked up his old Norelco Double Header and ran it automatically over the crags and creases of his cheeks and chin. For a second he found himself wondering what someone like Rena saw in him, then he switched off the razor, leaning over the sink and supporting himself with both hands. He'd spent the night with her twice, and they both seemed to have enjoyed the experience, and yet here he was being a cop and thinking about motives. Maybe she didn't have a motive beyond simply liking him, or would it be just too goddamned strange for a pretty woman to take a shine to someone like him? On the other hand, lady luck sure as hell hadn't been shining her headlights in his direction lately. He pushed the whole thing out of his mind, straightened up and finished shaving.

With all that done he went back to the bedroom, threw on his old tattered terry-cloth robe and collected the address book he'd found at Schwager's love nest and his own notebook. He took them both back to the kitchen, switched on the dowdy old Emerson 541 he kept on the counter tuned to KRLD and poured himself a second cup of coffee. This morning, instead of talking about Kennedy, they were going on endlessly about Oswald, who was apparently going to be transferred from the holding cells at HQ to County, a few blocks away. Ray switched the radio off and sat down at the kitchen table. Maybe getting him out of the station would ease the congestion in the corridors and everyone could get back to work.

Ray opened up his notebook to a clean page, noting the date, then flipped back through his previous notes. It still didn't amount to a whole hell of a lot, but he transferred the whole thing under the new date and then added a few more lines to his list.

PINOCCHIO
TIME
CARE
PETER PAN
PLANNED
OLD LAMP
CORVAN
ARTS & MONUMENTS
OLD BOOKS
OLD PAINTINGS
OLD LETTERS
SCHWAGER
RUBY
ARMY RECORDS CENTER
KIDNAP
KOOP

Ray stared at the list, then took his pencil and began re-arranging things into blocks of information that seemed to go together, striking out "Pinocchio" because he was reasonably sure it had no real relevance except as to the method behind the murderer's madness, and occasionally underlining another word:

~~PINOCCHIO~~
TIME, CARE, PLANNED, <u>PAST</u>
<u>OLD LAMP</u>, OLD BOOKS, OLD PAINTINGS,
OLD LETTERS
ARTS AND MONUMENTS: SCHWAGER, PRICE,
VALENTINE, <u>KOOP ARMY RECORDS CENTER</u>
<u>PAST</u> AND PRESENT: KIDNAP, MURDER, CORVAN

Ray looked down at his new list and tried to connect the dots. Less than an hour before she was kidnapped, Lucille Edmonds had told her brother about an old fringed lamp she'd seen, but where? Not the school, because her brother, Marcus, would have known the lamp she was talking about, and not Mrs. Pinkers's place for the same reason. At the time Ray had been more interested in the man who drove the hearse for Todmorden's Funeral Home, but now he remembered something else Marcus Edmonds had said. Ray had asked about who'd gone by that day and Marcus had mentioned the junk man. A junk man might have had an old fringed lamp in his truck and a junk man might have made a promise to that little girl about making sure that she got that lamp she liked so much. A junk man who traveled a regular route from town to town, picking through garbage dumps for abandoned treasures. A man who could take the time to plan his conquests, a man barely noticed as he drove the back roads of the northern counties. A man who might have come upon all sorts of antiques, even the occasional old book or painting. Excited now, Ray flipped through the pages of his notebook and found the telephone number he'd jotted down for Amanda Pinkers. He looked at his watch; just past eight; early, but not too early, especially for a little old lady with arthritis who probably didn't sleep well. He went out to the hall and got the operator to make the long-distance call. It rang five times and then he heard the woman's cracked, dry voice.

"Yes?"

"Mrs. Pinkers?"

"Who else would it be? This is my telephone and I'm the only one here."

"It's Ray Duval, Mrs. Pinkers. You remember me?"

"Of course. The policeman who was asking about Lucille."

"That's right. I said I might want to ask you some more questions."

"Then ask."

"Marcus Edmonds mentioned a junk man who traveled in your area."

"There have been several over the years. These days they seem to be interested in automobile parts. Tires and such."

"In the past, Mrs. Pinkers. Around the time Lucille was murdered. Was there a regular junk man that you can recall?"

"Certainly."

"Can you recall his name?"

"DiMaggio, like the baseball player who married that unfortunate movie star."

"Do you recall a first name?"

"Martino. He was Italian, of course."

"What do you remember about him?"

"Very little. He often smelled, either of the dump or of wine. I would say he was almost certainly a heavy drinker."

"Do you remember how old he was?"

"Specifically? No. He never mentioned his age." She paused. "I would say that he was in his sixties or seventies. He had a large stomach and very little hair. What he did have was snow white. He had bad teeth and equally bad breath."

Ray's spirits slumped. Martino DiMaggio was obviously not his man. "You're sure about his age?"

"Certainly." She paused again. "Of course, his assistant was much younger."

"Assistant?"

"Yes. From time to time Mr. DiMaggio was too drunk to drive his pickup, so his assistant did. The boy sometimes even covered the old man's route without him, especially toward the end."

"End?"

"Mr. DiMaggio died in 1939. January, I believe." Just when the murders stopped.

"How old was this boy?"

"Eighteen or nineteen. Quite a pleasant-looking young man, dark hair, strong hands. What we used to call a pianist's hands."

"Do you recall his name?"

"Certainly. William Cooper, but—"

He saw it in a clear bright light, just like Rena had said the night before—the wisdom of the bones. "Everyone called him Coop," said Ray.

"That's right," said Mrs. Pinkers. "How on earth did you know?"

"Just a guess."

Koop.

"Shit!"

"I beg your pardon?"

"Sorry, Mrs. Pinkers." He thanked her for her help and hung up. William Cooper had traveled up and down those back roads with old man DiMaggio like a smokescreen all around him. It was DiMaggio's junk business and no one really cared about them one way or the other. The police were looking for a solitary killer, not the young assistant who sat beside the junk man. William Cooper, the one everyone called Coop, would mark his victims, and when the old man was too drunk to make his route, Coop would make his move.

Ray went back to the kitchen and his list. He crossed out and underlined until he was sure of what he had.

~~PINOCCHIO~~

~~TIME, CARE, PLANNED, PAST~~

~~OLD LAMP, OLD BOOKS, OLD PAINTINGS, OLD LETTERS~~

ARTS AND MONUMENTS: SCHWAGER, PRICE, VALENTINE, WILLIAM COOPER KOOP

ARMY RECORDS CENTER

~~PAST AND PRESENT: KIDNAP, MURDER, CORVAN~~

William Cooper and Koop were one and the same. And somehow Jennings Price had uncovered his secret and written or called the Army Records Center in St. Louis to confirm his suspicions. He'd left his assignation with Futrelle and gone to meet his death at Cooper's hands. It all seemed to fit the facts, or at least his personal theory of events. Personal theories, however, were about as far from evidence as a cop could get, at least when it came to making a case to the district attorney's office.

Not that Henry Monasco Wade would give him the time of day anyway; he was an ambitious politician, a schoolmate of Connally's and he was going to try to ride this poor son of a bitch Oswald into the governor's mansion all on his own. He wasn't going to have time for Ray Duval with less than a week before his ticket got punched and a harebrained story about a lunatic who went around killing little nigger girls; no votes there, and fewer votes still if he threw Paul Futrelle into the Mixmaster. Ray glanced at his watch. Almost nine o'clock now, and on a Sunday. It was bad timing but he had to get some kind of help from Fritz, and at the very least he could use the sheriff's directory at the office to try and find out if William Cooper had any kind of record in the northern counties back in the 1930s.

Ray suddenly had another bright idea, prompted by the list. He took his notebook back to the telephone in the hall and called Douglas Valentine at his home number.

"It's Duval."

"Detective, I'm just watching the preparations for Mr. Oswald's transfer to the County Jail on television combined with Mr. Cronkite's description of Mr. Kennedy's coffin being taken from the White House. An odd juxtaposition to say the least. These are terrible times, Detective."

Even worse for Zinnia Brant if he didn't do something soon. "Quick question for you, Mr. Valentine."

"Certainly."

"Koop."

"What about him?"

"Did you know his actual name?"

"Of course. William Cooper."

"Out at Schwager's place in Blackstone, Schwager said that Jennings Price liked hiring local boys."

"I remember."

"How local was Cooper?"

"Lubbock, I think. Or Decatur. One of the two." There was a pause. "That it?"

"One more thing."

"Yes."

"The Arts and Monuments group . . ."

"Monuments, Fine Arts and Archives, Detective Duval. MFA and A."

"Okay."

"What about them?"

"A lot of army units have associations, the Rangers, the marines have half a dozen, most divisions have them."

"And you're wondering about the fairies in Monuments and Fine Arts?"

"You said it, not me."

"Yes, there is an organization. Sort of an alumni group. It was a pretty small bunch."

"Is there a secretary, or a treasurer or someone I could get in touch with on a Sunday?"

"Jannie."

"A woman?"

Valentine laughed. "Hardly. Jan van Plaut."

"German?"

"Dutch. He spoke just about every European language you could think of. He'd been a curator at the Rijksmuseum before the Nazis invaded, and when we came along he was working for the Rijksbureau voor de Monumentenzord or something of the sort. And he was no fairy."

"I'm supposed to call him in Amsterdam?"

"No, no," said Valentine. "He emigrated after the war. He's a director of the Addison Gallery of American Art in Andover, Mass. Teaches at the Phillips Academy. Dutch Masters."

Ray had never heard of either the Addison Gallery of American Art or the Phillips Academy. "You have a number for him?"

He did, both home and office. When a woman answered the home number, presumably Mrs. van Plaut, she told him Jannie was at his office. Her accent was as broadly Boston as Kennedy's had been. Clearly Jan van Plaut had married an American after the war. Ray called van Plaut's office and got through on the fifth or sixth ring. The connection was poor and Ray felt as though he was shouting down a well.

"Where did you say you were calling from?" Van Plaut's accent was flat, formal and mid-Atlantic, the voice of a man who'd learned English at school or from a stack of Berlitz records.

"Dallas," Ray answered, and for the first time he heard the cold, hesitant reaction to the name of his city.

"I see. And you are a detective." The academic liked to repeat everything for himself, as though fixing it in his mind.

"Right. Douglas Valentine gave me your name and number."

"You are investigating a murder."

"Yes."

"I would have thought that the Dallas Police Department would have other concerns at the moment." The tone was like a winter wind.

"I'm working on this alone, Mr. van Plaut, and I'm running out of time."

"Correct me if I am wrong, but if this is a case of murder, then the victim is already dead and time is no longer of any concern to him."

"This victim isn't dead, yet, or I hope she isn't. She's a twelve-year-old girl, Mr. van Plaut."

"I'm sorry, I did not know. I am presently immersed in writing a book comparing the themes of Winslow Homer to those of several Dutch Masters. It takes up a great deal of my concentration."

"I'd just like to ask you a few questions."

"Hopefully I will be able to give you the answers you are looking for."

"Do you remember a man named William Cooper? A member of the MFA and A unit like yourself?"

"Yes. Although to be truly accurate Coop was never actually a member of the unit."

"How did he become attached?"

"I have no idea. Jennings Price simply appeared with him one day. Said he was good with books and documents."

"Did he wear a uniform?"

"Yes. That of an infantry corporal."

"Can you remember the unit he was with?"

"Just let me wander in my memory for a moment," said the Dutchman. There was a long echoing silence. "Eighty-second Airborne," he answered at last.

"So how does someone from the Eighty-second Airborne wind up with an art unit?"

"According to J. P. . . ."

"Jennings Price?"

"Yes. According to Jennings he had been seconded by the Art Looting Investigation Unit."

"This was part of your Monuments and Fine Arts people?"

"No, no!" van Plaut answered. "Most definitely not. ALIU were part of the Office of Strategic Services. We were under the umbrella of Army G2 Intelligence."

"Cooper was in the OSS?" Christ, now we've got the CIA involved, thought Ray.

"I do not think he was actually with them per se, Detective. He was just extremely good with books and documents. He could tell vellum from paper at a glance and had an intimate, expert knowledge of the structure of books and how to fix them, sometimes invisibly. That's what he was doing at Alt Aussee for the Art Looting unit — repairing damage to books and documents."

"So Price stole him away?"

"It wasn't difficult. From what Jennings told me, Coop was not well liked."

"Why not?"

"With the exception of an officer from the Naval Intelligence Department who tended to day-to-day operations, the ALIU was entirely made up of academics. Theodore Rousseau from the National Gallery of Art, Lane Faison from Williams College, John Phillips from Yale. Coop had one of your Texas drawls and no formal education. They looked down on him. He was something of an idiot savant, I think."

"Like someone who can play Mozart on the piano two-handed but can't wipe his own ass, right?"

"Something like that, but Cooper was certainly not so . . . extreme. He seemed perfectly capable of dealing with his own bodily functions, for example."

"So you guys didn't mind him?"

"He did his job and he did it very well. Much of the time he kept himself to himself, but he was always personable and friendly."

"Schwager said he disappeared in Berlin."

"That's right. Both our group and the Art Looting Investigation Unit were there simultaneously. That was late July of 1945, shortly after the end of hostilities. The Russians were stealing everything they could get their hands on; we tried to save what we could. That's when Cooper had his unfortunate accident."

"Accident?"

"He had talked to someone who told him that they knew where there was a cache of rare books from the State Library, including a Schrifft Bible from the fourteenth century and a copy of Cavalieri's *Portraits of the Roman Pontiffs*."

"Valuable?"

"Worth millions, even then. Virtually priceless."

"So he went off to fetch them and never came back?"

"No. He went off to fetch them and was murdered."

"He's dead?"

"Without a doubt," said van Plaut. "He was found by the local MPs the following day in the ruins of the Nollendorf-platz Theater in the Shoneberg District. Someone had covered Mr. Cooper's body with debris and set fire to it. The body was badly burned but he was easy enough to identify apparently."

Ray saw his entire theory spinning down the toilet bowl. William Cooper might well have been killing little children in the thirties but he wasn't killing them now, or knocking off Jennings Price either. He thanked van Plaut for his help, then let the art historian get back to his Dutch Masters.

He still wasn't willing to let go of the theory entirely; too many of the pieces fit. He decided to get dressed and go down to headquarters. Somebody would be in the County Sheriff's Offices up in Lubbock and Decatur, and maybe one of them had information about William Cooper that would point the way to a living killer instead of a dead one.

Chapter 22

Ray dressed in pants and a white shirt, threw on his shoulder rig and shrugged into his tweed jacket. He pushed his swollen feet painfully into his old loafers, then went back to the kitchen, where he picked up Schwager's address book and stuffed it in his jacket pocket. Before leaving the house he switched on the TV for a minute. Every station was showing the same thing: the President's flag-draped coffin heading down Pennsylvania Avenue to lie in state under the Capitol Dome and shots from inside and outside headquarters as they waited for Oswald to be transferred over to County Jail. Ray switched off the TV and left the house. If he was lucky he'd arrive after all the fuss was over.

He spent the ten-minute drive thinking about William Cooper and his friends, especially Jennings Price. Why had Price been carrying an envelope from the Army Records Center? With Cooper dead, whose records would he have been searching and why? The only thing Ray could come up with was that perhaps Price knew who Cooper was going to meet that night, and somehow managed to get hold of the supposedly priceless books, the Bible and the book of papal portraits. Maybe Price had been lurking in the ruins of the

Nollendorfplatz Theater that night, and perhaps he had seen Cooper's murder.

Jump ahead eighteen years to the present and suddenly Price runs into Cooper's murderer and starts to blackmail him, or is simply killed for recognizing the man. A new dealer in town, or perhaps a new client. But if that was the case, why would Price's killer be running around kidnapping little girls like Zinnia Brant? It was the continuing bugbear about the case—making the past line up with the present.

When he got to headquarters the Commerce Street ramp was blocked by an armored car, presumably to carry Oswald, or more likely to act as a very visible decoy as well as completely block off that entrance to the basement. There were two uniforms walking back and forth in front of the heavy-jawed vehicle and a scattering of reporters. Ray kept on going, turned left on South Pearl, then turned left again on Main Street. Halfway down the block he turned down the Main Street ramp entrance to headquarters, waving at the pair of uniforms and flashing his badge.

He slowed at the stop sign painted on the floor at the base of the ramp and honked his horn a couple of times to get the crush of reporters to move out of the way so he could park. As he turned left into the basement level of the garage he waved again, this time at a detective friend from Robbery Division, Rio Pierce, who was piloting a black unmarked car out of the lot and up the ramp.

Ray parked the Bel Air and sat behind the wheel for a moment. He realized he'd picked just about the worst possible time to arrive at headquarters. There appeared to be at least fifty uniforms and more than twenty Stetson-wearing detectives in a human corridor that led from the jail office door to the foot of the ramp. Behind the cops there were a

dozen film and TV cameras with their lights as well as another thirty or forty reporters and technicians. It was a zoo,
and it meant that the jail elevator was going to be tied up.
That in turn meant he'd have to use the basement stairs to
get up to the first floor and the main elevator bunk, or sit and
wait it out. He decided to wait it out and rolled down his
window.

He glanced at the clock on the dash in the dim light and
wondered how long he'd have to wait. It was 11:20. He'd
managed to find a parking spot between a DPD paddy
wagon and a cherry-top Ford Custom cruiser, which gave
him a perfect view of the scuttling mass of humanity focused on the door leading out from the jail office. He leaned
back in his seat to enjoy the show and at the same moment
he was startled to hear a car horn echoing from somewhere
behind him. It wasn't the sound so much as the methodical
sound of it: short, short, long, short. There was no mistaking
it—dot, dot, dash, dot. Morse code for the letter *F*. The
only people he knew who even used Morse code anymore
were him and R. T. to announce their arrival at one another's
homes, something they'd been doing for years. He turned
around in his seat and peered out through the rear windshield, almost expecting to see Odum's banana-yellow
Corvette, but it wasn't there.

Ray turned again as an expectant rumble of voices came
from the reporters. He looked out the windshield and saw
that the lights from the cameras were all focused on a group
of figures coming out the door that led back to the jail office
and the elevator. One of them was Fritz, his craggy, jowled
face serious and his Stetson pulled low. Behind him, and
towering above the homicide captain, was Leavelle, also
wearing a Stetson, handcuffed to a much shorter man who
Ray vaguely recognized as Lee Harvey Oswald. It was hard

to believe that a skinny little pissant like him could have killed the president of the United States and then pumped a street cop like Tippit full of bullets. He looked more like a janitor in a high school, or give him a few more years and he's "Peachy," driving an elevator in some government building.

Somebody in the crowd yelled out "There he is!" and all hell broke loose as the pack of reporters and camera people surged forward, bathing the whole area around the jail office door with blinding light. Suddenly, out of nowhere, hidden by the glare of lights, a short dark figure in a fedora pushed through the throng of press men, his arm extended. From the first movement of his locked forearm Ray knew who he was and what he was going to do.

"Jack," he said softly, staring in horror. "Jack Ruby, you son of a bitch, you're going to kill him."

Ray had his hand on the door handle but it was far too late. There was a single hard familiar popping sound. A .38 Police Special. Oswald grabbed his guts, dragging Leavelle's shackled hand toward his belly and staining the detective's jacket sleeve bloody red. A dark green car, probably the one they were really going to use to transport Oswald, hit the mobster in the back of the legs and thumped him down on the floor of the garage before he could get off another shot.

A split second after that Lou Graves from Homicide and Billy Combest from Vice dropped down on Ruby, Graves pulling the handgun away from Ruby and turning it away out of his reach. People were yelling loudly and milling around but Ray could clearly see Leavelle down on his knees beside Oswald, still handcuffed to him. His hat was tipped back on his head and the detective was looking around wildly, trying to make himself heard over the roar of the crowd all around him.

"An ambulance! Let's get an ambulance here!"

The car that was supposed to take Oswald to County went rocketing up the Main Street ramp and away and Ray watched as Ruby was hustled back through the jail office door with half a dozen detectives in tow, a phalanx of uniformed cops stopping the news and TV people from following. For the first time it occurred to Ray that he had actually witnessed a homicide in his life and a moment later he realized that it was almost certainly the first murder ever broadcast on network television.

For some strange reason he felt tears welling up in his eyes at the simple awfulness of what he'd just seen and the things preceding it. It was as though the killing of the President was just the first ripple in the pool and this was the next, both inevitably leading to a new world where this kind of violence was the rule and not the exception anymore— an America that would be changed forever.

A pale green O'Neal's ambulance backed down the Main Street ramp, siren wailing and bubble light twirling. Two men got out, opened the tailgate of the slightly remodeled Ford wagon and pulled out a collapsible stretcher. The crowd of reporters and cops parted before them and a moment later they came back out of the crowd with Oswald on a stretcher, one hand dangling and dragging on the ground. The two men loaded the stretcher into the back of the wagon, climbed into the front seat, then went tearing back up the ramp, siren screaming, followed by a tattered line of cops and reporters.

Within five minutes of the shooting the basement was almost completely empty. No one was making any effort to block off any area as a potential crime scene. It was as though nothing had happened at all. The body had been removed, the perpetrator taken to jail, the evidence of his crime so overwhelming that nothing else needed to be done. Ray knew the shot was fatal from the instant he heard the gun firing. A .38 fired point-blank into Oswald's mid-chest from that angle would have ripped through every major organ in the man's body, including heart and lungs. Oswald might not be officially dead, but he soon would be, and if Ray knew Chief Curry and Captain Fritz, that would be the end of any real investigation into the assassination of John F. Kennedy. Dallas would do its time in purgatory silently, but it would also do its time with a suspect apprehended in minutes, and the suspect's executioner in less time than that. Curry and Fritz would assume they might endure a lot of ribbing about letting a prisoner get shot while he was handcuffed to one cop and surrounded by a hundred more, but maybe that wasn't so bad compared to being the focus of a trial that might go on for months, if not years.

Staring out into the empty, now-silent garage where murder had just been done, Ray knew that Curry and the captain would be wrong in their assessment of what lay ahead. Ruby's single shot had turned Oswald from a suspected killer into a myth, and myths, as Ray Duval well knew, had a tendency to last forever. A million questions would be asked by a million people and would remain unanswered. Years would pass, decades perhaps, and the mystery would endure.

Ray smiled thinly, thinking about the myth of his own life, the myth of sitting with his nonexistent grandchildren, telling them the story of how he'd actually been there and seen the blood on Jackie's suit, seen the President's blood and brains leaking into his makeshift plastic shroud, seen Jack Ruby lunge forward into the TV lights and history, putting a single shot into Lee Harvey Oswald and starting a never-ending story with an infinite number of good guys and bad guys, beginnings, middles and endless endings.

Ray finally climbed out of the Bel Air, locked it and walked out of the lot and up onto the ramp. He crossed the spot where Oswald had been shot and took a quick look, noting that there was no blood on the floor, probably meaning that there had been no exit wound. Ray stopped where he was and thought for a moment. Unless it had hit bone, Oswald's spine maybe, a .38 fired from that range should have gone right through him. Ray reached into his jacket and took out the bullet he'd picked up off the floor at Parkland on the day of the assassination. Definitely a rifle round, but smaller than he'd originally thought and unjacketed. What if Ruby had been using the same kind of ammunition, a "sabot," as it was called, where a smaller caliber, unjacketed bullet was fitted into a larger casing; such a bullet was lighter, would travel faster and would do a great deal more damage as it tumbled through the meat of the intended target.

He put the Parkland bullet back into his pocket, went through the entrance to the jail office and rode the elevator up to Homicide. This time he took his chances and bullied his way through the crowd of reporters, nodded to the two uniforms standing guard at the door and then stepped into Homicide-Robbery for the first time in days. There was no sign of either Ruby or Curry but Leavelle, his long horse face still looking shocked and horrified by what had just happened, was tagging some evidence at his desk, including Ruby's gun. As Ray had assumed it was a .38 Police Special, in this case a Colt Cobra Hammerless. Leavelle was handling the weapon carelessly, not paying any attention where he put his fingers.

"Karl been over it yet, Jimmy?" Karl Knight was the head of the DPD fingerprint section.

Leavelle answered with a sour look on his face. "Naw, and I got a suspicion he ain't never going to go over it. Who needs fingerprints when you got ten or twelve million witnesses on TV?"

"I didn't see Carl Day or any of his people down in the basement either. Shouldn't there be some kind of crime scene perimeter or something?"

Jimmy Leavelle's tone was bitter. "Well, it's funny, you know, Ray. We get the President killed and there's about a thousand cops running around with their big goddamn shoes messing everything up, and today there's a guy shot right there on TV with my goddamn hand cuffed to him and there's no crime scene there either, because we just know what we're doing so well that we don't need people to pick up bullet casings or mark things up right, or maybe even interview a few people about where they were when the gun went off, or who that fool was who jumped in and started giving the poor bastard artificial respiration after he's been shot in the belly and the chest and probably has both his lungs shot through."

"Missed that," Ray paused. "Where's Ruby now?"

"Up on five in his underwear. What do they expect, he's got a machine gun shoved down the back of his fat-ass pants?"

"Can I see the gun?"

"Sure." Leavelle looped the tag through the trigger guard of the handgun and gave it to Ray. He popped open the cylinder and emptied it into his hand. There were five live rounds that looked like standard Remington-Peters 158-grain loads. The empty shell casing was a Remington-Peters .38 as well, but the neck of the brass had been crimped as though to take a different bullet. Ray reloaded the gun and was in the process of handing it back to Leavelle when Fritz came out of his office, smacking the door against the wall behind him, the venetian blinds clattering.

"Just what the fuck do y'all think you're doing, Duval?"

"Looking at Jack Ruby's gun."

"This your case, Duval?"

"No, sir."

"Well then what the fuck are you handling evidence for?"

"Ruby's part of my case."

"No, Jack Ruby is fucking well not part of your case, Detective. In fact as far as you're concerned you don't have a fucking case, you understand me."

"No, sir. I don't understand you, because I do have a case."

"Bunch of little nigra girls killed way back when that nobody gives two shits in the wringer about and I've got the fucking crime of the century on my hands. You know that, Detective Duval, they're calling this the crime of the century in the newspapers. Used to be the Lindbergh baby back in New Jersey but now it's the fucking crime of the century, Duval, and I don't care about your little nigras, and I don't care about some dead queerboy chopped up in a refrigerator. What I do care about is the fact that Lee goddamn-his-fucking-eyes Harvey Oswald is probably dying up to Parkland right this minute and all I got to show for it is some Jewboy strip club owner who thinks he's fucking Al Capone or something *and* I got the world thinking' this good ol' boy is personally responsible for arranging Dallas as the best place in the world to kill the president of these United States, so I don't need any crap from you about nigger babies, Detective Duval, and in the middle of all this I most certainly do not like being given personal shit by Mayor Earle Cabell about why one of my detectives was going around slandering one of his school supervisors. *Now* do you understand me, Detective?"

"Yes, sir, I suppose I do."

"No more cases. You're on medical leave. You're going to go to your checkup next week and you're going to be given a meritorious discharge from the Dallas Police Department with a recommendation for a full disability pension and a bonus for early retirement. How does that sound, Ray?"

"Just peachy, sir."

Fritz's eyes went to little slits behind his black glasses and his heavy lips flattened out. "You backtalkin' me, Detective Duval?"

"No, sir," said Ray. "You want me to, I'll come right out and say it."

"Suit yourself."

"You got Lee Harvey Oswald bleeding to death at Parkland and I've got one of your so-called nigger babies who might just still be alive. If I can find her in time I might just be able to stop some crazy bastard from tearing her little body apart and ripping off pieces of her skin before he wires her head back onto her shoulders, which part we don't know is if he fucks her in the mouth *before* he cuts her head off or *after*, so you can just go fuck yourself, Captain."

Fritz stared at Ray for a long moment, his hands visibly shaking. Then he turned and went back into his office, slamming the door behind him.

"Man's under a lot of pressure," said Jim Leavelle.

"So am I."

"Always thought the phrase 'he went white as a sheet' was just a saying. Now I've seen it for myself."

"Cap'n's got all sorts of experience with sheets and going white from what I hear."

"Careful," Leavelle cautioned, looking around the room. "No way to talk in this place."

"Ask me if I really give a shit, Jimmy; one of the benefits of my condition—having absolutely nothing to lose."

Chapter 23

Leaving the squad room, Ray turned left down the hall, pushing through a thinning crowd of reporters, and took the regular elevator in the lobby up to the fourth floor and the Records Bureau. Normally the big room would have been full of clerks and stenographers but on a Sunday the only person there was a patrolman manning the front information desk. Slaughter, the captain who ran the bureau, was nowhere to be seen.

The patrolman at the desk was reading a copy of *Time*. He put the magazine down on the counter as Ray stepped up.

"Hep you?"

"Maybe. I'd like to know if you have a jacket on a guy named William Cooper."

"Probably more than one," said the patrolman without moving.

"DOB maybe around 1918, '19."

"Heps." The patrolman turned away and drifted back among the endless rows of filing cabinets. He was a third of the way back before he hit the C's. He slid open a cabinet, rummaged, checked a file, slid it back in, checked a second file, slid it back in and finally came up with a third. He pulled it out and brought it up to the counter. He flipped open the file. "One arrest. Public drunkenness and aggravated assault. Charges were dropped when the person bringing the charges discovered that your man had just enlisted with the Citizens' Military Training Corps at Fort Bragg."

"What was the date?"

"December fifteenth, 1938." Escaping into the army where he'd never be noticed.

"He have a driver's license?"

"Yep."

"Registered where?"

"Dundee. Denton County." Less than an hour's drive.

"Is there a mug shot?"

"Sure."

"Can I borrow it?"

"Of course not. Gotta stay with the file, Detective, you know that."

"Anybody ask for this file since December 1938?"

The patrolman checked the yellowing log sheet pasted to the front of the file folder. "Nope."

"They likely to in the near future?"

The patrolman shrugged. "You did."

"I need the mug shot." Ray pulled his wallet out of his back pocket and laid a five-dollar bill on the counter. It vanished into the patrolman's breast pocket.

"I'm going for a leak," said the patrolman. "I piss quick, so I won't be long."

"I'll hold down the fort."

"Y'all do that," said the patrolman. He pushed the file to one side of the counter, opened the flap and went to the door. He opened it, paused, then turned, frowning slightly.

"This doesn't have anything to do with the Kennedy thing, does it?"

"No."

"Well, that's one good thing anyway. Don't want nothing more to do with that shit. Sticks to you like flicked snot. Damn Secret Service and FBI and anyone else with a badge damn near emptied out the O filing cabinet yesterday. Few others too."

"Nothing to do with me," said Ray. "I swear."

"Then that's okay at least."

The patrolman sauntered out of the room, letting the door swing shut behind him. Ray took out his notebook and went through the file quickly, jotting down Cooper's date of birth—March 9, 1919, which would have made him nineteen when the 1938 killings happened. He looked at the mug shot for a second or two. Dark-haired, narrow-faced with a bruise on his left cheek and a line of stitches on his forehead. He tugged the mug shot out from under the paper clip and slipped it into the pocket of his jacket. He closed the file, then left the Records office and headed for the pay phones beside the elevators.

Dundee, it turned out, was not only a duly incorporated town, it had a mayor, a town marshall and a volunteer fire department. Ray managed to track the marshall down at his home, and when Ray mentioned the name William Cooper, Sheriff Andy Grant was only too glad to meet with Ray in his office next to the old Dundee State Bank building on Front Street. Ray said he'd be an hour; in fact, with the very light traffic, it only took him forty minutes.

Dundee was a flyspeck on 377 North near the old Texas and Pacific tracks about forty miles out of Dallas. A sign on the outskirts proudly touted the town's incorporation the year before and gave the population as 125. It looked as though Dundee had about ten businesses, including a hair dresser, a bar and a hardware store. At the far end of Front Street there was a large brick building that might have been a small factory sometime in the past, but which had long since been abandoned. The old window frames were blackened and charred, the roof had collapsed and there were weeds everywhere.

The Marshall's Office was right where he said it would be, a small wood-frame building huddled beside a much more imposing brick-and-stone edifice that had clearly once been a bank but which now seemed to be doing business as an office block. One of the upstairs windows advertised a lawyer in gold leaf, while the one across from it offered accounting services in plain black lettering. A sign over the marshall's door said TOWN MARSHALL, and the two windows facing the street had bars on them. The only thing missing was wooden sidewalks and women in hoopskirts. Ray parked and climbed out of the Bel Air, looking for a hitching post to tie up his nag to. Any second Gary Cooper was going to show up, the clock was going to strike twelve and a train's steam whistle would shriek in the distance.

Ray stepped into the one-room office. Andrew Jackson Grant, a very lean man with thinning, nicotine-blond hair, was sitting behind a desk filling out forms. He was wearing blue jeans and a faded denim shirt with his marshall's badge pinned to the left pocket. On the wall beside him was a gun rack with three good-sized deer rifles and a shotgun padlocked into a safety frame, and behind the man's desk was a metal-strapped door that had the word *CELLS* stenciled on it. As Ray entered the office a little bell tinkled, just like the one in Pop Mercier's candy store. The lean man looked up.

"Ray Duval?"

"Marshall Grant?"

"That's me." He smiled. His face was seamed and split by a lifetime of sun and cigarettes. He looked very much like an aging cowboy. He popped a pack of Marlboros out of his right shirt pocket and lit up with one of the kitchen matches he kept in a little tin tray at the head of his desk. He pointed to a wooden armchair on the opposite side of his desk. "Take a load off." Ray sat down. "Terrible thing about this Oswald killing."

"Pretty embarrassing," Ray agreed.

"You see it?"

"I was there."

"I'll be damned. I was doing the vacuuming in my living room and I saw Ruby just step up and shoot. Amazing thing. Doesn't look good for Texas. Kind of shoddy, if you know what I mean."

"Shouldn't have happened."

"No, sir, it should not, and if you don't mind me saying it's going to bring out all the little ghosts and goblins for about the next thousand or so years."

"That's what I've been thinking."

"So how'd you come up with a ghost and a goblin out of my past?"

"William Cooper?"

"Billy Boy. Charming Billy. That's what he was called around here."

"He get into trouble?"

"Right from the start."

"How?"

"Used to hunt people's animals."

"Animals?"

"Cats and dogs. Occasional Four-H pig. Catch 'em in this net thing he invented so he wouldn't harm them. Then he'd kill them and stuff them. Found a whole lot of them after he left town. Buried in his daddy's basement."

"That's the extent of it?"

"I could never prove anything, but a couple of kids disappeared. Found them a long time later weighted down to the pond at Graveyard Knob."

"Negroes?"

"Uh-huh."

"Girls. Ten, eleven?"

"Uh-huh."

"Anything else?"

"His daddy."

"What about him?"

"Billy's momma was no good—everyone knew that."

"Everyone knew it?"

"This is a small town, Detective. It's not built of bricks and boards. It's built of rumor and hearsay. Some people even said Billy was servicing the woman from a young age."

"Incest?"

Grant smiled. "Some of my Negro friends have a more expressive description of it, but yes, that's what people thought."

"What happened?"

"She disappeared, just like the little girls and all those pets. Never could lay it at anybody's doorstep. Billy's father said she just left him and good riddance."

"How old would he have been?"

"Fifteen or so. Little younger maybe."

"What happened to the father?"

"Took Billy out of school. Apprenticed him at the bindery."

"Book bindery?"

"That's right. This is the biggest school district in Denton

County and there's seventy-one others. It was a good business here. Employed a bunch of people, even through most of the Depression. Billy's old man had bigger plans, though. He wanted Billy to learn the old-fashioned stuff, hand binding for rare books, special editions and such. Then there was the accident."

"The burnt-out building I saw?"

"That's the bindery, all right, but it's not the accident I mean. Accident was Billy's old man trying to fix one of the wire pullers and the foreman switching on the machine to check it before Billy's old man was completely out. Cut him to pieces, and right in front of Billy too."

"Christ."

"On a crutch, uh-huh. Old Doc Wagner stitched him back together like a jigsaw puzzle just to get him into his coffin."

"And Billy?"

"Went to the funeral and that's the last anyone ever saw of him. Bindery burned down two nights after they put his daddy into the ground."

"You think Billy torched it?"

"He had good reason, I guess, and it was arson. Smell gasoline all over the place, especially on what was left of the foreman."

"There was someone in the building at the time?"

"Tied to a chair with wire. Didn't stand a chance."

"Figure Billy did it?"

"'Course he did it, Detective. But we both know motive isn't enough. No evidence at all. And no Billy." He shrugged. "We went through the house, found all sorts of bookbinding tools, some beautiful books and a bunch of stuffed animals buried in the basement. Didn't find his mother. Didn't find the bones of the little girls who disappeared for years after that. Had people spooked for a long time, just like that Hitchcock movie a while back."

"*Psycho*."

"That's the one. Billy down to his toes. Even looked a little like that Norman Bates character. Real soft talker."

Ray took the mug shot out of his pocket and pushed it across the desk toward the sheriff. "That him?"

"A little older, a little banged up, but yup, that's him." He looked a little closer, reading the date on the card around Cooper's neck. "Nineteen thirty-eight. What'd he do to get his snapshot taken back then?"

"Drunk and disorderly. Assault. Before that I think he was killing little girls all over the northern counties."

"Sounds like our Billy."

"Surprised you didn't hear about it, put two and two together."

"What year?"

"Nineteen thirty-eight, spring and summer."

"March 'thirty-eight the unincorporated town of Dundee took a vote and decided they couldn't afford a sheriff that year. Went to live with my brother in California. Guess I missed it all. Called up in 'forty-one, spent the war as a drill sergeant at Fort Rod. Got out in 'forty-five with everyone else. Good people of Dundee wrote me a letter and told me they needed someone to stop all the beer fights so they re-elected me and gave me a raise. Also gave me the old Cooper house since no one else wanted it." He shrugged. "Suits me fine." He squashed out his cigarette into a tin ashtray. "Even got a pension now."

"Headed in that direction myself," said Ray. "Just wrapping up a few loose ends before I go."

"Billy's a loose end for you? How?"

"I think he's in Dallas and he's killing little girls again."

"Shit."

"Yeah. I think he takes them and he holds them for a few days, then he kills them."

"He's got one now?"

"Yes. But not for long. I want to find him before he kills her."

"He thinks you're close, he's going to run. Sensitive boy, Billy was. He knew I'd been watching him for a while. He's not one to hang around."

"You ever get the sense that he was queer?"

"A fairy boy?"

"Yeah."

"I suppose he could have been. Didn't pay much attention to that stuff back then."

"He was fifteen or so. I remember those days."

"So do I, barely." The sheriff laughed. "I don't think he had any girlfriends. Like I said, he was too spooky. Not ugly or anything, just kind of . . . strange." The sheriff lit another cigarette. "Why do you ask?"

"It seems to be part of this whole thing. A lot of homosexual connections."

"How long do you think you've got?"

"Twenty-four hours. Maybe less."

"Good luck to you."

"I need more than luck. I need a miracle."

"Precious few of those in our business, I'm afraid."

"Maybe none," Ray answered.

Chapter 24

Ray made it back into Dallas by four o'clock in the after-noon according to the big Hertz billboard on top of the School Book Depository. He went across Dealey Plaza, through the triple underpass and headed for home. By the time he reached it he was pretty sure he'd put most of it to-gether, with the exception of a few details and one or two things that only hung together on a flimsy theory that would be hard to prove in a courtroom.

He parked the car just before it started spitting rain again and went into the house. He mixed himself a drink of half Jax and half V8 juice. According to the Old Man it was the only way Ronald Reagan would endorse it back in the for-ties. He drank it down standing at the sink, mixed a second one and drank it down as well, then headed for the tele-phone. He made two fast phone calls, the first one to Valen-tine's shop. The man picked it up on the third ring.

"Duval."

"Detective."

"A question."

"For you, anything."

He listed off the measurements he'd jotted in his notebook. "Mean anything?"

"Of course. They're paper sizes. Old ones. Foolscap Folio, Duke and Large Post Quarto. Also applies to the book sizes themselves."

"Second question," said Ray, feeling the bile rise up into his throat, burning at his chest. "Is any paper made out of animal skin?"

"Two," answered Valentine. "Parchment and vellum. They have paper versions now, but originally parchment was made out of goat- or sheepskin. Vellum was a finer paper and was made from young animals, goat kids, lambs, very young calves."

"Covers?"

"Same thing," Valentine responded. "The younger the animal, the finer the leather for the binding."

"Thanks," said Ray, his voice choking. He hung up the phone and stumbled toward the bathroom, remembering the buttery feel of the dark brown leather book he'd picked up at Schwager's love nest. The rich look of the vellum letter from Davy Crockett. He dropped down in front of the toilet and emptied his belly into the bowl.

When he was finished he got up on unsteady feet, rinsed out his mouth, brushed his teeth, then brushed them a second time. He made it halfway back down the hall to the telephone, then paused, using one splayed hand to support himself while he caught his breath, fighting to keep the terrible images out of his mind.

He eased his way along the hall and dropped down into the kitchen chair that stood beside the telephone table. He picked up his notebook and called Futrelle's house in Kessler Park. Once again it was Andrews the "personal assistant" who answered. This time he fetched Paul Futrelle without question.

"Why are you calling me at home?" His voice was brittle, with an edge of fear behind it. In the background, distantly, Ray could hear the sound of laughter and clinking glasses.

"Party time?"

"A few friends."

"Celebrating Mr. Oswald's demise?"

"My anniversary, as a matter of fact."

"I won't keep you long."

"All right."

"It seems likely that you were the last one to see Jennings Price alive."

"A supposition."

"Who left the apartment first, you or him?"

"I did."

"And went where?"

"Home. Andrews and my wife can both confirm the time."

"When we talked before you said you didn't know where Price was going."

"That's right. I still don't."

"You're sure he said nothing?"

"Nothing."

"You also told me he had several old-looking books with him as well as the letter from the Army Records Center."

"That's correct."

"You mentioned as well that he was having a book rebound for you."

"That's right."

"Do you have any idea who he used to do his binding and repairs?"

"No." There was a pause. "He did mention it once. Some-one Schwager had just discovered. Someone new in town. The name started with a *G*, I think. Gregson, Grillson. Some-thing like that." The school supervisor paused again. "Any-thing else?"

"One more thing."

"Yes?"

"Did either Price or Schwager recently redecorate the apartment? Paint, rugs, that kind of thing?"

"Not that I know of. Are we finished?"

"For the time be—"

Futrelle hung up before Ray could finish the sentence. He went back to the kitchen and began leafing through Schwa-ger's address book. Since it was Schwager who found him, the name and number would surely be in the address book. There were twenty G's listed in the book, their names neatly printed along with the phone numbers, but with nothing to indicate which were friends and which were business ac-quaintances. He decided to take a different approach and went back to the telephone, this time taking his own note-book. He found Betty Finch's number listed under her hus-band Frank's name and dialed. Frank answered on the second ring, the chaotic sounds of his several children screeching and screaming in the background.

"Hi, Frank, Ray Duval."

"After my wife again?" A huge guffawing laugh fol-lowed.

"Absolutely."

"Good. Take her. Big pain in the patootie anyway." He turned away from the receiver and bellowed Betty's name. A few seconds later she came on the extension and her hus-band hung up.

"It's Ray."

"Oh God, you want something else and me up to my armpits in laundry."

"Frank thinks I want your body."

"I wish you'd take it. He sure as hell doesn't pay much attention to it." Ray had been hearing the same banter between them for years. Frank Finch was a six-foot-five interstate trucker and Betty was a five-foot-two Kewpie doll who seemed to have no trouble keeping her man in line. The fact that they had five kids and another on the way suggested that Betty's comment about Frank not paying much attention to her body wasn't accurate. At one time Betty had been an ambulance dispatcher at Dallas Methodist, which was where she and Ray met, back when he was a patrolman. Fifteen years ago she'd transferred over to a supervisory position at the telephone company, and she was by far his best contact there.

"You want me to do something illegal again, don't you?" she asked.

"I'm not sure if it's illegal or not. I need to find out about a new telephone account."

"What's the name?"

"I don't have it."

"Helpful, aren't you?" Betty sighed. "Residential or commercial?"

"Commercial."

"A little better. What's the name of the business?"

"Don't know."

"Jeez, Louise, give me a hand here!"

"It's a bookbinder, doing custom work. Antique stuff. I think his name starts with a G."

"Is this important?"

"Life and death, Betty, and I'm not blowing smoke."

"Please tell me I'm not getting into the Kennedy thing."

"Everybody's starting to ask me that."

"I hear the FBI's taking people into custody as material witnesses and then no one sees them again. Some bums out by the tracks behind Dealey Plaza got picked up and no one's seen them since. Some guy went to Parkland in an ambulance just before it happened and now he's gone too." Like caterpillar to great black butterfly Dallas was being transformed from Texas cow town to the center of some universe awhirl in clouds of death and conspiracy. Come to Dallas and die.

"I didn't know that."

"*Is* this the Kennedy thing, Ray?"

"No. Scout's honor."

"All right. Give me ten minutes. You at home?"

"Yup."

"Back at you."

It was eight minutes, not ten. "Ray?"

"Betty. Find anything?"

"Only one binding company opened up shop in Dallas in the last four months. Name is Gerritson Fine Binding. Owner is William Joseph Gerritson." William Cooper. Koop. William Joseph Gerritson. Charming Billy.

"Where?"

"Marilla Street. Down where the railyards and the old cemeteries meet."

"What number?"

"Telephone or address?"

"Both." Betty rhymed them off and Ray jotted them down in his notebook.

"There's another one," said Betty.

"Another what?"

"Gerritson. Mrs. William Joseph. According to the exchange she lives in Oak Cliff."

"Better give me those numbers as well." Betty did. Ray thanked her for her help and hung up. He stared down at the page in his notebook. Charming Billy with a wife and kids didn't fit into the puzzle at all; in fact it threw it completely out of whack. He tried to imagine a man who could slice up little girls and then go home to a bowl of yummy Campbell's Cream of Tomato Soup with the missus, watch *Captain Kangaroo* with the kids and play golf at Bob-O-Links on Sunday. He knew it was getting away from him at the worst possible time, knew his theory was falling into little pieces, and unless he could stitch it back together it was going to be too late and Zinnia Brant was going to die a terrible death because he was missing something as plain as the nose on his face.

What was it Rena's mother had said?

The wisdom of the bones. Maybe it wasn't working for him, or maybe it didn't exist, or maybe he just wasn't listening hard enough to what it was trying to tell him.

Or maybe he didn't care.

Ignoring his notebook he reached down onto the shelf below the phone and pulled out the White Pages. He went through it, flipping pages hard until he found the page and the number he needed. He dumped the White Pages back onto the shelf and dialed.

"Bill Harcourt."

"Ray Duval."

"You're phoning me at home now? Jeez! I already made the list for you. Took it to police headquarters myself this afternoon. Left it with the desk sergeant."

"Never saw it."

"Did my best, Detective."

"You have a copy with you?"

"As a matter of fact I do. In my briefcase. Hang on."

Ray waited. A minute later the Chevy dealer was back on the line.

"Got it."

"Find the G's."

"Okay, just a sec." Another moment passed and Ray could hear pages flipping. "G. Okay, what now?"

"Look for the name Gerritson."

"Spell it."

Ray did.

"Not here."

"It has to be!" Ray said furiously. He could feel the vein in his neck swelling hard and his breath began to hitch. He couldn't be wrong. "Look again."

"I can look until my eyes bug out. No Gerritson. Goes from German, Edgar to Gettler, Martin."

"Shit."

"Why don't you try Hertz? They rent them."

"Christ, that must be it. Thanks." Ray hung up and scratched the name HERTZ down in big letters, filling up half a page in his notebook, then underlined it and threw in an exclamation mark. Why own the vehicle you kidnap little girls in? Why not just rent? It would take days to track down Gerritson's rental of the Corvan. He'd just have to take it as a given for the moment. There was no time to waste double-checking now. He went back into the kitchen, threw on his rig and his jacket, then headed out into the rain.

Chapter 25

The Old City Cemetery, the Jewish, Odd Fellows and Masonic Cemeteries were a group of four burying grounds bordered by South Akard Street, Desoto Street and Masonic Avenue, located a few blocks south of the downtown district. The cemeteries, dating back to the time when Dallas was little more than a frontier town, lay long forgotten and forlorn in an out-of-the-way cul-de-sac surrounded by warehouses, squatters' shotgun shacks and dilapidated rooming houses that provided accommodation for some of Dallas's less-fortunate prostitutes.

The Jewish Cemetery was the best preserved and best taken care of, surrounded by a black-painted wrought-iron fence. The Old City Cemetery, or what was left of it, was guarded by a small cottage with a weather-beaten American flag on a pole in front of it. The cottage was occupied by an elderly watchman hired by the city whose only real job was to raise and lower the flag each morning and evening.

Behind the cottage was the overgrown remains of the Odd Fellows and Masonic cemeteries, which had once looked down over the now-vanished Santa Fe Railyards. The centerpiece of the forgotten quadrant was a thirty-foot-high fluted granite column topped by a huge stone eagle, wings spread, dedicated in 1918 to all the members of the Fraternal Order of Eagles who died in the Great War.

To the rare visitor the most surprising thing about the monument was its continued existence intact, still standing after almost half a century of pollution and vandalism had run rampant through the rest of the area. There had been various groups and committees trying to salvage and rejuvenate the old graveyards since Ray had come home from his adventures in Europe, but everyone knew that land in Dallas these days was far too valuable to be left to the dead and it was the inevitable that the eagle would eventually fall in the name of progress.

Where Marilla Street curved up to Young Street, a flat-roofed, three-story brick-and-stone warehouse had been crammed into a small triangular space not included in the original land grant deeded by the Odd Fellows and the Masons. Originally built as a machine shop for the nearby Santa Fe Railyards, it had lain vacant since the end of the Second World War, when the yards had been moved downslope toward the narrow Trinity River, closer to the edge of downtown. With buildings like the Old Courthouse, the Thomas Block, and the Life Building screening the squalid area from view, the warehouse and the other buildings around it were almost invisible.

Ray drove south on Akard, coming at the warehouse the long way round, turning off Akard onto Short Street, little more than an alley with small factories and clothing warehouses on one side and a row of sagging-roof town houses on the other. At least a third of the decrepit houses were clearly abandoned and several had been burnt out, leaving holes like a gap-toothed grin in the row.

He parked the Bel Air at the end of the street, leaving the

engine running for a minute, letting the wipers slap back and
forth as he took in the warehouse address he'd been given
by Betty Finch. Number 9 Marilla Street had a rough sand-
stone first level, topped by two more of brick. All of it was
being darkened by the steady shower and the last of the
evening sun. It was longer than it was wide, the windows
facing Marilla Street done up like bay windows on a house.
A white-on-black sign had been painted up the corner of the
building facing Ray and the Bel Air: COMMUTATOR. There
were two chimney stacks and an air vent poking up from the
roof. On the main floor, taking up the corner of the warehouse, was a large-windowed storefront or office, the windows painted black halfway up to the top. There was a
narrow recessed door leading into the office and a rough
brick patch where there had once been a door on the side of
the building facing its narrow, packed-dirt parking lot. The
lot was empty and so was the curb in front of the building.
No cars. No white Corvan.

Procedure said that he should find a telephone and call
for backup to help him raid the warehouse, but after his
dressing down by Fritz it was unlikely anyone would come
to his aid; besides, he didn't have any of the paperwork he
needed to go busting into the place. On a Sunday it was unlikely he was going to get it. All too late, but that would be
the right thing to do, the cop thing to do, the safe thing to do.

To go into the warehouse alone was more than foolish, it
was possibly a fatal act. The windshield slapped and wiped,
slapped and wiped, leaving a long streak in the center where
the rubber had frayed and worn down. He put his hand over
his chest and let his body speak to him in quiet whispers.
Each incident, each movement, each risk was anguish now,
bringing fear up into his despairing chest. Death was personal now, no longer something in the future; it was attached

to him like a shadowy dream, a part of him, waiting to be summoned up at the final moment.

He switched off the engine and got out of the car anyway, his hair instantly matting down with the rain, the heavy droplets smearing his vision. He wiped his face and looked around, seeing no one, a tiny flicker of memory rising like a bright star and fading from sight almost before he realized it was there.

It was the fourth of August 1944 and the First Army had finally broken from the beaches at Essay. Alone, separated from his men, Ray Duval lay in the soft cover of fallen leaves and small plants that covered the floor of the Foret de Sever, a mile or so north of their target, the tiny village of St. Pois. Ray knew they held the line from Fortain to a junction with the Second Army just north of Vire, but at that moment he felt utterly alone, dreadfully aware of his singularity and the fact that no one in the entire world had the slightest idea where he was right now, and few people, if any, cared. Even a cough or a sneeze from some other soldier nearby would have been enough to keep his terror in check, but there was nothing except the sounds of birds and the rich graveyard smell of the soil an inch from his face.

Ray slipped back into the car, popped open the glove compartment and rummaged around in it until he found what he was looking for: eight inches of a thin metal ruler, the lopped off end wrapped with electrical tape so he didn't cut himself. He slipped the steel strip into the inside pocket of his jacket, climbed out of the car again and locked it. He looked around again—there wasn't another soul to be seen. Over the roofs toward downtown there were only the darkened windows of office buildings. The sounds of traffic were muted by the rain and the mourning city. Alone in his dream, Ray knew he might as well have been walking across the mountains of the moon.

Crossing the street, his heavy, waterlogged legs taking him toward COMMUTATOR and what perhaps might lie inside the wet-stained building, he could hear the sneering tone of Paul Futrelle's surprise at him seemingly knowing Cicero. Well, he knew a bit of appropriate William Butler Yeats too:

> *I balanced all, brought all to mind,*
> *The years to come seemed waste of breath*
> *A waste of breath the years behind*
> *In balance with this life, this death.*

He smiled. Who was he trying to kid; he wasn't that much of a hero, although he was contemplating his own death, just like Yeats's "Irish Airman." He reached the sidewalk and stepped up over the crumbling curb, his eyes fixed on the narrow door of the storefront. It was painted black from the inside like the window, but all the way to the top so there was no way of seeing what lay beyond. Without even bothering to look around the rain-swept street to see if anyone was watching, Ray took out his metal strip and ran it down the outside of the door frame until it reached the lock. He waggled the strip up and down gently, and the door popped open. If the metal strip hadn't worked he would have put his elbow to the glass.

He put the strip back in his inside pocket and took the Browning out of its shoulder rig as he pushed open the door with his free hand. He sensed no movement or any danger in the darkness beyond so he stepped forward, his hand brushing the wall on his left for a light switch. Eventually he found it, an old-fashioned brass toggle. He flipped it up and closed the door behind him. Overhead two old-fashioned pan lights with green glass shades flickered on, throwing a pale weak light down into the room.

Ray found himself standing directly in front of a broad wooden counter that ran three-quarters of the way across the room with an opening on the left. There was a modern cash register to the right of the opening and a rack of three-ring student binders beside it. Ray put the Browning down on the counter, pulled one of the binders out of its wire rack and leafed through it. Inside, slotted into plastic protective covers, were photographs of various binding types and examples of book repairs with before and after pictures on opposite leaves. Ray closed the binder and picked up one of the business cards stacked on a small brass tray.

WILLIAM GERRITSON
Fine Binding, Gilt Work
Antiquarian Book Repair

There was a Brooklyn, New York, address and phone number neatly crossed out and an inked Dallas address and phone number that matched the ones given to him by Betty Finch. He stared into the area behind the counter and saw a neatly laid out shop with a heavy wooden bench running almost the whole length of the room. Above it was a long pegboard rack that held the tools of Charming Billy's trade: knives, needles, oil stones, a huge pair of heavy shears, a collection of tinned iron plates to put between the leaves of books when they were being rethreaded, weights, a variety of saws, hand drills and drill bits, and a collection of small, almost jewel-like planes.

On the bench itself was a large vise, a pair of lamps on swinging armatures, and at one end, a lying press, used for holding books and individual parts of books being glued, and a sewing frame for stitching the separate signatures of paper together to make the finished book. Ray could also see a small stack of old books off to one side, waiting to be worked on, as well as one that had already been taken apart, its various pieces spread out in front of a tall stool. The whole bench was obviously made to be used with the book-binder standing.

To the right of the bench, pushed up against the wall, was a small table with some kind of special vise that held a book spine toward the person working on it. To the left, in a custom-made holder, were a dozen or so wooden-handled engraving tools with long U-shaped chisel blades for cutting into the leather. These were the instruments that had created the delicate U-shaped killing wounds in the eyes of his victims. There was a book of dull-looking gold leaf beside the viselike object and far off to one side, bathed in the light from a green gooseneck lamp, was a family photograph of a young blond woman, her hair cut in a bob, and two smiling children under her arm, one a boy of eight or nine, the other a girl of twelve or so.

Without any warning, a square of wood in the center of the floor came up soundlessly as a trapdoor opened. A man in his fifties stepped up into the studio, several large squares of leather interwoven with sheets of dark green felt in his hand. He looked startled to see anyone in the shop and stopped cold, half in and half out of the trapdoor opening.

Ray picked up the Hi-Power and aimed it loosely in the man's direction. "Come on up. Slowly."

The man did as he was told, his eyes on Ray and the muzzle of the pistol in his hand. Ray had a brief moment to study the man's face. He was mostly bald, the hair he did have fully white. The left side of his face was covered with a red-skinned burn scar that went from the base of his neck to his forehead. The right side was gaunt, skin pulled down tightly over misshapen cheek- and jawbones. The eye on the burn side was not quite the same shade of blue as the one on the right and had the dull sheen of glass. For the first time in all his years as a cop, a monster actually looked like one. Quasimodo without his hump. The man came up out of the trapdoor. Ray smelled a faint, musty basement smell come up with him but nothing worse. Nervously, the man put his hands in the air as he stepped around the open trapdoor.

"Nothing much to steal here, mister." His voice was cracked and dry with a permanent rasp to it that was probably a result of whatever had caused the burn on his face.

"That's the second time in four days someone's accused me of being a thief."

"If you're not here to rob me, why the gun?"

"I'm a cop."

"What did I do, steal a book from the library?"

Ray ignored the comment. "You're working on a Sunday."

"I work every day except Christmas. Lots of work in my trade, believe it or not."

"You're William Gerritson?"

"That's right."

"Ever heard of someone named William Cooper. Also known as Koop?"

"No." The answer came too quickly but without inflection, although it was hard to read the man's facial expressions or the tilt of his words.

"Jennings Price?"

"Yes."

"How?"

"He brought me books to repair. Some gold-leaf work as well."

"He was murdered."

"So I understand."

"Hasn't been much about it in the papers, what with the Kennedy assassination."

"Dick Schwager told me about it."

"Schwager comes in here?"

"He has done."

"Where do you know him from?"

"Here. He brings in books and documents for me to work on from time to time." Gerritson sighed. "I really wish you'd get to the point."

Ray nodded in the direction of the picture on his desk. "In a hurry to get home to the wife and kids."

"We're divorced," said Gerritson. "That's part of the reason I moved down here from New York."

"Stay close to the family?"

"Something like that." Which explained why the name in the telephone directory was in her name and not his. Gerritson was beginning to fade as a suspect.

"How'd you burn your face?"

"That's none of your business."

"Why don't you tell me anyway. Save us a lot of trouble and paperwork and lawyer's fees."

"A fire."

"I can see that."

"I had a shop in Brooklyn. There was a fire. I got burned."

"The damage to the other side of your face?"

"For Christ's sake!"

"Humor me."

"A two-by-four. I was wired up for almost six months." His face twisted into an ugly grimace and he ran his hand back through his hair. It fell back over his forehead almost immediately, but Ray saw the old scar there. He could feel his heart begin to thump erratically in his chest and he tightened his grip on the Hi-Power. He hadn't been wrong after all.

"What about the scar on your forehead? The old one."

"What about it?"

"Where did that come from?"

"I fell off my bicycle when I was a kid."

"No."

"What? I'm lying about falling off a bicycle?"

"I think so." He transferred the Hi-Power to his left hand and took the mug shot out of his jacket pocket and laid it on the counter. Gerritson took two steps forward and looked down at the old photograph. "Assault charge and a drunk and disorderly. December 1938, just like it says on the sign around your neck, Mr. Cooper."

"My name is Gerritson."

"You originally come from a little place called Dundee, not too far from here. Your father worked in the local bindery and you went around killing small animals until you graduated up to pigs, and then little black girls. Two of them, both found later weighted down in a pond near some place called Graveyard Knob."

"I was born in Ogdensburg, New York. I don't know what you're talking about." But he did. The one good eye was wide with apprehension and there was a faint line of perspiration in the bristly hairs on the man's upper lip.

"Word is you were also fucking your mother," said Ray, pouring gasoline on the fire to see if he would react. He stiffened visibly and took a step away from the counter. It actually seemed as though the scar on his face was turning a deeper red, almost a purple.

"Watch what you say, mister. Watch what you say about my mother."

"Okay, Charming Billy, what about your father? After your momma disappeared, and we can go into that too if you want to, your daddy had an accident. Got chopped up in some kind of machinery at the bindery. Maybe that's why you chop up little girls now, who knows? You thought it was the foreman's fault so one night you tied him to a chair and poured gasoline all over him and lit a match. Took out the foreman and the whole damned bindery. Which is when you disappeared."

"This is insane."

"No," said Ray. "I think you are."

"Then why don't you charge me?"

"Don't worry, I'll get around to it. I just want to get my whole theory out on the table where you can see it. Maybe you can come up with something to prove me wrong. Do that and I'm willing to listen. But let me tell you, Charming Billy, we've got your prints from the drunk and disorderly, and we've got your prints from when you enlisted in the Citizens' Military Training Corps. All we have to do is match those to your prints now and you'll be done like dinner, Charming Billy."

"I'd appreciate it if you didn't call me that, Officer."

"Get your goat a bit?"

"I just don't like it." The man was using every ounce of energy to control himself and Ray knew it. He also cursed himself for a fool. He really was alone with a madman and there was no way to summon help.

"I guess Moran and Durkin were making you nervous."

"Who?"

"Two Texas Rangers who were on your tail. You'd stuck to killing black kids like Luci Edmonds you mighta got away with it longer, Billy. Those white girls, though, they got people pissed. Smart thing, joining the army like you did. Good place to hide. Too bad about the war, though. Or maybe it was good. Maybe it let you do all the things you liked for free. Lots of little kids to kill and no one was going to notice, were they?"

"I think you'd better leave now."

"Who was it who recognized you? Price or Schwager? Probably it was Price. You did business with him before the war, didn't you? You were a picker and he worked at his uncle's bookstore in the summers, didn't he? Did he find out what you were up to that summer of 1938? Did he keep your secret? Why? Because you'd bring him things? Special things?" There was a long and very empty pause with nothing but the sound of the slanting rain outside to fill it.

Finally Gerritson spoke. "Because he didn't have the guts," the bookbinder said, his voice almost too soft to hear.

"Guts to do what?"

"Kill the old man."

"The old man who ran the bookstore?"

"Yes."

"Why did he want to do that?"

"Because the old man was . . . doing things to him that he didn't like. Because he wanted what the old man had."

"Books?"

"Rare books. Valuable books. He used to tell people that his family had lots of money but it wasn't true, they just had one of those old Atlanta names that got you into the right places."

"What happened?"

"At the end of the summer he made sure everyone knew he was on his way back to Atlanta, but he wasn't. He came back to the old man's store and so did I. We killed him and made it look like an accident. I had DiMaggio's truck. He was dying by then anyway. Didn't know what was going on. We took the best of the stock and drove it to Atlanta. He said we'd let things cool off for a while and then we'd open up a store."

"But then there was the war."

"They were getting too close, those two Rangers you mentioned. One of them even interviewed me. Moran, I think."

"Not about the little black girls, though. Not about Luci Edmonds."

"Who?"

"Your first. The one you threw in the dump at Oklaunion. The one you took on her way home from school near Haynesville."

For the first time the bookbinder smiled, the smile broadening, pulled down by the scar across half his face into a joker's leer, and then he actually laughed, a strong, slight wet laugh as though he'd heard some terribly funny joke.

"Her? The tight-twat little nigger? My first? She wasn't my first. She wasn't even my tenth, you idiot!"

The move when it came was terribly fast. Reaching out almost blindly with his left hand Gerritson plucked one of the engraving tools from its block on the desk and brought it down onto the back of Ray Duval's right hand, which was resting flat on the counter. The engraver sliced like a trough-shaped scalpel through tissue and tendon, carving down between the metacarpal of the middle finger and the carpal wrist bones before it sank a full inch into the soft wood below, impaling Ray's hand and pinning it to the counter.

Screaming in agony, Ray managed to get the gun up, thumbed the safety down and got off a single shot before Gerritson vaulted down through the trapdoor in the floor.

Suddenly the weapon felt as though it weighed a hundred pounds and he let it drop to the counter, his attention completely on the wooden knob of the tool pinning him to the wood below.

His heart was pounding with a strange erratic rhythm he'd never felt before and it was as though the hand of God Himself was reaching into his chest and squeezing for all He was worth as bright red blood began to pool beneath his hand and wrist. Ray could feel his vision begin to fade and knew that he was going into shock. The only thing to stop it would be to stop the pain and the only way to do that would be to pull the blade out of his hand and free himself. He grabbed the wooden grip of the instrument, closed his eyes and took a long shuddering breath. Then he pulled, straight up and straight out. He threw away the engraving tool as hard as he could, then used his free hand to loosen, then pull off his tie. He managed to wrap it around his hand, pulling the knot tight, stopping the flow of blood. He wrapped the rest of the tie around his wrist and put in another knot, squeezing hard like a tourniquet. Almost magically the pain in his chest began to recede as the episode passed. He stayed where he was for a few seconds, leaning on the counter, staring at the bright red stain of his blood, tasting its coppery scent in his nostrils. When he'd gathered strength enough he picked up the Hi-Power, went around the counter and headed across the room to the trapdoor in the floor.

Chapter 26

Ray was one-handed now so he went down the steep flight of stairs leaning his back against the railing, moving clumsily, one step at a time, trying to forget the terrible pulsing pain in his hand. He kept the gun pointed downward into the gloom at the bottom of the stairs but saw nothing. Faintly he heard footsteps disappearing into the distance toward the rear of the building, a strange sound, like someone walking on crunching gravel.

He reached the base of the stairs and found himself in a small, very low ceilinged room that was shelved on three sides. On the shelves were hundreds, perhaps thousands of pieces of leather kept between layers of dark felt with what looked like lead weights holding them down. Ray edged over to the nearest shelf, reaching out with his gun hand to feel the leather. It was smooth and fine, hairless and small pored. Horror. He jerked his hand back. There were cheap blue and brass trunks on the floor, half filled with more piles of the felt and leather, as though Gerritson was leaving, preparing to disappear again.

Stepping through a low doorway into a second, much smaller room, Ray paused, sniffing the air. There were tables here as well as shelves, the shelves piled with various supplies, the tables set out with paper. Another doorway and a third room, set, it seemed, at right angles to the second. Here there was only a single light and a huge, zinc-topped table. At the end of the table there was a gigantic cutting arm, four feet across, the full width of the table, a foot pedal and some kind of spring mechanism connected to it, probably to even the pressure as the blade came down. In the center of the table there was a pile of heavy card stock or board, thick enough to be for the making of book covers. The floor here was pea gravel, unlike the concrete of the other two rooms.

An exit from the third room led into a narrow, twisting passageway, the walls rough plywood, tacked to the ceiling beams with long nails. Stapled at intervals were stretched pieces of leather, fat side out, ready to be scraped, taped and tanned. The leather patches were grouped in series of half a dozen swatches each and penciled in above were dates, comments and color references. "October 9/ #4 umber. Light tanning, very fragile." Once again the floor here was pea gravel and for the first time Ray noticed spots of blood on the ground. His single shot had been lucky but he had no idea how badly Gerritson was wounded. His bad hand brushed against the plywood and he had to bite back a scream as the pain roared up through his hand and arm. His tie was soaked with blood now and dripping continuously. Enough blood loss and he'd pass right out.

A smell was in the air now, thicker and darker with each step—the reek of the monster's charnel house. Ray paused for a moment, wondering if his heart could take what he was about to see, wondering if after all this he had failed at the final moment, come too late.

There was a plain wooden door at the end of the corridor,

grotesquely cut down to fit the low ceiling and the narrow passage. It was fitted with an old-fashioned cut-glass door-knob with no lock. He paused, bent his bad hand across his chest and nestled the automatic in the crook of his arm, pulling back the slide sharply with his free hand, recocking the gun. He took the gun back into his left hand and fumbled with one finger to push down the safety. He'd fired once so there were twelve rounds left; plenty of firepower to kill the monster. He pushed open the door.

Worse, oh dear God in Heaven, much worse than he could ever have imagined in the most frightening night-mares. *Worse even than the beaches of Normandy where the bodies floated in the shallow water by the hundreds, always facedown, rocking, cradled on the tide, anonymous.* The room was small, the walls delicately covered with a floral wallpaper, the floors done in a sunny yellow flecked with red linoleum that belonged in a kitchen. There was a false window off to one side, fitted with a poster of Hawaii and lit from behind, just like Donna Reed had done in that scene on her wedding night in *It's a Wonderful Life.* A small spotlight on a bare wire shone like a hot sun down onto the surface of the brass bed below. A hidden speaker behind the backlit poster was playing a scratchy rendition of a slack-key Hawaiian tune from the thirties called "Little Brown Gal."

For a heartbreaking moment, though, he was looking at all that was left of Zinnia Brant, but then he knew it couldn't be. This girl was much older, at least fifteen or sixteen, her breasts and hips fully formed, looking nothing like the inno-cent child in the strip of photos taken in the photograph ma-chine. Looking nothing like a human being now, every part of her body separate from every other, the eyes in her sev-ered head half open and milky, the tendons and veins and ar-teries hanging down from the hole beneath her chin like the white and red and blue plastic ignition cables of a car, touching but not really belonging to the torso an inch away, the breasts fallen away to either side, a huge square of flesh hacked out of the midsection beginning just below the swayed dugs and stopping just short of the navel. Below that the horror escalated. Like a cored apple the reproductive organs, labia, vagina and all had been pulled out and lay between the woman's legs in inverse horror, the horror intensified by the blood and fecal matter and urine that stained the pale pink bedclothes. A thick, twisted rubbery tube pushed up out of the mess and slumped down over to the floor on the opposite side of the bed. Ray took two steps and gazed at the smaller horror on the floor. The woman had been pregnant and the fetus lay sprawled on the floor, its brown belly sliced open into a pair of flaps to reveal the abdominal organs. The child would have been born a boy, but now its severed penis and scrotum were held in one curled hand.

Below the purged torso on the bed were the thighs, their ends like ham bones, and below that again the lower legs and then the feet, fallen left and right in a gruesome Charlie Chaplin step. There was blood everywhere, dark and dried, caught and still where it had dripped from the sheets and pillows down the sides of the bed and finally to the floor. He knew if he rolled her over he'd find sections of skin taken from the back and buttocks as well. Flies had begun to gather at the eyes and the neck hole and there were already maggots squirming in the gore between her legs.

There was another door on the far side of the bed and Ray stumbled toward it, pushing at it with his left shoulder, a deep growling sound building low in his throat and finding its way through his pain. The door led into the darkness of what must once have been the furnace room, the Hawaiian music echoing from somewhere off to his right. He gripped his pistol in his sweat-slicked hand and moved forward. He could see a faint patch of light and followed it to a set of rain-slick metal chairs that led up to another open trapdoor beside a coal chute. Jamming his Hi-Power into the pocket of his jacket he grabbed the handrail and began to haul himself up into the rain and the silvery fading light of late afternoon.

He reached the top of the steps, retrieved his weapon and climbed out of the basement. Parked up against the wall on his left was a white Corvan with white-painted bumpers. There was a dealer's decal on the rear door. Someplace in New Jersey. He'd been wrong about the rental. The plates were New York commercial. White, just like Texas plates. Directly in front of him, choked with weeds and high grass and broken stone, were the remains of the Old City Cemetery. Through it Ray could see the crushed undergrowth that marked Gerritson's path, and as he followed it he saw spots of blood leaking away in the rain.

He found him halfway across the dreary, desolate field, most of its headstones broken or abandoned, pushed over, names worn off by time and neglect. Gerritson was slumped down, leaning against the eagle column, a huge bubbling stain of blood spreading out across his shirt. A lung shot. Given time it would kill him, but for the time being he was still alive. Ray dropped down beside him, wiping the rain out of his eyes.

"Where's the girl?"

"You must have seen her." Gerritson coughed and blood flooded out of his mouth and nose. "Hawaiian Sunset."

"Not her. The little girl. Zinnia Brant."

"Why—" he stopped and choked and coughed again. "—should I tell you?"

"Because if you don't I'm going to call an ambulance and get you sent to Parkland, where they're going to fix you up and get you to stand trial, and then by Christ they'll put you in Huntsville for a hundred lifetimes. Not that you'd last a week before the inmates did to you what you've been doing to their sisters and their daughters."

"And if I do tell you?"

"I'll put a gun in your ear and pull the trigger and that'll be the end of your sorry fucking life, but at least it will be quick."

Gerritson coughed more blood. "The house," he said finally. "She's at the house."

"Your wife's house?"

"There is no wife." He coughed more blood, dark red clots from deep in his lungs. The single shot must have taken him side on and gone through both the organs, maybe even knicked the heart. "I found that picture in an album I picked up somewhere. Makes me look more . . . real."

"Is the girl alive?"

"Yes. Hadn't started on her yet."

"Lucky for you."

Ray put out his gun hand onto the gray, dirt-mottled column and started to lift himself up.

Gerritson suddenly looked terribly frightened. "What are you doing? I told you where to find the girl. You promised me."

Ray boosted himself upright and stood over Gerritson, looking down. "I lied, Charming Billy. I lied."

"Bastard!" With a flourish, Gerritson dug under his bloody, rain-wet shirt and pulled out a long, thin knife that was actually a ground-down jigsaw blade used for slitting uncut pages in finished books, one end of the razor-sharp tool covered with a wrapped leather pad. Gerritson swung the blade, aiming for Ray's upper thigh, but exhausted as he was, Ray managed to lift his shoe and kick the blade away. It arced into the air and disappeared into the undergrowth on the other side of the eagle column.

Ray lifted the automatic and drew a wavering aim on Gerritson's head, then lowered the gun again. He turned and walked away, wiping the rain and the tears from his eyes, paying no attention to the blood leaking down his wrist and hand or the feeling of terrible dread that filled his chest. He heard Charming Billy's voice calling out to him weakly as he headed back to the street.

"You've got to keep your promise. I can tell you something. I didn't kill J. P. It wasn't me, but I know who did it!"

"So do I," said Ray softly, and kept on walking.

Ray called Jimmy Leavelle at home and got him to make the call to headquarters. An ambulance and a squad car were dispatched to pick up what was left of William Cooper, also known as William Gerritson, and a few people from the Crime Scene Search Section, including a photographer, were sent to go over the basement of the Commutator warehouse. He also asked Leavelle and a squad car to meet him at the address Betty Finch had given him for the mythical Mrs. William Gerritson and to bring along an ambulance there as well.

The house turned out to be a perfectly ordinary bungalow on a perfectly ordinary street in Oak Cliff. It took Leavelle and two uniformed officers almost an hour to find the secret soundproofed room in the basement, hidden behind a false wall of stored books. Zinnia Brant was naked, tied to the four corners of a makeshift bed and gagged. She had urinated and defecated in the bed more than once and was both dehydrated and in shock.

The ambulance attendants cleaned her up as best they could, gave her a small dose of Demerol and transported her to one of the Negro hospitals even though Methodist Hospital was much closer. At this point, with the vinyl on the Chevy's seat between his legs covered in blood from his wound, Ray Duval finally passed out. Leavelle called for a third ambulance and Ray was transported to Parkland Hospital, where he was given first aid and three pints of blood.

Doc Rose came up to tell him that the shot from Ray's big automatic had pierced Cooper's left lung, nicked the heart in passing and then blown out through the other lung. By the time the ambulance boys reached him he was just another dead boy in the Old City Cemetery. Rose made a joke about digging a hole and just dumping him into it, but Ray wasn't in the mood for humor. He also wasn't in the mood for Rose's suggestion to keep him overnight for observation. Ray told him that being under observation by the county medical examiner was too much like being under observation by the Grim Reaper himself. He asked Leavelle to accompany him on one last errand. Then he'd go home to bed.

Leavelle agreed and they left the hospital. They walked to the parking lot, Ray going slowly, Leavelle supporting him at one elbow. "Sure you want to do this, Ray?"

"Don't do it now it'll never get done. Strike while the iron is hot and all that stuff."

"All right, Ray. You're the boss."

"Even if I only found a murderer who killed little nigger girls?"

"Now don't go on like that, Ray. Not everyone in a white Stetson is part of the Klan, you know. And anyway, Ray, I hear from the Crime Scene boys this guy killed babies, ripped them out of women's bodies. Black or white, something like that matters."

"Two bucks says it doesn't make page ten. Five bucks says it doesn't make the paper at all."

They walked along to Leavelle's unmarked. As they reached it Ray stopped, his hand on the handle of the passenger-side door. "Question for you, Jimmy."

"Sure."

"What the hell's a commutator?"

"You got me, Ray."

They climbed into the car, slid back onto the freeway and headed north.

"I'm not sure what your point is, Detective Duval."

It was Sunday, and Dick Schwager, dressed in his loose dark trousers and a striped silk shirt open almost to the waist and wearing his blond cancer wig, was dusting in his apartment. Leavelle was waiting in the parking lot.

"The point is William Gerritson, or more properly Koop, or William Cooper, said that he didn't kill Jennings Price, but that he knew who did."

"You also told me that he was the child murderer you've been looking for, correct?"

"That's right."

"So why believe him?" Schwager slapped the bouquet extra hard with his duster.

"I didn't have to. I already knew."

"Really? Is this like some Agatha Christie Hercule Poirot novel where all is revealed by the detective to a roomful of enthralled suspects?"

"I'm no Hercule Poirot and you and I are the only ones in the room, Dick."

"You're accusing me?"

"That's right. You killed him right here in this room, just after Futrelle left and you arrived. He was waiting for you, telling you that he wasn't going to put up with the blackmail anymore. You hit him, probably with something heavy, and then you got the bright idea of chopping him up and making it look like old Koop was back in town, which of course he was, and you knew it."

"Sounds very circumstantial, Detective."

"How many of these carpets do I have to kick aside before I find dried blood you couldn't quite scrub up? Or take some of that blue paint off the walls to find the blood spatters. I smelled fresh paint when I was here before, but I didn't make the connection. Beginning to sound like real evidence?"

"Go on," said Schwager.

"How long will it take me to find out where you bought the plastic to wrap up the pieces, or the paint, or the piano wire? It might take a little time, but I'd put it together and you'll go to jail."

"Seems rather pointless. I'll be dead in a few months anyway. I wouldn't live to see my judge and jury."

"I won't last that long myself. Heart. Probably not as long as you."

"We certainly make a pair, don't we? The dying murderer at the hands of the dying detective." He paused. "So why our little confrontation?"

"I want to know why. Simple curiosity."

"Is that all?"

"I want to know that I've tied up all the loose ends before I go."

"Perhaps that's why I did it, because J. P. was a loose end in my life as well." Schwager gave a long sigh and sat down in a chrome-and-leather chair close to his glass wall of antiquarian objects. Ray dropped down into a chair across from him.

"I suppose it started when we were very young," said Schwager. "I knew J. P. in Atlanta, we both came here during the summers to make a little money."

"That's when you met Cooper?"

"Yes. Love at first sight, of course, but he never even looked at me sideways. It was crushing."

"But you helped with killing his uncle, the bookseller?"

"Yes. I didn't think it was necessary to kill him, I thought we could just sneak in and knock him out or something, but Cooper was the leader. He was always the leader, and I would have done anything for him then. He made me put the pillow over the old man's face while he and J. P. held him down."

"And then you met again during the war?"

"Bad luck, fate, karma, call it what you will. The whole thing replayed like a fucking record. It was like I was a puppet on a wire. When J. P. came back with Koop that day, started calling us the Triumvirate, I should have just fled, run away forever."

"But you didn't."

"No."

"This has to do with the Bible salesman, doesn't it?"

"You know about him?"

"I talked to a man named Jan van Plaut."

"Jannie! He was at the reunion a few years back. I wore a blond wig and everyone was utterly dumbfounded."

"The Bible salesman," Ray reminded. The painkillers they'd given him at the hospital were working to dull the pain in his hand, but he could feel the steadily growing pain in his chest again. He tried to ignore it.

"Koop had met a man. A German named Grosskurth, Christian Grosskurth. He had all sorts of things to offer, including a Schrifft Bible and Cavalieri's *Portraits of the Roman Pontiffs*."

"He went to the meeting and someone tried to kill him."

"Not so simple."

"Explain."

"J. P. and I beat him to the punch. We had dozens of things to trade with Grosskurth. Portable things, jewelry, mostly."

"You double-crossed Koop?"

"Yes. And asked Grosskurth to get rid of him for us. Paid him extra."

"That's where he got the burn and all the rest of it?"

"Yes. They beat him half to death and then set him on fire. I don't know how, but he managed to escape and killed Grosskurth in the process. I have a sneaking suspicion he left his own dog tags on Grosskurth. Then he disappeared."

"Did you know about the dog tags at the time?"

"Just a guess."

"But he came back. To Dallas."

"Yes. A few months ago. I recognized him and so did J. P. At first we didn't know what to do. Koop knew everything about us, all the forging work, the smuggling of artwork out of Europe after the war. He could have brought all of us down. He told us that was exactly what he was going to do, but that he wanted to see us squirm a little first. He even said he had evidence."

"Such as?"

"Records that the Schrifft Bible belonged to the Quedlinburg collection. Records that J. P. had sold it for a huge profit after he smuggled it back to the United States. Even records of previous dealings he'd had with Grosskurth."

"So you decided to kill him?"

"That was J. P.'s idea. I refused. It was too precipitous.

We didn't really know what Koop had come back *for*, don't you see? It seemed as though he was going to blackmail us, but we couldn't be sure." He shook his head, then ran both hands through his thinning hair. "J. P. even went to Army Records to see if they had any background. They came up empty. According to them he had died in the ruins of the Nollendorfplatz Theater in Berlin. Death by misadventure. Graves Registration has him interred in Invalidenfriedhof Cemetery in Berlin."

"So what happened?"

"We argued. He insisted. Killing Koop was the only way."

"So you hit him."

"I didn't mean to kill him."

"But you did cut him up to make it look like Koop had done it. Or at least some psycho."

"And to let Koop know that it might have been him. I even used an engraving tool I stole from his shop."

"You thought you could *scare* a man like that?"

"I thought he might leave. If he was coming here to get his revenge on J. P. somehow."

"And what if he wanted his revenge on you?"

"He knew I was a follower, not a leader. He knew I had cancer as well. There wouldn't have been any point. He would have left me alone. Even though I knew most of his dirty little secrets."

"How did you know?"

"I made it my business. Followed him. Saw him in the ruins, buying chocolate bars for little girls. Then taking them away. The same girls who showed up in the MP's incident reports a few days later. Butchered, just like the children up north before the war."

"You made the connection?"

"Just because I'm queer, Detective, doesn't mean I'm stupid. After a while it all started to fit together. The police were getting too close so he joined the army and disappeared. He wasn't the only one, believe me."

"Did you ever confront him?"

"I made sure he knew. Dropped a few hints. I wasn't in a position to throw stones, Detective. I had my secrets too and Koop knew it. Being homosexual in the army is a crime. They send you to Leavenworth." He smiled weakly. "Kansas has never been my favorite place."

"So it was a standoff?"

"I guess you could call it that."

"One more thing," said Ray.

"Of course."

"Killing Price is one thing, maybe cutting him up, but what about the rest? Wiring him together, getting him into the refrigerator, all of that?"

"I had help, obviously."

"Who?"

"Not telling."

"I'll find out eventually."

"You won't live that long, Detective, and neither will I. Let's just say it was someone who had a vested interest. Someone who'd go to jail if he was ever exposed as J. P.'s accomplice in crime."

Errol Timmins.

"I didn't think the little bastard had it in him."

"You'd be surprised at the depth of the young man's talents," said Schwager. He grinned, his face turning into a death mask topped by the ridiculous wig. "But you didn't hear it from me."

"He's an accessory."

"I didn't give him much choice. Leave him alone, Detective. He's harmless."

"So what are you going to do now?" Ray asked. He levered himself up from the chair, the pain in his chest increasing. He felt an overwhelming sense of fatigue and something close to despair. He'd managed to save little Zinnia, but how many had gone unsaved before her? How many like Luci Edmonds had there been over the years?

"I suppose that depends on what you're going to do, Detective."

"Nothing. William Cooper is dead. Jennings Price was punished for his crimes, and you'll be punished for yours, sooner or later." He shook his head. "Five days ago I didn't know anything about this. Tangled lives and deaths, lies and deceit. Five days from now it probably won't matter at all."

"No," said the man in the silk shirt. "It probably won't. Lost in history. The unfortunate death of President Kennedy has seen to that. Nobody's ever going to remember any of this, or any of the people involved."

That evening, lying in bed with Rena, letting her gently rub his back with baby oil, Detective Sergeant Horatio Duval suffered his second heart attack of the day and was taken by ambulance to Dallas Veteran's Hospital in the southern part of the city.

11/25/63
MONDAY

Chapter 27

By noon the following day the various doctors at Dallas Veteran's who had attended to Ray pronounced that while still suffering from acute congestive heart failure, the damage done by the two heart attacks—the first at the Commutator warehouse and the second in his own bed—had done no serious damage. They put him on a light diet and a continuous intravenous dose of Diuril, the most effective diuretic available at the time.

At one o'clock, when visiting hours began, Ray and Rena went down to the TV lounge and watched the Kennedy funeral in Washington, D.C. The lounge was filled, mostly with aging men in bathrobes, a few visitors and several nurses. At least half the people in the large, dingy room were crying, and an orderly took it upon himself to walk around the semicircle of TV watchers offering tissues directly from the box.

As the funeral procession reached the gates of Arlington National Cemetery, Ray sat forward in his uncomfortable chair and stared. Just inside the gates there was a thinly treed rise to the right of the roadway with only one or two stones in place.

"That's it," he whispered to Rena. "That's where I want to be buried."

"In Arlington?"

"I'm a veteran, that's my right."

"How do you make it happen?"

"Get in touch with the Veterans Administration, I guess."

"Can you pick your own spot?"

"I don't know."

There was a lot of "shushing" going on so Ray and Rena went back to his room. There were four beds in the small ward at the end of a long green corridor, three of them occupied. There was Jacko Munro, who'd been gassed at Passchendaele in 1917 and who'd been in and out of veterans hospitals for the better part of forty-five years, his condition deteriorating with each passing decade; Nick Childs, legless and blind and plagued by diabetic ulcers, not to mention being in his seventies and well into dementia; and there was Ray, the youngest of the three. The fourth bed, the one directly beside Ray, was empty.

Both Jacko and Nick were sleeping when they got back to the room. Ray parked his three-legged IV pole and eased himself into bed, letting Rena fluff up his pillows and then steal a third from the bed beside him so he could breathe better. She sat on the bed and reached out, just touching Ray's outstretched fingers, the rest of the hand now properly covered in a long-wristed cast.

"I don't like this talk about funerals and graves," said Rena. Her voice was thin and Ray knew she was close to tears.

"I don't like it much either," Ray answered. "But if it's going to be done it's going to be done right. The first thing is, we've got to get married as soon as possible."

Rena's eyes went wide. "What?!"

Ray wiggled his fingers. "I'm still a cop. They would have bounced me on Friday, but it's too late now. I got this in the line of duty. It's my shooting hand, my writing hand. I'll get full disability. It's fifty percent more on my pension. Brings me up almost to full salary."

"What does that have to do with us getting married?"

"When I die, you get the money, every month, regular as clockwork."

"You want me to marry you for your money?"

"No, I just want you to have it. The house too. Everything."

"But I don't want anything, Ray. I just want you."

"You've got me for as long as I'm here, but I'd like you to still have a bit of me after I'm gone. Just tell me you'll think about it."

"I'll think about it." She stood up and leaned over the bed. "I've got to go to work now. I'll be back after I get off. The nurse said she'd let me in after regular hours." She gave him a long sweet kiss and he brought up his good hand and let it slide lightly down the front of her blouse. She leaned into the caress and deepened the kiss for a moment. Then she stood back, her eyes a little wet, smiled and gave him a little wave. "Love ya," she said, surprising him, and then she turned and left, making her way between the beds almost before he could answer.

"Love you too." Surprising himself even more.

He spent an hour composing and then dictating a handwritten last will and testament to one of the nurses and the rest of the afternoon finding a pair of doctors willing to witness his signature. One was a major who specialized in cancer and the other was a full-bird colonel who was a surgeon and who seemed to think that being a witness along with a major was beneath him, and worse still, witnessing it on be-half of a sergeant.

They brought dinner around at five, just as it was getting dark outside, but Ray found he wasn't hungry at all. The tiredness he'd felt the day before was threatening to over-whelm him, and the only thing keeping his eyes open was the sound of Jacko's ghastly breathing and the clicking, whirring sound of the esophageal tube in his throat and the strange, almost coherent mumblings coming from Nick Childs's bed, a whispered muttering rant that never seemed to stop. He knew that he had to stay awake, though, because Rena would be coming and he had to tell her about the will.

He closed his eyes, resting them for a moment, listening to his favorite radio, the Philco 90B that looked like the pol-ished wooden arch of a cathedral. The volume was turned down very low and he could just barely hear it, that old Irv-ing Berlin tune he'd liked so much and for so long, "Putting on the Ritz"; a circus tune, part funny with its up-and-down calliope rhythm, but something rich and dark and sinister behind it like the Hall of Mirrors or the Freak Show. Half Man, Half Lizard, see Chameleon Boy!

The radio was still playing and he found himself in the painting from Rose Cottage, seeing details he'd never no-ticed before, the turn of a leaf on the bush to the left, the un-derside faint pink, the texture of the sandy road leading down to the launching place, summer hot between his toes and somehow comforting. In the distance, close to the heav-ily wooded point, there was the small cottage that he knew was theirs, and then he knew the truth, felt the thwarts of the old flat boat in one hand and the rod in the other. He was the one in the boat, the one going fishing with Daddy, and as if to prove it the old Evinrude burst into life, and behind him, without even looking, he felt the thump and rock of the boat as his father stepped over the transom and sat down, the throttle in his hand.

Twisting the throttle to give it more gas his daddy turned the boat up the lake and away from the launching place, leaving a V-shaped foaming wake behind them, taking them away to the places he'd never fished before, the bright sun from the clear blue sky skittering over the broken water, turning their passage into a trail of shattered glass and diamonds until finally they were almost invisible against the horizon. With a final twinkle of light and faint laughter, Ray Duval reached the dark point at the painting's end and rounded it, disappearing at last. Forever.

Epilogue

Detective Sergeant Ray Duval of the Dallas Police Department Homicide Division died sometime on the evening of Monday, November 25, 1963, three days after the assassination of John Fitzgerald Kennedy and one day following the assassination of Kennedy's reputed killer, Lee Harvey Oswald. The time of Detective Duval's death is approximate since his passing was not discovered until a visit later that evening by his friend, Rena Michelle Abson. According to his wishes Detective Duval's remains were transported to Washington, D.C., and he was buried at Arlington National Cemetery, plot 224A, Section 3, which stands on the small knoll just inside the gates to the cemetery. Miss Abson was the only person who attended the funeral.

William Cooper, also known as William Gerritson, was buried in a pauper's grave on Wednesday, November 27, 1963, in Fort Worth's Rose Hill Cemetery three plots east of the grave belonging to one William Bobo, an itinerant and indigent cowboy. The actual occupant of the grave was Lee Harvey Oswald.

Ray won his bet with Jimmy Leavelle. The story of his discovery of William Gerritson's atrocities and the rescue of one of his victims never made the papers at all. Leavelle anonymously donated the five dollars to the local Dallas chapter of the beleaguered NAACP.

A week after his visit by Ray Duval, Richard Schwager went up to his sister's place in Blackstone, sat down among his roses and with a glass of perfectly brewed iced tea as a chaser, took a massive and lethal dose of morphine. He was dead before he'd fully swallowed the first sip.

R. T. Odum, once Ray Duval's partner, was killed in a hunting accident in East Texas on November 30, 1963, under mysterious circumstances. Although some interest was shown in Mr. Odum by the Warren Commission, when Mr. Odum's house was searched it was found to be completely empty of all furniture and documents.

A year after Ray Duval's death the first of a series of heart medications was introduced that would have extended the detective's life. By the mid-1990s such drugs were commonplace and millions of Americans enjoyed near normal lives while living with congestive heart failure.

Joseph Civello, purportedly the mafia boss in Dallas and the man who met with Jack Ruby, R. T. Odum and others at Jack Ruby's apartment, died of an apparent heart attack while awaiting trial on federal narcotics charges in 1969.

Jack Ruby died of cancer on January 3, 1967, sure that the cancer had been "given to him" by various people in authority who wished to keep him silent.

After a protracted legal battle with Ray Duval's father and brother, Rena Michelle Abson, with the help of the two military officers who witnessed Ray's holographic will, eventually inherited Ray's entire estate. While going through clothes to be given to charity, Rena discovered the sabot bullet Ray had picked up off the floor of Parkland

Hospital in one of his tweed jackets. Not having any idea of its possible significance, she threw the bullet into the trash.

Claudius Duval, Ray's brother, never became governor of Texas and divorced his wife, Cynthia, after she had a very public affair with a local state senator. Claudius Duval died in an alcohol-related accident in 1974. Ray's father drowned three years later while fishing on Lake Arrowhead, a few miles from the town of Henrietta, Texas.

Each year between 1964 and 1994, the year of Rena Abson's death from acute ovarian cancer, she came to Washington in November and placed a single yellow rose on Ray Duval's grave in Arlington. From 1973 onward, Rena sometimes noticed that a red rose had been placed on Ray's grave as well, and often wondered who the mysterious visitor was. She never found out and never really tried to, although she had her suspicions and respected the other person's privacy.

On the fortieth anniversary of the President's death, November 22, 2003, an attractive middle-aged black woman, Dr. Zinnia Brant Hellman, a practicing pediatrician and also junior senator from Tripp County, South Dakota, went to the JFK memorial and grave in Arlington Cemetery. She placed a bouquet of yellow roses and one of red close to the grave along with the hundreds of others already there, reserving one flower from each bouquet. She walked back down through the winding paths in the blustery air and then climbed up the knoll as she had so many times before.

She reached the stone, weathered now, the inscription and the dates steadily wearing down, knowing that he wouldn't care. She lay down the yellow rose first.

"From Rena."

And then the red.

"From me. Zinnie. For my love, for my children, for my work." She stopped then, unable to keep back the tears, thinking of all the hours and the days and the years he'd given her. "For my life," she whispered, smiling as the cold wind shook the last leaves from the trees around her, scattering them down on the grave and then skittering them away across the sloping winter grass, almost as though they were alive.

ACKNOWLEDGMENTS

During the writing of *Wisdom of the Bones*, the author consulted hundreds of documents and books. He would especially like to acknowledge the definitive information provided by the Dallas Police Department; the Dallas Archives; *Treasure Hunt: A* New York Times *Reporter Tracks the Quedlinburg Horde* by William H. Honan; *Regicide: The Official Assassination of John F. Kennedy* by Gregory Douglas; *The Day Kennedy Was Shot* by Jim Bishop; *The Search for Lee Harvey Oswald: A Comprehensive Photographic Record* by Robert J. Groden; *Death of a President* by William Manchester; and *With Malice: Lee Harvey Oswald and the Murder of Officer J. D. Tippit* by Dale K. Myers. And last, but certainly not least, I would like to thank my editor, Doug Grad, for helping me get the cars right, among other things.

AUTHOR'S NOTE

All of the information stated as fact within *Wisdom of the Bones* is true. There were a number of child mutilation murders in several northern Texas counties in 1938, and one of the victims' fathers was lynched for the murder of his own daughter. The murders and the mutilations took place as they are described within the novel, and to this date they remain unsolved. The homicide files relating to the black children killed are limited to basic information about the victims and the details of the crimes. There is virtually no information relating to any real investigation of the crimes by the various county authorities involved. The names of the victims and their families have been changed out of respect for their surviving relatives.

Details included surrounding the assassination of President John F. Kennedy are accurate and the majority of named characters, such as Captain William Fritz, head of the Dallas Police Department Homicide-Robbery Division, and Dr. Earl Rose, Chief Medical Examiner for Dallas County, are real people. Details concerning the arrest and interrogation of Lee Harvey Oswald for the murder of both President Kennedy and officer J. D. Tippit are also accurate.

Immediately prior to the assassination of President Kennedy, Jack Ruby, owner of the Carousel Nightclub on Commerce Street in Dallas, really did meet with the organized crime figures mentioned in the book, and really did attend a late-night news conference at Dallas Police Headquarters on the night of the assassination.

Only a few minutes prior to the killing of the President there really was a man who apparently threw an epileptic fit on the sidewalk in front of the Texas School Book Depository building on Dealey Plaza, thus removing one of the strategically placed ambulances on the motorcade route. After arriving at Parkland Hospital the mysterious epileptic disappeared and was never identified or found.

Thirty seconds prior to the arrival of Lee Harvey Oswald in the basement parking garage of Dallas Police Headquarters someone really did tap out the letter F in Morse code on his automobile horn, generally accepted to be a warning to Jack Ruby that Oswald was on his way down to the garage. Following Ruby's killing of Oswald an unidentified police detective wearing a white Stetson bent down and administered CPR to Oswald, although it is assumed that any police officer would know that CPR administered to a gunshot victim with a sucking chest wound such as Oswald's was actually exacerbating the situation and almost certainly hastening Oswald's death.

Although Ray Duval is a fictitious character, congestive heart failure, the disease that killed him, is very real and as of the writing of this book affects almost thirty-five million Americans, most of them over the age of forty. In 1963 there was almost no therapy in existence for the disease other than the limited-use diuretics described in the book, and its diagnosis was inevitably a death sentence.

Descriptions of racism and the Ku Klux Klan within the

Dallas Police Department are accurate for the period involved. In November of 1963 there were no black police officers of any kind on the DPD, although the population of Dallas at that time was approximately 34 percent Negro. There were also no women police officers at the time.

In 1963 there were 232 homicides in Dallas, 584 reported rapes and 27 kidnappings. Between January and December of that year there were 428 missing persons reports filed. Of that number 64 were black, and of those, 31 were children under the age of twelve, 26 girls and 5 boys. Three of the boys were found but nineteen of the little girls simply vanished.

Of the 232 murders in Dallas during 1963, seven took place between November 20 and November 25, not including the deaths of John F. Kennedy, Lee Harvey Oswald or Officer J. D. Tippit. Of those seven murders three were described as domestic, one was a rape-murder. The remaining three were "simple" homicides. Only one of the four nondomestic murders that occurred during the time frame covered in *Wisdom of the Bones* was ever solved. In light of this Ray Duval's rescue of little Zinnia Brant can only be described as fantasy.

Like all young countries, America embraces its history almost as much as it embraces change. Much in Dallas has been transformed since that day in 1963. The big Hertz sign no longer graces the roof of the Texas Book Depository, and the sixth floor of that building, the floor from which Lee Harvey Oswald allegedly fired his deadly fusillade, is now a museum, almost certainly the only museum in the world dedicated to a split second in time. The Carousel Club is long gone, just like Jack Ruby, although the Texas Theatre where Oswald was captured is still there and still showing second run movies. The old warehouses and the cemetery where Ray Duval fought his last battle have completely vanished and are now an open space called Pioneer Park, a place where office workers eat their lunches and where children play.

—Christopher Hyde
New York/Dublin/Nassau